In the Days of
Simon Stern

a novel by
Arthur A. Cohen

 Random House New York

In the Days of
Simon Stern

All rights reserved under International and Pan-American Copyright
Conventions. Published in the United States by Random House, Inc.,
New York, and simultaneously in Canada by Random House of Canada
Limited, Toronto.

Library of Congress Cataloging in Publication Data

Cohen, Arthur Allen, 1928-
  In the days of Simon Stern.
  I. Title.

PZ4.C6768In [PS3553.0418] 813′.5′4 72-11429
ISBN 0-394-48303-0

Portions of this book have appeared in
Commentary, Midstream, Response and *Works in Progress.*

Manufactured in the United States of America

First Edition

for Elaine

and to Harvey Swados (1920–1972)

Book 1

Prologue

The Messiah is at last uptown. He is tired by the events of the past few days but he is uptown and that is something. He has left the confinement in which, until now, he had lived. Once again events have conspired to delay him: the community is dispersed, the Temple destroyed and the section of the city in which he lived condemned by the authorities after the fire. But since he is uptown, there is hope, for he is now in the open. He is sad, but he is not despairing. I emphasize that. Jews who resemble Simon Stern (and the resemblance is everywhere circumstantial) are never despairing, only sad. I will not speculate about his condition. I have never before; there is no need to begin now. What's done is done and he is uptown,

sitting quietly in the park, before the artificial lake where I
am told children sail boats and, nearby, others dance and perform plays. People from all over the city—and from as far
away as Cleveland and Montreal, it is reported—have heard
that he is there and have come to call. That's good. Simon
Stern needs them now.

Simon. Show your glory!

Well, even if you don't, on your own behalf, I will. What
choice have I? I am pledged to it. The Nazarite vows of
abstinence I took some months ago—my ridiculous beard,
untouched, untrimmed—oblige me. Yes, I'll do it. Blind Nathan will do it for you, Simon Stern. I'll start as soon as I've
finished writing up this account of you and your exertions—
well, not yours—his then, the Holy One, blessed be He! But
then you bear it all, don't you, Simon? You're not a poor man,
not by any means. The fire? What did it cost you? Ten,
twenty million dollars. I have no precise idea. There are
millions more, millions. It doesn't depress you, Simon, does it?
All that money lost in smoke. What does it matter to you?
You lost more than money.

Admonition to Nathan: disregard Simon's money. You work
without pay. People like Simon don't pay disciples. And that's
what you are: *disciplus primus* among equals, but special: his
secret fool and jester, his hubris checker, his friend, his scribe.
And what's more, his proclaimer.

It is no delight to prophesy and prophecy is dead in this
land and it is foolish to think me a prophet. But what else is
a proclaimer of visions? Barker. Impresario. Shill. What am
I then? Nothing fits. The English language is helpless before
such requirements and I write all this in English. Simon required English of us, believing it the second language of the
world, the language of exchange and intercourse, carnal
union, embracing everyone finally. Hebrew he reserved for his
testaments, for his chapters of the history of the universe,
for prayer and thought; but it's in English, he said, that the
world heaves and groans. English: language of the fallen
angels. Hebrew: language of anticipation, honey in dew,
tongue of new beginnings and salvation.

It was I, at a council meeting of the Society for the Rescue
and Resurrection of the Jews, who first professed publicly,

just after the Black Fast Day of Av, that Simon was the Messiah: "Listen, Klay, don't you understand that Simon's the Messiah?" I had whispered to Fisher Klay—he was Simon's first conscript and the director of the Society's work—after Simon had called a council meeting at three o'clock in the morning. "Simon's the one we have awaited all these years. He's the Messiah." Simon had thought better of his impetuous summons, and although we were assembled in night robes and slippers, he did not appear. But I spoke my feelings, aware of his mood and our disappointed expectancy—for in the middle of the night one is awakened from sleep only for news of death or birth. No one spoke. They had heard my urgent whisper.

I must stop now and go uptown to visit with Simon. He sent word that he wishes to speak with me. Only to me. I must go now to cut my quills, mix the ink and bathe away my impurities. I will delight to share his presence and hear him speak to me.

Blessed be He who has permitted the Messiah to go into the world.

It is not the depth of the well of the past, but the spectrum of time—that dumb show in which the past is frozen, the present flickers and vanishes, and the future rises in dreams and prophecies—which moves through me. I am the medium of their suspension, for in me, blind Nathan Gaza, they are drawn together and held like snowflakes in a glass globe.

I read a mute map, a map without markings and designations (or rather those that exist are already faded and overlaid with other scribbles and jot marks). I give to all my sources the gift of my imagination. It is I, finally, who must make the myth and make you believe it. Others, the many others who figure in this narrative of the coming to light of a redeemer, are unaware of what they are obliged to be. I select. I present. They are the actors. They know only their lines and they improvise the intimacies that whirl them through their lives in touch with others, yet blind finally to what sustains them. They speak the lines they must speak, for they can imagine nothing else. They are actors.

Even redeemers are victimized by art. Or rather, otherwise put, even redeemers succumb to the laws of their destiny. Only artists are free. And I am the artist of this narrative. Actors do not record the history of their dramaturgy. That task is left to critics. The critic can always tell us of the alternatives, but can never describe the right way. That is a risk too great for criticism. For this good reason I am content with my blindness. I have ceased to be a critic, for I cannot ravage with my sight. I am forced into dream, and everything I see, I alone am responsible for seeing.

Ruth bas Yaakov Yitzhak, the mother of Simon Stern, came of ordinary Jews: Yaakov Joseph, an attendant in the ritual bathhouse in Polnoye, himself a Hasid named after the great sage of Polnoye—may he be blessed for eternity—and Judith, like all the mothers from Sarah to our own day, a sensible, generous, practical woman who kept a stand in the market and sold undesirable vegetables with a truthfulness and enthusiasm that often moved the women of the village to buy from her rather than the more perfect vegetables offered elsewhere. She would cry, "Have pity on these carrots. God in his wisdom formed them for our need. Should they go un-

eaten?" And pious women, hearing her moral, would sometimes stand in line to have mercy on her miserable produce.

Yaakov Yitzhak was now dead. His wife and helpmeet,
Judith, had also died. And Ruth, an orphan in Polnoye, became a ward of the community. She was fortunate in being
an only child. Her mother had labored more than a day to
give birth to her and when her agonies had passed and the
child, slapped and crying into life, was brought to her by
the midwife, she was told: "Never again. Never again."
Yaakov Yitzhak was advised to divorce his beloved Judith, for
a woman who could not bear sons was less than a woman,
defective and unusable, but Yaakov Yitzhak did not believe the
pearl of his name would be missed in future generations;
moreover, his love for his wife and his reliance upon her
was more than enough joy to his life.

Their devotion to one another was enormous. They tended
each other lovingly during a summer's plague that went
through the *shtetl* in the first year of the last decade of the last
century. Ruth had been sent away to another village to visit
with Judith's cousin for the weeks that followed the end of
the Fast Day of Av until the season of the New Year. When
Ruth returned it was with clothes torn in mourning and
without shoes upon her feet. ("If only he had divorced her,"
it was said, "one of them might be alive." "*Shta*," another
answered with anger, "they will hear you and punish us."
"But what devotion! what devotion!" they marveled.) Found
together, fallen upon the floor, a dish of herbal tea within
reach of her fingers, a cool rag moistened with vinegar near
his, it was supposed that each, hearing the moans of the
other, had struggled up and he coming from the tap in the
garden and she from the hearth had died within reach of
the other.

Ruth was fourteen when her parents died. For several
years thereafter she worked in the kitchen of a Rebbe of
the village, preparing cakes, supervising roasts, tending to
the garden, assisting in all manner of work which the Rebbe's
wife could not take time to perform, busy as she was visiting
the sick, taking care of women in childbirth, rushing about in
her skirts and peasant boots from house to house extending
the greetings of the Rebbe to strangers who passed through

the village and had stopped at the houses of wealthy grain and timber merchants or taken refuge in the smoky huts of the poor. There were always twenty people at Sabbath table, the family of the Rebbe and a dozen or more guests who were sojourning in the village for that most supreme of routine days. Ruth, having finished waiting upon the family, would join them at the table, for she was honored in the memory of her father and her mother. The other servants, girls from peasant families who worked in Jewish homes, stood at the sideboard and ladled the soup or brought in second dishes of beet preserve or potato pudding, cleared the table and then withdrew when the steaming tea was served and song and holy discourse began.

The Rebbe attended to Ruth, for though he prized his children and saw in them the redemption of his seed, it was to Ruth that he showed a tenderness his busy wife could not patiently receive. He taught her to read Yiddish and say her prayers; he reviewed with her those sections of *The Prepared Table* which dealt with the obligations of women in Israel; and even taught her enough Hebrew so that she was able, with effort, to read the Five Books of Moses, the Prophets, and the Writings accompanied by the commentaries of Rashi of Troyes. She sat beside him on a low rush stool while he held open before her the books of study, and he dreamed while she read. When she would read a particularly difficult passage and interpret it correctly to him, he would delight, his lips curving downward in constraint of satisfaction, while the crease of pleasure wrinkled the skin puffed around his eyes. He would give her a fruit or cake and send her away, for at those moments he wished to stroke her head, but she was by then more than sixteen, a grown woman, with the marks of her maturity, and he was frightened of his affection.

When she was seventeen, already beyond the age of betrothal, the Rebbe offered to supervise the selection of a husband. Though she was poor, she was not destitute, for her mother had left behind a small chamois bag which contained, besides a wedding band in which two twisted hands of gold clasped together the *Yud* and *Heh* of the divine name, a small ruby which years before an itinerant householder

6

had left with her as a pledge and never redeemed, and a brace-let of semiprecious stones which her paternal grandmother had given as a present to her mother upon the birth of Ruth. Besides these were two small amulets crudely beaten in sil-ver and the filigreed mezzuzah which had announced the entrance of her parents' house. It might be thought that these trinkets were of no consequence. Indeed not if one com-pares their infinitesimal value to the vast wealth of her son-to-be-born, but they were of consequence in those days. Pledged, they were worth several thousand zlotys—less, of course, for the worth of the jewels and the gold than for the intricate and subtle workmanship of eighteenth-century craftsmen, whose tapered fingers and exquisite taste could execute the little links and minute facets which gave the jewels their elegance.

The Rebbe had called Ruth on the evening of her birth-day and given to her the little bag, opened it, checked its contents against a list he had prepared three years before and proposed for her consideration several indigent, but gifted and industrious, young scholars whom she might marry. He went so far as to extend to them the customary privi-lege of spending some years at his table, protected by his roof and counsel, while they pursued their studies and made ready for their examinations and ordination. But Ruth was unwilling. Two of the young men she knew. They were worthy, and although she was obedient and grateful to the Rebbe it seemed to her that other things were called for by the events of her life than to marry a young Talmudist and repeat the ordinary generations of the history of the Jews. Something—in later years she claimed to know—warned her against the suitors the Rebbe proposed. Intimate details (un-suitable to this narrative) which proclaimed the excellence of her body persuaded her that she was a special vessel and, indeed, that she would find her husband in a special way. The Rebbe remonstrated, even raised his voice and brought down a fist emphatically upon the leather binding of the folio which lay before him. But Ruth was adamant. She thanked, thanked, and praised and praised, but with that meeting her closeness to the Rebbe strained. No longer had he time enough to study with her. Another servant was ordered to bring his tea and jam at twilight. Even the Rebbe's wife—a formal but considerate woman in the past—began to carp at her behavior.

One night, therefore, as you would expect, Ruth left Polnoye, and set out along the highway that led from her village into the larger world where there were millions of Jews who would protect her and millions upon millions of others, fashioned as well in His image, whom she feared would do her violence. She believed as do we all that there is a monstrous divide which separates Jews from the others of this world.

Some months later Ruth came to Warsaw and found employment as reader in the women's gallery of a synagogue of the Opponents—those who stood firmly against the enthusiasm of the Hasidim—and there, each day, she would arrive before the sun had risen from its rest, and opening the prayer book she had carried with her from Polnoye, read aloud the service being offered below, punctuating with an elevation of her voice those special phrases at which the community (women included) should stand and glorify, or responding to the *hazzan*, offer their amen of confirmation. Each week the women would hand her various sums for having been their guide in prayer and special gifts for remembering the day of a *Kaddish* or coming to their homes to assist them in the preparation of holiday foods. In time they came to call her the Little Rebbetzin, for Ruth conducted herself with that solemnity and special knowledge which was commonly associated with the wives of rabbis.

During those Warsaw months the chamois bag hung from her neck secured by a tallow-colored leather thong tied with a double knot. She would, from time to time throughout the day, touch the spot where the bag hung between her breasts. When her dress was loose it would pass unnoticed, but when she walked in the park on the afternoon of Sabbath, she would wear another dress, long and tight, and the little bag was remarked as a deformity, as though growing there between the feasts of nature was another, a third and stunted breast.

The chamois bag was a talisman, a remembrance and evidence to herself that she, like other children, had once been sustained and loved by parents, and her unpremeditated touching of the small bag was less to covet her wealth than to make contact with her childhood. She had told no one of the bag or its contents, fearing that if they knew, the poorer women of the community would begrudge her the few zlotys they gave to her each week, and the rich women, made jealous by her imponderable wealth, would disdain her and withdraw their patronage. She had no idea what those little jewels and bracelets were worth, but remembering them on the wrist of her mother or exhibited like lost treasure to her childish gasps of delight she believed them infinitely valuable.

One afternoon in springtime, four months after she had come to Warsaw, Ruth was sitting upon a low bench in the kitchen of the wife of a lumber merchant to whose house she had been called to prepare dishes for a feast to honor the betrothal of their only son, who was to be married that evening. She was tired. She had stood for hours, mashing almonds and dates into a sugary paste with which to cover a large wedding cake she had put to bake. The little bag hung down before her and with familiar fingers she had withdrawn and returned the ruby—a gesture of tiredness, distracted and unaware. She did not notice that the bag had caught in the folds of cotton beneath her breasts and turned upside down. The bag was slightly open and the ruby fell into the mash with which she covered the cake before putting it to cool and settle into iridescent stillness.

It was not until evening that Ruth missed her jewel. The guests had begun to assemble, the musicians were tuning in the hallway, and the tables were set for the guests to share the benedictions of the marriage and eat the nuptial feast. Panic gave way to melancholy and a sadness which she knew to be grief. The ruby, the most precious of her keepsakes, her most valuable inheritance, was lost. But she had no time to weep, for the guests were now seated. The fish, trout and pike, cold and hot, seasoned and bland, covered with sauces and naked in their skins blue and clear like fresh water, were carried to the table and distributed. The guests—there were more than sixty, all relatives, aunts and uncles of the bride—came from as far as the borders of Russia and the fastnesses of the mountains to the south, collected out of the enclaves of the diaspora to celebrate and rejoice in the good fortune of Reb Mendel, their only Warsaw relative, a poor carpenter, who, failing in the country, had sought his fortune in the city and now, in this blossom of his life, was fulfilling the promise of his seed. They liked Reb Mendel though they abused his failure. There were successful Jews and failed Jews, and the excellence of a Jew was estimated by the proportion and the degree to which he struck a bargain between piety and prosperity. Now then, the blessing was spoken over the wine, for on such joyous occasions a *Kiddush* is always in order and bread was broken, but Reb Abram, the bridegroom-to-be, had not raised his eyes from the table. His eyes seemed tangled in the thickets of his young beard. He looked down, his neck stretched forward taut and strained, like that of a bird offering itself to the knife of the slaughterer. His hat lay back upon his head, so that if one caught his profile it was a chaos of uncongenial angles, brim up, chin poking down, eyes withdrawn, all whites, focused upon a world which the celebrants ignored.

Reb Abram's father came forward to his son and whispered in his ear, and Reb Abram listened, his eyes rising from the table for an instant, brushing the forehead of the bride who sat opposite him pinioned between an aunt shaped like a wooden tub and her mother, whom it would appear God had quite literally formed, as he had formed Adam, from blood and earth. Reb Abram considered the face of his betrothed and though he recognized her, acknowledging that it was she, in fact she alone, whom fate had brought forth for him to marry, he knew that it was not she who had been appointed for him.

Reb Abram, who you must guess already was to become the father of Simon Stern and was not going to marry the daughter of Reb Mendel, three years before, in the late hours of Purim evening when all the Jews of Warsaw—indeed, Jews everywhere in that day—put on masks and pretended to be kings and viziers, Persians and princes, Mordecais, Vashtis, Esthers, and, even, young scoundrels, Hamans, and visit strange houses where food and strong drink were offered to precisely such youthful visitors and pranksters, had become separated from his friends with whom, full of recklessness and abandon, he had been roaming the streets.

Young Abram swirled through the city, flushed and lightheaded from a tumbler of brandy the *Rosh* Yeshiva had given him before he and his friends had left the House of Study. Crossing a park in the center of the ghetto, a park surrounded by houses that leaned across to each other, he became aware that he was alone. Ahead of him he could hear his friends. They hooted, sounding horns and clashing cymbals, darting in and out of the shadows, leaping benches and calling out to the lights of the houses for cakes and steaming tea. But then they were gone and the night silence enveloped him. Abram stopped. Before him he saw a light unlike any other. It beamed, not as do candles or gas, coming and going, waxing, waning, but was strong and unbroken, piercing down through the crack between the buildings from which the park received its patch of sky. He was enveloped by the light whose circumference expanded until it encircled him and contracted until it seemed powerful enough to burn into his chest. A hallucination, he thought, and muttered a formula to protect himself from evil. But then the light seemed to lift itself, curving back away from him, receding until it was withdrawn to its source. When he looked up, wrenching himself from his fear, he saw in the window of the wretched tenement a woman of indefinite age—how young, how old he could not make out—looking down at him, not with a lascivious smile as he had been taught Lilith would look, but with a smile of gentleness and consolation. She beckoned to him and pointed to the street entrance to the house. Abram thought to flee and called out for his friends, but the park was silent. His friends had long since disappeared and he was alone, now tired, his head whirling from the brandy and the excitement of the evening. He determined to greet her; he was pure and God would protect him. He made his way up the dark stairs to the third-floor landing, feeling his way, hugging the wall, and as he pushed his hand forward to grasp the newel that capped the landing post his hand was seized and held firm.

A woman's hand had taken his own. The skin was soft

and firm, a young hand. It drew him into the room from which the sourceless light had beamed. Abram could not fix her age. Hers was not the age of his mother, although his mother's hands were as smooth and hairless as that which tightly held his own. But his mother was young; while this woman wore the semblance of age before death, her face clear as a cloudless sky, her hair abundant and white. Erect and unbent, she continued to draw him toward her with remarkable strength. Abram tried to resist but relented, giving way to her tenacity, for he could see in the small light of the single candle that stood upon the window ledge that her eyes, powerful eyes, burned with a passion that is not made in a day, but is succored and conserved by a lifetime of energy and pain. He realized then that it was her eyes that must have cast the beckoning light to him below.

Abram was terrified. He could not speak, but stood before her, wetting his lips nervously.

"What is it you want?"

"I ask for nothing. I have something to give."

"And for what payment?"

"None. Simply hear me and having heard, accept that your life will be changed."

The woman explained quite matter-of-factly that she was undoubtedly mad but that her madness was a gift, that she could read the mysteries and that on the eve of every joyous festival of the Jews she would call to someone in the park below, and having drawn him to her, read out to him his future.

"And the light?"

"The light of concentration," she answered. "Unnatural," she went on to explain, "only because my mind can touch the rim of the spheres, harness its light and bend it for an instant to the park as a signal to the one with whom I wish to speak."

Abram thought to test her, but he was still too frightened, for she knew more than he dared to admit. She told him of his circumstances, his parents, their dreams for him, his piety, his studies, even the page of the Talmud that he had studied that very afternoon. He was baffled, and under his breath continued to mutter oaths and imprecations, but at

12

last desisted, for she did not disappear in smoke as the stronger oaths promise, if indeed one is tempted by the devil or a witch. No. This woman could speak in tongues; even prophesy. At last the singsong recitation of his life came to an end. Confirmed in trust, he awaited the substance of her vision. While she spoke she did not see him, for her eyes showed only white, the pupils hardly visible, hidden now in the carapace of her skull where she consulted tissue, blood, muscle to draw forth her truths.

"Young *bachur*, child of Abraham, our father, you shall bear a son in your days, and he shall be a beacon and a ransom for Israel." Abram gasped. He could not believe her words. "And the woman who shall carry that fateful treasure will be revealed to you by an accident. What is it?" Her body shook and she groaned slightly. "At the hour of your betrothal to another, the true one that is appointed for you shall be made known. You will marry her. The other, the one you desert, will not comprehend—nor could she, no matter. But she will be satisfied according to his will, may his wisdom be unconfounded."

Abram struggled to leave. One foot turned toward the door, but the other acquired such weight as to be immovable. He surrendered to the hearing of her blasphemy. A messiah and redeemer? Miraculous revelations, betrayals?

"And last"—she paused and began to weep—"my dear stranger, this son of yours, this son to be, ransom of Israel, I have called him, ah, he will be, forgive me"—she strained now against her own words and they came slowly, attenuated, each interrupted by heavy groans and sighs—"this son will, beyond himself and his capacity (God forgive me for seeing his secrets), he will kill you (God forgive me), you and your wife-to-be. He will die into you and become the ransom and light to the nations out of his grief for you. Dear boy, forgive me, but must we not all suffer?"

At that instant her face turned blue, her lips quivered and she fell, fainting, to the floor. Abram ran to her, and knowing that one loosens clothing to give the gasping air, he went to unbutton her tight bodice. He tried to unhitch the clasp, but his fingers were cold and clumsy. He tore the garment apart, and seeing her weary breasts heave beneath the folds, he beheld the specter of his death, the red marks of her self-infliction upon her neck, the scales of the ancient reptile upon her shoulders, and he ran from her side.

Three days later a police inspector visited the home of Abram's parents and informed his astonished father that the name of his son had been found inscribed in a ledger of names which the old woman kept on her night table. There the last of the names was installed—Abram ben Belim Stern. It was then that Abram's father learned the explanation of his son's unaccounted absence on the evening of Purim.

It appears that the following morning a tinder merchant hearing a strange sound—he said it was like gargling—entered the woman's room and found her hanging near death from a gas pipe, a rope covering the bruises which Abram had observed. He cut her down, but she died minutes later before a doctor could be summoned from the neighborhood. Among her possessions several documents were uncovered— a *ketubah* dated forty years before and a certificate of death for an infant son born and died within the hour of his birth. That woman, her neighbors testified and the ledger confirmed, had, to be sure, told and foreseen, counseled and complained, for decades summoning to her quarters on the festivals of joy young men of the neighborhood to read their foreheads and tell the future from the lesions of their skin, predicting this and that, all accurately, except that to each and all the birth of the Messiah and redeemer was vouchsafed.

Abram's father called him to his study and, in the presence of the inspector, questioned him. Abram replied forthrightly, satisfied the curiosity of the official, but guarded the secret of the encounter, for it was only to him, it is certain, that it was told that his wife would come forth out of the ordinariness of the everyday to become wife and mother, and only to him was it told that the child to be born would be not alone Messiah (an annunciation which his father regarded as foolishness and blasphemy) but the instrument of his parents' death.

It is no wonder that Abram should sit, enclosed by melancholy on the feast day of his betrothal, drifting by the face of his bride-to-be, talking in a low voice, undistracted from the memory of his destiny by the whispered counsels of his father. If it was to be shown forth, it would come in this moment, during the next hour, for later that night, at the hour of ten, the marriage contract would be signed and witnessed, the rabbi would speak the seven benedictions, the glass broken, and tears poured into wine would be consumed.

You will have no choice but to forgive the interjections of the scribe and narrator of this tale. Or, if angered by them, to ignore them and pass on. And yet, I advise against such a dismissal, for Nathan Gaza, that is I, have a purpose which is served by these occasional interruptions.

This is not alone a tale, intended to divert or even, as is the common way with tales of saints and heroes, to instruct. What I am telling is truth and truth requires a canon, for my truth may not be yours, and for that reason alone, I am obliged to disclose to you, reluctantly I admit, the argument of my truth. Take it or leave it, as I've said, but I cannot permit you to hold against me that I have not revealed my premises and my sources. Therefore it came to pass.

What is it that the language of Scripture and the hagiography of our saints and martyrs intend when they emphasize "And it came to pass?" And what do I mean when I write this, serene in undifferentiated darkness, my left hand acting as guide to the pen my right hand holds, moving down the page a half inch at a time, while the nib scratches at the border of my guiding hand?

Might I not write "And it came to pass" and be done with the narration of these particulars? Might I not as easily write "God spoke. It came to pass. The Redeemer is come to Zion?" I could, but I have my vanity and my craft. Seeing Simon Stern, who can disbelieve him? He is what he appears to be. But then numberless eyes in the presence of their salvation would report to themselves only the salvation they desire. If God wishes to save each of us in our particularity he would commission one Messiah apiece, for each of us comes into the world cast from the same mold but flawed by the individuality of our stamping.

It is not the perfection of the mold that marks our difficulty but the eccentricity of our casting—that for each of us there is one womb and one electric spermatazoon, the universal receptacle, the universal fecundator. The issue of the womb bears the form of universality, striated by the definitions of history and race, the specifics of accident, shading, weighting, outweighing, balancing, organizing the viscous substance of the womb into a creature that is very creaturely and nonetheless first Adam all in one.

This is the predicament which I confront. I am obliged to render the event as if the necessity consisted in the universality of the form under which Simon Stern appears in flawed particularity, whereas in fact the necessity of Simon Stern consists in the particularity, not in the generality, of his being human. The humanity we may take for granted, for God is in that respect a peasant drone, fashioning vessels at his wheel (all are round), blowing glass at his glass works (all are breakable), striking coins at his mint (all are metallic and debasable). There is the necessity of the form and it is a boring and repetitive necessity. The artistry consists in the necessity of the mistake, the alteration of the form, the roughness, uneven texture, graininess of the execution. And the pride of man is in the uniqueness of his flaw, not in the similitude he bears to the model, and his anguish and despair proceeds from the definition of the flaw, the hardening of accident into habit.

So it is that when a man beholds a redeemer what does he in fact behold: one who contains all the flaws, whose compassion ranges the defects, encompassing them.

The Redeemer, like the shamans of the East, descends into the most populous regions of the underworld and there among his familiars contains all wretchedness. The Redeemer elevates wretchedness by being all-wretched. The something "more" that makes him redeemer rather than merely wretched is that he makes wretchedness a part of the model, that he ransoms wretchedness from necessary particularity and makes of it something universal. How else to explain why King David is the prototypical Messiah of the Jews? Was he not cruel, proud, lustful, unstable, discontented, abundantly vain? Indeed. Who else but he, consummately Man, should be the Son of Man? The Redeemer in David is the incommensurability of his manhood to ordinary man, for David gathers to himself all the dust and lint of the universe, and from that disorder of broken shells, refuse, chips, offal, he willfully produces an order.

The "And it came to pass" is the fortuity which permits the need of the hour to be fulfilled as it is, as a desperate need. Not a moment later. Not a second earlier. The present is abundant with the need and the circumstances of its being met. That's the miracle. That's all there is to the miracle.

My own prayer is for the Annunciation, the coming to day. It is a prayer released by a heart that knows nothing of theurgy, possesses no magical devices, is even terrorized by the fear that perhaps there is really no one to hear it and nonetheless doggedly, pertinaciously prays, "O Lord let it be done," and adds surreptitiously, "according to your Will," or even more dramatically, but incredulously, "and if not for our sakes, then for your own." Something invariably happens, does it not? Something does happen in answer to such a prayer. Something ordinary and unimpressive to the lazy sensorium—a cat cries in the alley or the moon is obscured by a black cloud. Such things, in themselves hideously pedestrian after the exertions of prayer, do occur. What do we assent in our hearts? It depends on the heart. The heart that willed the prayer, that wanted to influence God's will, is confused and disheartened, and says to itself, God wasn't listening or else God was too busy, or perhaps, worse yet, what's the use, why bother? But another heart, less urgently practical, wanting not this or that, but only a wisdom to withstand, a strength, a general courage (no less needs than others more specific), exposes the linings of the heart, and says, "Be present to me, as I am to you," and to itself perhaps but one phrase—"Compassionate One"—and to such a petitioner the cat whining in the alleyway, the effaced moon confirm that something has happened.

The whole of life is a concatenation of signs and wonders which we are disposed either to receive or to ignore. After the fact, when the miracle of the need, the prayer, the event are past, then we can explain. The cat's in heat for her lover, the sky is overcast by a murky fog. What good's the explanation? The heart has no need of explanations. The

17

magnificent fortuity of anything happening the hour that our hearts break in need suffices.

And it came to pass that Abram departed from Ur of the Chaldees; that Joseph's brothers descended into Egypt in search of food and provender for their cattle; that the Children of Israel stepped into the swirling sea at the moment when a blast from the desert wind, heavy with the heat of day, powerful from the gathering fury of wasted days flaying the sands of Sinai, directed themselves, as they had done perhaps thousands of times before and cleared the water from beneath their feet and they passed through to dry land. At that moment. At that moment. At that moment. Nature and history don't go together. Nature hides her reasons. History is the pursuit of reasons. The miracle is that the impossible in defiance of reason should occur at the hour of history's demand.

We need Simon Stern. We do. He must come to life. He must be born. He is here now among us undisclosed and our need for him is so great that he should be born.

And it came to pass as she had told it. Is not the gift of prophecy but another exertion of man's combat with the spark within his nature, his unwillingness to be any less than God and his panicked understanding that he does not endure forever? The only way to eternalize himself, without forgetting that he is mortal, is to encompass the past and draw the future into the present. The ancients divinized, necromanced, compelled miracles by dissimulation, but we are the first people with enough sense of history and eternity to have prophesied and we go on. Good and bad prophets. True and false ones. Detailed rules and procedures for discerning the genuine from the spurious, but it comes to the same thing—we risk our necks into the future, straining until the pain beats at our shoulders, rising above the scaffolding of the past until we see something of the future, its configuration, its accumulating weight and power, and those we read out to the yawning heart.

And so it came to pass as she had told it to the father of Simon Stern.

Abram succumbed. He gave up believing the unfortunate

woman who had announced his grand and miserable destiny. An hour from that moment, at the most two or three—for weddings are interminable—he would be married according to the tradition, to a lovely girl whose eyes only he had seen, whose hand he had touched but once so lightly, when her father and his own had presented them to each other after agreeing upon the terms of the dowry. Abram should have been filled with joy and expectation, should he not? But then you would miss the essential characteristic which Abram maintained throughout his days until his untimely death, a sense of the weighty miracle of his own life. And indeed it was a miracle.

Can you imagine a child born to a proud and wealthy merchant's family coming into this world with a disease later to be diagnosed as tuberculosis of the lymph glands? Would proud and wealthy parents turning to the cradle of their first-born delight in beholding such a wretched creation, a face pallid and lifeless, a forehead moist and mottled, legs and arms scrawny and unfleshed like an abandoned fowl? Reb Belim, Abram's father, became a blaze of anger and in his rage with heaven he denounced God for his betrayal and denied a pledge he had made to the Holy Congregation to pay for the carving of a pair of lions to surmount the Ark. There was no respite to his anger. His wife, the mother of Reb Abram, a wraith of a woman, as though she had been raised in the shadows and had never seen her own face, cried until it became raw with tears, and from her husband she received no consolation.

In truth, it must be acknowledged that Abram survived into life by a handbreadth. Poultices and cool waters flavored with rose petals, unguents and goat's milk kept him tied to the thread of breath for many months and during that time not a single pound was added to his meager body.

And Abram cried. How he cried and how his cries set up the crying of the neighborhood. Dogs bayed, cats howled, all the beasts of the community would thrash and writhe when Abram would cry out during winter nights, for Abram, however smothered in quilts and warmed in the cradle set before the hearth, would cry from cold and in the morning his lips and ears were blue from cold, his hands and feet frozen like the Vistula. In the days he would be thawed by the breasts of his mother, but by nightfall when his father had returned he would be cast back among his swaddlings and left to moan.

It was a year before his parents realized that perhaps not Providence in its majestic indifference but disease, selective and precise, was the cause of Abram's inability to grow and his refusal to laugh. It was late summer and the family went to the watering spas in western Poland where Hasidic dynasties and German doctors went to cool themselves from their exertions. Passing their table in the large café which fronted the esplanade of the resort, a German doctor (fortunately he was a Jew and, though emancipated, not wholly disdainful of Poles or Jews from the East) dropped his glove near the table where Reb Abram's parents sat, his mother rocking the carriage in which Abram lay twisted in sleep, and as the doctor bent down he caught sight of the swelling behind his ear, the slight blueness of strangled breath which showed about his eyes and lips, the unsavory pallor of his skin despite the radiant warmth of the sun.

"Dear friends," he spoke uncertainly, using German with ever so gentle an indication that he could and would retire into Yiddish if they desired. Abram's father and mother looked up, he from the glass of tea into which he had just descended and she from the reveries of her unhappiness.

"Dear friends, your son is not well." Reb Abram's father was about to snort in annoyance, but he was constrained by the tone of gentle concern with which the doctor spoke. "If I may be so bold as to be urgent and alarming, your son is not well. He should be looked to immediately."

The family brought Abram to the doctor's suite the following morning, and there the doctor examined him carefully, feeling and pressing, touching and smoothing, noting carefully in a little book the observations he was accumulating. The parents could not have known that the doctor (his name was Litvin) was an expert on obscure forms of tuberculosis, that little Abram had indeed in the early hours of his life contracted a rare bacillus which reproduced and fed upon his vital glands and they, in rebellion against a death which would have come had they not ferociously resisted, drew to themselves all the meager resources of Abram's body in order to contain the disease which ravaged them. For one so young, the doctor could only prescribe total rest, mountain air, a variety of known medicines, constant attention. The parents of Abram were grateful, paid him magnificently, and followed his advice.

Abram was sent that very autumn to live in the village of a distant cousin who owned a forest in the mountains near Salzburg, and though his mother, once a year, at the conclusion of Passover, would visit him, bringing him paniers of chocolate, glazed fruits, cookies flavored with anise and dotted with sesame seeds, woven scarves and embroidered shirts to be opened amid smiles, kisses and admonishments, six years were to pass before the disease retired and Abram could return to Warsaw, to the home in which he was born.

The years he passed with Cousin Max, an older brother of his mother, were exquisitely happy. Tuberculosis is a disease of languor—it patches the spirit with joy and sadness and it is only when the time of healing approaches that the ravages of the disease are missed. Until that time, the questionably welcome time of health, the body is a warm thing, fevered and redolent, flushed beautifully as only youth is flushed, succumbing gratefully to attentions and succors.

Cousin Max was a gentle giant—a big man, with hands like lion's feet and fingers that gnawed at kindness, stroking Abram at nightfall with an ingenious containment of power, for fearing his blistered and warted hand would irritate Abram's sicklied flesh he wore a pair of cotton gloves, thick enough to secure Abram's flesh against the bruises that would never come, yet thin enough to communicate his love. Cousin Max had no child, indeed no wife, though occasionally in the sinning intervals of the year, a day or so before the great planting and harvest festivals, it is told, he would go to Salzburg to waste his seed, leaving Abram in the care of a fiercely devoted housekeeper. He would return to Abram and in the pleasure of seeing him once more would enfold him in his arms, raise him up and carry him into a pine forest near the house where they would chatter and play until night fell.

When Abram left to return to Warsaw, he was brought to the Salzburg railway station by Cousin Max. Max held his hand tightly. He did not wish to lose Abram or to lose himself in his emotion at their parting. As they approached the entrance to the station an old man, a man beyond seventy years, came toward them. His face was yellow like ancient paper, foxed brown, and creased as though it had been crumpled and flattened out once more, his arms were bandaged and he walked laboriously with a cane. He had not seen them. Nor had Abram seen him. Cousin Max, from some feeling of the preternatural, raised his free hand to cover Abram's eyes and gripped his hand more tightly.

"Why, Cousin Max, why?" Abram cried out, suddenly afraid.

The old man heard the child cry and turned toward them, raising his cane in his own fright as though to beat off the attack of predatory birds. Cousin Max stopped and dropped his protecting hand, and child and protector saw then the dead eyes of the old man, black like charred roots. They hurried away, turning back only once as they were about to disappear into the marble cavern of the station when the old man had begun to sing a joyous song in a language Abram did not yet know.

Belim ben Aharon, the father of Abram, paced his bedroom, kicking against a Bokhara rug with impatience. Puffs of dust rose and settled. He observed an unclean spot and grimaced. Reb Belim required things in place; he made a habit of cleanliness, precision and work. And now his sick son, his first-born, was returning home from the mountains. Two daughters had been born since Abram had gone away, but they were girl children. Abram was his heir, his gift to the nations, his longevity and length of days, his produce and his legacy. What a sick child God had given him. He kicked again and dust rose once more and settled.

"Where is he?" Belim spoke aloud to himself. The train is late? The coach he had ordered to take his wife and servant to the station broke down? An accident (God forbid)? He thought of a dozen things and discarded them one by one. A simple thing. The trains do not come on time. No point agitating. He sat down and began to read a book, the *Musar* of Rabbi Israel Salanter, and his annoyance passed and he resolved to study an extra page of Talmud on the coming

Sabbath. He dozed, his eyelids fanned like the wings of small butterflies, black with fatigue, closed. He heard the front door open and suddenly the room burst with light—although it was evening the shutters were flung wide and sunlight from the square flooded the room. Before him he saw his son, standing, it seemed, in a patch of darkness amid the light. He called to him to move, to step outside the circle of darkness and come to him. The boy struggled to move; he tried to lift his leg to force himself against the ring of darkness abrading the light, but he could not, for wherever he moved the darkness moved with him. Belim perspired and tugged at his collar to relieve his fear and awoke to find his son approaching him. He kissed his father and Belim wept to see him.

The day after Abram's return, his father called him to his study. He lost no time coming to the point.

"You will become a scholar."

"What is that, Father?"

"A scholar, my son, is one who has learned the whole of the Torah, its commentaries, the Law and its traditions."

Abram looked wild-eyed and frightened. "All of God," he exclaimed.

Belim smiled, "All of God, my child."

"All of God, all of God," Abram continued to repeat incredulously, rubbing his eyes.

"And when you have learned 'All of God,' my son, then you will learn from me and become a merchant, and sell grain and timber and become a rich man who knows all of God."

"But I will be old, Father."

"Young, my son, Abram. The words are sweet as honey and gold and silver will sweeten them more."

This was the hope of Belim and his dream for Abram. Abram studied and learned well. He studied and learned for twelve years and he was accounted a genius in the Law, for he progressed more rapidly than could be imagined. His father, accustomed to notions of work popular among merchants and entrepreneurs, could measure the exactions of labor only by the weights and standards of achievement and the visible signs of exhaustion. He could not really comprehend Abram. Abram was by sixteen grown to a height that no longer supported his head nor what it contained. His head was large; his cheeks, though still covered by a wisp and straggle of a beard, were pale as a winter snow upon which a few drops of blood have fallen. But more than his face, which he wore as an ancient tragedy mask, blank but for the wrinkling of his brow when he studied or spoke of the mysteries, it was his manner of bearing himself before the world which prepares us for his future.

Abram walked as though his legs were fettered, took short and painful steps, each movement accompanied by tightness of breath which concluded after several beats in a deep sigh which came from some distant recess of his body. It was a weight which Abram bore, a weight unfathomable which bent his shoulders, which forced his muscular stomach into a perpetual cavity of containment, which pushed his head forward as though it were to his head that had been assigned the task of feeling out the air before him.

Abram was in pain. Not that he suffered. We do not wish to give the impression that Abram was a young sufferer. He knew pain, and pain had been his intimate since his birth, but not suffering, for suffering, you know, can be undertaken without pain. It is a painless wound, suffering is, and one prepares for suffering like a runner before the race, undertaking short bursts of speed, pacing the energy, training the mechanism by containment in anticipation of that bursting explosion which sets the whole body into violent motion.

Abram first knew the significance of this distinction when he became intimate with the conventicles of the Hasidim, particularly the Hasidim of Levi Yitzhak, the Berditchever, for Levi Yitzhak had not prayed that God explain to him his pain, but only that He reassure him that the sufferings he undertook he bore for no vain and vulgar reason, but only for His sake, for His sake. Suffering was like a crooked finger calling Abram to follow.

It was a bitter winter, the year of Abram's sixteenth birthday; the cold was severe beyond imagining. It entered the warmest homes, froze the healthiest bodies, coming around corners in a blast to enter through the greatcoats of thick wool and through skins of Russian wolf and seal. The cold had lasted a month and fuel was scarce. The rich paid exorbitant prices for coal and cut logs, while the poor took to sleeping together in their beds, sharing their bodies with an abandon made serene and childlike by the absence of carnality.

Abram left the courtyard of the Yeshiva after dark. He had been studying near the large stove which sizzled in the center of the study room, but his hands, despite gloves, were chapped and red, and the skin had cracked between the thumb and second finger of his writing hand. He was wrapped in a fur coat made of bearskin and his head was buried in a fur hat; around his face he had tied a scarf and only his grey eyes were visible to see the way. He hurried along, his body turned toward the wind, bent forward in his familiar posture. As he came around a corner toward the square in the center of which stood his home, he tripped and fell. Regaining his balance he turned back and saw lying upon a mound of matted snow an old man. His coat had blown open and his undergarments showed, frozen and stiff; his ritual fringes had turned into icicles, and his beard was like a rock of dirty quartz, black, white, grey, and hard. Only the eyes told Abram that he was still alive and an occasional moan from his tired lips, still moist from the dying breath of his life.

Abram lay down over his body to cover him with a panic of warmth, and as he bent his face toward the face beneath him the old man struggled up to draw breath. Abram put his lips to the lips of the old man. The face quivered and the old man seemed to revive from the intensity of Abram's breathing, but the wind continued to beat against their bodies and Abram began to feel the cold enter into his own body. He removed his lips for an instant from the mouth of the old man and he saw the body shake with convulsive violence and the eyes look up to Abram to wonder at his deserting the kiss of life. Abram shuddered and bent down, exhausted, once more. The old man, however, had stopped breathing, the heart had stopped beating, the old man had died. He lifted himself from the body of the dead man and moved slowly into the darkness of the square.

It was not Abram's wish to be free of the death of the old man. He took to himself all responsibility for his death—guilt, if you will, but not ordinary guilt, for Abram knew well enough the doctrine of his ancestors to recognize that in no precise sense could he hold himself accountable for the old man's dying. Quite the opposite. Mathematical ethics would exculpate him; but Abram chose otherwise, for he did not believe that anything comes into the way of man without intention, either to seize and hold him prisoner by force or to compel him, as the Patriarch, Jacob, was compelled, to struggle to regain his freedom. Abram had become familiar with something no longer mundane, a fissure in the universe, which he came to regard as factual, but no less fantastic.

The words of the Torah came to Abram flying like birds, and he would open his mouth and they would pass into him. But it could not be known that these same birds did not come to rest within him, but in the night hours would flutter and shake Abram from his sleep. In time Abram became melancholy and sad. At night he did not sleep and nightmares assaulted him.

"Ach, he is a nervous child, a high-strung child," his father would say with disgust whenever his wife would speak to him of the strain under which Abram seemed to labor. "He needs a worldly distraction. Too much of God! It isn't healthy," Reb Belim muttered. The parents determined therefore that Abram should be married on his twentieth birthday. A suitable bride was found, and although her family was not wealthy, Reb Belim found their circumstances desirable, for he had no intention of losing his son to another's family and he was persuaded that the girl's good manners, education, and pleasing appearance would be quite enough. If his son went to live with the family of his bride for the customary years while he completed his studies, he would still be called upon to contribute to his support and for that breach of custom he could exact his price, that Abram and his wife should pass the Sabbath at *his* home. That would be enough, for though Belim loved Abram in his fashion, he loved the more that he remained empowered by his wealth to order Abram's life.

Music sounded in the hall.
The double doors of the dining room where the wedding

feast was set and the bridal canopy installed were thrown open and the musicians entered. They were an aged and groaning ensemble of violins and balalaikas. A single horn player, whose face was blotched with pimples, blew upon a dented cornet. They strummed, whistled, sang, turned handsprings, played pranks, told stories to tunes. They had come to amuse and divert the wedding celebrants. The guests smiled, laughed, drank their wine, picked at assortments of fish, salads, and platters of meat and vegetables.

The servants reeled about the room, threading through the tables, carrying trays of hot tea flavored with brandy, removing dirty dishes and replacing them, refilling empty tureens and platters. An hour passed and the time came for the nuptial cake to be cut by the groom. The pimply horn player paraded an ascending blast upon his instrument, and the guests lapsed into an expectant silence. The center lights were extinguished and only the candelabrum on the table at which Abram sat with his parents and his sisters remained lighted.

Once more the double doors opened and Ruth bas Yaakov Yitzhak, Ruth of the Lost Ruby, appeared bearing the wedding cake she had decorated several hours before. The cake sat upon a silver tray whose handles were shaped like decapitated swans, and she gripped the tray with a fierce strength and bore it high above her head while she passed down the lines of admiring eyes to the center table and placed it before Abram. Abram looked up and nodded thanks to her and his eyes fell once more to the table, averting their gaze from all. Abram sat immobile. He slowly moved his hand toward the knife, inching his fingers like an insect across the white tablecloth until they found its handle. He lifted the knife and assessed the surface of the cake seeking out the spot into which to insert its point. His eyes squinted to measure its quadrants and he noted a point near the center which seemed to glisten beneath the surface of the sea of frozen sugar and the islands of dates and nuts which dotted it. He could see there, at that point, there, to the left of the center, a faint glow, as though the composure of the sea were broken by an agitation moving beneath its calm. Suddenly alive with excitement, the knife descended with a vicious energy as if, of a sudden, the gentle Abram were cutting the throat of a calf. The knife descended and rose once more, bearing upon its flattened side, amid dough and fruit, a small but glowing and perfectly cut ruby. Ruth cried aloud and, clutching her throat, fainted. Abram rose from the table, erect, and with the gravity of princes came to her side, bent down and kissed her upon the forehead, lifted her in his arms and carried her from the company. A gasp of horror, subsiding into the petrifaction of the amazed, attended his departure.

"You will not do this thing. You will return immediately and the wedding will proceed as I have planned."

"It cannot be, Father."

"It will be. I say so and I say it for the last time."

"I do not wish to cause you grief, but if you must grieve for me let your grief begin now. I shall only marry that girl, that girl in the next room."

"You don't even know her."

"I know her."

"Impossible."

Those were the last words which were exchanged between Abram and his father. Reb Belim left the room and did not return. Abram left his father's house that night and did not return. His father compensated the family of the bride and when the ceremony of nullification had been completed, he rent his garments and declared his son dead in disobedience to his will. Belim suffered. Of course he suffered, but he did not know nor would he understand had he been told what it was that obliged his first-born son to listen to the sign of the ruby, to determine to take to be his wife a poor orphan of a pious family of Polnoye whose parents had died of the plague.

There is no doubt that Jews are mad. Do you have any doubt? Look here, the survival of the Jews is a madness. I know all the reasonable reasons.

The fact is that the survival of the Jews is senseless. I'm not talking theology here, so I won't invoke the divine name (although you know perfectly well that I think it's His doing and His alone). What I'm saying is that any people who go into mourning for a disobedient son, who cut cloth, sit on low benches, put ash on their foreheads because a son has made up his mind to be different from his father—such a people is mad. But remember this, will you? What did Abraham, our ancient father, do: he broke all the idols in the workshop of his own father, Terah, and went walking after a windgod voice which spoke to him in Ur of the Chaldees and ended up in the Land of Israel, running a whole people. Now, that's a monumental disobedience.

It is a question whether Ruth fled the home of Reb Belim or was driven off by the screams and shouts of the rejected bride and her family or the rage of Reb Belim, who disappeared after his final meeting with Abram and turned over the cake, smashed the glass of wine with which the marriage was to be sanctified and screamed, "It's off, it's off. Go home. Get out. Go away," and then sat down and wept.

Nothing more is known about Reb Belim or his wife, the father and mother of Abram, father of Simon Stern. It must be that they lived out their days and died in grief. No further mention of them is made by Simon Stern in his recollections of his parents. It is only the case that their lives end and the life of Abram and Ruth begin during a night of winter in Warsaw.

Ruth returned to her room on the sixth floor of a tenement in the ghetto. She entered her room, lit the wood-burning stove, and sat down upon her bed exhausted. She had worked in the house of Reb Belim three days and had received nothing for it. She was owed a hundred zlotys which she could not return to collect and the ruby was now in the hands of a possessed young man of whom she was frightened. She fell asleep in her coat. The night passed, and as morning came a chill passed through the room. The fire was spent and the windows were covered with frost. Her stomach ached from hunger and she felt a rancid taste in her mouth as if bile had risen in her throat. She groaned and opened her eyes. Above her, wrapped in a fur, only a small beard streaking the black of the bear coat with ruddy brown, stood the young man of the night before. He looked down at her and smiled.

"You. my God," she gasped.

"Don't be afraid," he said quietly.

"Go away."

"Impossible," he replied, leaving no doubt.

She sat up and wrapped her coat around her. "What for? What for?"

"For what, you mean?"

"For what?

"For you. For you."

"You've done enough. You've cost me everything. A hundred zlotys. My ruby."

He reached into his coat, and withdrawing a leather pouch, opened it and put a packet of money on the bed. "More than a hundred zlotys. More like twenty thousand, I should think. The ruby. The ruby is something else entirely. You shall have it back when you have done what you must do."

She looked at him and her eye twitched. "What? What's to be done?"

"You will marry me. We will go to my rebbe this afternoon. No. That's not possible now. No matter. I know another to whom I went sometimes for Torah. He knows nothing of me."

The young man thought aloud, indifferent, it would seem, to Ruth.

"You're mad."

"Yes?" He seemed recalled from his distraction. "Mad, is it? Mad it may be, but it's done. It's settled. Let me be clear. I have no choice but to marry you. If I do not marry you, my life is as good as finished. My marriage to you was settled up there, by others more grand than you or I. They make up their minds what's to be and it's done. We don't cross them. Yes, it's quite true that for others, for most others, for all the Gentiles, for most of the Jews, it doesn't matter. They all believe in God and angels, and devils, and sages and saints. Correct. They believe in them. And why shouldn't they? They don't get in their way and everyone minds his own business. Occasionally it's different. Occasionally, word comes that someone is wanted, that an appointment has been made, and a messenger arrives and reads out the message. Now, unfortunately, young lady, that messenger came to a prophet three years ago and she told me exactly how and why and to what end I would meet and marry a young lady like you.

I have no choice." He finished and flicked his tongue over his lips, wet them, and gulped. There were dots of saliva at the corners of his mouth. He sat down on her bed and stared at her for a minute or more, watched her, estimated her shaking body, her quivering jaw.

"Your name." It was a command, as though at the frontier a guard was ordering a stranger to produce papers. She did not answer. "Your name, I asked?"

"My name? Ruth bas Yaakov Yitzhak of Polnoye."

"And your father?"

"Dead."

"That doesn't answer the question," he continued peremptorily.

"Does it matter?"

"I wish to know."

Ruth began to narrate her life. That is how I know the details. Abram told his son. Ruth did not. I learned all that I have recorded here from Simon's telling. When Ruth had finished, Abram seemed satisfied. "It is well."

The blue-black of night was taking refuge in the courtyards and alleys of the city and a sepia light was spreading like a stain over the rooftops. Ruth got up from her bed when she had finished her telling and went to the window. Abram remained seated, his back to her, weariness licking the bones of his body like a brush fire. They were silent for a long time. The sun was coming out of Russia into the sky above Warsaw.

"But why me?" she turned and faced his back.

"I explained. It was foretold. It must be that way."

"But do you believe these things, these omens and portents?"

"Has the Messiah come?"

"No, but do we need him?"

Abram turned toward her. He smiled, but the smile was pinched with sadness. "I have a confession. Without the Messiah I would have died. I wait for him like others wait for their lovers. I stand on street corners and examine faces in the streams of people. I watch passers-by, strangers, tramps, hawkers, fish peddlers, looking for that unearthly transposition of passion and wisdom which is Messiah. The flesh

31

clarified like melted butter, spooned of impurities. Wisdom made into an unconscious habit. It is looking for the reversal, the turnabout, the descent of the high and the elevation of the earthly. Do you see?"

Of course she did not, but she was moved by the intensity with which he spoke. His words were spoken like nails hammered into a board—hard, deliberate, permanent. "I gave up the Messiah. That is my confession. I don't believe in him. He doesn't come when he's needed. We should stop worrying about him."

"Ruth," he said gently, using her name for the first time, "Ruth. I know you have suffered. But you have never despaired. You may thank God for that. But I *have* despaired and from despair I have conceived my love for him who comes, but has not appeared. I have no choice but to give myself up to the madness of that prophet. She knew despair as I. She killed herself from despair. But out of her limitless desperation she told me something of the invisible bands which join heaven and earth, which the Messiah will one day walk. I do not know if we shall be the bearers of that gift, but she promised and she spoke and she took her life to seal her prophecy. We can do no less than try."

Abram had swayed her. He was pitiful and beloved in his pitiableness. If she was to be a bride of heaven, at least she would be fed as she had never been, and clothed and treated by the father of Messiah as a heavenly Queen, until at least the revelation had come to pass or forever abandoned as a delusion. But once more, half-hearted, she pleaded against him, acknowledging his right, but claiming for herself no less the right to decline such honor. She knew that for him there was no choice, but that for herself, "I don't want this madness. It's mad. There is no messiah to be born to us."

The young man took a pistol from his pocket and put it to his temple.

"What are you doing?"

"It's obvious, isn't it?" His finger cocked the hammer and he quivered with terror.

"Don't! For God's sake. Don't!"

"Will you marry me?"

"I'll marry you. You're mad. I'll marry you."

Abram put away the pistol and went to Ruth and took her hand into his. It was the first time that he had ever looked openly upon the face of a young woman, the first time he had dared to take the hand of a woman into his own. He was twenty, a disciple of the wise, a sage in Torah, a Hasid, but he was now alone in the world, cast out from the house of his father.

When Reb Belim had stormed from his study, Abram had gone to his desk, removed twenty thousand zlotys, which had been set aside as a gift to the family of the bride he had rejected, and his father's pistol with which he had intended consciously and with premeditation to terrorize Ruth or to use against himself, and departed. He had searched throughout the night, asking all the cab drivers of the district, the beadles of the synagogues, the kitchen maids of homes in which she might have worked, and from a scrap of information here, a smile of recognition there, a word of direction from one and a recollection from another, had come to the tenement in which at dawn, quietly opening and closing doors to each apartment, he came to the top floor and found Ruth once more.

The sunrise opened into day. Abram went to synagogue and said his prayers and met Ruth later at a small café facing one of the many squares of the ghetto. They had tea with bread and jam. They scarcely talked. Ruth looked up at him circumspectly, dropping her head quickly when his eyes rose to meet her own or turning aside to watch a sleigh fly through the snow. But during the hours that passed, circumspection gave way to curiosity and curiosity to question and question to that mystery of entanglement which is human talk, the ebb and flow of language, where passion licks the letters of words and burns into them warmth and feeling. By nightfall Ruth had come to trust Abram, and Abram, strengthened by his victory, had passed from desperate necessity to willing desire.

They resolved to marry. A week after the evening of their meeting, at a small feast to which Abram invited three beggars from the synagogue, the beadle and his wife, the landlady in whose tenement Ruth had lived, and a drunken coachman who had come into the restaurant where the feast had been arranged, Abram made the benedictions and completed the ceremony that had been begun an hour before under a canopy held by four ancient scholars in the study of an unknown rabbi in the livery and coach quarter of the ghetto. At the feast's conclusion Abram put down on the table two tickets. "In the morning," he announced, "we shall leave by train for Vienna. From there we will travel to Genoa in the country of Italy, and by boat in five weeks we shall land in the United States of America. There is nothing left for us in Poland." Ruth looked up to her husband, Abram, and began to weep.

"Too much, too much," she cried, but Abram, silent and assured, stroked her head and laughed. At the conclusion of the feast, while waiters hurried to close the shutters for the night, while the drunken coachman snored in the corner, while the landlady and the beadle drank their last cup of tea, and the other guests were exchanging gossip and stories, weary of wine and cutlets and cakes, Abram slipped upon Ruth's nuptial finger, obscuring the thin metal band that had bound them earlier in wedlock, a silver ring in which Ruth's small ruby was buried.

Ellis Island is stripped to bare necessities of humanity, its monumental stone buildings, chipped and carved and buttressed like a castle of the industrial age, built for a siege, but never besieged except by the millions who clamored through its chambers and waiting rooms to the tugs and ferry boats which chugged them from quarantine to the new land.

Reb Abram and Ruth bas Yaakov waited their turn in line. Nearly three months had passed since that day in Warsaw when Abram announced that they would leave Poland for America. They had made their way south to Genoa. That had taken more than a month. They had lost their suitcase when, during a night stop, gas extinguished, they were trapped in a tunnel between Switzerland and Italy. Someone had picked it up and made off with it. It was found three cars down the next day, emptied of its contents. Possessions, possessions. It wasn't their value—Reb Abram kept his money on him and his own prayer book, *tallit, teffilin* he kept in a paper bag, like a body amulet, always at his side. It was rather like

34

losing some sentimental nosegay—irrelevant, useless, but of the past, a mnemonic of a history of lives and associations about to be irrevocably abandoned and yet carried away in the guise of possessions, an old wool sweater, a pair of leather boots, a kaftan of black silk, a frivolous dress of white cotton with puff sleeves which Ruth wore on holidays, and three kerchiefs of bright color that Abram had bought for her at the station as the train was about to leave Warsaw. Abram converted part of his money into Italian currency and the rest into gold. The fortune in zlotys, though still considerable, was no longer in zlotys but in some anonymous international metal that signified to both of them the end of Jewish days and Polish nights.

The ship left Genoa the following month—a steamer with a mainsail, one of the last in the Italian merchant fleet. The decks and hold screamed with people, mostly peasants from Calabria and Sicily and Polish Jews who found it more convenient to embark from Italy than from Odessa. The trip cannot be described. It need not be. Harassment, stench, depression. Abram began to cough and Ruth became afraid that the disease of his youth had begun again. But Abram remained quiet and unafraid, reassuring her that it was only the dampness, the crowded bunks, the stifling water-laden air that made him ill.

They reached New York in sun and disembarked to dock hands flinging suitcases and trunks into a jumbled heap and officials seated before tables upon which stood the alphabet letter to which one's name assigned him.

Abram's name was Sternguecker. His great-grandfather, who had been born in one of the towns contested by Germany and Poland since the seventeenth century, had been appointed by the council of his region to survey the boundary marks which divided the emperor's realm from that of the king. He had surveyed and surveyed, using plumb lines and sightings, marching over the hills as a young man and traveling by horse cart as he approached middle age. He made the task endless, since he feared that if he finished he would be expelled and his permit card, then required of Jews living in border towns, would be revoked. It was for this reason that he managed to protract his inquiry until a conspiracy of anger and politics obliged him to make a final disposition of the matter. More than twenty years had passed since he had begun his surveyal. As he neared his fiftieth year, weariness with the task made him less anxious of its consequence. The majority of his village were German-speaking, but he disdained German Jews for their laxness of observance and considered the new currents of free-thinking sweeping out of Germany to the East a threat to solid Judaism. It was his mission to take his region out of Germany and lodge her securely in Poland. He accomplished this, but when the survey report became public the cry of perfidy that rose from his superiors and the anger of his neighbors was so great that it seemed prudent to depart the countryside in which he had lived his life and move closer to the heart of Poland, to Warsaw in fact.

The day of his departure, as the cart was being piled high with his furnishings, a crowd of boys gathered around it and parodying his name—already Stern from earlier but now unknown associations, and his profession as land surveyor— called him Sternguecker. He did not despise the attribution, having always thought, as the Psalms proposed, that the stars in the heavens gave more praise by their numberless twinkles to the one who formed them than to men who, as he had been for nearly a generation, kept their eyes upon the ground, that they might protect, divide, and die for some spot of dun-colored earth. He did not mind being a stargazer and it was as a stargazer that Abram ben Belim Sternguecker and his wife took their place in line "S" to pass into the United States of America.

"Name?" the official with the walrus mustache barked. Abram did not understand. He had no gift for languages and his ear was so cluttered with the singsong rhythms of Talmudic study that he did not readily translate from the sharp "a" of English, to the broad "a" of German.

"Name, name? Damn them. They really don't understand English," the official grumbled. He called to an assistant who stood behind him. "I've had them. Time for lunch." He disappeared into the mouth of the grey building that loomed behind him, and the young assistant with sandy blond hair and wire eyeglasses replaced him. He was a precise American. He began briskly, inflecting his German with what he took to be its Yiddish parody, but all without play or amusement.

"*Name*," he tried again.

Abram understood. "Sternguecker."

"Impossible," the young man replied. "You want all that? Excuse me. *Sie willen das?*"

"*Warum nicht? Es ist mein Name.*"

"*Aber dies ist Amerika, nicht Heimat.*"

"*Heimat ist wo bin ich*," Abram replied proudly, but his face became red and feet shuffled impatiently behind him. He coughed.

"Stern is enough," the official said, settling the matter and taking up his pen.

"Sternguecker," Abram said and began to spell out the name. The official ignored him and returned to his paper, filling in the port of embarkation, the name of the ship, the port of entry.

"Where are you going? I mean, *wo gehen Sie von hier?*"

"New York."

"Every one of you say New York. It's not milk and honey, you know."

Abram smiled. He didn't understand. Ruth smiled. She didn't understand. They signed the document "Sternguecker," but quite clearly their name was now Stern. It would remain Stern as it had been in the past before the Stargazer.

Abram and Ruth moved from one line to the next. The lines were endless—the inspection of their documents, the retrieving of their luggage, the inspection of their luggage. They had been in lines now for six hours and before them was the medical officer, neat in blue serge, his grey smock flecked with dots of dandruff. Ruth was first. She was in excellent health. Abram, however, was apprehensive. The official looked into his ears. He heard. And his eyes. His pupils dilated and contracted. No glaucoma. His reflexes showed genius. He nearly kicked the doctor. He apologized. At last the stethoscope was picked from the table and the rubber tube wriggled toward his heart. "Cough," the doctor ordered in German. Abram coughed. He coughed once and stopped. He coughed again. He coughed three times in succession. He began to cough and continued in a paroxysm of coughing. He pounded his chest to stop the cough but he continued to cough. Finally he was helped to a chair and the coughing subsided. He had lost his place in line. It was nighttime and the doctor left. All the doctors left and officials of the Hebrew Immigrant Aid Society appeared—Jews in suits and ties and women in skirts and blouses with uncovered heads. They spoke among themselves in English, although occasionally a matronly superior would order them about in German. Soup and bread were distributed and a little pamphlet printed in English, German, Yiddish and Russian was passed out describing the procedures of the day.

Abram finally understood what had happened. He even noted that sometimes names were incorrectly set down, but that later if one wished one could go to court to have the incorrect name set aside and one's ancestral patronym restored. It seemed unlikely that he would take advantage of the opportunity. New land. New name. That's that. He continued to read. The medical examination was critical. Immigrants could be returned to Europe if it was found that they were of unsound health or were incubating communicable diseases. He remembered his days with Uncle Max. The tuberculosis. The cough. He shuddered and passed the night in dread. With morning the doctors reappeared and by seven the reception hall was filled once more with surging lines of petitioners.

The doctor with flecks of dandruff was not assigned to "S" but Abram saw him three letters away. While he finished saying his morning prayers and putting away his *teffilin,* he concentrated particularly hard on asking God to blind the eyes of the doctor to his presence in the line, to stop up his chest from uttering a sound, and to pass him through to the land of respite. His turn came. The same examination again. The stethoscope. He coughed again. It did not recur. The nemesis doctor passed his line, stopped and conversed quietly with his examiner. The examiner looked up at him and frowned. Abram fibrillated with fright. The doctor frowned again, but signed his papers, and passed him through. Abram looked back to see if the doctor's eyes were following him. They were not. They were looking at another immigrant.

Abram and Ruth Stern, the Sterngueckers of Warsaw,

38

settled on what is called the Lower East Side, that swollen membrane of the city. Both registered for English classes at the Educational Alliance; both applied for assistance from the Hebrew Immigrant Aid Society and with their kindness found a cold-water apartment consisting of a tiny room and gas stove. After several months of this, Abram, already speaking English in spasms of ungrammar, found steady employment as a tailor in which craft he soon excelled. Moreover, he continued to study, arising before dawn so that he could spend an hour with his beloved Alfassi and the Turim, whose compendiums he had borrowed from the rabbi of the yeshiva across the street from the apartment. With money that Abram saved, they moved at the end of the year to a somewhat larger apartment with one front window and a small bedroom. A portion of the gold sovereigns had purchased a pushcart and a supply of vegetables and underwear which Ruth sold in the streets—the vegetables for women and the underwear for men and boys. Time passed, and though poverty had not withdrawn, it was now contained, and poverty, like wealth, entails a ritual of adaptation. The poverty of the Sterns was neat and orderly, without color, but also without odor.

Children were never discussed. They would pass children in the streets, boys with side locks, girls with black stockings, boys with hoops and sticks, girls with jump ropes, boys with broad noses and cropped heads, girls with black curls and high foreheads and Ruth would reach to touch them and Abram would busy himself with his footsteps, avoiding mud or potholes. Never children. Homes, houses, apartments, bedrooms, bathtubs, heat, light, the corodies of domestic contentment, but of children—the most critical of assets, those for whom the sages and saints prayed into the years of their wrinkled impotence—of these no word. Often Ruth would raise her head from her plate and wish to speak of the child of a neighbor or a Son of the Law who had been inducted into the covenant the previous Sabbath, but always at the last minute she averted the subject, turning back to her piece of fish and picking at a bone.

They had been married nearly five years. It was a winter of discomfort—the gas main had broken and had not been repaired, a cord of wood piled in the kitchen for the stove was nearly gone, and the lumberyard near the river was waiting for a delivery by cutter from upstate, as the roads into the East Side were clogged with snow that had not been cleared away. The bottom of the city, cut off and aloof, sustained itself upon ingenuity and atavism. Jews who had forgotten the use of Polish or Russian put on their high boots and trudged out into the streets calling to each other like muzhiks of the Old World, safeguarding Yiddish for a glass of tea or a greeting in synagogue.

Abram returned from the tailor shop two miles away, across the bridge in Brooklyn. He panted from the iciness of the air and his body shook with weariness. He lay down upon the bed and Ruth brought him a glass of tea and a sip of brandy. He gradually fell into sleep. For some time Ruth watched him, his hand moving in familiar struggle from brow to groin, slipping from one to the other, drawn away as though by another hand to return to unencumbered rest upon his forehead. It can only be surmised what transpired between the sleeping Abram and the watchful Ruth, but shortly thereafter when Ruth made known to her husband that she was bearing his child, his mood of anxious circumspection vanished and in its place an order of acceptance dropped like a collar around his life. He prayed no less than before, but he became more punctual at synagogue. He returned home no less expectantly nor departed for work no less ambitiously, but each coming and going was attended by a formality and deliberateness—his coat and cap going on with the care of an arthritic afraid of dislodging a bone—which suggested, all observed, an altered sense of self and situation. Abram divined that all would come to pass, that all that had been promised had thus far been, that this too, this final grace, would then be his, that no terror of finality, no avoidance, no nervous finger-drumming, no cough, no racing heart, no thing of this frightened world could set aside what had been determined and inscribed.

Ruth enjoyed no luxury of confinement. Had she been the daughter of a living sage, a child not of humble parents died in a plague but of prosperous and learned Jews, she would have been obliged by custom to retire into quiet the last month of her pregnancy, to sit in repose among her friends, to tend flowers and sew clothing for her infant, to plant seedlings, and say psalms. Instead she was in the streets at an early hour, buying her produce, stocking her small cart and arranging the beans and cabbages, sprinkling them with water and pushing the prepared cart to her stall on Hester Street. She wished no concession and received none. Once, at noon, Abram appeared from nowhere, put his hands on her shoulders and squeezed them affectionately. He had traveled the whole of his brief lunch period to see her, and had stood for some minutes hidden in the crowd watching her cry her vegetables and wrap those she sold in newspapers gathered and cut the night before. At any hour Ruth might pull down the wooden cover of her stand, lock it and walk quietly to their room and send a neighbor for the midwife. The world harbored no terror for her as it did for Abram. He watched her, smiling, marveling at her containment. He had been cutting a lapel that morning, attaching the fabric to its lining, and about to sew the whole to the body of the garment when, of a sudden, the voice of the visionary returned to him and he remembered her prophecy as though it had just been spoken. His hand began to shake and he almost drew the needle through a finger of his hand. He put the garment down, sat back on his stool and closed his eyes, and all he could see was a small child, an infant, in fact, setting fire to his bed. He left the shop and told Mr. Manger, his employer, that he had an errand to do for his wife and he would be back in an hour. He had to see Ruth, to know that she was all right, that nothing had happened.

"You here?" Ruth had said with delight.

"I had to see you," he answered.

"Good. It's the right time for a surprise. I think it may be this evening. The baby turns and turns, kicks at me like he's dancing. Tonight I think."

Abram clasped his hands together and then clapped them with pleasure. "He will be born tonight. Our little Messiah will come tonight."

"Why do you say that?"

For a moment Abram was embarrassed. He had never spoken of the prophecy since the day he had tormented Ruth into accepting him. She had never referred to it, fearing it, determined to have no explanation of Abram's madness.

"You remember," he said.

"Two pounds of fresh beans," a small woman demanded, pushing a ten-cent piece at Ruth.

"Not now," Ruth answered the woman. She went away. "I don't remember. I don't want to remember. It's no Messiah, this child. No Messiah. It's only a baby, our baby, that's enough. Nothing more. You hear, Abram? Don't you make our baby into a Messiah."

The conversation ended. It should be noted, however, that both had assumed from the very beginning that their child would be a boy. Granted, a common assumption, but messiahs are not women. Sages can be women, like the wife of Rabbi Meir or the sainted women of the Hasidim, or even in the company of the thirty-six righteous who bear the world as an ass bears a burden, but never messiahs. Abram and Ruth at least assumed the condition without which the prophetic destiny could not be. That was a beginning. Abram believed the mad prophet. Ruth struggled to forget her. Abram knew the whole of the prophecy. It was enough for Ruth to know only a portion, the portion of joy and promise, a portion already too magnificent for her to abide.

Ruth bas Yaakov Yitzhak of Polnoye, the wife of Abram ben Belim Stern (né Sternguecker) of Warsaw, began to labor the birth of their first and only child shortly before midnight, the eve of the commencement of the penitential month of Elul, when it is thought that the world recollects itself, in stasis, entranced by its own immediacy, cautious before its shadow. Ruth began to cry out as the contractions shortened; the midwife came; boiling water was readied; blankets opened and toweling heated and prepared. Women stood in the hallway of the tenement listening to her screams. Abram, on the other hand, having by the early hour of the new day completed his reading of the entire Book of the Psalms of David, had begun to write a letter, a letter which he folded, sealed with wax dripped from a house candle, and gave the following morning into the hands of the *gabbai* of the Klausenberger Rebbe, one of the most saintly of Hasidic rebbes, whose court was established near the shop in Williamsburg where Abram worked. The instructions to the *gabbai* were clearly stated, and for his services or those of his successors until the event should come to pass, the sum of two dollars a year was to be paid annually on the first day of Elul. The document (which I did not see until many years later, when Simon showed it to me) was to be delivered to Simon Stern at the conclusion of the period of mourning, if it were the case that both he and his wife perished in a common accident for which Simon could be in any way implicated, whether by commission —God prevent and forbid—or by negligence or dereliction.

Simon Stern was born on the first day of Elul in the five thousand six hundredth and fifty-seventh year after the Creation of the World, in the year 1899 of the ordinary calendar.

It is our tradition that on that day the Holy One paused from his meditations, and during the afternoon service of prayer, that which is called *minchah*, delivered a homily to the Congregation of Saints. The words of the homily that have been reported to us are unreliable and we cannot credit them (what value is the report of a young boy whose heart stopped beating and with electrodes and hand massage was restored to life?), but the point is well taken. The Holy One took account of the fact that on that day, many years before, an event had occurred in our world. Whatever its credibility, the only complete sentence the young ressurect could recall (the rest was fragmentary, like the text of a corrupt manuscript whose words have been effaced by wind and rain) when we questioned him was, "Is it not time, my beloved, that I should have mercy upon them?" The scholars of our Society take "beloved" to mean God's filial address to the community of sages, prophets, disciples, saints who studied in his presence and conversed of destiny in his midst. The singular, then, not the plural. But "them": who can this be other than the broken House of Israel? for we are not one, but many, and yet correctly God might confuse numbers for our sake, offering a single mercy to ease the pain of many. We understand this mercy to be Simon Stern. It need not be completely precise. It is enough that the young boy who died and was restored transacted his journey to the regions of the blessed and descended once more on the first day of Elul, forty-two years after Simon Stern had been born on this earth.

Early in the first year of our habitation at the compound of the Society for the Rescue and Resurrection of the Jews, whose origins and destruction describe the perimeter of this narrative, Simon was asked by the librarian of our community—one of several functions performed by Rabbi Steinmann, whom you will encounter later—to prepare a memoir of his childhood, since little was known of his origins, and the many hundreds of those whom he had rescued continually besieged the leadership of the community for information about their benefactor.

It was Rabbi Steinmann who, prudently, but unromantically I confess, besought me to intercede with Simon Stern for the composition of this memoir, knowing that it was I, as just described, who had free access to his quarters and with whom Simon spoke unhesitantly and without guard. (Simon always confused sight with ravagement, I believe, and regarded my blindness as a species of protection.) It came about, therefore, that Simon began to speak aloud his recollections, speaking the words and then writing them. Had our community relied upon him alone, however, no memoir would have been produced, for his interest in the project was short-lived; consumed by the energy of his person, the words of his past flooded from his mouth, stained the pages before him, and were crushed daily in a fist of irritation and thrown away. Fortunately, I was near at hand and each afternoon of his brief engagement with the task, I remembered, noted, stored, and then taking my leave with that excruciating casualness which dissimulates the wish to flee, would go to my room and transcribe what I had heard.

The memoir which follows, interleaved with other documents, contains as much as we have come to know of the childhood of Simon Stern, and for the fact that it is virtually in his own words, however pruned and strained by me of needless repetition and underscorings, is presented here as though quoted from the source.

"My childhood was pedestrian, uneventful. It was quite simply the childhood of an immigrant. No less, no more pedestrian or uneventful than that of any immigrant childhood. The

44

only occasions that recollection preserves with particular fervor are those otherwise unpredictable, but no less ordinary, moments when the glass surface of our childhood seas are rippled, even broken, but turbulences rising from the cold depths of the uterine past. Moreover, the variations of childhoods are those traditionally proposed by culture, environment, habituation—the lingering illnesses of Continental esthetes, the private schools of English gentry, the fierce winters and flaxen summers of The Steppes, the city heat and subway confusion of the New World.

"My boyhood—a Jewish boy set down in unexceptionable poverty upon the pocked pavements of New York—was not different, but for the fact that in my youth—no, at the age of five (for five is still childhood)—I was obliged to study and that not simply in deference to an inherited passion to be superior (and superiority for us had no relation to power), but more for the conviction that by means of study we—that is, I—might become equal to our past, draw level, one might say, to the extraordinary heights of our ancient progenitors (and in our imagination Mount Sinai is less a mount covered with a beard of stubble than a fast of Everest, unscalable, crevassed, treacherous, exceedingly high).

"We do not regard it, we Jews, as either an unnatural obligation or, for that matter, as impractical, foolish, irrelevant to break our opening years in study of a useless literature. That literature is for us a *mysterium*, a datum of love upon which I feasted like a beauty mark, an ecstasy of communication between the divine beast of heaven and this flock of unshorn lambs. I have always seen it as a struggle between the beast that wants more and more to consume that over which he is lord and the timorousness of the lambs who seek by dissimulation to pacify him.

"I did not know in those early years that this was my intention and, indeed, even now, I readily grant that all my belief is only a rationalization for my fear that there is finally an irreconcilable enmity among things. Nothing can abide its neighbor and the most loved deny themselves love. Knowing this, I have been obliged to labor doubly hard to disguise the chasm between men.

"It began in my childhood, when I commenced to study. It

45

is a happy conceit of parents that the learning of the sacred Law begins with honey and apples and ends with wisdom and grandchildren. It is not so. Let me assure you that it is not so. It begins on a cold morning many years before one can remember it as a fairy tale. It begins with chilblains and ends with loneliness. My father took me by my hand and brought me to the synagogue. While he stayed in the *shul* to put on his phylacteries and say the morning prayers I was delivered into the custody of a young rabbi with a beard red and ridiculous. And it was he, without a dip of apple into honey, who forced us to learn the alphabet with which God created us. I learned Hebrew as if I were learning to stay alive, as I would someday learn the streets that were dark and dangerous, as I would learn the difference between the clout of the Irish and the truncheon of the Pole, as I would learn the difference between Fourteenth Street and Houston Street, between Williamsburg and Brownsville, between pious Jews and Jews who were poor, or between pious poverty and jealous poverty, between pious wealth and envious poverty, between rich Jews and poor Jews, and the most important fact that once one knew all the differences, there were really none, that all letters of the alphabet were sweet and brutal, that none was higher or lower and that for a five-year-old in winter, with only tea and oatmeal in his stomach when the rabbi pinched his cheek to praise, it hurt as much as if he had rapped him on the ears.

"I endured those days and surrendered myself to them: in the evening, after supper, my father would sit himself down before my bed, and leaning back, his eyes closed, encourage me to sing aloud the lesson of the day and picking up the rhythm of my chant would join me until often both of us, rocking back and forward, were together shouting out to God his alphabet, crying aloud *aleph* and *bet, gimmel* and *dalet, heh* and *vav*. It was easy to sleep on those nights. The cold gave way to springtime and however tired he was my father would take me on walks on those warmer evenings through the streets of our world and point out to me the wonderful and the forbidden, all the time bringing me back again and again to a passage of the *Mishnah* and later the Talmud and after that the *Tosefot* and the Codes and then, by the time of my bar mitzvah, into the lighter mysteries of the Kabbalah.

"On vacation days when the intermediate days of Passover yawned empty, the feasts past, the massive trays of gefilte fish reduced to solitary balls of blended whitefish and carp floating in a gelatinous sea, dotted with islands of carrot or floating rafts of parsley; and the hard and mottled *matzot* of affliction which my father bought at the bakery of the most strict of rabbis, whose wheat was grown and harvested in a guarded field of New Jersey, and winnowed and beaten into the purest of flour which became the round bread, bleached of tenderness and the ease of the world, were almost consumed; and ahead lay only that last outburst of the Seventh and Eighth Days of the festival, when the Jews, subdued by pious gluttony, humbled by abstention in the intermediate four days when nothing divine would occur and nothing profane was permitted, would take courage once more to face the Almighty—on those in-between days, those of Passover, or those of Succot, or the days before the New Year, as his very own disciple, I studied with my father. Our small apartment was filled to bursting with our study. Nor would my father's employer, Mr. Manger, the pious Jew who owned the tailoring establishment in Williamsburg where Hasidim and observant Jews throughout the land purchased everything from long black silk outer coats to business suits, all certified to be free of *shatnez* (that mixture of wool and cotton which suggested license, perversity, the confusion of the world which the ancient pious of Israel avoided so passionately), raise any objection if my father sent word that he would be absent from work because his beloved Simon (that is, myself) needed him that day for holy study and conversation.

"On the ordinary days (and they were so many and so routine) my father would rise at the first suffusion of light, wash, bless, eat, bless, hurry to synagogue and bless once more and climb aboard the streetcar to Williamsburg, often saying: 'What shall I say to the Holy One when he asks me a question? Can I tell him that I had no time for the *Mechilta* or the *Yerushalmi*, that I had to mend garments, cut lapels, sew inseams? Master of the World. Forgive me.' The little monologue, addressed to the air, blustered at street

47

lights, overheard by shopkeepers, would make his world smile. And indeed it was the case that my father made some of the world smile.

"Excepting the days of festivals and the between days when the world was suspended in indecision, my father had little time to study. On festival days, however, Abram ben Belim the Levite (for he was known in all his world as Abram, even as Reb Abram, though it was New York, and a new century had begun, and the winds of different times coursed through the settlement of the Jews as heady and elevating as they did through the centers of Christendom in that land) would begin to study, and he would study and he would study until his eyelids, like wax thinned to transparency, would redden and tear, and only then would he put off his reading glasses, groan at his labor, and say aloud the *Kaddish* reserved for scholars finishing the deliberations of the day. So intent was he on making himself a holy vessel that in his clumsiness he was inattentive to the swirl of the universe about him.

"It was in this way, through the community of joy which my father and I celebrated, that I came to be educated.

"Secular learning? The very phrase meant nothing to my father. It was of little consequence to me. Learning was learning. The letters of the Bible were no more exquisite than the numbers of mathematics or the commas and semicolons of English. Of course I went to public school. So that's clear."

It is appropriate to introduce here a documentation of more than circumstantial relevance to the narrative. In the last year of the Society, before the end, as a blind to other and more dangerous inquiries, Dr. Fisher Klay—whose presence will be felt later at the appropriate juncture in the narrative—retained the services of a firm of private investigators to research and account for the unknown years in the life of Simon Stern. The Lubrice Detective Bureau, whose principal investigator was Harold Gusweller, assisted by Leopold Pan, was paid generously to help us enflesh the bare bones of Simon's memoir, for as we have seen, these are more of a pious celebration of his father, Abram, than a revelation of himself and his own origins and education.

The testimonies of Miss Gloria Lavine, Rebbe Yaakov Mangel, and Milton Rubino are, for the reason given, all the more illuminating.

Depositions and Accounts

DOCUMENT #1

Miss Gloria Lavine

Fifth-Grade Teacher, Public School Number 2, located at Essex and Stanton Streets, New York City.

Miss Gloria Lavine, present residence: Winter Park, Florida. Miss Lavine was interviewed in the public mango garden of Winter Park. She and the interviewer sat across from each other, while she exercised on a stationary bicycle, whose seat, shaped like a trough (or was it like a baseball glove?) received her amply. She seemed relaxed, tanned, her face shone with coconut oil.

She remembered the subject of the inquiry and spoke of him without hesitation. It did not seem to us that she was forcing herself to remember. No lips pursing in thought, no neck, scalp, or face scratching, no finger raised to forehead to stimulate intellectual effort, nor did it appear that she was hedging truth with the decorative bushes of fantasy, for at no point did Miss Lavine employ the convention of the dimpled smile or eyes lowering into an appeal for credulity, nor did she, but once, as you will note in the body of the report (at a minor point, we believe), refer to her age as an invitation to charity.

We think her testimony particularly valuable. It appears subject was remarkable even at an early age.

Signed: Leopold Pan
Staff Investigator
Lubrice Detective Bureau

"How could I ever forget little Simon. Wherever did he come from and whatever became of him? I can see him now, Mr. Investigator. He was a mite of a boy, standing just over the rim of his desk, only thing showing were those big eyes, and those long Jewish-looking black eyelashes. (I'm Jewish, you know, but down here it don't make sense speaking of it

49

too much. Why, Winter Park don't have but a few and we keep it quiet. You understand, don't you now?)

"It was a murky morning—my Lord, must have been near forty, forty-five years ago. Not completely sure, but don't you worry, Mr. Investigator, you got the right Gloria Lavine. Yes, sir, I remember that little, little boy. He just came in that morning, opened the door, and announced that—what'd he say?—always remember that line—'Simon Stern reporting for school and homework.' Loved that. Why, we didn't give those little ones homework. Happy to keep 'em off the streets and away from their mothers. Quite enough, that. I laughed. 'No homework, son. Lots of fun here.' The children laughed, too. At me, I guess. They didn't think it was much fun. But he answered, pert and snappy, 'I have no time to waste.' That sort of stopped me. All that serious talk from such a little one. Made you think he had something special on his mind. What'd you say he was doing? I mean, what's he done that you're asking me all these questions?

"His intelligence? All children, you know, all of them are intelligent or at least terribly fanciful. Why, they just love mind games and I loved playing them. Thought games, I called them. 'Now, children, pay attention, we'll have a thought game.' Simon really loved them. But sometimes he frowned, 'cause, like he told me once: 'That takes no thought, Miss Lavine.' He was right. I never made a mistake in one of my thought games. He said, 'Without a mistake, Miss Lavine, there's no thought at all.' Now, that sets you thinking, don't it, Mr. Investigator? Simon's aptitude? He learned everything, first time out and then rest of the period he'd just lay back in his seat and look around, smiling to himself. Sometimes I'd snap my fingers at him. Listen here, Simon. Just 'cause you're a smarthead. You listen here. 'Yes, ma'am,' he'd say, and snap up.

"Show any religious bent? That's a strange question, mister. Don't really know for sure, but I will tell you this, and I call it religious—maybe you don't, because you're a big man, but me, well, I'm not much taller than Simon was and so I think it's religion for us small people. Well, once a big strong boy, Timmy Shawn, rushed in late for homeroom and didn't see little Simon standing back of the door—you know, those

homeroom doors with frosted glass, you only see the shadow
of things—well, in charges Timmy and knocks over Simon,
knocks him clean out—I always thought he elbowed him,
but you never really know. You're what extract, Mr. Investigator? You don't know? Well, Timmy, he was Irish. All events,
knocked little Simon on his ass. When Simon came to, he just
looked up at us all: 'There's no hope for the meek, you know.
None at all. And I'm not meek, even if I am small as a gnat.
Watch now.' He got up and threw out a flat hand at Timmy
which in a twinkle bunched into a fist. Hit Timmy on the
shin. He doubled over in pain. No idea where he learned that,
but it sure worked. Timmy never made for the little ones
again. That little meek boy, Simon, inherited the earth, didn't
he now, Mr. Investigator? Kind of reverse religion, I always
thought. Not the Jesus kind, but some kind for the little
people who don't go to church. It's hard to think you're meek
and small and disinherited from the things of this world when
you got four hundred millions of one kind and three hundred
millions of another, all saying, 'We're meek, boy, are we meek
and disinherited.' Don't remember much more. Yes sir, Simon
Stern was smart and kept his own counsel."

DOCUMENT #2
Concerning the learning and piety of Abram ben Belim Stern
(né Sternguecker), father of the subject, Simon Stern.
Yaakov Mangel, the so-called Pintele Rebbe, from the village
of Pintel, Hungary.
    The Pintele Rebbe is semiretired, living in a home for
aging rabbis of the Hasidic Jewish persuasion. When this investigator called upon him he was at first refused admittance.
It became necessary to buy a black fedora (a bill for which
will be attached to expenses at the end of the month), as
the ordinary nakedness of my head was doubly unappealing
to these *Obgehitene Yiden* ("Guardian Jews," as this phrase
was translated to me by the director of the institution, the
only official, it appears, at the Shomrei Torah Home for Aged
Hasidim who spoke English with competence), who, it seemed
to me, did more to cover their heads than most people
nowadays do to cover any other part of their body.
    The Pintele Rebbe, nearing ninety-three I was told, was

wheeled into the recreation room—so called because it was the
only room with no beds, being regarded as recreative because
the walls were lined with learned tomes which an attentive
younger scholar would lift and bring to the table of a visitor,
open, find the page desired and sometimes even read aloud
to the infirm and blind who gather there before the afternoon
services—for our interview.

What follows is, I am afraid, an inadequate report, but it
is all that could be secured.

Signed: Leopold Pan
Staff Investigator
Lubrice Detective Bureau

"He was so pious. He was a *grosser hasid* ("a great and
pious Jew") until his son was born. Before his son's birth he
was almost a *shtickel rebbe* (meaning one who partakes of the
intrinsic thoroughgoing holiness of a *rebbe*). His son made
the difference, but I avoided seeing Reb Abram after the
birth of his son. There was something strange about all that.
Before, when he first came to this country, he was climbing
the rungs like a Torah athlete, one rung of piety after another.
And then, suddenly one day, he didn't come to my study
period. I was teaching the *baalei batim* (the householders)
the Laws of *Sotah*—about adulterous women, may they all
swell and burst—and he didn't come. I knew that he had
already mastered the tractate and all its commentaries, but
he was to me like a whelp to a lion. I needed him at my side.
But he didn't come. As I walked home from the house of study
that night I passed a library where they have forbidden books
in English and other languages and I saw him through the big
glass window sitting at a table reading. He didn't see me. But I
saw him. I saw that his beard was trimmed and his earlocks
were tucked behind his ears. I knew at that moment he was
lost to us. I didn't see him again for more than a year. I
mourned him. But you can't go on mourning lost Jews."

DOCUMENT #3
Milton Rubinc
Library assistant at the Carnegie Free Library, now Public
Library Branch at 415 East Houston Street for more than

a generation, presently the proprietor of a secondhand book-store specializing in occult literature.

Mr. Rubino was familiar with Abram ben Belim as well as with Simon Stern. When Rubino was contacted he was in the process of arranging a window in his bookshop on astrology. He is a corpulent man in his early seventies, with a face like a nectarine, soft, rotund, roseate. He stood in his white sweat socks in the window and padded through the mountains of books like a circus elephant. He smoked incessantly.

Signed: Leopold Pan
Staff Investigator
Lubrice Detective Bureau

"Yeah, I knew Abram. We were both young then and new to the country. I confess I was a greenhorn. Not Abram though. He was damned smart, although he didn't know a word of English the first time I met him. But between the Alliance and me he got an education.

"The first month he was here he came into the library around closing time and stood near the checkout desk. He didn't say a word. Finally I said to him, 'You want something, mister?' He didn't answer, not even a diffident smile. Nothing. I thought maybe he didn't understand, so I spoke to him in Yiddish. (Sure, I know Yiddish. I can see you don't believe me. Name like Rubino. But that's just Rubin with an 'o' tacked on by my mother—a fancy *yenta* she was.) Polish Jew just like Abram. I was older, though, and had been in the States about five years.

"Anyways, he finally said he wanted some books about the origins of man. And I thought, Hell, he can't read them. I explained we didn't have any books in Yiddish. He said that he read Hebrew, Russian, Polish and German. Didn't have many of those either. But I dug out one or two things in German and brought them out—something by that biologist Uekull, and a little vitalist stuff by Rudolf Eucken and prob-ably some others. He thanked me, asked if he could come back regularly and I said Sure, laughed, didn't think twice about it. That was the beginning. Came back every night before we closed for more than a year. Only on holy days he didn't show. But I was used to that. Sometimes we'd have a tea together and talk about the old country and about the new one. I realized that he was very well educated—a brilliant Hebrew scholar and very knowledgeable in the Enlightenment literature—you know, standard stuff, Eugène Sue, Zola, Tolstoy, Dostoevsky, a little Goethe and Schiller, and the good solid modern Jewish classics, along with Kant, Mendelssohn, Krochmal, Luzzatto, what have you? But he didn't know English. So we went to work. Got him and his wife to the Alliance. Before you knew it, he was talking and reading. Told me he used to study every night until one, two in the morning and then after synagogue on the way to work. Read everything—signs, pamphlets, advertisements, papers, anything with an English word on it got Abram's attention. Used to say to me: 'It's hard in this country, harder than Poland, even if you do make more and buy more things. There nobody forced you to work if you wanted to starve or beg. Here nobody needs to, you do it yourself.' How'd he put it? *'In Amerika, man yogd sich alein*—in America you chase yourself all alone.'

"Then his kid was born and off the kid goes at five to Hebrew school, and then when he's six or seven, and reading holy tongue like a little genius, Abram starts bringing him in. The kid was really something. He was a fright—face all blue veins crisscrossing dead white—but a genius. He'd read like a buzz saw. Take out six, seven books at a time and bring them back next day. Then I noticed something curious about the kid . . . Simon, yes, Simon, that's right. Simon concentrated. He didn't just pick up a book, look at the title, sample the story, check for pictures, and if it pleased him borrow it. No. He'd come in and say—I guess he was about eight then —'Mr. Rubino, I'd like everything you have on prehistoric animals.' I'd get him ten or eleven books and away he'd go. Just on dinosaurs. Then it'd be the stars, then geology, then plants and invertebrates, then mammals, and so on until he'd digested a whole bite of human knowledge.

"The big thing when he was about eleven was the history of commerce: gold, real estate, stock markets, and not just the easy pablums they feed out now, you know, things like *Books to Begin On: Your First Book of Money.* Not for him. He wasn't interested in the why, only the how. I asked him once what all this practical turn was about and he answered with no fuss: 'God is why. I am how. That's the way it is.' "

There were other depositions and documents which Messrs. Gusweller and Pan presented to us—to Dr. Klay and myself that fateful week before the end—but they were less relevant to our inquiry into Simon's origins and growing up to manhood. No need to tell about the neighborhood shoemaker who remembers fixing the family boots and shoes or the gabbai of the synagogue who recalls Simon cleaning out the shul one winter's morning ("as a penance," he said) or the stall-keepers who spoke kindly of his mother, Ruth. These depositions and many others were asides of obfuscation, embellishments which Mr. Gusweller had instructed Leopold Pan and his staff to assemble to keep attention away from the main issue. As it turned out, they weren't even necessary and many of them may well be fanciful or even untrue. Those I have just presented and several others which will appear in due course I regard as having weight, setting off and affording contrast and highlight to the remainder of Simon Stern's own brief memoir, which follows.

"From the dawn until nine in the morning I would be in *cheder*—learning Talmud—and from nine until the middle of the afternoon I was a citizen.

"When school ended and children ran into the streets to shout and throw balls at each other, I would go to a park and sit there, looking at trees. Looking at trees is innocent, or the flowers, or the children playing stickball or roller-skating. I would just sit. There was no point trying to join in the games of the children. For one thing, I disliked games and never found it necessary for my recreation to play them. But I guess, to be more truthful, no one would play with me. In the time of games, I was so diminished in form and capacity that I would appear, were I to run in the streets or jump into the air or balance myself on a stoop, more like a yapping lap dog than a growing boy.

"I was a speck, beautifully formed as specks will sometimes be, reflecting all the symmetry and undulation of the molecular composition of the wood or coal of which they are now but the black remains, but specks are not desirable in games. It did not matter to me that I was regarded with disdain, sometimes with anger. It could not be helped that I was disastrously small and enormously smart, that I could barely see above the top of my wooden desk, that my feet did not yet touch the floor, that my head was disproportionately large, that my hands were thin and tapered, that my eyes were brown with flecks of red like pomegranate seeds, and that my substance, my weight, my density were as a speck, nothing. And so I would watch from the bench of the park the flood of youth wash into the streets all the joy and disappointment, the competitive idolatry, the agility and grace, the loyalties and antagonisms out of which, of necessity, the normal man and the enviable mediocrity of the species is matured.

"What else for me but to dream? In those days my dreams were all of power and glory, money and success, glory and money, success and glory and money and power. I dreamed those dreams to revenge myself.

"Vengeance is ignoble. Even God is embarrassed by His vengefulness. He repents of having drenched and nearly drowned Creation. He promised to cease and desist. I recall that narrative often when I become vengeful, but unlike Him—and the chasm between us is vast—I have none of the genius to make a world nor the strength to destroy it. I have only the human truthfulness to admit that I have wanted both to create and to destroy. Thus my vengefulness. And why that?

"It began at the time I am now recalling, when I was a child of eight. I did a generous act—no, more than that, a lordly act—and the consequence was a disaster for my mother and father, may they rest in peace.

"In the summer of this city, heat is unimaginable. I think it must be like Rangoon during the rains or Bombay or the steaming jungles of South America. It is less the heat—that would be sufficient, or the absence of air—all that, too—than the moisture, the humidity, the condensation which clings to one's face and eyes like jelly, droplets so thick with the filthy stuff of the air that they hang suspended, unable to fall away. At that time of year—the windows open, the fire escapes crowded with bedding, the iceman coming with chunks of ice already smooth from melting, the tepid tea standing upon a table with a single lifeless chip of lemon floating, the bedclothes sticky with sweating bodies—the whole disgusting spectacle of the human is spread out before one's eyes. In that time of year people speak little, and when they speak, their anger is in their eyes and in the clipped, scarcely articulate issuing of commands and acknowledgment of being commanded.

"It was Friday afternoon in August. The Black Fast of Av was the following week. My father was not yet home from the tailor shop in which he worked. My mother was at her stall, closing up for the Sabbath, disposing at mark-down prices of the few perishables that would not survive until the following night.

"I was alone in the apartment. The sun flashed orange-red through the room which was our living room, dining room, my bedroom and portion of the kitchen. The weight of heat made movement an encumbrance, and motionlessness a respite and for that fact cool and quiet. Cool and quiet; heat and motion. I read. I had discovered a novel by a Russian translated into Yiddish. It was under my father's pillow. I should have studied the rabbinic commentaries on the Book of Lamentations. An appropriate scourging of the soul in preparation for the fast to come or the Sabbath portion or even my mathematics homework. Novels were frivolous and forbidden, but my holy father studied novels, so why not I? I read at random, curious to discover what it was that my father was reading. It seemed a laborious work—that impression I retain—long disquisitions on human fatuity and corruption, punctuated by scenes of incredible drama. One I recall: a man throws a bundle of rubles into a fire, and another, at the last moment, reduced to vulgar incoherence, rescues them.

"The light began to fade in the room. My mother had lit the stove at noontime, and the soup of beans and meat which was our Sabbath fare was simmering slowly. Later a gentile woman would make the rounds to check each Jewish household, to do chores forbidden on the Sabbath. (I disliked this custom, but the exigencies of the Law made it a mandatory arrangement.)

"Where was my mother? She was late. The room began to steam. I returned the novel to my father's bedside, but failed —deliberately, I imagine—to hide it once more beneath his pillow. I was eight but discriminating. He had no need to fear that I would succumb to the finicky world of the imagination.

"There was movement in the hall, a shuffle, a cough. A voice spoke somewhere in the corridor, muffled by the heat, undulant and indistinct. Yiddish, English? I wasn't certain. A rap on our front door. My mother never knocked, but perhaps her arms were full. She would often arrive home from her stand laden with packages and parcels, particularly if it had been a prosperous day and she had sold all her produce. But this was not her sound. I opened the door slowly, unafraid but circumspect. An old man? Not old as old men ultimately become, but old to my eyes. Fifty, sixty. Somewhere between those extremities of age. But more than his age or the indefiniteness of his age was the smell that rose from him, a smell of fish and urine and perspiration. There was a stain on his pants running from the crotch to the cuff of his canvas trousers and he wore socks. Not shoes, only socks. He moaned and said nothing. He could see that I was a small boy, a terribly small boy, and so he moaned. He moaned more insistently and then stopped.

" 'Open the door wide,' he commanded. I slammed the door shut. Silence resumed. I pressed myself against the door. My heart pounded and beads of perspiration fell from my matted hair into my eyes and stung them. I could hear his breathing through the door, the shuffling of his padded feet, a moan.

" 'What do you want?'

" 'Nothing, dear child. I want nothing. A Sabbath charity. All I want is a Sabbath charity.'

" 'Stay where you are. I'll bring you something.' I went to my parents' closet and felt the pockets of my father's good suit. Nothing. I went through my mother's change purse—she carried a leathern purse tied with a thong about her waist when she was working—but there was nothing. No pennies. No nickels. I had no money. There was no money in the house. 'I have nothing to give you,' I called to him remorsefully.

"The old man moaned once more. 'I don't believe you,' he whined. 'A Jewish house without a penny for the poor. I don't believe you. Well, then,' he said sternly, 'give me something else.'

" 'What?'

" 'A coat, a shirt, a sweater. No. Better. I want a pair of shoes. Old shoes. It doesn't matter. Old shoes. I have no shoes.'

"I ran to the closet in my parents' bedroom where I had looked for money. Above the closet there was a shelf filled with wrapping paper, the canvas bag which my parents had carried from Europe, and five, maybe six, shoe boxes, with old shoes of mine and my father's. I pulled one out. Another fell from above it into the space it had vacated. I lifted the cardboard lid. A pair of black shoes, scuffed and dirty. I ran to the door, opened it and pressed the box into his hand. I shut the door again. He laughed. The moan ceased. He laughed and his laugh was filled with spit and mucus.

" 'Shoes. What do I need shoes? Have a pair tied around my waist. Stupid boy. Sell them for a quarter, maybe fifty cents. That's a living?'

"I became angry. He didn't need shoes. I would have run after him and grabbed the box from his hand, but he would have hit me. It was charity. He didn't appreciate it. So much the better. Don't humiliate the poor. All the laws of charity despise the humbling of the poor, the pride of the donor. Just as well. An unwanted gift, reluctantly received, converted into coin, into food, into well-being for a disgusting, perhaps even an evil, old man.

("For a drunk, a quarter; a blind man, a quarter and pat his German shepherd; a confused old lady, directions; a cripple, an arm on which to rest; a melancholic, a smile— for all these, the disabled of our world, small gestures, bestowed from the reservoir of our largesse, deep and cool, endless, from which we draw dollops and pat the faces of men. Our charities, our benefices. And we believe them. For us they are gifts. We give them easily. They are easy to give. Hurt yourself when you give—the advice of those who delight in the gift less than they delight in the pain of giving and who, for the pain they suffer in the gift, demand so much more from the receiver. They want the recipient to throw away his crutches and dance, blind men to see. Celebrating the charity they demand for it has pained me. No. That's quite wrong. Worse. They want the cripple to bend more heavily, to limp more profoundly, to cry out his anguish more unselfishly, demonstrating his misery like a reward.

" 'Give that beggar a quarter,' the man said to his child. Let the child reply, as he should, as he should, 'Give it to him yourself.' But that's not the way. 'You have from me,' the father admonishes the child and 'you must learn to share it with the unfortunate.' The child takes the coin, tentatively. He walks toward the beggar. The beggar sees him approach and because the beggar begs he holds his cap open for the child, he thrusts the cap to the child, he may even bend toward the child and the child averts his eyes, and perhaps in supplication, even asks permission of the beggar to address to him his coin and puts the coin into the hat. The child turns and runs away, flees toward his father. What has happened? The father has strengthened the bondage of the child by establishing a moral culpability between them as well as injuring him in that he has obliged the child to acknowledge the similitude that joins his own fragility to the human wreckage of the beggar. Not love brings the child to the beggar, but torment dropped like an iron mask over his face. Torment and obligation. You possess. He does not. But the child possesses nothing but his openness and vulnerability. Children. Tell your parents to give to beggars by themselves. Reply to the admonitory parent: 'I will give to my own beggars in my own time.')

"But that was not the case with me. I gave to that beggar, whom I feared, who set upon me like a carnivore. I have given many pairs of shoes to beggars in my life since that hour (although I never wear shoes of leather any more and sometimes the beggars refuse my canvas shoes and sneakers), but I have always taken them from my feet and I have handed them to the beggar and I have said nothing nor inquired of their fit nor of their comfort. And I have walked away in my self-possession, indifferent to the utility of my gesture. Mine, yours. You want, I provide. But I will permit the gift no savor of moral transaction. None. Cold-blooded and reptilian, the aloofness of the world that is today, in our time, so much more brutal and devastated than it ever was when St. Martin gave a cloak or St. Francis stripped himself in the square of Assisi.

"And my mother returned at last and kissed me and hushed me when I began to speak of the beggar's visit. She hurried and bustled, for the Sabbath hour, late on that summer's evening, would shortly arrive. My father returned and he, too, tired and discomforted by the heat of the trolley car and the walk through the cemented caverns of the below city, would hear nothing of me or mine until he had bathed and changed his clothing. The hour came. We went off to synagogue, his clammy hand holding mine. We prayed and bowed, opened our arms to the Queen of the Sabbath, saluted her, returned, kissed our mother, praised, blessed, broke bread, ate, sang, blessed and died into the evening heat.

"It was late. It seemed that it was another day, when at last they turned to me and inquired of my news. I told them of the hours in *cheder* and the school hours and the hours in the park and the hours in the library and my hour, my last hour before they returned home, and of the beggar. 'And so finally, having no money to give him, I gave him that for which he asked.' 'And what was that?' my father asked kindly, delighted in my story. 'A pair of shoes.'

"The silence began. The silence mounted like the night heat, and fireflies and mosquitoes sat upon that silence as upon a fetid breeding ground. Its heaviness, its desperation. Both my parents, as one, burned their eyes into me. There was no word. My father rose, slowly, lifting himself from his chair, his hands pressed against the white tablecloth. The Sabbath candles threw shadows upon his face. I wanted to sing another song. I would have shouted, but the silence and heat choked me. My father walked to the bedroom. My mother sat, frozen, pillared to rigidity, the pulse in her temples bulged like the throat sac of a frog. And then my father screamed. We rushed to him. White, white as though dead, he sat upon the floor, his nails digging into the sides of his face. 'Dearest son, dearest son, you have given away everything—the gold sovereigns, your mother's ring, your mother's ring. Aiiiii. It all begins.'

"I knew nothing until that moment of gold sovereigns or of jewels. I was a poor boy, and poorness, like all things vague but omnipresent, was a bitter liquor distilled from many grains. It was nothing of itself. To me now, as then, it was not even an essence, an abstraction, but a condition whose character was lack and depletion, whose language was composed of impossible, even inconceivable, nouns such as chicken (which we ate but once in my childhood), glazed fruits (which I have come to adore), theater (which I despise but know to be a luxury), automobiles, planes, ocean liners, and most of all, works of art (which I accumulate the way other men buy dozens of shirts or silk underwear to repay the memory of nakedness clothed in tatters). Gold sovereigns? Jewels? These were inconceivable. As my parents wept is it any wonder that I stood amazed? They sat upon the floor; they tore at their flesh. I stood beside them trembling with wonder and confusion.

"Could I have understood then that the loss of possessions is not to be mourned or could I have learned then that the acquisition of possessions is to be prized more than any legendary valorous woman or the children she might bear me? I have no certainty of this, but I continue to scrutinize myself through the magnificatory loop of recollection. I was only eight, but even then I had the power to impoverish.

"They sat upon the floor: my father slapped his face in grief, my mother with one hand sought to stay his scourging and with the other circled my neck and drew me close, hugging me, kissing my forehead, my hair, my eyes. At last the amazement dissolved into remorse and I wept, crying aloud their names, Father Abram, Mother Ruth. For some hours we sat and wept upon that Sabbath evening. With the sovereigns, it was not more than three, four hundred dollars. Three, four hundred. That was all, and yet for those sovereigns and that ring and the trinkets of their ancestry my parents wept as though abandoned.

"The weeks that followed were painful beyond reckoning. What I recall, now—an image of an image of memory, distorted and amended by the brutal education given me by that obscene beggar and my crippled parents—is scarcely complete.

"In the weeks that followed, the Fast of Av, which we observed more in mourning for our real devastation than for any symbolic grief over a destroyed Jerusalem, my father went out each morning and returned, wrapped in a shawl of silence and yet we—my mother and I—feared for him. His silence was prescient. Like a dry leaf closed into a book, he seemed frail and ready to crumble. We dared not speak around him, moving like aliens in his midst, we made no noise, cast no shadow on his place, laughed not, neither did we smile. He groaned occasionally, taking bicarbonate of soda in a hot glass of water to clear his knotted stomach of smells and odors. But he did not speak. Twice, the Sabbath after our loss and then again two weeks later, he tried to speak. Once when my mother announced happily that her diligence and energy had earned for us in the week three dollars more than in any previous week, he replied dryly, 'What's three dollars against thousands.' He thought that we had lost thousands. And another time, returning from our visit to the library—we interrupted none of our routines, only conducted them without conversation—I saw in a pile of disused furniture a brass pot which my mother recognized to be of fine Russian quality and used thereafter for making our Sabbath gruel; he commented sourly, 'Would that it was filled with gold.'"

It is at this juncture that my scribal transcription of Simon's memoir ends. He lost interest? No. I think not. The enormity of the remembered pain was too vast. It was left to me to complete what he would not finish himself, although he often alluded to his ill-fated charity when others made reference to his exaggerated wealth.

A General Observation:
As early as can be authentically documented—that is, about 1920, when Simon was approaching twenty-one—he was observed to wear canvas shoes with rubber soles. From that time forth Simon only wore canvas shoes. It is quite possible that he began this custom much earlier, perhaps even in reaction to the disastrous gift of his eighth year, although

there is no direct evidence for such an assumption. It is only known that from 1920 to the present the wearing of leather in any form ended. Some have thought that this eccentricity signified that like the High Priests of ancient times he regarded himself to be a priest, all life a sacrifice, and the world a sanctuary. Too neat. Or that Simon opposed the killing of animals. Not at all. He enjoyed fish and chicken, though it is true he disliked the flesh of quadrupeds in general and bovines in particular. I think only that it was a crotchet, though I know he had poor arches and canvas upon thick gum and rubber soles is softer by far than leather. It may be something else, however. Everything is possible with Simon Stern.

DOCUMENT #4

Concerning the recovery of an unintended charity.

Attanasio Santucci, retired night watchman of a lumber, coal and ice yard on West Houston Street for nearly sixty years, lives with his youngest daughter, unmarried, on Mulberry Street. The questioning of Mr. Santucci was extremely difficult due to interviewee's extreme age (eighty-seven), his patent senility, and the absence of all teeth.

I put the question as simply as possible, but only after innumerable variants—each time shifting and compounding words, syntax, meaning, in the hope that by some deft contrivance I could cut through the fog of age and charge the faltering battery of his mind. At last I succeeded. Mr. Santucci stopped drooling, his daughter wiped his mouth with a dustcloth, and he spoke: "Yes. Insect child. Yes. Insect child. Stand with Jew lady. Rain. Snow. No matter. Four hours. Five hours. Every morning. Sun rays. Sun sky. Speaka da bums. Bum bastards drunk. No capisce. Back next sun ray. Hours. Weeks. Months. Whole year. Long ways back. Insect boy."

Signed: Leopold Pan
Staff Investigator
Lubrice Detective Bureau

At dawn in the city, at the moment when blue streaked black and clumps of red huddled behind the folds of night,

Ruth would come to Simon's room and kiss his forehead. He would rise, wash his hands in the tin basin beside his bed, yawn the prayer of awakening and dress quickly. They would be gone before the light had come. Ruth had set a kettle on a low flame and in an hour its whistle would awaken Abram. Descending to the street the first heat of the day, sullen and recalcitrant, would break from the night embrace of buildings and alleys, and stale odors of hops and garbage would descend with the humidity of late summer.

The end of the August of their impoverishment. They would walk swiftly—Simon's hand enclosed by the hand of his mother—toward the lumberyard on West Houston Street where beggars and bums of all faiths passed the night. Ruth would pass a drunkard sprawled in a doorway and demand of Simon: "Him?" "No, too old," Simon would answer. Or fall upon a greybeard starched with coal dust, and pull his head up by the beard, leaving behind his hat like a receptacle propped against a doorpost, and thrusting his face into Simon's, would ask, "Maybe him?" But it was not him and it would never be him and in a rage Ruth would release the beard and the insensate head would fall back into the receptacle hat and crack against the post. They would never find him. Sometimes, in frustration, Ruth would scream at Simon horrible imprecations, "Little scum, wretch," and other times deliver moralisms about the cruelty and untrustworthiness of the world. They gave up a month after the loss of their wealth. They knew they would never find the beggar, but one month ended the time of rigorous mourning and eleven months remained before the mourning time was past. They mourned the loss as though a living person had been taken from them, and though they did not set forth to seek and find as early, and sometimes on beautiful days when the fall sun was veiled with grey-white frost they did not go out at all, on hideous days when it was wet and damp or in the days of snow, it was all the more necessary to rise early before the blue had streaked the black of night and hurry to the lumberyard to stand beneath the portico that sheltered cut boards and beams and watch the beggars lurch up and struggle to shelter and surround them under the portico and suffer their disgusting smells and filthy clothing like a penance.

A year from the day of the loss the mourning ended. Ruth prepared a feast of potatoes and carrot sharlat and a small piece of boiled beef with an onion and there was a twist bread freckled with caraway seeds and a bottle of sweet wine, and although Abram did not say a concluding prayer glorifying the mysterious and controversial ways of God, it was clear to the three of them that a cycle of mourning had ended, that a tombstone chiseled with letters of commemoration ineffaceable to time, was installed in the loam of their memory.

During the year of their ravagement, when the tremor and shock of accurate prophecy was recorded in the life of Simon Stern, the world passed no less relentlessly through its own cycles. An abortive attempt made to overthrow the tyrannies of the Czar had failed and Russia gave itself over to a lecherous monk and the Ochrana; a Viennese doctor, employing new and radical techniques of therapy, relieved a woman of hysteria; Germany was consolidating an army to conquer Europe; the United States marines occupied a Caribbean nation and despoiled her; a novelist of Jewish extraction commenced to write a monumental autobiographic expostulation of his public and private fantasies; and there were, besides, famines and earthquakes; children were born deformed and there were uneventful births, and people were hanged, burned, murdered, strangled in their vomit and there were countless quiet deaths.

The year of 1908 passed and successive years passed.

It is my confession that I have no patience with the legends of childhood. It does not seem convincing to me that the child gives birth to the man. I know that the logic of the organism and the prejudice of parents and the presumptions of science contradict my hostility, but I remain no less hostile, no less unconvinced. I grant willingly, no, more, aggressively, that grown men are infrequently little more than the extension and protuberation of childish proportions. Should one think otherwise of slovenly adults, grotesque in their exaggerated infantilism, that they are more than the child written in

66

elephantine majuscules? Since, however, I am a scribe—moreover a Hebrew scribe for whom all letters are square-cut, majuscules, not minuscules—all is evenness and undiscrimination. Accent and emphasis are achieved not by stylistic variants of the scribe, by the elaborate flourishes of his pen, his delicate thins and elegant ascenders, descenders, his bravura serifs. None of these. For me, a Hebrew scribe, the lowest-paid religious profession of my people (it was written in the time of the ancient rabbis that scribes should be prevented from growing rich lest they give up the writing of scrolls and other holy artifacts and indulge their leisure in less exalted and eye-saving occupations), the joy of transcription is precisely in the fact that the opportunities of embellishment are limited.

The gentile scribes signed their manuscripts. Their handicraft was known and sought out and they competed one with the other for the affections of lords and princes, but Hebrew scribes signed their works rarely and did so more that God might register and remember the name of the one who had written so precisely, so carefully, mounting the columns of lettering with attention and concern, than that the public might track him to his room and commission his services. One scribe (and I have in my youth done similarly) signed a Scroll of the Law with his name and a petition (I completed mine on the day before the season of penitence) that his benefactor and his family (mine paid me in the third decade of this century the trivial sum of eight hundred Turkish drachmas) forgive him his transgressions if by failure to transcribe so much as a cantillation mark correctly he should bring his benefactor's house to sorrow and to grief. (I did not. I transcribed perfectly. My patron Jew—he was originally from Ephesus—died in the riots of 1929, his house being set afire by Arab incendiaries who roamed the streets of Jaffa. His death was an accident.)

The scribal vocation obliges a sense of measure. In our work there is no more or less, only fidelity, neither great nor small, prior or successive, acorn, tree. We are not morphologists, since we do not believe (in other than a rudimentary scientific sense) in the boring endlessness of evolution.

Simon grew, but this is not to say he became more, that the man was consequent to the child, his quintessence or distil-

67

lation. The process of growth as I have implied is meaningful only when one reports upon mediocrity. The mediocre grow. Their very irrelevance demands the man be discriminated from the child by observations of bulk, expanse, elongation, muscular dexterity, physical agility, manual excellence. They are the maturation of their natal equipment, unadorned by conceits of intelligence and passion, freed from the perturbations of spirit which vision and an impractical and foolish sense of destiny exact.

Mediocrity is not regarded by me with disdain. It is myself and it is the numberless billions of the species. But it is not Simon.

Simon Stern is whole and complete at every moment of his life. At any moment but the right moment his death would be an accident. And only at the moment will his death be required. For others, for myself and them, death is always a visitation of providence, a recall of the unrewarded to their reward, a summons from heaven that the poor be made rich, that the sick be made healthy, that the orphan be set among the angels. The familiar liturgies which record the optimism of men and impute it to God are correct in their short-sightedness. It is a pity that God always summons out of season, that for no man other than the extremely rare is death appropriate and accepted. There are always tears and lamentations, always wailing and the wringing of hands. It is the exact contrary.

Death is never an accident for the mediocre. It is simply a random event in which God has no part or interest, a happenstance shuffling of nature, an irrelevant end to an irrelevant beginning. Its irrelevance makes its occurrence no less grievous, but my purpose in setting down these Lucretian observations is, unlike those of Lucretius, not to consign the life of ordinary creatures to the mindless conflagration of atoms, but rather, by making the distinction between the ordinary and exceptional so extreme, to justify the absolute criteria I have employed in setting forth the years of the life of this blessed and exceptional man.

Since he is complete and since his excellence is ritual and immanent in all the actions of his life, the narration of events is at best a concession to the semblance of reality, an obedience to temporality (when in him all is eternal present), to emphasis and embellishment (when in him all is undifferentiated evenness), to mortality (when in him there is no death but our forgetting makes him die).

Simon Stern was an integer at birth. The task of living his life, of immersing himself in the nagging whine of the real was not that he might learn more, but that we might become accustomed to the light of his presence, that beholding him small and uncompleted, we might, bit by bit, illumination by illumination, train ourselves to his presence, blinded, that we might see by the means of his light.

The difference between destiny and fate in reckoning the fortunes of men is but a few miles, a few dollars, a few minutes, a few inches. For instance, ideally suited young man takes train to challenging city, there to make his way in the world. A road runs adjacent to the railway tracks. A bus speeds along the road carrying ideally suited young woman to same city and to similar ambitions. Beholding this scene, conjured as it would be by the sentimentality of cheap cinema and even cheaper fiction, we would be obliged to acknowledge sympathetically, "If only she could have afforded the train. They might have met. Oh, they might have met." But no. That's the sentimental fallacy. The difference between bus and train is a universe of distance. He might as well be coming from the veld in an oxcart to Johannesburg and she in a a droshky from a snowy plain to Moscow. They are fated, quite simply, never to meet. The distance is but an irony appealing to the emotionalism of the world, which wants all youth and beauty to meet youth and beauty, even though, quite probably, they would despise each other if they met.

It is a fatum, not the fate of universal instruction, but the particularity of fate, a specific gesture of incommensurability meaningless in the grand spectacle of nature, but deadly serious to the young man who remained a bachelor or the young woman now withered into old age by unfulfillment. For them fate is the protest of mediocrity against their failure to grow. But if, indeed, it were the case that both had sat next to each other on the train, exchanged magazines, perhaps offering a piece of chocolate to the other and receiving in return a diffident smile, and then failed, out of that despairing fright which blocks the searching of the eyes and the gentleness of language from penetrating the natural camouflage of strangers to meet and discover their harmony, we must appoint that destiny.

The youth reflecting the next day in his boarding room, the girl in her cubicle at some woman's hotel would think of the other with a shudder of regret, but dismiss the episode as an occurrence of chance, an explanation familiar to the unimaginative. But it is not chance. It was an occasion of destiny, missed, and now irretrievable.

And of money, no less the same. The man of the middle class, with eyesight enough to envisage wealth, but lacking the ambition or the occasion to secure it, will always survey the broken furniture of his world with sullen anger. For him all should have been provincial excellence, turned on the machines of today in the styles of earlier gentility, durable but with palpable elegance. It was fate that kept him from the higher post, that made him sell prematurely the valuable lot on which oil would soon be discovered, that obliged him to offer his savings to secure an operation for his mother-in-law from which notwithstanding she did not recover.

These incursions of the stars, these permutations of the galaxies, these gestures of the heavens—these obscured his destiny and obliged him to begrudgingly accept the fate which leaves him now in toothless age, complaining of the missed, the passed, the lost, the wanted, but never secured, emoluments of the world.

And of minutes the peripeteia is the same. But for the breakdown of a watch, the faulty mechanism of an alarm clock, the misreading of the timepiece in the tower of the skyscraper, she would have kept the rendezvous, he would have been first in line, she would have become a lady pilot and he a millionaire, but when they arrived, the lines were closed, positions filled, the wealth distributed.

And of inches, inches to the body, inches to the biceps, inches to the waist, those inches which describe the atmosphere of weight and occupancy in the world, no less the same. Take, if you will, a giant of a man. Is it any wonder that when you reach seven feet in height freakiness becomes

70

an asset? Begin as an athlete and end as the stockboy in a grocery store who can reach the highest shelf or a weight lifter with biceps monstrous and waist like a mannikin and from Mr. Universe one declines to hauling scrap steel.

The body, perhaps more than other things, is a frailty, but even then it is not a fate. A man who has, let us say, five feet and several inches almost, but not quite, in the neighborhood of normalcy will, it may be observed, be more desperate in his pursuit of stature and authority, raising his heels along with the volume of his voice to command the world to behold him. But another, like the one of whom we speak, whose childhood was spent beyond normalcy, not short but diminutive, not dwarf but yet midget, will be obliged to follow another course, for to him it is not a fatality, but an option which is offered. Surely it, too, can be fate, but only if he fixates with obsessional stupidity that about which nothing can be done. He, too, can explain failure in the world as fate, the employment lost, the love abandoned, the wealth denied and all because of what—too few inches in a world that requires the unexceptionable. Fate and fate again. Over and over the man without money, the man without time, the man without place, the man without power will berate the eccentric intersections of his life as though some indiscriminate but malignant genie had prepared the conditions of catastrophe, conditions which cannot be amended, conditions which—like gravity and death—are absolute and indifferent to worth and excellence. They try hard; they exert themselves; they struggle upward; they congratulate their exertion; they disport their achievement, but then, in the dead center of night, in the silence of all worlds within and outside of themselves, they acknowledge their fright, that it is hopeless, that they know that nothing can be done, nothing can be helped. It is then, just then, that they caress their faces, and in a mime of immemorial maternity, comfort themselves and calm their fears with the lullaby of fate.

In the order of the extraordinary, those gifted with a native excellence, there can be no fate. The excellent disobey the ministrations of dumb excuse. Indeed, failing to accommodate the resolute insistences of the world, the stoniness of secure traditionalism, the demands that man in com-

71

munity always puts to the gifted young that he give over, accede, make common cause with the commonplace, too often, alas, there is a garbled "no"; the sad and discomforting refusal, the intuition which is compelled to deny before it has had the chance to discover what is its own, its proper, its best. The morgues are filled with broken no's, asylums with broken spirits and minds broken by illusion, and hearts made perverse by the fatal exactions of the ordinary. Against these exigencies there can be no complaint. If those who might have become great are broken, it is less a denial of their promise than an affirmation that the fortuities of destiny needed to be courted longer while impatience and despair cozened her prematurely.

And so of them. Of those others, that handful of arrows in the quiver of God, fashioned one by one, and discharged in the midst of the crowd of history, how should one speak of them?

It is believed (and why should such a belief not be ours?) that there are in every generation thirty-six human beings who sustain the world. No one knows their names, where they live, what they do. They can be field workers, ritual slaughterers; one was an attendant in a theater, another perhaps cleaned out ritual baths or swept the boudoirs of Viennese brothels, another may have professed philosophy in a German university. Who knows? But these are the true arrows whom God sequesters in His quiver. It is they who are launched as the vanguard of the Messiah. Call them little Messiahs. They are the sotto voce *of divinity, when God mutters or clears the throat of the heavens or flushes the* anus mundi. *All tasks, all works, all duties, humble and exalted, these the secret righteous undertake for the sake of us and to His own glory. They, they are perfected destiny. In them—since the conditions of life in the world are of no consequence— all is destiny and they salute it with the same welcome and delight as other men greet a plate of hot soup on a winter's day or a blazing fire in a storm.*

And it is from such modest and uninspired origins, from the womb of an orphaned housemaid with a smattering of learning and the seed of a youthful scholar who forswore family and wealth that into this time, amid the poverty of the exile, set down into the damp concrete mausoleum of the New World, another righteous one (another little Messiah who we believe is more, not just another beside others forgotten or never known, but he through whose hand the final work will be done) has been born.

These are reasonable times, and fanaticism and repression in the name of God are no longer common among us. We give our energetic unreason to other causes which men contend are more of moment and importance and in this time God has been spared deadly service. The murdering for heaven is done, although assuredly our revulsion proceeds from the orgy rather than containing it before its start. Survivors are always nauseated by what they themselves have done or countenanced others to do, and that nausea remains for a while, settling over the world like stinking air. For a time we will loathe the hands that can murder while they make, but this queasiness passes. It remains, then, always, to hope that we may learn a bit from what we have done. And there is for this occasion the service of our little Messiahs to prod and instruct us and of the single Messiah who is born but once in every generation. To that last Anointed, that Single One, who is the head of the body, the superb among the superior, the first and exalted amid a secret conventicle of servants, we turn now. Him we lead out into the fields and plazas of the world, as a bride is led from her waiting room to the canopy of her betrothal. No bride comes forward without her escort, without horns and cymbals, without the men in smiles and her friends of childhood, each one garlanded with a circlet of roses, and if the sun is bright and the sky blue like a tropical sea, and the wind gentle like the breath of a ewe, there is an augur of promise recorded like a shudder of pleasure in the groin of the earth.

My task, therefore, is to lead him forth as a bride is led to the altar.

Simon's passion became money. It is hard to imagine an eight-year-old boy giving his energies to the pursuit of money. It seems so foolish to us, those of us who have grown beyond or never succumbed to this passion in the first place.

But it was the case.

His time was organized, planned like the timetable of a battle maneuver, little tolerance for delay, none for dereliction. His religious studies commenced several hours before public school and resumed several days of the week for three additional hours until the early evening. That left Simon the hours before seven in the morning and those after six in the evening (exclusive of Sabbaths and Holy Days on which he rested) to hunt money. He managed. He was the first boy in the neighborhood to sell magazine subscriptions by mail. He arranged with an agency to consolidate and transmit subscriptions for him and to make available all of their grand bargains, their two-for-one specials, their only $1 for 40 weeks of this and that, their samplers of various magazines for the undecided. Simon deposited with the agency $5 as an earnest which he had earned from errands, from carrying water and ice in the buildings of the neighborhood, from running messages between shops and distracting the drivers of the horse-drawn carriages for the benefit of aging ladies who would give him (he stipulated) a penny for each approximate minute he delayed the driver with Bible questions and Yiddish antics while they climbed aboard.

Simon wrote out in ink on a gelatin-coated sheet, which was then hectographed, a brief announcement of his venture into the world of magazines, and having already borrowed without permission a list of all the people in his district from the local Tammany headquarters, he sent to them the following: "*Jews.* It's not enough to know the geography of the Holy Land. You have to master America. Geography for new Americans with suggestions for how to improve your English, your business and matrimonial prospects, and your share in the American Life to Come." There followed then a list of all the magazines with a one-line description of their contents and a price set in a Jewish star topped by a crown resting on its points.

The first week, from two hundred letters, all addressed in capital letters to disguise their crabbed immaturity, he received orders for fourteen magazines, five from a Polish immigrant doctor on Hester Street, who wanted in addition to the ones ordered and paid for, two medical journals translated, he wrote, "into either Polish or Hungarian." Simon had earned, after the agency price was remitted, $6.60. Enormous. He bought his mother a peacock feather and his father a velvet skullcap and put the rest in a tin box under his bed. From there it was up. Magazines, not errands, and after magazines a few appliances and household remedies and some books, and by the time he was twelve years old he ran a small mail-order business which grossed nearly $600 annually, from which he earned sometimes $140 or $160 depending upon whether people were staying put and sinking roots or moving to the Bronx or Harlem and mail had to be returned.

Nothing about his *bar mitzvah*. It is expected in hagiographies such as this and is for that reason irrelevant. There's no need to underscore the obvious. Simon was meticulous, astute, but dispassionate in his performance of the Law. His *bar mitzvah* marked no change. It signified only that he was obliged now to do more. He made no speech praising his parents. That, too, would have been irrelevant. He adored his parents. Standard.

His *bar mitzvah,* unlike the bacchanalian fantasies of our own time, was nothing more than going to synagogue the Monday of his birth date according to the Hebrew calendar, and there, in the company of the congregation, thirty-seven men ranging in age from fourteen to seventy-nine, all covered by the tent of their prayer shawls and armed with the frontlets of their phylacteries, putting on his own *tefillin* (a scribe had written the parchments and prepared the little black cubes protected with a cut of skin from a permitted beast, razored the leather thongs that bound the arm and circled the hand and dropped like plaits from the portion which stood between the eyes as monitor to the brain), which he withdrew from a wine-colored velvet bag covered with an appliqué of baroque flowers among which a regal lion of Judah stalked. His mother had made it for him in a week and had presented it to him that morning before they left for the synagogue. Was it his mother whom he heard crying softly in the women's gallery, concealed from the congregation of men below by a linoleum table covering into which a lattice of boxes had been cut for peering and gossip? It must have been his mother. The other lady who had come to the *shul* that morning coughed, indeed coughed so persistently that the president of the congregation sent an assistant to present her with a handkerchief and ask that she please choke a little until the *bar mitzvah* boy had finished reading his portion.

Simon was called to the Torah and there, standing upon a three-legged stool, his head level with the raised lectern on which the Scroll had been untied and exposed he blessed the Torah, and receiving the silver pointer from the hand of a smiling worshiper began to read the portion, singing the words, dancing the phrases, until without beginning and without end, seamless, the whole of a simple and translucent joy swelled and with the closing word subsided and died away. When he finished he stood upon his toes and saw his mother's face, an eye, a section of forehead, a portion of cheek pressed against a rectangular opening in the linoleum divider. He put both hands to his lips, and with a theatrical gesture, not unlike him, rushed a kiss toward her. His father said to him quietly in Yiddish, pinching his shoulder with affection, "Well done." And he stepped down, completing the recitation of the names of his parents, receiving the blessing of the reader on himself, on them, on the congregation, and upon all the House of Israel. That was a *bar mitzvah*. He became mature before God because it was the appointed time. There was no surprise that one should become responsible, and without surprise there was no need to celebrate the event.

Simon completed high school before his fifteenth birthday. He was finished with school, absolutely finished. He had no doubt that he had learned something, but he was not persuaded that what he had learned even interested him. Mathematics he had learned, but adding and subtracting money bore no relation to geometry and calculus; and he had mastered English, which he spoke in that gestural cadence immediately recognizable as Yiddish in origin, and history, geography, biology, physics, chemistry, some French (a language whose spirit eluded him) and Latin (a language which he regarded with ambivalence). He decided he wanted no profession, not law, not medicine, nothing that resembled accommodation to power without power itself. It was money, but it was power more than money, that interested him.

The summer had come and it was time to plan. He had accumulated in the seven years since he had begun his enterprises nearly a thousand dollars. A thousand dollars, he would think, looking at the coins and bills sorted and distributed in little piles upon his bed.

Abram and Ruth did not admire his industry, or praise his persistent avarice. His father would sternly demand, not often but often enough, whether a dollar could learn a page of Talmud. But Simon would reply indifferently: "That, too. What's one to do with the other?" "You'll learn in time. Everything. A man can't whore with God. It's either Torah or money." His father also wanted him to marry. A marriage broker told him that a wealthy merchant who lived above his dry-goods store wanted Simon to marry his harelipped daughter and promised him lodgings and an allowance for five years so he could continue to study Talmud at the yeshiva. Simon was incensed at the suggestion and stamped his feet in rage. His father told the broker that he was too young to marry. "He's old enough to be a genius, he's old enough to marry," the *shadchan* said, shrugging. "That girl will be taken, so think it over," he muttered confidentially as he left. "So she'll be taken," Abram replied, annoyed that she, not his own son, was regarded as the prize.

Later that summer Abram and Ruth devised a campaign of seduction. Their difficulty was that they were uncertain of their own wishes and its end. They felt only their fright, and not the conviction of their strategy. For Ruth, having incomplete knowledge of the prophet who had divined the destiny of Abram and Ruth and of their son, the anxiety was practical. Simon was a do-nothing, without profession, without an apprenticeship. He was a vagrant genius with a thousand dollars. How could he marry with nothing, but on the other hand, how could he afford not to marry?

In the summer of 1914 it was inconceivable to go to college. You went to college if you lived in the Bronx (and then it was a struggle), but not if you earned $1300 a year and lived in three tiny rooms in a cold-water apartment in one of the poorest neighborhoods in the whole of the city. The clever boys who went from the Lower East Side to the great world did it by other means: a good voice, a comic gift which gentiles admired and ridiculed, acting on the Yiddish stage, writing a book, becoming a union organizer or a radical. In those days before the Great War, people didn't expect to get out. They wanted to get in. They wanted only to be contented, hard-working, secure Jews, who didn't have to worry about Cossacks or tax collectors. All right, they said, it's America, and for that we are happy and respectful and we won't break its laws unless they're bad, or abuse its customs unless they're foolish, or get in the way of the gentiles unless they get in ours. But Simon wanted more. He wanted to have everything, to have more than any Jew had had since King Solomon, but he wanted it without having to entertain a Queen of Sheba, any foreign dignitaries, any viceroys or princes of the other world. And so when his mother began leaving about the apartment handwritten descriptions of neighborhood girls given her by the *shadchan,* or when his father would talk about the sons of their acquaintances or other householders in the *shul* who were working as an assistant in a law firm or training to buy piece goods for a garment factory or buying a pushcart to sell the shoes or shirts bought at a fire sale of an uptown department store and how much money they were earning—$11 a week, $13 a week—Simon would laugh and say again, "No, no, no," and stamp a foot and leave the apartment to take a walk.

Simon's intractability before his parents' reasonable concern about his life persisted until the day before the New Year, shortly after his sixteenth birthday. "Shimen, *kleyn kindele,*" his mother said early one morning while blowing on her steaming tea, "we can't afford you scheming for a living. Now, maybe, you should help us a bit. Your father's doing fine. It's not money we need. It's money for twenty years from now, when your father will have, God forbid, a bad back or poor eyesight and not be able to work twelve hours a day. Then it would be nice to have some money put away for us. But on schemes, Shimen, on schemes, we can't live." Simon didn't reply, but went to his bedroom, took the tin box from under his pillow, returned and counted out $500 which he gave to his mother. "For when you're old, but in the meantime I want one more year to scheme." She looked at the money and then at his face and began—it's no surprise

—to cry. Not much she cried, but enough to release her pleasure and her sadness, that from her only son should come $500 for their old age. "We're not old yet, Shimen. Keep it for us. I'll tell your father and let him decide." That night after supper while the three sat at the table playing silently with bread crumbs, Ruth told Abram of the gift and the request. "I disapprove, but I consent." They understood and nothing more was said. Simon had bought his moratorium.

His days were crowded with inactivity. To be sure, he continued to study with the rebbe, learning Talmud and the Codes with familiar proficiency, but now with disinterest. He was admired by his fellow students, praised by the rebbe, encouraged by the householders of the block, but all this commendation only strengthened his resolve to become a master without disciples, to learn the right ways without the obligation of teaching them. He had no wish to be righteous and certainly never to be holy. He simply wanted to be above reproach and with the license of the Law to be in a position to command deference, even when, as the time would come, only he would know that he did not deserve it.

The hours at the yeshiva—three, sometimes four daily—provided him the fence or, more accurately, the shroud to his passion. Money was his passion, as I have said; however, it was money accumulated to no end. Simon recognized that money meant the transformation of his physical condition, the ending of his poverty, the repayment of a debt which he construed to be not only literal but figurative as well, the debt of life. In the way of things, less became more, reality became the enemy to be subdued or transformed, the self became the neutral camp, to be loved and despised in turn. One could not have been a learned and pious Jew, a midget at sixteen years and the possessor of a thousand dollars unless all things whirled in the dizzying kaleidoscope of ambivalence, one moment rosied wtih affection, the next moment yellow with terror, the next green with splenetic rage, the next blue with melancholy and despair, and the next black with the auguries of death.

Late one afternoon Simon went out for a walk. He had

finished posting fifty letters to magazine subscribers, soliciting renewals and stuffing the envelopes with offers for a new Jewish encyclopedia. He was tired and bored—more accurately, depressed. Four months of his year of grace had passed, and although his little mail-order business thrived, it had proved no more profitable than the year before. He was making the same money, but his father was making more and his mother still worked long hours. He was no closer to his destiny. He put on an old fur coat of his father's which his mother had shortened to the point that the bottom was scarcely six inches off the ground and pulled his cap on and went into the dirty dampness. He walked mindlessly, looking up at window shades pulled down against the coming of winter, at the lights beginning to flicker from gas jets that illuminated billboards at nightfall, read over and over, in unconscious imitation of his father's method of learning English, every poster, every sign. At the corner of Grand and Delancey, the border between the Jews and the gentiles, those Irish and Poles, he rested, turned around several times, undecided whether he would continue across the street into the forecourt of the enemy when he saw, written in greying whitewash on the window of a storefront, a notice: *Wanted: Sweeper and Runner.* Simon walked closer and looked up at the chipped black paint which announced *Baumgarten & Fitzsimmons: Realty and Rents,* and considered whether he would enter and interview them for the job. His mind convoluted. He might sweep floors, but then, but then, he might, yes, he might at the end of the road collect rents and then earn them himself. He made up his mind, turned the doorknob and entered.

A middle-aged woman with bright red hair, clumped and tied at her ears, wrote in a ledger at an oak desk. "You!" she said, without raising her head. Simon didn't answer. He was still examining the office. Three desks, including that of the woman with red hair. "You!" she repeated, "what do you want? We have none."

Simon was taken aback by her rudeness. "How do you know what I want?"

"They always send their kids to beg for one of our apartments."

"Why's that?" Simon queried with interest.

"We're the best, that's why. The cleanest apartments for the least rent. That's our reputation," she said, slamming the ledger and looking up for the first time. "Well, if it's not an apartment, what is it? Rent late? Want an extension? No extensions. Out with you first. That's why we're the best and cheap. We collect rents first of the month or by the tenth, it's into the streets. Riffraff is what you are."

She screamed at Simon, but Simon didn't move. His confidence grew with her madness. "Lady, you're nuts, you should pardon me."

She opened the ledger again and slammed it even louder. "Scare you?" she asked.

"No. Why do you want to scare me?" he responded with amusement.

"I'm tired. It's goddamned awful work, this. I sit here hour after hour," she imparted confidentially, her voice sounding like a scraper on fish scales, "while sweet-and-dumb and loud-and-fat, that's Fitzsimmons and Baumgarten, are out milking it from the poor. Oh Christ, it's a lousy world. And I get the sweet-ass job of sitting here and taking it off them when they come in person to offer me halfsies and homemade cookies for an extension. You know what I'm instructed to do. If they're Micks I give them a little printed card with Fitzsimmons' malarkey all over it—the old-sod crap and there's lots more good, hard-working Irishers waiting in line if they can't make a go and keep up the rents—and if it's Jews I give them one of Baumgarten's God-of-wrath manifestoes. It's a melting pot all right, but we melt by boiling them first. What do you want?"

"You finished?" Simon asked quietly.

"Don't be fresh."

"I'm not. I'm the new sweep-up and runner."

"You are?" she questioned incredulously.

"I am. As of now."

"Who says you are?" she parried, her suspiciousness returning.

"Nobody but me."

"So what's your qualifications? You're a runt, I can see that. You can't lift heavy things, that's for sure. You'll rupture *everything* if you do," she laughed, slapping a roll of fat which thumped on the desk.

"What's to lift. You throw the people out. You don't move the apartments."

"Don't be a wise ass with me, kid."

"I'm not. I'm being funny."

"You are," and she laughed again.

"So do I get the job?"

"There are lots of kids want this job."

"Come now. No one wants it. The whitewash in the window is filthy. It's been at least three weeks." Simon was guessing but he was right.

"True. Who would want to work for my bosses if they could help it and for six dollars a week and a daily cup of tea? Jeezus," she called, moaning. "Okay, I hired you. I have no right to, but I am. You're funny and small and won't be in the way and won't get fresh with me. I can stand you." Simon looked as if to ask whether the bosses would let her get away with it. "Don't worry about Fitzbaum—that's my name for them—they do what I want, because they know I have a lousy job and make only thirty dollars a week and don't steal. So you're on. Be here at eight in the morning. It's eight to six. Understand? Eight to six. Six days a week."

"Which six?" Simon wondered.

"If it's a Fitzsimmons, you get Sundays, and if it's a Baumgarten it's Saturdays. Which are you? Pair off. Choose up sides or you'll end working seven days a week if you're an atheist from Scandinavia like me." She grabbed her sides and roared.

"I'm a Jew."

"That makes you a Sabbath-off kid. Okay by me. I'm Hilda. Hilda Engstrom."

Simon went home that night with a job. He made up his mind to learn real estate and become a millionaire.

The Monday on which he began work he had arrived at the office an hour before Hilda. Baumgarten and Fitzsimmons never appeared much before noon. Simon walked around the neighborhood while he was waiting and noted the number of buildings with little zinc plaques—MANAGEMENT: BAUMGARTEN & FITZSIMMONS. He noted thirty-seven buildings in ten blocks. They were all in various states of decrepitude, stoops cracked and fallen away, knockers missing, gas jets in the hallways sputtering blue and dangerous, windowpanes smashed, paint peeling, and filth, every manner of filth—garbage, litter, stains, legions of bugs, rats, water bugs the size of rotten lemons, roaches like oily pinon nuts, scurrying from one deposit of refuse to the other. The Jewish tenements were suffused with the smells of fish and rotten potatoes, the Irish of hops and cabbage. He returned to the storefront a few minutes before eight and studied quietly from a little pocket edition of Maimonides' *Mishneh Torah*, concentrating with particular interest on the laws of lost-and-found property, damage of possessions left untended in the public domain, the complexities of that category of the law called torts. Indeed, he already envisaged the possibility that when he became the owner of buildings in the community he would manage them in the spirit of his ancestral law, according to the requirements of Babylonian equity and justice, avoiding controversy, making peace, and remaining separate from the encroachments of secular law. Only with the implacable, the irredentist, the recusant, would he go into American courts and then simply to redress the balance that he might begin again to do the work of reconciliation.

He did not hear Hilda come up beside him. He was sitting on the concrete door stoop, his feet tucked beneath him, his father's coat enfolding him like a blanket. He was reading the Hebrew aloud, singing it in a quiet singsong chant, nodding his head, praying, if you will, the text of the legal exposition.

A throat cleared above him and he looked up to see a red-rimmed orifice, larger, he thought, than the flaming mouth of a street furnace. It descended rapidly and his hands shot up to push it away. He was slapped and his face hurt.

"Damn you, midget dwarf, little midget Jew, little Jew dwarf," the face shouted.

Simon saw that it was Hilda. She was wearing a long black coat which ballooned about her hips and flared into a tent by the time it reached her feet. Simon toppled forward under its skirt and stayed there a moment, hidden in the cavernous dark of her clothing. She held him there with her hands, pushing down on his head until she forced it to the cold pavement, all the time belaboring his ingratitude, his ugly miteness, his Jewish indifference. At last she relented and Simon's head emerged from the opening between her buttons and he squeezed through into the day. He stood up and stepped back from her, replaced his cap on his head, retrieved his book, kissed it, and returned it to his coat pocket and waited silently, frightened of the big red-haired woman, humiliated by her aggressive fantasy. He would not be dominated, leastwise by Hilda Engstrom. She didn't apologize, laughing all the while she unlocked the door and swept into "Baumgarten and Fitzsimmons." Simon followed her suspiciously.

The hours passed slowly. He swept the floors, washed away the grime from the window, boiled water for tea and was drinking it quietly, sitting on the one chair that was detached from a desk when Baumgarten and Fitzsimmons entered.

Hilda had not spoken to him from the moment they entered the office until then. "On your feet, little one," she called menacingly. Simon stood up and remained motionless. Baumgarten entered first, his girth invading the doorjamb and passed through with a handbreadth to spare. He was all dark wool and beard. He seemed to have no face between beardline and black homburg, lip, nose, eyes, forehead shrunken with wrinkles and bloodless gave the appearance of a crushed parchment which could never be unrolled. He bellowed good morning to Hilda, taking no apparent notice of Simon's unfamiliar presence. Simon was quite simply there. Behind him, a pink face set off by a white silk scarf and a circlet of thinning red hair which stood away from his scalp like the aureole of a saint bespoke the genial insubstantiality of Fitzsimmons, a light man, a man of airy blasts, and fustian theatricality. They were ideal, Simon concluded after observing them throughout the day, for small power and dreary dominations but for neither magnanimity nor millions.

But it is true that Fitzsimmons liked Simon. Hilda scarcely acknowledged him. He was, as she had said originally but disingenuously, acceptable because he would not get in her way. He was neither lazy nor dirty and he did his work so quickly that however much she barked at him she could find no fault.

Baumgarten would have preferred to discharge Simon, particularly after Simon had corrected the Biblical citation included in one of his manifestoes to the derelict, noting in a precise hand that the passage quoted was not from Deuteronomy but from Numbers, and attaching the little memorandum with a pin to a printed example of his self-righteousness and leaving it on his desk. Baumgarten had seen it when he returned on that day, looked at Simon who was kneeling on the floor filing papers, snorted with anger, his face wrinkling down to the point of vanishing, and made no comment. But Baumgarten watched Simon carefully thereafter, particularly as Fitzsimmons apparently embraced him as a dutiful boy, a bright thing, a useful amanuensis, and a helpful colleague. And Simon was that. You see, Fitzsimmons could not help drinking a little too much, not often and not in public, but it did happen that the rents he would take in late on an afternoon were often miscounted and pocketed without the error being discovered. Fitzsimmons hated collecting rents and surrounded the chore with moralisms and homilies, advice and flattery, telling some poor old widow who couldn't even afford the price of lard and cabbage greens that she seemed fit and blooming.

Simon became Fitzsimmons' watchdog, heeling to his side as they stopped before each door of his tenements and listening as Fitzsimmons asked, received, counted, thanked, bawled, cried, hectored, pestered, whined, cajoled, threatened, extracted, and received the money from his hand in a gesture like feeding a pet at the dinner table, underhand and circumspect. Simon counted it, noted the amount against the list he carried and deposited it in a purse he carried. In this way Simon saw the insides of hundreds of tenement apartments, saw the dismal gloom, the broken furniture, the three-to-a-bed families, the chipped crockery, the unmatched, broken, flimsy, dank everything of poverty and he vomited inside. The second year, at Fitzsimmons' insistence, Simon received a substantial increase in salary—now twelve dollars a week—and one month Baumgarten had such a severe chest cold that he had to stay in bed for three whole weeks and Simon collected the rents for his buildings as well. He was now indispensable. He called the plumber when a repair had to be made, and argued with the gas company when they were slow about fixing a leak, and arranged for plasterers, paperers, hangers, painters, cleaners, handymen and carpenters when their services were required. He was quiet and firm; his smallness obliged a gentle tenacity and gradually the craftsmen and artisans with whom Baumgarten had screamed and Fitzsimmons weaseled came to rely on small Simon's clarity and fairness.

The end of his apprenticeship came by chance at the end of two years, during the summer of his seventeenth year. Simon had gone as far as he could go. He knew the outside of real estate, but none of its arcane mysteries, nothing about finance, mortgages, costs of operation, profits. Hilda stood between him and the ledger. He contemplated deception in order to see the books, tricking Hilda into leaving him alone after hours so he could study the records. It wasn't necessary.

Hilda had become more nervous and unpredictable (if that is imaginable) during the two years since Simon arrived. While she was writing at her desk, for instance, she had gotten into the habit of turning furtively and looking over her shoulder at the empty wall as though someone was lurking there to spring at her, or wrapping up her coat and tying it in a bundle, which she put under her feet during office hours. She had plausible explanations for these and other eccentricities—washing her teacup a dozen times, sharpening her nibs until they were like razor blades, taking everything off her desk and hiding her personal belongings at the end of the day to trick any burglars who might have been surveying the premises for a theft—but despite her gestures at rationalization, both Baumgarten and Fitzsimmons, frightened at her little derangements, knew that she was going off in the head.

One Monday morning during September of the second year of Simon's employment, Hilda did go insane. She had not come to work that day and Fitzsimmons went looking for her in the tenement apartment she rented from them.

He found her under her bed, the linens piled about the brass posts like a fortress, and Hilda sleeping quietly in her own refuse. He called an ambulance and she was taken off. They did not speak of her again, although occasionally Fitzsimmons would say that he missed a woman about the office and that Hilda had had lovely penmanship. Simon inherited her position and her salary while continuing to be sweeper and runner. He now set himself the task of mastering land, buildings, and money.

His first months as accountant, assistant rent collector, scourge of the delinquent, and still sweeper and runner for Baumgarten and Fitzsimmons, were full of surprises. For one thing—perhaps the most immediately shocking—was his discovery that his employers were, like himself, wage earners. To be sure, they earned much more than he did. They managed in a prosperous year like 1915, with the beginnings of wartime inflation, to earn as much as $150 a week, but they did not, as Simon had believed, own the buildings from which they collected their rents. This explained their parsimony, their unwillingness to maintain the apartments they managed in reasonable repair, their constant bribing of officials to overlook grotesque violations of the casual fire and sanitation codes of the city. They owned nothing. The banks owned everything, that is, the banks held the mortgages despite the ownership of genteel Smiths, Walshes, Lowenthals, a stray Vanderbilt, an aunt of the right Carnegie. The banks financed ownership and closed their eyes to the disgrace of their properties; the uptown and out-of-town owned the land and the buildings; Baumgarten and Fitzsimmons were employed to collect the rents. In those days the owner gave them a flat percentage of the rent roll out of which to maintain, heat, light and superintend the buildings, and whatever corners they could cut, they did. Heat rose at nine or ten in the morning (and sometimes not at all if an unrepaired pipe could be blamed), and was turned off at six in the evening. Gas repairs were made fitfully, since it was cheaper to turn off the gas than to repair a pipe or clean out the jets. From rents they made a living, from chicanery a profit.

Simon sometimes joined Baumgarten and Fitzsimmons

87

when they would sit down in their hats and overcoats to drink a cup of tea and discuss business. Why not pay a living wage for one superintendent who really worked rather than practically nothing for several who didn't earn enough to do anything? Or buy coal by the ton and store it, rather than buying it by the carload whenever needed—cheaper and better service? But this was the extent of Simon's suggestions. Without the intimacy of ownership, capital was unimaginative. Simon realized that he would have to wait for his opening. Occasionally a property owner—someone from New Jersey who owned a single building and wanted to sell out—would come to the office and ask his employers' advice. They invariably told him of a bank, the Bank of New York or the Morgan Guaranty, that administered the holdings of other of their clients who might be interested in purchasing it. Never once did they offer to buy it themselves. It never crossed their minds. It did cross Simon's.

It was a late morning in the spring of 1918. Simon had been called by the draft board, had reported, been rejected (a sergeant, in fact, had laughed at him when he came up to his desk and had to ask that the paper he was to sign be given to him so he could fill it out on the floor), and returned to the office in time to meet an elderly woman with a fox stole held by a diamond clip.

It was a Miss Quick, Letitia Quick. Baumgarten had ignored her, and she sat waiting patiently for someone to take note of her. Simon asked politely whether he could be of assistance. With diffidence approaching embarrassment she said in a low voice, her hand cupping her mouth to ensure the secrecy of her words, "Is this the right place to sell a parcel of property?" Simon became as secretive as she. He asked if she would wait a moment while he completed an inconsequential piece of business, hoping that Baumgarten would leave for lunch at the dairy restaurant a block away and leave him alone with the gentle lady. He did shortly. Nodding to him briskly, tipping his hat to Miss Quick, Baumgarten departed. Simon pulled over a chair and sat down before Miss Quick, his knees rubbing the lining of her coat, his ear cocked with energetic seriousness.

"I am a wealthy but, I am afraid, hopelessly confused spinster who does need some help," she announced with immoderate directness. "I own a great deal of property here and in Youngstown, Ohio, where I was born, but there is one piece of property I am afraid I despise and would like to dispose of. It's quite near here—in fact, three blocks away. It's a small house of three floors, not more than fifty handbreadths in frontage and built to the depth of a small carriage house. I visited it this morning and was assaulted by a pack of rats. It's a breeding miasma, unoccupied for more than two years, invaded by vagabonds and drunkards in wintertime, disused other than by rodents in summer. It's worth nothing to me and I hate vermin. Might you buy it?"

Simon knew the house. It was nasty, but it was situated curiously. The reason for its shallow depth was, as Miss Quick explained, that its original owner had been the widow of a sea captain who lived alone in that house during the middle part of the nineteenth century when the area was quite different, when craftsmen and artisans of the sea made their homes in accessible distances to the port. The widow's husband, who had gone down with his ship in a Pacific storm in the 1840's, had built her this home with the assistance of his own shipwright and had intended at the conclusion of that final voyage to retire to it with her. It had not come to pass and the widow had lived there until the 1880's when she died. The property was sold by the city for payment of back taxes and bought by Miss Quick's father during a hysteria of land speculation which preceded the panic of 1887. Miss Quick had managed the property herself—in a manner of speaking—rented it and been cheated by her tenants, evicted them, acquired first an Irish family, then a Polish family; and the last tenants, a family of fourteen Italians, had cooked at an open fire in the living room and nearly destroyed the building. It was now empty, seemingly worthless, a source of plague to the neighborhood, an apparent pestilence to Miss Quick.

"I would sell it for five hundred dollars," she suggested, her voice inflecting disbelief at her own daring.

"We would be interested," Simon said quickly, adding, "that is, I would be interested in acquiring it."

"You?"

"Of course, I am quite able to purchase it. I have the money, although my parents will have to sign the documents, since I am not yet of age."

"You look hardly twelve."

"Miss Quick, you would not be speaking to me in such a trusting and confidential way if you really thought me twelve. I am simply tiny, but I have the imagination of age, and, at the very least, the experience of someone who is on his way to nineteen."

"In that case, I would be willing—"

Simon interrupted, his mind coiled like a serpent. "I doubt you would wish the property to remain an insult to its history, that of the sea captain's widow and the Quicks of Youngstown. I propose to refurbish the building, clean it thoroughly, make it not only habitable but hospitable. To this end, I shall have to invest perhaps another thousand or more dollars. I will buy the building and deliver to you the cash today, but I must acquire it for not more than four hundred and twenty-five dollars." She blushed with chagrin, blew her nose soundlessly in a lace handkerchief and her eyes agreed to the transaction.

A hasty contract to purchase was prepared, with the necessary safeguards warranting ownership and title search— a difficult matter in properties as old as this one—and Simon brought the paper to his father in Williamsburg to sign, returned with his tin box of savings and counted out the money from the now nearly sixteen hundred dollars he had accumulated. Simon suggested that she might wish to consult her lawyer, but she averred that the sum was so insignificant that is was unnecessary.

They met late in the afternoon in the empty office to which his employers had not returned, and there, having exchanged documents, deeds and warranties, monies and receipts, the purchase was completed. The following day Simon recorded the transaction at the County Clerk's office and set to work cleaning the building, converting it from a one-family dwelling into three comfortable but minuscule apartments, each of which was rented within two months for the handsome sum of $12 per month. At this caculation, his investment would be returned in something under four years, and with luck he could now sell the building to someone more prosperous and enterprising than he. The entire transaction was done without the knowledge of Baumgarten and Fitzsimmons, although from that moment he began to regard himself not as employee but as self-employed—moreover as self-employed with a more distant horizon than either of his employers.

It was at this time that the first and only natural miracle of Simon's life occurred. The childhood and adolescence of Simon Stern was marred, we have noted, by his excessive, indeed extreme, diminutiveness. He was a midget, a tiny, a mite and minuscule, and it was as such that Simon had come to regard himself. His smallness had consequence, for it carried with it a sense of self—crabbed by books and constrained by narrow ambition, becoming wealthy was regarded by Simon as the only way by which he could aggrandize, that is, make himself large.

"I aggrandize," Simon would announce when people asked his profession. Most of his friends and associates did not know this word, but he had studied its root and was well familiar that its French origin entailed the meaning of taking substance from the world and attaching it to oneself. Sometimes he dreamt that money and buildings stuck to him like glue and plaster, and it was his conviction that beginning small he would be swollen by wealth until he was become a large man. It is fortunate, then, that before his millions were made, the fantastic underpinning of aggrandizement should be rendered irrelevant by the fact of growth. He had not grown since he was twelve. His height was reached then and all believed it was fixed and unsurmountable. He was four feet eleven inches and that was that. No amount of nourishment nor medical consultation could alter that fact. The doctors recommended abundant protein but Simon's family could scarcely afford red meat, and the drinking of warm blood which one doctor had advised was considered cannibalism. No. No. It was settled that Simon Stern would be a small thing in the world.

But then, unaccountably, in the wondrous ways of providence (which means only that beneficent fortuity is miraculous), Simon began to grow before his nineteenth birthday. Perhaps it happened because he was out in the world, and nature had taken mercy upon his vastly increased vulnerability, deeming it wise to equip him more generously for his exposed profession or perhaps it was because, as the Sterns became less poor, the quality of their diet improved, or perhaps it was the case that God had simply grown tired of looking for Simon Stern and not being able to find him. In all events, shortly after his purchase of the house of Letitia Quick, it was noticed that Simon began to grow. Ruth noticed it first. One day she went to cut down the trousers of her husband to make them suitable for Simon's wearing and observed that instead of having to roll up the pants four cuffs' worth in order to accommodate Simon's smallness, three was enough.

"You seem to have grown, Simon," she said cautiously. Simon ignored her. But it was the case. The caution gave way, over the following months, to confidence and elation, and by the time of his nineteenth birthday, Simon Stern had passed five feet and was well on his way to the settled height he achieved a year later, that of five feet six and a quarter inches. And with height came other marks of maturation. He confided to me, with a shudder, that until the age of eighteen and a half, when the growth began, he had virtually no hair about his body, not a single hair—a scruffy down he could see under a magnifying glass covered his groin, but it could not be called hair—and under his arms, upon his chest, across his stomach, nothing. Only a single hair grew from a beauty mark upon his thigh. That was it. But by his twentieth birthday he had stepped forth into manhood.

Of course, this transformation from midget into ordinariness was not without its unfortunate side effects. Simon could no longer look to the world for concessions. He could not trade upon his spectacular smallness; he had no recourse any longer to embarrassed shoe-shuffling or face-shielding. The world, that is, the world of tenants, bankers, renters, servicemen, could not be relied upon to excuse his brashness because of stature. Indeed he had traded upon his tininess, but that was done. He was as most men of the world of such average and mundane complement that no excuse would be offered or contrived to spare him the consequence of his action. He wasn't big, but he was no longer small.

Simon Stern had become an ordinary man.

The years, like the tables of interest and amortization, compounded and grew, time passing and sums growing, properties accumulating, rents increasing. By 1928 Simon Stern owned pocks and holes of the Lower East Side, several warehouses near the Customs House and flanking Wall Street. His premise had remained unvarying—to buy the unwanted and abandoned, to identify its proper use to the neighborhood, whether private or commercial, and transform it to that use, reselling it thereafter as quickly as possible. Every property that he owned he improved at little expense, since solicitude and consideration cost nothing. He did not evict; rather he improved properties and raised rents, the aimless poor vanishing to make room for the industrious poor. He managed everything he owned, owed little or nothing, but was owed much on properties he had already sold and on which he held the mortgages himself. His holdings were in excess of a million dollars, but still he lived with his parents in a somewhat larger apartment in the same building, no more luxurious than the last but fitted at least with a large stove that heated the living room more adequately than in the past. There was no privacy, no plumbing to speak of, but for the first time there was adequate food and clothing and his mother no longer worked. That was enough for a decade of enterprise.

The economy collapsed in 1929. Six properties on which Simon had been paid nearly fifty thousand dollars in cash and on which mortgages were outstanding for more than one hundred thousand more went unpaid and Simon reclaimed them. (One of the purchasers who had defaulted committed suicide shortly thereafter.) Simon was all cash and real estate, nothing speculative, hard rock and concrete. It was time to consolidate and be patient.

The depression deepened. Simon allowed several of his empty buildings to be occupied by destitute families and provided them daily with steaming cauldrons of hot soup and potatoes which his mother distributed. But throughout these years Simon did not personally detach himself from poverty. The more elaborate the poverty of others and the more wealthy he became, the less inclined he was to leave the tenement in which he had grown up. He made his own poverty into a talisman to be witnessed through the holes in the rotten fur collar of his coat, his battered cap, his bagging wool trousers, his crepe-soled canvas shoes, laced up and tied in a double knot. Simon walked through his little village and knew that he owned nearly two-score houses, that he owned empty lots and garbage dumps, that he owned warehouses and small office buildings, but that most of these were empty, awaiting better times to fill and flourish and produce. The money he preserved he would lend to small loan companies and insurance funds, collecting from them high but legitimate interest, receiving from them options to purchase their stock at very low prices, options which years later would be worth fortunes. He had quite simply mastered the art of making each dollar do the work of five and waiting patiently while it did.

Spring was upon the city the day Simon made his way to the borders of his ancestral world. It was the right day to make the largest single acquisition of his life. Fourteenth Street was crowded. It was the season of the Holy Days, and Jews from all over the city, Jews more venturesome than he, had come to that screaming street to shop, to buy new suits for their sons and for their daughters taffeta dresses with long sleeves and puffs. On the street, pushcarts were heaped with windup toys and remnant dolls, and strangers with odd faces and alien colors idled and pushed their way to kiosks that shined shoes and offered magazines and up to stands for fat frankforts and cheap orange drinks and into stores where counters hugged goods and women tore at them to ferret out an unnoticed bargain.

Simon came to the corner and peered around. He had never crossed that avenue. He was almost thirty years of age, but in all those years he had never gone farther than Williamsburg to the south, to see his father, or the borderland of Fourteenth Street in the north. When he was just a small boy and smallness had not passed from small or stunted into midget/dwarf/pygmy, he would sometimes come up to Fourteenth

Street and put a foot out into the street and pull at his mother to cross and listen to the workers milling in the park, but his mother would hold on, telling him in a shrill whisper: "The forbidden world. That's the forbidden world. *A treyfe velt.*" He would step back to the curb, frightened as a trolley lurched past. He would watch the people looking at the crowd among whom he stood, unmoving, and a finger attached to the hand of a little girl with a red face and blond hair would wag at him and the words "Look at the tiny Yid" rush across his forehead and pain him. Why do they speak of me this way? He would review the variety and the inventiveness of contempt: sheeny, kike, yid (generic forms of designation; like simple denotative nouns, they pointed out without describing), but cockcutter, bloodeater, waterpoisoner, Christkiller, these were more, particular, sharp, combining the absolute unbearable monotone of history (a magnified decibel screech which only Jews' ears might hear) with desperate particularity: Shimen the killer, the poisoner, the cutter, the Christkiller. In those childhood days Shimen would run home, tears rushing down his face.

But now, years beyond childhood, Simon had come to Fourteenth Street and stopped. He had no interest in crossing to the other side. He had power on his own.

More than a decade had passed since the first million, stitched out of crumpled bills and defaulted mortgages and court judgments, had been amassed. Simon no longer emptied his monies upon his bed and counted the coin and paper. He relied upon savings accounts and safe-deposit boxes. Some days he went to the bank vault and would sit for hours in the cubby room, sorting the money and marking the larger denominations with his initials, and later when the ritual enterprise had been completed and the money returned to the gunmetal box, he would spin his fantasies of power and become so excited by his vision of such tremendousness, tremendousness he could no longer even count—the sums were so large—that he would contain himself by withdrawing a hundred-dollar bill, noting its removal in the ledger he kept within the box, and upon leaving the bank, present the bill, enveloped, sealed, unmarked, without return address for thanks to the first pushcart woman he met in the street. These benefactions did not occur often, but over ten years, from the time of the economic collapse until the days before the decimation of the Jews, he held himself at bay by massive accumulations, countings, and minor generosities and gifts.

In his pocket, that autumn day of 1940, Simon carried a certified check for $52,000 with which he was going to buy five buildings, the largest single purchase of his life. Simon Stern had cash.

He walked up a flight of stairs and entered the office of Lebentraum and Levinsky, Attorneys at Law and Realtors, on the third floor, overlooking Union Square, in full view of Klein's clock. Lebentraum, something like Simon, bought buildings out of forced sales, cleaned them up, reduced the mortgages, increased the rents and primed them for sale. Levinsky handled the paperwork and the closings. They danced about each other, the one talking values and equities, the other talking deals and profits. They were smart and rich down to the gold that flickered in their mouths.

People still starved all around town and particularly on Grand Street, where Simon was buying, but what Simon knew was that on the next street the Elevated was going to be torn down, a subway station was coming—and with it, increased business and some minor species of prosperity (pushcart prosperity he called it). Simon knew it and was smart. Lebentraum and Levinsky didn't. He entered their office, and a spindly woman, her hair masked by a green visored cap to screen away the direct light, was typing a long document—his contract to purchase, he assumed.

"Stern for Lebentraum and Levinsky," Simon said briskly. She buzzed, feet scuffed an inner carpet, and a glass door rattled open. Lebentraum emerged, squeezing through the door sideways, his immense fat folding around the doorjamb as he came through. He extended his arms and gripped Simon's small-boned hand in a moist clasp. "Stern, Stern, a great pleasure to meet you." Simon was severe; but he secretly smiled. Who's having whom? he thought smugly. It was over in an hour. Levinsky told him he didn't need a lawyer. "Dealing with us is like *mishpocha*. Who needs a lawyer to talk to *mishpocha*."

Simon learned later they had cheated him, but who cares,

who would have cared? There were building-code violations on all five buildings and such a whittled-down warranty in the contract of purchase and so few representations by the sellers that he had no recourse but to shrug shoulders and wag fingers. Lebentraum and Levinsky had made a fat profit and thought Simon would make little or none. The facts were otherwise, as they soon found out. Six months later, after the property had already been sold to Consolidated Edison for a new power station, Simon was visited by Lebentraum in the small office he kept for calls and mail.

"Mr. Stern," Lebentraum addressed him deferentially. Simon retained his seat, his feet wrapped around the legs of his swivel chair. "Let's face it. We took you the last time."

"You *took* me?" Simon replied, laughing. "Nothing of the kind, Lebentraum. Nothing of the kind. *You* cheated me. *I* made a killing. That's the difference."

"It's a difference," Lebentraum conceded.

"So what's the reason for this visit?"

"I have a building on Varick Street which I'm handling for sale. A large six-story office building, big windows, good for a factory, or subdivision into large mercantile offices."

"The price?"

"Three hundred and fifty thousand dollars with sixty thousand dollars cash and a nice take-back mortgage for ten years."

"The rent load presently?"

"Only one floor's rented and that's for nothing."

"So what's the bargain?" Simon shrugged. "I'll tell you something, Lebentraum. I don't need it, but since it's you, the man who started me off in big-time real estate, my sponsor, so to speak, for you, I'll buy it. But my offer is two hundred and fifty thousand dollars *in cash.* Your client can make the other hundred thousand if he invests properly and no need for him to wait ten years."

"You're *meshuga.*"

"I am *meshuga.* Agreed, but I'm rich, Lebentraum, and you, you and Levinsky, are widow *ganavim,* thieves and small-time crooks." Lebentraum looked at his fat stomach and heaved a deep sigh. He suddenly felt sorry for himself. "While I, Lebentraum, am not a crook or a thief. I am only *meshuga.* I make the glue that keeps dollars stuck together. When I met you, friend Lebentraum, you thought I was crazy. You know now I wasn't. I had information. It was unreliable, but it helps to have a friend in City Hall with an ear like a redskin, always to the ground. I gambled and won. You cheated and lost. And I've gone on and on. Now, sir, I'm rich. In these lousy days, this Jew is worth quite a few millions of dollars and each day it grows and grows."

It was true: in those lousy days. It was 1940, near the end of 1940. The war was on. France had lost, England was on her knees, Germany was running Europe, and America was thinking aloud, unsure as to whether it should remain a benign giant or become an active one. In the meantime, business was sluggish, the poor stayed poor, unemployment was severe, agitation was intense, but nothing really was done. Only capitalism had been saved by Roosevelt. In those days Simon Stern was single-mindedly acquisitive. He bought and sold like a Rockefeller, although his taste and talents weren't a Rockefeller's. Would a Rockefeller drink soup out of a paper cup or carry crackers in his wallet for afternoon snacks? Of course not, but then Simon Stern hadn't had a Rockefeller's advantages. For one thing, his name wasn't Rockefeller and that can be an advantage when you need banks and loans, business advice and counsel. And what's more, Simon never went uptown. He did it all downtown. "For my money, let them come downtown," he would shout into a phone when he had closed a deal to buy something on Broadway or was invited to inspect a property in Cleveland or Chicago. It didn't matter that his associates often didn't know what "downtown" meant. How should a steel scrap dealer in Indianapolis from whom he had bought the frames of ten thousand junked automobiles know what Simon Stern meant when he said from a phone booth in New York, "Bring the papers downtown or I'll give my attorney power and he can sign them"? How should they? They didn't. But in the meantime, they obeyed him.

In October 1940 he bought two wrecks in the Indian Ocean and sold them almost immediately to a buyer from the Nippon Trading Center who claimed he wanted them to make agricultural machinery. How should Simon know? Simon knows a lot, but I don't think he could have known then what he found out later, that the Nippon Trading Center fronted for the procurement division of the Japanese navy. By the summer of 1941 Simon was worth over sixty million dollars. He was in real estate, junk, scrap, stocks, bottling plants, commodity futures. It was a one-man business, a business with a few accountants and lawyers, a part-time secretary, some file cabinets, and Simon's blue notebook in which he made entries of his transactions, his purchases, his properties, his investments, his loans.

The peripeteia and discovery, fond to the imagination of the ancients (the occasions by means of which the multitudes of pagan divinities inseminate the history of men) are acceptable only upon the assumption of inexorable fate.

It could not have been otherwise, that King Acrisius of Argos should die at the hands of his grandson Perseus while attending in disguise the games at Larissa. The discus finds the forehead of the old man. It is an unavoidable conjunction. The gods fix the course and the course is accomplished. It is curious, of course, that when the oracle speaks, her words are ascribed to no single god. It is not churlish Zeus, not waspish Hera, not the fatuity of Poseidon, nor the confederations of demigods who are charged with the oracle's inspiration. The oracular spume covered kings and petitioners from head to toe, dyeing the skin of their days with an ineffaceable pigment of terror. Acrisius tried, so did King Laius of Thebes, but however their interventions gave to time the semblance of a mime reducing its speed, breaking the fast step of fate, bringing the unravelings of the mechanism to a near standstill, their devisings were only delays. Indeed, they endured to old age, but what was spoken to them in their youth came to pass, when they were old.

It is not that they sought to avoid death, to pretend as later did the Emperors of Rome that they themselves were gods and entitled to immortality, but rather that they despised a life sucked dry by the unavoidable. They gave the whole of their days to confounding the oracle, to making certain that the conditions of their end would not exist—to hiding away virgin daughters so that male murderers would not be born—but however hard they strived, a god or a man (ignorant, it would appear, of the admonition spoken by the oracle) would circumvent their elaborate ruses of escape. Did Zeus know that when his golden loins copulated with the beauty of Danaë he was setting in motion that propulsive energy of history that would end, many years later, in the throwing arm of Perseus at Larissa, that history would curve back, that the two lines, symbolic asymptote, would actually meet at that point in infinity to which the oracle alludes?

I am mystified by these matters. But the oracles of the Greeks were the stuff on which the tragedy of the Greeks depends. Those seers spoke; their words, riddles, conundrums, glossalalia, were reported, early in the drama, and by the end, the tragedians had brought down whole dynasties to ruin, women to withered virginity, wives to barren old age, kings and their brothers to murder and to blindness and to mourning and to silence.

With us, there are prophets. They are oracles no less than those of Delphi. They speak to us with ephod on their breasts, they divinate with urim and thummim, and later after these holy artifacts are dispersed or, later still, put to rest in the sanctuary and worn on feasts, less as marks of special powers which threaten by their presence but are not used, than as mnemonics of earlier days of terror, other men come forward who speak only from the wisdom of their possession. Those other prophets hardly prophesy as do the oracles. They announce what is already done but is not yet visible. Their instruction is not addressed to the single man as a mindless confusion.

What else could Acrisius do? But there is much that Hezekiah could have done and much that he did do and much again that he did not. And all the Kings of Israel and even the prophets themselves, Jonah for instance. They were given not only the consequence—that is, the issue of the prophecy in death and destruction, the fall of the royal house, the murder of fathers and sons—but a choice that they could change their lives, abandon their miscreancy, repudiate the cheap gods, the temple whores, the corruptions and peculations of their reign, and more: lead back their people, that's the point, make the way straight for their people, and avoid for them, by their repentance, the consequence which is in store for the whole nation, stored up in the rage of heaven like a volcanic crater awaiting the fault to dislodge and spew forth molten fire upon all.

In September of the year the United States entered the war Simon's mother developed pleurisy. Dr. Rufeisen came to visit her and prescribe, but the pleurisy worsened and, after a week, he insisted that she be taken to a hospital. Ruth refused, saying that she would die at home, that she preferred to die at home, drinking soup from a cup her son spooned to her, listening to her radio in the dark, holding Abram's hand. She refused even though her temperature was now dangerously high.

The third evening of her illness, convinced that she would not survive the night, Ruth forced Abram and Simon to swear that if she did, by some miracle, pass through the crisis she would not have to live any longer in that tenement, that Simon would get her a decent, warm apartment where she wouldn't have to go at rats with a broom, or drown roaches in hot water, where she would have a proper toilet and a proper bathtub.

"Enough of being poor," she wailed, "enough of being poor. I'm tired of your punishing us, Shimen." Simon was horrified. What did she mean? How could she say that? She never explained. She sank into a deep sleep murmuring tearfully, but incoherently, throughout the night. "My blood stone," she was heard once to say.

The doctor remained at her bedside throughout the night into the afternoon of the next day. By early evening beads of perspiration began to form upon her forehead and her nightgown was soaked. The fever broke and a few hours later she awoke and smiled.

In November Simon kept his promise and moved his family two blocks away to the small house he had bought more than twenty years before from Letitia Quick. It was occupied now only by a Polish gentile named Krawicz and his daughter, Lubina, an eighteen-year-old girl crippled from childhood, who dragged herself on steel braces and rarely left the apartment. Lubina kept house, cleaned, cooked, and cared for her middle-aged father, a revolutionary who had fled

Poland after—the story was told—he had assassinated the director of a large bank and had robbed him as well of the considerable monies he had been carrying. Both his fellow conspirators and the police had tried to catch up with him, but he had escaped, and coming to the United States had taken a common-law wife by whom he had had Lubina. The woman disappeared shortly after the child's birth, and Krawicz had given himself over to brandy and writing endless briefs and justifications of his aborted revolutionary career.

The Krawiczes lived on the top floor of the small building, and Simon installed his parents and himself in the lower floors, furnishing the house comfortably, modernizing the bathroom and the kitchen, and on the first Sunday in November of 1941 he moved his family. His mother cried while his father carried up to their bedroom on the second floor the small Torah he had caused to be written several years before and installed it in the cabinet of an old-fashioned standing clock from which the works had long since been removed to make way for the sacred scroll. The mezzuzahs were affixed, the psalms sung, cake and wine consumed after the ceremonial bread, salt, and sugar had been presented by Simon to his parents, and the family spent the day delighting in their home.

The lives of Ruth and Abram settled like the earth. Dislodged, blown from their natural place, carried by accident and fortune to another place, set down again, an irregularity in the landscape, they were now, nearly a half-century after their flight from Warsaw, joined to new soil. Soil of the city. Apartment. Home.

Different people have different ways of giving body to their estrangement and their hard-won adjustments. They give up Yiddish and chicken fat and seltzer bottles at the table; they give up the neighborhood *shul* and travel on Sabbath to a synagogue outside the neighborhood; they give up finally what they call the Old World synagogue for one with an organ and lights on a rheostat; they give up oilcloths for plastic and then plastic for linen and finally plastic returns as place mats; they give up pickles from a barrel for pickles in a jar—the same with herrings, the same with halvah, the same with green tomatoes and black olives; they give up cooking and cleaning and become supervisors and gourmet specialists who go to work only for an occasional cholent or sweet-and-sour gizzards; they give up *Oi veh* and *Gewalt* for "So what else is new?" maybe just a shrug; they give up wearing gigantic prayer shawls in which to die and instead curl decorous silks of blue and white about their shoulders; they give up blowing the nose during "Cast me not off in my old age" and become stolid parishioners who tear not neither do they mourn; they give up bestowing blessings upon their children on Holy Days and start worrying about them in naked anxiety. What they give up they think is unbecoming, indecorous, *kleynshtetlekh* and perhaps it is, all these little customs and contrivances—just that, indecorous. But giving up is simply not enough. It's more like giving over than giving up.

The Sterns had nothing to give up, absolutely nothing. It's not giving up to keep coal in the basement near a real furnace rather than keeping it in a bin near the stove which isn't in a kitchen but in the center of a living room, which is also a kitchen, the dining room, the sitting room, the parlor, the library, and Simon's bedroom. Giving up? Nothing of the kind. They gave up the slow depredations of rot and filth and replaced it—mind you—not with an apartment in an apartment house, but two small floors in a very old house that had been built by New Englanders one hundred years before. Yankeefied? What could be more astounding—the Sterns of Warsaw in the house of New England seafaring Yankees acquired from the wealthy Quick family of Young-town, Ohio? Better than moving to the Bronx, better than moving to upper Broadway, better by far than leaving the city altogether. They gave up nothing. They wanted to give up nothing. But they became suddenly obsessed with the passion to have more than the nothing they had. Their son was a success, they might have thought. But they didn't. They didn't think of Simon as a success. Simon's wealth was what the Jews used to call *parnossa*—fodder and supplies. "Without sustenance there can be no Torah," it is written. Poverty is no curse if you can study on an empty stomach. Most people can't. That's a fact, a simple human fact with which not even God argues. It's hard to keep your mind on

God or on anything else if you haven't eaten for a few days. So Jews worked out a simple, practical notion: you've got to eat in order to think; you need a coat on your back in order not to freeze; you have to have some place to put your head down—preferably, but not necessarily, a bed—in order to sleep. Food, clothing, a bed—that's enough, that's minimum, that's what you need for your own Torah work. More than that, that's success. How so? You can provide food, clothing, bed for someone else. Charity, you say? Right, charity is a Jew's success—having something extra—not for a rainy day, but for someone with a leak in his roof.

Abram quit the tailoring shop in Williamsburg. Quit? That's not correct. Jews like Abram ben Belim don't quit. They go to the owner of the shop and say, as Abram said late one Friday afternoon, about three o'clock when shops in Williamsburg begin to shutter up because Sabbath comes early in the winter, "Reb Yonah. I am able to give all my time to Torah."

Yonah Manger smiled and looked up from the pattern book in which he had been pasting down swatches of cloth he had just received from a kosher textile company in Mexico. "That's a blessing, Reb Abram. I wish I could."

"One day you will, Reb Yonah. But I can begin now. I'm nearly sixty-five and it's time."

"That's very good indeed. Good for us. These are times when more Jews should study." The Japanese had overrun the Philippines. Hitler had invaded Russia. "Do you think, Reb Abram, it is as *Sefer Daniel* speaks, the time of beating wings? At night, I think sometimes I hear them above our heads, winging out over Brooklyn, shuddering the buildings. I awake and it's a streetcar. But I hear the beating." Reb Yonah closed the pattern book and drank some cold tea. "It could be. It could be. The Jews are beginning to suffer once again. It's always a sign."

"Do you say *Tehillim*, Reb Yonah?"

"Every morning, every evening. I used to say the whole book every day. But, with all this"—he motioned with weariness to the sewing machines, which now stood idle in the workroom—"who can say the whole book? Fifty psalms, sixty, sometimes a hundred when it's quiet and a page of

Talmud. There's so much to do speaking to God. It's not that He says a lot, but He wants to be noticed. You can't blame Him?" Reb Yonah always spoke of God like a neglected parent.

"You understand then, don't you?"

"What?"

"That I won't be coming into work any more."

"Oh that, yes, of course. But you wouldn't mind, would you, if from time to time I send you some special pieces to sew for me? You alone put on a collar perfectly. Some of my customers are special—the great rebbes, mostly, you know, the Hasidim of the Gerer—they need the silk cut like a diamond. You do it best."

"Of course, of course. Anytime. Send them to me on Sundays and I'll give them back in a few days."

"Fine." Reb Yonah stood up. He was a short man. Reb Abram took his hand in both of his and drew him toward him. They embraced. They had worked well together. Not a cross word. In more than forty years never a cross word. And that was that. Reb Abram left the tailoring shop of Reb Yonah in Williamsburg, Brooklyn, recrossed the bridge for the last time, and returned to his house to study Torah.

Ruth did not take up the study of Torah. She could have, but she didn't. She knew more than she knew when she was a young girl, just come from Polnoye to Warsaw, but that much more, no. And it wasn't necessary. She was happy that God had formed her according to His will and caused Abram to cleave to her that they might become one, each drawn by warmth and struggle to share the intimacies of their lives. But with Abram home now, singing to himself the words of Torah, shuffling back and forth between the kitchen, where water boiled continuously, filling his glass with tea and returning to the desk in their bedroom behind which stood the grandfather clock protecting a scroll of the Law, she had less of him than before. In the past, when both returned tired to the tenement, she from her stall in the streets and he from Reb Yonah's, they would talk a bit about the world, discuss the serial in the *Forverts* or a Torah sermon in the Orthodox paper, but now Abram was in his workroom climbing up the rungs which led to the Chamber.

He rarely visited the Bet Midrash to study, contenting himself with his own argumentation. Sometimes Ruth would hear him shout out the conundrum and listen, leaning on the kitchen table, while he replied in a slow and patient voice. He was a disciple of the dead rebbe, the Bratzlaver, who died more than a hundred years ago, leaving no succession, but whose followers endured, gathered in small conventicles honoring his active leadership of their mystical ascent. He had no need of a living rebbe, since all that mattered was there, given, and bequeathed in his actual writings and the hagiographic literature which clustered about his name.

Ruth didn't complain. In those early months of her passage from tenement to home, Ruth would sometimes address her long-dead parents at nightfall, when she head Abram singing quietly to himself in the study. She would say: "Can you see me, Father and Mother? Have you found me after all these years? I know you must have looked for me and not discovered me. I was so young when you died. How could you find me among all the pushcart vendors of New York. I looked just like them. Heavy sweaters, scarves and kerchiefs. And me, a girl from Polnoye crying vegetables and underwear in New York. But now you recognize me, don't you? I'm taking care of a proper house, and a Torah scholar and a genius son. Would you have believed it?" Ruth conversed thus with her parents, but when her headaches would begin she would lie down to rest.

The headaches often began in the evening and raged until the morning. But Ruth refused to see a doctor. There was nothing wrong with her she insisted. Too many years of hard work catching up, she temporized. Old age. Tiredness. The brain gets tired like everything else, she believed. There was no cure excepting rest. But Simon realized that it wasn't rest she needed, but companionship. Whenever he came home, his hours irregular and undisciplined, his mother would set a cup of coffee before him and sit down, clasping her hands under her chin while he told her of what had occurred in the world below.

Those conversations relieved her headaches. "Such a nice talk, Shimen. I feel so much better." A month after the headaches had begun, Ruth disappeared from the house and was gone nearly the whole day. "I've been uptown," she explained in the evening when she returned. "It's so busy uptown, so many stores, so many people. I was frightened a little, but I made a friend." She explained that when she was returning downtown she was about to board the wrong train, and a rosy-cheeked woman had said to her, "It's the wrong train, Mrs. Stern."

"Yes," Ruth had smiled, not noticing that the woman had addressed her by her name. But Ruth had followed Mrs. Weiss into the train and sat beside her.

Mrs. Weiss took her arm and held it gently. "Never take that other train. You'll end up, heaven knows where, in Brooklyn. This is the right one," she continued, pointing to the little metal signs which indicated the train's ultimate destination, Coney Island. "And I know you, Mrs. Stern. We all know you." Ruth was confused and did not reply. "I'm Mrs. Weiss. My husband owns Kimmel and Weiss, the big hardware and appliance store on Delancey Street. Come visit me."

Every morning thereafter Ruth went to Kimmel and Weiss and hunted through the shelves. She came to know the store by heart. Every shelf, every bin. She would enter the store, wave to Mrs. Weiss, who sat on a high stool in a cage near the cash register, and look around. Toasters. Beaters. Sabbath clocks. Roasters. Rotisseries. Washers. Dryers. Refrigerators. Electric knives; electrical frying pans; electric scrapers, peelers. Hair blowers. Curling irons. Radios. Phonographs. She looked and looked. "I need this scraper, Mrs. Weiss," she said, picking up a small knife with an electrical attachment. "It's hard cleaning the fish," she apologized and purchased it. And then she felt she had earned the right to sit with Mrs. Weiss and have a cup of tea and a visit.

Her headaches abated. By the beginning of March she had bought almost two thousand dollars' worth of equipment. She would carry the appliance or wheel it in her wicker cart or ask Rosie, Mrs. Weiss's daughter, to deliver it later in the day. Returning home she carried the purchase to Abram to inspect. He would look up and smile distractedly. "Another appliance," he would say, without recrimination. "Good. Life should be easier for you." That would be enough for Ruth.

Abram knew that her life had not been easy. It was a permission to ease. Let there be ease and contentment in Zion. She carried away the purchase to the kitchen and plugged it in, hanging the device, the gadget, the mechanism, from a peg on the wall. There were two electrical outlets in the kitchen and from each outlet there was a multiple socket and into each socket there were plugged the cords of four appliances.

Simon noticed his mother's diversion. It pleased him that she had finally come to rest, that she would sit in the kitchen, her beater beating, her refrigerator cooling, her oven baking. It pleased him, but once he tripped over a cord and fell on his face. He hit the ground and a red knob swelled on his forehead. "Mamma," he cried in pain, "can't you hide the cords? Today it's a bump, but one day I'll be strangled by a cord." His mother put ice in a rubber bag and pressed it to his forehead. Another day he came into the kitchen and noticed that five appliances were going at once. A whiff of smoke came from one of the wires. He turned them off and warned his mother, "Not more than two on an outlet at one time." He reminded himself that he should have more power brought to the house and add other outlets in the apartment. He reminded himself. That was all.

The winter was hard. Snow fell on the city like a murrain, melting away one week, returning in a fury the next. Simon was gone from morning until late at night, buying and selling. He was involved in the syndicate which bought the Sixth Avenue Elevated and disposed of the steel to West Coast interests which in turn shipped it out of the country to South America. He bought and sold, bought and sold. The money grew from hillocks into mountains. Reb Abram studied. Ruth bought appliances. The money grew and so did the distance and the silence. Simon came home and his mother fed him, but Reb Abram stayed in his room studying. Simon would join him at midnight for *Tachanun* or to welcome the New Moon and stay with him until two, sometimes three, o'clock in the morning, reading and talking holy conversation together. They would forget Ruth in the kitchen or in the living room until they would look up and observe the black purple of the night, the glistening quiet of the early hours and awaken Ruth where she had fallen asleep over a cake she was decorating or find her in the living room asleep on the couch, her hair unrolled, the pins in disarray upon the floor.

"What becomes of me while you make love to God?" she lamented to Abram late on that evening in March.

Snow was on her hair. She had walked in her knee-length rubber boots until evening, kicking snow, flailing at the wind. Her rage mounted as she recalled the day long ago when Abram had sought her out in the early morning of a Warsaw winter and she had succumbed to his despair and to his promise. What had become of it all? All that had been built seemed to her worthless. All those years, for what? Abram had loved her only as a rung up to the love of God and now she was left alone.

"What becomes of me while you and God talk back and forth, while you and Simon make up to him?"

Abram stood up in anger. "Don't talk like that. I won't hear it." He bunched his hands to his head. "I won't hear it."

"You will, you will," she shouted louder.

"I can't. No. Not now. Ruth, stop. I must go on. I'm almost there. I must plead with Him. Simon and I both plead with Him. He must know what's going on."

"What's going on? What's going on? I'll tell you what's going on," she screamed, tossing her unkempt hair, drops of water falling on the open folios on Abram's desk. "You're killing me. That's what. I'm drying up. I'm drying up. I haven't spoken to you in a month. Yes. Yes. A month. I slip food and tea to you like you're a walled-in monk. *L'havdil.* A monk. That's what I said." Her eyes were red from crying and her voice shrill and reedy. Abram turned his back on her and began to sing the *Hallel* psalms. He pounded the wall, calling out the words of the psalms to drown out the cries and weeping behind him.

The silence came. Abram continued to speak the psalms, his voice slowly dropping, the psalms of ascent to the Mountain of Zion becoming more quiet. He listened while he spoke. He looked tentatively over his shoulder. Ruth had gone and the door was shut. He heard a humming sound. A *bzzzzzzz* came under the door. The noise rose in the other part of the apartment. A menagerie of appliances. They were all going. He stopped his speaking and opened the door. The smoke hit him and he fell back coughing, his eyes smarting and then he smelled the fire. The kitchen at the other end of the apartment was aflame. He tried to call to Ruth, but his voice gagged. He rushed to his desk and flung the folios to the floor, hunting a scrap of paper on which he had made kabbalistic notations. He went to the window to open it, but the ice had frozen the casement. A chair to break the window. He couldn't lift it. The Torah. The Torah. He rushed to the clock, opened it and struggled to prise out the scroll. It stuck. He couldn't move it. He put his head into the cavern of the clock and shoved and pulled at the scroll. A scream from upstairs. A fire engine wailed below. He could not dislodge it. The Torah was firm. His hands were clenched about its rollers.

Several hours later Ruth was found on the kitchen floor charred like leather and Abram in his study suffocated by smoke. In the apartment above, Lubina, the crippled daughter of Krawicz, was rescued, her face and neck severely burned.

Simon had stood before the little house and watched it burn. He had walked slowly downtown from Houston Street, where he had been negotiating with an Italian family for the purchase of an empty lot on Mulberry Street, and heard the fire engines. The sound of their sirens seemed pleasant, and the reveries of childhood, of men in peaked hats and high boots and rubber hoses and red engines with a barking Dalmatian, had come back to him. A house was burning somewhere in the neighborhood. Simon approached his block and saw the engines, their lights circling in the dark, the crowd of people, the police cordon. His house. The water played in cascades, hitting the building with a smack and dropping slowly. Firemen ascended ladders, smashed windows, clawed at casements with crowbars.

Simon stood by the lamppost before his house and watched. The electrician whom he sometimes employed came over to him. "It's a tragedy, Mr. Stern. My real sympathies, but I told you many times to fix those power lines and I told your mother, too." And he remembered that it was true,

110

that he had noted in his blue memo book that he must bring more power to the house, that the wiring was faulty and inadequate. He had forgotten. When his parents were carried out, wrapped in canvas bags, and the fire captain had approached him and informed him officially of his parents' death and Lubina's burns, he turned away from the house.

The month following the burning of his parents Simon gave up the world. The inquest was over and judgment had been passed. He had been remiss, but he was not found guilty of criminal negligence. The district attorney of the city had not even bothered to seek an indictment. It was enough that it was a tragedy.

There was no place for Simon to mourn. The house in which he had lived with his parents was burned out. Two were dead; a third, already crippled from childhood and abandoned by her drunken father, was now marked with the scars of the fire.

Simon returned, therefore, from the cemetery, to the room behind the office where he conducted his business. It was a storage room. Cartons of documents, accumulated for nearly fifteen years, lay piled against the wall that separated the room from an alley. A naked electric light hung from a wire in the center of the room. An old desk stripped of varnish. A green file cabinet with a broken lock. Piles of newspapers and magazines. Books on Judaica and philosophy which Simon had bought at random from the stalls that ascended Fourth Avenue to Union Square were scattered in the room, in small piles, unsorted, everywhere. A container of rancid milk. A cot with a blue-and-white striped mattress and an army blanket.

So it was that Simon announced in the Yiddish newspapers that he would observe, he alone and by himself, the required days of mourning in the disused storage room behind the small office that he maintained two blocks away from the site of the tragedy. There, from the early hours of the morning until late in the night, people by the hundreds came to call. He was already legendary in the neighborhood. It was known that this curious high-domed eccentric was a big man in the world, a super-millionaire, who had millions upon millions, who never left the Lower East Side, never visited with the gentiles or, for that matter, really comprehended that they existed, who was pious and learned, who kept his money in little packets and envelopes hidden about his office, who rarely slept and was never seen to eat in public, who had no friends but his mother and father and the young crippled girl who lived above him, who was known to leave donations tied with ribbons in the seat of whatever synagogue he happened to visit for his prayers, and who now, seated on an egg crate draped with a silk shawl his mother had forgotten in his office some months before, his head resting in the cradle of his hands, studying the laws of mourning or reading from the Psalms, absolutely silent, was receiving visitors to comfort him.

They did come. The ladies of the neighborhood brought candy and cakes, dishes of herring in cream and filets of herring in vinegar, puddings of potato and dishes of carrot and prune, hampers of fruit, apples, plums, pomegranates blood-red, kasha with onions and mushrooms, and kasha in butter and sour cream, salmon, and whitefish, and these ladies, those to whom Simon had once or twice nodded, arranged an order among themselves ("I live next door. I say hello to him every day and he smiles at me," or "He came into my shop and bought a newspaper not more than a week ago"), and having established the hierarchy of proximity to the bereaved, determined who should stand by his chair in the back room and tell the indifferent Simon the names of those who came to speak to him their comfort, while other ladies cleared the large desk in the front and spread out the food, while others carried in and out the laden dishes and the dirty dishes, and washed them and returned with them once more.

In the morning before the sun had risen, thirty, sometimes forty, men would gather in the front room, leaving Simon seated on his crate in the doorway between the storage room and the storefront, and there in *tallit* and *tefillin* they would say the morning prayers and Simon would rise alone to say the *Kaddish* and in the late afternoon the men would return and having said prayers once more, would drink tea and brandy until the early night and leave to make room once more for ladies who came to sit and talk and laugh and give comfort to the mourner.

Many rabbis visited the storefront, rabbis who had known Abram, rabbis who knew of Simon, rabbis and rebbes, and ritual slaughterers and scribes, and marriage brokers, and yeshiva directors, and simple idlers who sat for hours in synagogues and at the gates of cemeteries, offering their prayers for hire and, when unemployed, prayed and talked and studied. They came, some leaving their calling cards, others writing their names in a ledger which had been opened as a guest book for the mourners. The ladies accounted the *shivah* a prodigious success—more than eight hundred people had called to greet the mourner and more than four-score bottles of liquor had been emptied.

In the late afteroon of the last day of the seven days of mourning, to the surprise of the eight or ten visitors who still pushed cake into their mouths and sipped at tea, Simon stood up, and with a wave of his arm as though calming raging waters, brought the company to silence.

During the days that had passed since his parents' death he had scarcely spoken, he had scarcely closed his eyes. He talked quietly, to them, to the oncoming night, to his parents: "I have come to an end. That life is completed. A new life begins. They are dead. I am something else, undescribed. And now, good night to you, and may you never have to mourn again." He turned and shut the door that led into the storage room, unscrewed the naked bulb that shone in the room, and went to sleep. He slept for a day and a half. He was left undisturbed. Several times a visitor would knock at the door, and hearing no sound, would enter, look about, observe him sleeping, and perhaps, as some rumored, rummage furtively in the piles of paper near the door, hoping to find a sequestered banknote (several were found, it is said) and then depart.

The following weeks were times of intense activity. Simon did not know what would come, but he was certain that a change would be indicated. His accountants, three of them, gathered in the office each morning and Simon would issue instructions to them to buy and sell, to liquidate or acquire, to prepare detailed reports of his wealth, to dispose of odd

113

parcels of property, consolidate ownership, amass and strengthen, draw together and unite. He spoke now of money in an oddly abstract manner, as though money were no longer property and cash but devices and weapons. He daily visited the young Lubina, who languished, weeping quietly into the folds of bandages that covered her face and neck, and to her he promised succor and protection, but of that we will speak another time, for the story of Lubina and Simon brings us to the borders of another kingdom.

The principal occupation was wealth, and when the week was over and the reports delivered—$103,000,000 in real estate and other investments, securities and cash; liabilities $27,000,000 in secured bank loans and mortgages—he felt at ease. It was defined. He sent the accountants away, telling them to return again in three weeks. In the meantime he determined to start upon a modest fast of reflection. Each morning the regimen was the same. He would arise, say his prayers in private, eat a cold breakfast of cereal and milk, and begin to study, first reading in the *Tanya* of Shneur Zalman of Liadi, and concentrating to bring his body and his mind into harmony, subduing passion until he felt his head glowed with clarity, and then turning to mystical works of Isaac Luria of Safed and Moses Cordevero, with whose charge to redemption he reckoned himself equal, and at last at the end of his morning studies he would read the newspapers, the Yiddish press, the New York *Times*, the *Herald Tribune*, the London *Times*, and turning the pages slowly he would note down on a pad of paper events and episodes which confirmed that the clouds of redemption were gathering, that the times were accumulating those portents which signaled the right moment, that there were gathering in the heavens those vapors of disaster which in an eye blink would rain down upon the fortunes of men. He thought himself ready. The afternoons would pass in silence. He would sit upon his cot and alternate thoughtful gloom with study of the Talmud; first thinking about himself and his wealth, its undisclosed potency, and then turning to the disused laws of sacrifice and the instructions for the building of the holy sanctuary, and in the evening, following a boiled egg and a glass of cold tea, he would walk through the enclaves of the city, stopping only to sit in the

114

park and listen to the sounds of an unconcerned world. He continued to await a moment when a bolt of instruction would call to attention the casual wanderings of time.

One night, shortly before the end of the obligatory thirty days of mourning, Simon Stern believed himself asleep. He told me plainly and without hesitation, "I am certain that I slept. It was certainly a dream." But despite his unwavering disclaimer, it has always seemed to me that it was no dream. At all events, whether asleep in the order of the world which sleeps and scarcely sees with one eye or awake and fully conscious and prescient in his reporting, it seems that Simon became conscious of another person in the storage room. He awoke, let us say, and looked about him, but the naked light blinded his discrimination and he could not see the lineaments of the boxes and papers which hugged the darkness of the walls. A voice, thick with an unfamiliar accent which impeded its clarity, spoke slowly. The voice appeared to emanate from the region of the white porcelain sink which stood next to the door that led into the alley. It was cold and Simon noted that the door to the alley was open, although it remained invariably bolted from the inside by an iron bar. But that night it was open and the voice said quite distinctly, "I'll be right there. I'm washing my hands." He could not hear the water tap, but no matter, as the faucet habitually dripped a continuous but insignificant stream of water.

A moment later the voice came from behind the door and a portly gentleman, wrapped in a fur coat and wearing a large hat about which whipped a dozen foxtails, became visible. He was not frightening, only unfamiliar. He stamped his booted feet against the cold and shut the door. By this time Simon had drawn his thin legs against his body and pulled the green army blanket up to his shoulders. The visitor sat down at the end of his bed, crossed his legs, withdrew a pipe from the patch pocket of his coat and lit it with a wooden match which he struck against the floor.

"I shall not tell you who I am. There is no need for you to know. If you know, fine. Fine. You should know. If you do not know, it doesn't matter. Eventually you will." The visitor's voice was uneducated. It was a peasant voice, harsh, guttural.

"Who are you?" Simon asked, ignoring the admonitory advice of his visitor.

"Heh, heh," he laughed, "always the same. A typical Jew. Tell him not to ask, and first thing, right away, he asks. I told you. Don't you hear, Shimen? I'm not going to tell you who I am. You'll guess soon enough."

"All right. Agreed. Have you come to harm me?"

"Again. Typical. An old woman. Maybe I've come to the wrong place." He withdrew a pouch from the other pocket of his coat and examined a piece of paper. "The address here?" he demanded peremptorily. Simon told him. "Right. No doubt about it. Absolutely right. You are the one. I've come to visit with you."

"Where do you come from?"

"A long way. A very long way. I travel a great deal. In fact, you might say I am, by profession, a traveling man, and not only a traveling man, an inveterate visitor. I'm always showing up unannounced, unexpected, dropping in and having a chat."

"How did you find out about me?"

The visitor laughed again. "I've known about you for some time. I mean that. Quite literally. Ages and ages, before all of this and that were made." He motioned vaguely to the room, and Simon assumed that he referred to the building of the tenement, perhaps even to the founding of the city, but that was too long ago.

"All right then. You haven't come to harm me. You've come for a visit. So visit then."

"I am. I'm visiting exactly the way I want to visit. I'm looking very carefully at you. I confess I don't see what they have in mind, but I am simple and uneducated, as you can see (and I trust you will believe that). It isn't for me to figure out. I go where I'm told. That's the situation of a traveling man."

"So why me?" Simon shrugged. It was warmer. The warmth of the blanket and the warming of his fright. He released the blanket from his mandibled grasp and it slid to his waist. He was in his undershirt.

"Sit back. Calm yourself. I'm going to be here for some time. You see, my friend, I have come to tell you a story. A very

116

long story. But direct and uncomplicated. It hasn't happened. That's why it is a story. But it can happen and that is also why it is a story. Stories like I tell are not simply stories. You seem quizzical, uncertain about me. Quite natural. Most people are. I'm a storyteller. All successful traveling men are storytellers. How do you think we get food and drink on the way if we don't tell stories? I can't sing or dance or play a tune. I tell stories instead. Stories that I heard years and years ago, bring them up to date, tell them again and again. I'm very good at it." He cleared his throat, drew upon his pipe, and pushing back on the bed, leaned against the wall. His feet no longer touched the floor. "My friend, Simon Stern, listen to my story."

THE LEGEND OF THE LAST JEW ON EARTH

In the region of Catalonia, beside the rivers Ter and Onar, in the city of Gerona, on the Calle de la Disputacion, which commemorated a long-forgotten controversy between his kinsman, Rabbi Moses ben Nahman, and the convert Pablo Christiani in the presence of King Alfonso and his court in the capital city of Barcelona, there lived in our time the last Jew on earth. He went by the name Acosta, a respected and honored patronym among Spaniards, but he was as many, if not all, Acostas, descended from secret Jews.

Don Rafael Acosta owned, as did many citizens of Gerona, a shop that specialized in the leather goods for which the region is famous. He inherited the shop from his father, who died when Don Rafael was a young man; however, his mother had managed it with such meticulous efficiency that by the time of his twenty-fifth year, when it was fitting that his apprenticeship end and he assume control, it had grown to be one of the most prosperous shops of its kind in the city, exporting cured skins to leather fabricators in France and England and distributing gloves, jackets, coats, hats and other articles of leather made by householders in the region to other parts of Spain and handicraft centers throughout the world.

Don Rafael became the director of a substantial business. His mother, now aged, her fingers gnarled by arthritis, sat in the study of their ancestral home, a stone house in the old quarter of Gerona, reading the Spanish fables in which she delighted, mending her son's clothing and overseeing Marietta, the cook, and Rosa, the maid, in the performance of their

117

simple domestic tasks. Don Rafael had no interest in marriage or in the fathering of children, although he was aware that in his ancestral faith celibacy was not a virtue and a man without wife and children was accounted but half a man. No matter. There were none of his people about him in the market of Gerona and none remained in the ancient judería where he lived. He was unafraid of reproach or disapproving stares; his fellow Jews had long since disappeared, disappeared before he was born, and of their memory only tales and legends remained; with these he was well familiar because his mother read to him on the Sabbath of the miraculous Toledans and Cordobans of earlier centuries who had caused the light of Judea to burn in that farthest reach of the Mediterranean. He knew of all the saints and philosophers, generals and poets, legists and mystics who had flourished in the land of Spain and of their trials and torments at the hands of Almohades and the Holy Inquisition, and of the pogroms and desecrations, and of the ghettos, and of the fiery preachers—converts and Jew-haters all—who picked off, one by one, from the stock of Israel the finest branches and grafted them forcibly to the numberless trees in the forest of Christendom. But, as with his lack of interest in marriage and in the fathering of descendants, so Don Rafael had no interest in the ministrations of the Mother Church. He had mother enough of his own, security enough in his business enterprise, youth enough to enjoy its fulfillment, and he counted it possible that in his later years, like an aging prince, he might take to himself a young woman for warmth and pleasure, and perchance, in the natural course, an heir would issue whom he would legitimate.

The people of the city of Gerona, set down by God in a plain of the north of Spain where mountains and valleys were verdant and productive, where peasants worked and were fed by their land, and industry and effort were rewarded by crops and produce, were generally indifferent to the dogmatic exigencies of religion. Catalonia was at the crossroads between Christendom and Islam, the way station from the shrines of France to the shrine of St. James of Compostela, the political cat's-paw of Louis of France, Henry of Aquitaine, Roger of Sicily. But that was some time ago. In recent centuries Spain had settled into withdrawal; a half-century or so behind more industrialized societies, she was at this moment restored to a constitutional monarchy, a regal church, an agrarian prosperity, and an uncommon calm. Spain loved to be at rest. It was in this most serene and comfortable corner of that peninsula of inactivity that Don Rafael Acosta was born and lived.

In his fortieth year, at the time of this narrative, his mother was gathered to the blessed and shrined in the memory of her son at the abundant age of eighty. Don Rafael was alone in his generous and well-trimmed world, walking in his black suit of heavy wool and his broad-brimmed Spanish hat to Casa Acosta in the Plaza España of Gerona, taking his lunch in the hotel on the square, joining friends in the bar behind the entrance to the ancient cathedral for a glass of wine and conversation or a game of billiards before returning to his home to rest and eat a late supper of Spain. His was the simple and uncomplicated life of the commercial gentry. It suited his quiet manner and gentle bearing, his shy smile which he covered with his hands, his black hair which sometimes fell with youthful indiscretion over his forehead, his slim and erect body which he bore with agreeable disdain. He was an excellent and unexceptionable man, and it was through no fault of his own that it came to him to enact the remarkable drama of being the last Jew on earth.

Don Rafael knew nothing of the world. That is the critical fact. The events of the larger world were quite simply irrelevant to him. Nothing beyond the precincts of Gerona engaged his attention, unless, of course, a famine in Uruguay or a pestilence in Argentina had destroyed so many hundreds of thousands of heads of cattle that the price of Spanish hides was forced by scarcity to unexpectedly profitable levels. Then Don Rafael would smile without covering his mouth and point to the newspaper in the bar behind the cathedral and announce the good fortune which was Gerona's through the bad fortune of South American cattlemen. It was a simple view of events and not unlike the view of most men. But aside from that, aside from the report of news that bore upon their lives directly and without the requirement of reflection, he and his associates and friends had no curiosity about the great world. It could not be known therefore or regarded with more than passing interest that in that year, Don Rafael's fortieth, the conversion of all the world to the Catholic faith had been completed. Assuredly, the Cardinal Archbishop of Gerona noted the event and delivered sermons about it, but his remarks were consigned to the back page of the Monday edition of the newspaper, below the results of the soccer tournaments and the corrida and it was hardly an event for prosperous burghers to note, perhaps least of all Don Rafael, who never read the *Noticias Religiosas*, and in fact was accustomed to avert his eyes in a millennial reflex at the sight of the person or picture of the Archbishop in his episcopal robes. It should be recalled, however—and this he remembered much later—that his mother on her deathbed had taken his hand and put it to her heart and demanded his promise that until his own death he would not depart from the faith of their ancestors. He had sworn and moments later she had died. The ancestors of Don Rafael Acosta had come to Gerona in the time of Moses ben Nahman, the Talmudist, the commentator, the grammarian, the mystic. Moses had lived in fact directly across the road from Don Rafael Acosta's paternal ancestor, who had come to Spain from the Muslim kingdom of Fez in the early part of the thirteenth century. The Acostas were a distinguished family, physicians and Talmudists, who served churchmen and grandees with uncompromised dispassion and rectitude while never neglecting the poor and sick among their own people.

It was at the time of the massacres of 1391, more than a century and a half after the Acostas had come to the city of Gerona, that the family publicly abjured the Jewish faith, renounced the ways of their ancestors, and took upon themselves the outer garments of Christian worship. They appeared to serve the Lord of the Christians mightily, observing abstinences and vigils, attending mass with regularity, receiving the sacraments of the Church, giving obedience to its laws and regulations. What was not known was that, foreseeing the possibility of just such times as these, the old patriarch of the Acostas, Solomon ben Jehudah, had drawn up and notarized a document, signed in his presence by all those of his family, binding them forever (despite any and all derelictions which might result from fulfillment of the commandment of our people, that we live) to obey in continuity and to death the seven principles of the faith of Noah. Moreover and wherever possible, they were sworn to the observance of the Sabbath and the Fasts of Av and the Day of Atonement. They were then commanded, even to the fiftieth generation of those who might live, to return in fullness and faith to all the remembered observances of the House of Israel, to remove from themselves the deceiving guise of the Other Faith and to obey the God of their fathers until the time of the true Messiah—but this only when true service could be accomplished in peace, serenity, and without threat to life.

The family swore to this document, affixing their names, some seen even in children's scrawl. The document was placed behind a vault stone over the high fireplace of the reception hall of their home, and each year, by candlelight, on the Sabbath preceding the Day of Atonement, it was removed and read aloud. In more recent times there was none who knew Hebrew, but no less faithfully the family gathered on what it believed to be the Sabbath before the fast (they had nowhere to turn for accurate knowledge of the calendar, and during the nineteenth century, although the fires of the Inquisition had long since been banked, the spirit of Spanish intolerance remained pure and uncorrupt), and no efforts were made to recover and return these secret Jews. They withdrew the document, examined it in silence, swore an oath of loyalty and returned the document to its hiding place. Correct Catholics— some of them, indeed (may they be spared in His mercy), believing Catholics—they nonetheless maintained this secret practice of ancestral obeisance. And so it continued to the time of the family of Don Rafael Acosta.

Change, in the guise of boredom and inaction, had come to the Spain of Don Rafael's parents. No longer obliged by law to be an *observant* Catholic, it being sufficient that one remain in the eyes of the world a Catholic, the father of Don Rafael began to educate himself in the practice of his ancient faith, obedient to the demands of his ancestor, Solomon ben Yehudah. He secured books of instruction in the Hebrew language and explained their presence in his home by the curiosity he felt for the life and times of the antecedents of his Christian Lord and Redeemer. In time he taught himself, his wife (a distant cousin whom he had married in her youth), and then his only child and son not only the language but the liturgy of the Jewish people. They were not meticulous in their observance, it being left to the declining years of his father and the fifteenth year of Don Rafael's life to learn by accident about the laws of the phylacteries (which they undertook to procure and don) or the mezzuzah (which they promptly affixed to their doorway concealed behind an iron cross).

Don Rafael Acosta could not have known then that he was the last Jew in Spain—indeed the last Jew in Europe—that no Jew survived in the Holy Land, that all the crypto-Jews, proto-Jews, aboriginal Jews, the few hundred Samaritans who clustered on Mount Gerizah, the black Jews of Harlem, the Falashas of Ethiopia, descendants of the Queen of Sheba, were no more; that the small community of Japanese Jews, the Karaites of Southern Russia, the Jews of New Delhi and Bombay, the surviving Chinese Jewish family in Shanghai had vanished, gathered up into the Holy Roman Church. But not these alone. Not Jews alone had vanished from the earth. Indeed, they had been the last to go. Some, to be sure—refusing the gentle advice of Franciscans and the hectoring Dominicans and Jesuits who had passed throughout the world in caravans of faith, distributing crosses and rosaries, instructing in the day and baptizing at nightfall—chose to die, taking poison or starving themselves to death in undemonstrative demurral. But they were few and their numbers were not reported. It was the case that after two thousand years of militancy and combativeness, what the Church had sought by sword fell to it now without effort.

It was a miracle of the Church Triumphant. Sikhs and Buddhists, Confucians and Shintoists, Taoists and Zoroastrians, Holy Rollers and Methodists, Adventists and Christian Scientists, Muslims of the Mutakallimun and Muslims of the Sufi, all these capitulated, singly, in family, in village, tribe, whole nations in an orgy of pacific espousal. Giant crosses played the skies of all the continents by day and night, radios offered masses and oratories of thanksgiving. The numbers of the recalcitrant were reduced gradually, with unapproachable tribes contacted and inundated by forces of missionaries. The tropical forests of Indochina, the tangled rivers of New Guinea, the green maze of the Amazon were all penetrated and their people converted.

The Reformed churches were the first to bow their knee to the Holy Pontiff, then came the Patriarchs of the Eastern Churches, then the Muslims of North Africa, the Near East and Asia, and then polytheists and pagans of Asia, and last, following the atheists of North America and Europe, came the picking off of the Jews, those wild fruits of the branch, the first flowers of divinity, the last witnesses to stubborn unbelief. It was done at last. The new millennium could begin. The reign of the child of God, the son of the Lord, the lamb of heaven, could begin, and ultimately, finally, at a moment that would still remain unknown the parousia would come to pass. The Christ would return in glory, and the world would be judged. All believed that they would be saved, nature transfigured, and the age of renascent beatitude, at the end as it was in Paradise at the beginning, would commence.

It so happened that a young priest from Saragossa, just returned from a triumphant sojourn among the tribesmen of the African grasslands, had taken his old mother and father on a tour of Spain. They arrived in Gerona late on a Friday afternoon and parked their battered car in the Plaza España before Casa Acosta. Don Rafael had been busy throughout the day. A convention of nurses had just completed its deliberations, and customers crowded his shop to buy presents for their families. It was late in the day and he had become accustomed to returning home early on the eve of Sabbath so that Marietta could serve his supper earlier than usual, depart, and leave him to a quiet evening of reading in the Torah and examining the rare editions of Hebrew works he had begun to collect. He had closed the door behind the last nurse, a pretty girl from Valencia in honor of whose long black hair he had offered a ceremonial discount. He had already sent off his assistants and turned out the lights in the stockroom when he heard a knock at the front door. He determined to ignore it, but the knock continued, followed by a low, muffled but insistent call for help followed by a plaintive *"por favor."* Annoyed, Don Rafael unlocked the door and opened it. The young priest from Saragossa stood before him.

"Sir," he said directly, "my car refuses to start. Would you be kind enough to push me into the street? Perhaps then I can encourage a passing car, if one chooses to come at this hour, to assist me further."

"There will be no cars at this hour. Not for two more hours. Those that come now are all rushing to go home. I doubt that even our gracious Geronans will stop for you, Father."

"You may be right. The problem is my parents." He motioned to an old couple seated erect, unsmiling, as though Egyptian dead, in the back seat of the vehicle.

"Indeed," Don Rafael commented. He thought he might show hospitality. It did not matter that it was the eve of the Sabbath. The young priest would not know or care. He seemed pleasant enough. He would bring them to his home and call Garaje Jaime to assist them. By ten o'clock they would be off and he could retire to his study. He proposed that the priest and his parents return to his home for supper. The priest smiled appreciatively, and after a brief and virtually inaudible consultation with his parents who even then did not speak but inclined their bodies slightly in an unspecific nod of acknowledgment, the proposal was accepted. Don Rafael called his housekeeper to inform her of his guests and arranged with Jaime to send someone to pick up the keys to recharge the battery of the old car. It was done.

His guests were left in the darkened drawing room of his

home. Rosa, the niece of Marietta, served them sherry while he rested. At eight o'clock a light supper was served. It had not been customary in his family for a large meal to be offered in honor of the coming of the Sabbath. The festive meal, as always among working Spaniards of the provinces, was at noontime. A simple soup, a fish turned in oil, and a salad were sufficient. And wine.

The priest (he had introduced himself and his family as Mendoza, his own name being Don Xavier Maria) was curious, but not astonished, to find Don Rafael seated when they entered, a small black-velvet skullcap pushed to the rear of his head, almost indistinguishable in the twilight. The priest, peremptory as is habitual to his vocation, made grace without deferring to Don Rafael's wishes, crossed himself, as did his parents, and commenced to spoon the soup, unaware that Don Rafael had not responded "amen" to his benediction nor, for that matter, crossed himself. Don Rafael pushed back the heavy oak chair, rose to his feet, poured wine from his drinking glass into a small silver thimble cup and incanted quietly, but without haste or embarrassment, the *kiddush* of sanctification, sat once more, broke off a piece of bread from a small loaf which stood before him and blessed it. Not until he was about to lift his spoon to begin his meal did he become aware that his guests were motionless, no longer eating, their faces ashen with incredulity. Of a sudden the old lady began to cross herself rapidly, hitting her forehead, shoulders, and chest in a frenzy of movement. The old man began to shake, one leg striking the table repetitively. Only the priest remained unstartled by the scene, though he regarded it as curious. He turned to his parents and with a gesture of his hands he calmed them. He turned to Don Rafael who had watched their consternation with amused confusion.

"Who are you, sir?"

"I, Father?"

"Yes, my friend."

"I? Indeed you must know. I am the proprietor of a leather shop in the Plaza España of Gerona, called Casa Acosta. *I* am *the* Acosta. Don Rafael Arturo Moyse Acosta of Gerona. Born in Gerona. And, with the grace of God, to die in Gerona in this house."

"I see. Yes. Quite so. But, tell me, Don Rafael, what was that rite you performed?" the priest demanded, wagging his finger theatrically at the silver thimble cup and the bread.

Don Rafael was abashed at the priest's unexpected rudeness,

but he replied. "That rite? Oh, Father. You must know it well. It is the ancient ritual from which the Eucharist of the Church arises. Wine. Bread. Blood. Body. You must know?"

The priest frowned and a tic appeared over his left eye, a slight irregular spasm. "I know of no such rite. Indeed, there were a people, the Jews, who until recently practiced such a cult, but they are either dead or converted."

"Indeed," Don Rafael replied.

"Completely. Yes, the last of them were baptized eighteen months ago. I, personally, was responsible for administering baptism to the remaining forty Jewish families of Fez, Morocco, two years ago while on my way south towards the tribes of the grasslands. I am finished with them now. Every Jew and every Bantu who came into my way has been baptized."

"In that case, Father, I must disappoint you. My family came from Fez more than seven hundred years ago. I am, if you will, a Spaniard from Fez, and moreover I am a Jew. It may well be that I am the last Jew on earth." Don Rafael began to laugh. The very idea seemed so witty, so preposterous, there was nothing left to do but laugh. He laughed a good while, his face reddening, his hand steadying the skullcap upon his head.

The priest frowned. Anger replaced curiosity. "I do not believe you, Don Rafael Acosta."

"Believe me, what?" Don Rafael replied, his laughter subsiding.

"That you are a Jew."

"But, of course I am. I am, as regards the world, an unobservant Catholic, a not unusual phenomenon in Gerona. No self-respecting Spaniard would go to church—that is for women and old men and parents of priests. I was born a Catholic of visibly Catholic parents. But my father and mother were both believing, practicing, devout Jews. I am as well. And now if you will excuse me for a moment. I should like to call Jaime."

Don Rafael rose from the table and left. The remainder of the meal was served, but Don Rafael's guests ate no more. The mullet in white wine did not please them, nor the salad, nor the fresh fruit. They were, permit me to say, thunderstruck. Don Xavier sat at the table without speaking. His mother suggested that he lead them in a decade of the rosary, but the young priest demurred. Something more drastic was called for.

Don Rafael returned to the table after it had been cleared and coffee and walnuts served. "It's done. Fine. The man from the garage was just here. I gave him the keys and he will drive your car here when it is repaired. There will be no charge. Hospitality, particularly Sabbath hospitality, is always complete."

"My dear Don Rafael, I do believe that what you said is correct."

"What, Father?"

"That you are the last Jew on earth."

"No, my dear Father, I was joking. I was teasing you. That's quite unfair. My apologies."

"No. No. You don't seem to understand. In all likelihood what you are saying is true. You are the last nonbeliever in the world, not simply the last Jew on earth, the last nonbeliever, the last non-Catholic."

"But if you wish you can regard me as a believer. I was baptized. It's there, as you would say, even if it can't be seen. It's only that I don't believe a word of the Catholic faith, not a word. I am a Jew, and that's quite enough."

"Quite enough for whom?" The priest spoke with solemnity.

"For me, of course. For me. Nobody demands more of man. I am a decent man, a good Spaniard. I support the government, endorse its laws, contribute to charity. It is only that I am stubbornly pledged to my ancestry."

Don Xavier did not persist. It seemed hopeless. His host seemed to have no interest in his anomalous situation. He was without curiosity, dull, unimaginative. It seemed irrelevant—more, wholly uninteresting to him that he might in fact be the last Jew and the last non-Catholic on earth. It was pointless to contend further with such proud and indomitable ignorance. The priest broke off the conversation, thanked Don Rafael for his hospitality, and left as soon as the car was brought. He did not neglect, however, upon arrival at his hotel that same night, to address a letter to the Cardinal Archbishop of Gerona, the Most Reverend Pedro Fernando Corazon y Iturbe. His letter read:

Most Reverend Father,

It is my duty to inform you that in your midst there is one, Don Rafael Acosta, proprietor of Casa Acosta on the Plaza España of your city, who remains, despite the visible triumph of the faith, recalcitrant and unconverted. He is, dangerous enough, a lapsed Catholic, having admitted to me that he was baptized at birth, but, more grievous than this, his heresy is not that of natural ignorance or libertinism with which we could more easily contend, but of active devotion and fealty to his ancestral faith, that of the benighted Jews.

There are, you are aware, no longer Jews in our world, may the mercy of the Lord be praised. He is, I feel confident to claim, the last. But it is not simply that he proclaims his faith (I witnessed at his table this evening the performance of antiquated rites which gave me and my aged parents who were the inadvertent victims of his hospitality a shiver of mortal terror) from the fount of simple ignorance. With such ignorance we have proved in recent years we are more than capable of dealing. It is rather that he, who bears upon his brow the waters of baptism, by giving allegiance to a dead belief, actively despises our truth. If he remains unrepentant he will corrupt others. Knowing as we do that the ways of truth are encumbered with thorns and stones, we cannot risk that one, even one, active unbeliever be allowed to thrive, lest his presence infect others who find the path of salvation hard.

I urge you to take action.

If for any reason you wish to contact me, I am shortly to return to my family home in Saragossa, where I am available at the Church of San Xavier, after whom I am named.

I am a priest of the faith recently returned from our missions in Africa.

Yours respectfully,
Xavier Maria Mendoza

Don Rafael, on the other hand, did not think further of his evening with the family of Mendozas. He had found the meal tedious, the priest ill-mannered and ungracious, and his parents superstitious peasants. Once they had left he drank coffee in his study until midnight, reading quietly from his father's Bible the portion of the week which tells the story of the righteous convert, Jethro, who was the father of Zipporah, who was the wife of Moses, who was the father of all our people.

The following days were uneventful. Twice Don Rafael observed that a middle-aged man in a black suit and white straw hat stood across the street from his shop, smoking small cigars, but he imagined he was an idler who fancied himself elegantly turned out and stood about to attract the attention of the girls promenading the Plaza España at noontime. On the fifth day his assistant, Pablo Henriquez, motioned to the idler and said laughingly, "We are being spied upon, Don Rafael."

"Who? Where?"

"There, across the street. He is there during the comfortable hours, but when I arrive early in the morning to open the shop, there is another, a bald, fat man who is relieved about eleven by this one."

Don Rafael shrugged without interest. "I don't understand, but if it continues I will see to it. I am well known and respected in Gerona. Why should anyone spy on me?"

The following Friday, when he arrived at the Plaza España to have coffee in the café which was directly across the square from Casa Acosta, he noticed a small crowd gathered before his store. He hastened toward the crowd, and pushing through, saw to his horror that the front window of the shop had been broken. Pablo and his fellow assistant, Benito, had begun to hammer a wooden beam across the window and clean away the glass, but the shock of this vandalism left Don Rafael stupefied.

Don Rafael called the police and the *Alcalde*. An inspector from the Police Department, with whom he often played billiards, arrived and explained apologetically that he knew nothing of the culprits, that, indeed, he would be vigilant in pursuing them, but he added as he turned to leave, "You may well have brought this upon yourself, old friend." Were it not that he knew this man's wife and children, having bought them ice cream each time they came into his shop, he would have lost his temper, perhaps even have struck the inspector. As it was, his rage increased and tears of frustration came to his eyes. He closed shop for the day, sent his assistants home, and sat in the darkened interior, occasionally stroking the finely tooled display cabinets, their stomachs decorated with carved flowers, their feet golden orbs covered with Empire ivy.

Nothing happened during the remainder of the day, neither telephone calls nor further visitations from the police. The inspector did not return. The mayor, who had once dined in his home, did not respond to his call.

Don Rafael was upset—gloomy, to be more precise. He had never experienced vivid fantasies of enmity or persecution, but the days which followed provided him with fuel enough for a furnace of suspicion. The window was only the beginning.

One night the shop was broken into and all the cabinets of ladies' purses and the glass counters with men's wallets and watchbands were overturned. Nothing irreparable, nothing broken, nothing stolen, but hours of restoration and inconvenience. A few days later a drawing of a Jew in sackcloth, his head surmounted by a medieval conical hat, a sign around his neck proclaiming him Marrano, and the flames of a bonfire searing his bare feet appeared in whitewash on the vitrine of the shop. A curiously scholarly insult, Don Rafael thought. He did not immediately discern its source. A leaflet—Benito and Pablo gathered up fifty of them scattered in the wind that circled the Plaza—denounced Casa Acosta as the purveyor of cheap, synthetic products, the leather imitated, the prices inflated. Business did suffer. The other merchants commiserated with Don Rafael, whom they liked, but professed ignorance of the origin of his misfortune. The harassment continued for a month—vandalisms, insults, graffiti, obscenities. Benito quit Don Rafael's employ claiming a nervous stomach. The matter was grave. To be sure, Don Rafael was not indifferent to the situation. How could he be? But he was ineffectual. He telephoned the Perfectura several times daily, but each time the *jefe* was unavailable and the duty officer answered him with bored rudeness. He wrote a dignified letter to the Alcalde of Gerona, but Don Francisco did not reply. It seemed hopeless, and Don Rafael, by now in genuine torment from many sleepless nights and undigested meals, contemplated leaving Gerona, even leaving Spain.

On a Thursday afternoon, nearly five weeks after the original visit of the itinerant priest and his parents, a limousine bearing the coat of arms of the Episcopal Diocese of Gerona appeared before the door of Casa Acosta. The chauffeur, a sinewy Spaniard with thin, dry lips, presented him with a letter, signed by a Monsignor Siguente, the personal secretary of the Cardinal Archbishop, requesting the presence of Don Rafael in extraordinary audience that afternoon, in fact in fifteen minutes. The chauffeur, without so much as an "Excuse me," went to the rear of the shop—indeed as though he knew it—and brought Don Rafael his suit jacket and topcoat, which hung in a small wardrobe in the wrapping room. Don Rafael followed the chauffeur to the limousine, entered and sank back into the refined comfort of the ancient Mercedes. The car started off, up across the bridge into the old city of Gerona, up the backstreets toward the cathedral and the palace of the Cardinal Archbishop. It was not a long ride. Six, perhaps ten minutes. The car stopped and the chauffeur opened the door for Don Rafael. Don Rafael hesitated. It was not that he was frightened. He had been to the palace many times, during the annual blessing of the city, at Christmas time when the Cardinal saluted the merchants of Gerona, and indeed at the investiture banquet of the present Cardinal. He hesitated then not from nervous unfamiliarity. Rather he dimly understood that perhaps not the *jefatura,* not the *Alcalde,* not even the few envious merchants of the Plaza España were responsible for his misfortune, but the Cardinal himself, and if the Cardinal, the whole of the Church. He struggled out of the car. The chauffeur walked ahead, his hand beckoning him from behind to follow. Damned impudence, Don Rafael thought. He was led through a dark vestibule lined with heavy furniture and bust portraits of the Archbishop's predecessors, men with lean jaws and small eyes or else jowls cushioned with flesh. They ascended two flights of stairs to an antechamber where a young priest sat in semidarkness writing entries in a large vellum-bound volume. The priest jumped up, looked at Don Rafael with a smile, rang a small hand bell which must have been concealed in the palm of his hand, and the vast oak doors before which they stood opened.

Don Rafael entered and the doors closed behind him. He stood alone in the darkness. A voice from within another chamber invited Don Rafael to enter. He did, advancing four steps through an archway into the room, which appeared to be a library, for there were tiers of shelves lining the walls although few books could be seen.

"Come closer," a small voice proposed. "You will not be able to see me, unless you come closer." Don Rafael advanced hesitantly. "Closer still. I am not well. Nor am I an easily visible man even if I were." Don Rafael walked toward the voice and saw a very tiny priest, who sat on a low divan covered in red damask. A single light from a lamp shone upon the table to the side of the divan. In the peripheral light which barely included the priest, Don Rafael could see a man of considerable age, his face a map of rivulets and creases, his skin the color of wheaten wafers, dotted with brown grain. "Do sit next to me, my son." Don Rafael sat upon the divan and clasped his hands before him. "Do you know who I am?"

"Your Eminence?"

"Not quite. I am no white eminence. Grey, black, scarlet perhaps, but no public eminence in the panoply of the world." The old priest chuckled. "No. I am a priest pure and simple

(I am Father Espinosa), but my responsibilities encompass the Society for the Propagation of the Faith, the Secretariat for the Promotion of Christian Unity, and until recently the nearly moribund Holy Inquisition. Note well that I have said 'until recently' and 'nearly moribund.' It would appear you intend to revive me."

Don Rafael did not understand, although he remembered well from history books the cruelties of the Inquisition. But no one had been burned in Spain since the eighteenth century.

"Father, I do not understand you."

"You will understand me terribly well, my son. Do you smoke?" The priest withdrew a packet of cheap cigarettes from the pocket of his soutane and offered one to Don Rafael. Don Rafael waved it way. He was becoming unnerved.

"Help me then, Father, to understand why I am here, why I am being persecuted."

"Are you a Catholic, my son?"

"The truth, Father, is this. I was baptized a Catholic as were all my family, but we have never practiced nor believed the faith. We are Jews descended from Jews who in this good Spain of our times are able, without giving public offense or disgrace to our friends and neighbors, to honor what we believe."

"You are a lapsed Catholic?"

The phrase came to his head, "Canonically speaking."

"In a word then, you are a Catholic in mortal sin."

"No, Father, I am an observant and believing Jew who, through the habit of centuries since our forebears were driven from this land, has been obliged to appear to be what he is not. I am the sole surviving member of my family. I am not married. My parents are dead, may they rest in peace. I am all that is left."

"Precisely!"

"Precisely what?"

"Precisely the point. You are all that is left anywhere, my son, anywhere in the entire world."

"I don't understand."

"Technically we could ignore you. We could say to ourselves, 'This peaceful Church has good Catholics and bad Catholics.' We could say to ourselves quite simply that you are a bad Catholic—no sacraments, no communion, no prayers and benedictions. That would be all right under certain circumstances—if you lived, say, in Zanzibar or Tanganyika. But here

131

in Catholic Spain it is a different matter. And in Catholic Gerona, founded even before the time of Rome, an ancient city of the faith, to have in the midst of Gerona, in the bosom of Spain, in the heart of the West, in the innermost ventricle of the heart of Christendom, not only a lapsed Catholic, but a believing Jew—no, my friend, that is quite a different matter."

Don Rafael clearly did not understand the priest. He smiled in dumb incomprehension. Father Espinosa shifted his inconsequential weight; his feet, hidden beneath him, covered by his soutane, appeared as small protuberances seated in red-velvet high-heeled pumps. They peeked out at Don Rafael, caught the light, and shone. The priest observed Don Rafael's curiosity. "My small feet," he said, lapsing into reverie. "My gazelles, I call them," he went on, first addressing them and then Don Rafael. A curious fellow, Don Rafael mused. "A different matter, my son."

"What? Which?" Don Rafael had lost the conversation. Feet. Shoes. The endearments of Egypt.

"We have returned, my son. From reverie to reality. You have not understood me, have you?" he said, extending his bony hand, white flesh, to pinch Don Rafael's leg. "Are you awake to my meaning?"

Don Rafael became dizzy; a small pain, hidden at the base of his skull, moved out of the moraine of buried impressions and memories into the whole of his head. He asked for water. A bell tinkled and a pitcher of water and tumbler appeared. He requested an aspirin. It was produced. He saw no one, but hands reached around him out of the darkness to set down what he had requested.

"Are you quite restored?" Don Rafael nodded. "In that case, let me continue. It should be clear by now. You are, my friend, not alone the last Jew in Gerona, the last Jew in Catalonia, the last Jew in Spain, the last Jew in Europe, but in fact the last Jew in the entire world. The very last." The priest struck his knee with two fingers. It was not an emphatic gesture, but it was emphatic enough.

"I see now," Don Rafael murmured. "Clearly now. It is for this reason that I am persecuted. First that priest and his family, and then the humiliations done to me and my establishment. Yes, I see."

"Those torments embarrassed me, I assure you, Don Rafael. I have put an end to them. Our Lord, the Cardinal Archbishop, is a peasant from Asturias, adamantine, to be sure, but somewhat crude. I persuaded him to put an end to harassment. He listens to me. No, no. There will be no further per-secution." The priest stopped for a moment and sucked on his lower lip. He swallowed hard and his throat clucked. The moisture gathered from his lips (like a bird sipping dew) was quite enough. "If you do not mind, it will all be satisfactorily completed when you sign this document." He took a letter from a drawer in the secretary which stood at the head of the divan and handed it to Don Rafael. "No, no. No need to read it now. It is perfectly clear. It is simply a document of faith, precise and crisp. By the regulations of canon law you must be genuinely free to examine it in quiet and contemplation. To submit to Christ is a choice of will. The will must not be constrained. I would not think to have you sign it here in my presence, under the constraint of my inquisitorial authority. No. No. You must have time and leisure to reflect. I think our interview is concluded."

Don Rafael took the paper, folded it, and put it in his pocket. "By tomorrow then. Let us say, three o'clock in the afternoon. At the cathedral. Tomorrow. You will return with the docu-ment, executed, notarized, if you please, and we will hold a small celebration for the last Jew on earth." The priest laughed. Don Rafael left the presence of the priest and descended to the small plaza before the episcopal palace. He thought to return by foot down behind the Arab baths, the long way, circling back to the small *rambla* of the city by way of Calle de la Plateria to the avenue at the center of which Casa Acosta had stood for more than one hundred years. But that was not to be. As he reached the bottom of the steps the same Mercedes hummed to a stop before him, and the chauffeur, this time with cap in hand, alighted and hurried around to open the door for him. He had no choice but to get in and be driven to his home. When he reached the door to his house and reached up to put his fingers to the parchment of the mezzuzah concealed behind the iron crucifix, both had disappeared and in their place a minuscule *ex voto* had been attached. He entered the house, and a painted statue of the Virgin, illuminated by a halo of colored lights, affronted his eyes. The living room was a gar-denhouse of white lilies, and where, before, the pictures of his family had addressed their love to his eyes now hung St. Francis being visited by the stigmata, St. Sebastian delirious in his pain, St. Stephen beheaded, and others and more in the ecstasies of their martyrdom.

Don Rafael did not even turn the pictures to the wall or order them covered. He let them be. He stared through them, indifferent. He took his supper as before. He made his blessing and he said his grace and he thanked God that he had been permitted the honor of this season and its trial and he went quickly to his room, not daring or even caring to ask Marietta, who had waited anxiously for his questions, as to how these disgraceful intrusions had come to pass. It was not her fault. Nor, he reflected, was it his. The maladjustments of fortune, the woundings of time.

It was nearly midnight when he emptied his pockets and took out the momentous letter. He sat back in his tufted chair, his bare feet cold upon the stained-wood floor, and poured himself a drink of brandy and then opened the letter. It read:

> I, Don Rafael Arturo Moyse Acosta, known to all as Don Rafael Acosta, resident in the most Catholic city of Gerona in the region of Catalonia, submissive to the grace of her protector and lord, the Cardinal Archbishop, the Most Reverend Pedro Fernando Corazon y Iturbe, do hereby declare in the presence of all the multitudes of Christendom that I abjure, deny, refuse, hold in contempt, anger and dismay, repudiate, reject and despise the congeries of errors and the magnitudes of untruth which are, have been and ever more shall be in the memory of man to the doctrines of the Old Church, the dead Synagogue, the withered limb of Christ which by this act I do cut off. Though I am baptized into Mother Church I have wandered with her ungrateful recusants and though I was availed the instruments of my salvation, I blunted them and cast them aside for useless and deceitful teachings.
>
> I am penitent. I implore the mercy of the Church and I repent my waywardness. In love and in faith I ask to be released from my sin, to have imposed upon me any penance the Church in its mercy deems fit to cover my stain.
>
> I, Don Rafael Arturo Moyse Acosta, the last Jew on earth, ask to disappear.

For many hours he sat and watched the paper in his hand until the letter wavered and disappeared into blackness. He read it no more. The paper passed from his sight, and the reverse, printed as images are printed in our brain, upside down for storage in the recesses of memory, was retained. He slept that night in his chair, and in the morning, cold, his feet icy, a sniffle in his nose, a huskiness in his throat, he pulled himself up before the sun and bathed himself in its winter rays. He said the morning prayers as he had said them many thousands of times before. He wrapped himself in his phylacteries and wound the knot of unity around the middle finger and draped his father's silk prayer shawl over his eyes, and resplendent before the sun, sang out the praise of God and the abundance of his manifold compassions.

The morning hours passed and at eleven he returned to the shop, avoiding the chauffeur whom he saw lounging before the house. He went down into the cellar, and through an underground passage which let out into the street three houses away, walked quietly to the Avenida, where, as was his custom, he took his coffee.

The noon hours came and the shop closed for the afternoon siesta. Don Rafael did not leave but ordered a soup and fish to be sent in. He waited and he thought. A desultory reverie. He rolled back the skin of the *merluza* and uncovered its skeleton embedded like a fossil in tender white flesh. Skin flayed from bones. A taste and it melted; his jaws worked slowly. He chewed long and distractedly until there was no flesh between his teeth and he bit his lip and cried out.

The shop reopened. An old lady bought an ivory comb in a tooled black leather case. Don Rafael sat in the rear of the shop and sipped his coffee, already cold. He knew the letter of recantation by heart and its words blew through his mind like rain-soaked winter leaves. At ten minutes to the hour of three, the Mercedes came to the corner of the Plaza España and stopped; its driver, now dressed in grey gabardine and black puttees, approached the vitrine, rapped and crooked his finger. Don Rafael rose and pulled on his overcoat. His assistant stood by quietly, averted his eyes, and busied himself with a feather duster when Don Rafael nodded his goodbye.

The *paseo* was quiet. A German couple was drinking coffee at the Montana Bar, but otherwise the shops were closed, the usual throngs of strollers were absent. The Mercedes turned around and passed to the rear of Casa Acosta into the narrow street which ascends through the Old City to the cathedral square. The car moved like a lizard, scuttering forward and stopping suddenly to avoid an idling pedestrian. As the car mounted the cobbled streets Don Rafael became aware of the numbers of people moving, it would appear, in the same direction as he. The last street before the cathedral square was packed with people; the car—the only car—moved with difficulty, but the chauffeur never sounded his horn. People stepped aside and the car passed through.

The automobile entered the square as a light rain began to

fall upon the bared heads of the multitudes, the thousands of Geronans, top-hatted dignitaries, choristers in black satin and white lace, the bishops—there were eight—in rose gowns, the papal legates, and high above them, at the top of the fifty-eight steps of the marble staircase that ascended to the doors of the cathedral, his Eminence, the Cardinal Archbishop of Gerona. At his side, holding his arm, was the withered priest, Father Espinosa.

The door of the automobile opened and Don Rafael stepped out into the warm rain. He looked about him, and dazed by the assembly, turned as if to reenter the car, but a chamberlain approached, and grasping him firmly by the elbow, pressed him to the base of the stairs and sternly whispered, "Go up. The Cardinal awaits you. No nonsense now." There was nothing to do but obey. Don Rafael put his right foot to the first pediment and hesitated. The leg abandoned him. It tingled with electricity, benumbed. Don Rafael struck his thigh with his fist. The leg moved and he followed. Slowly he rose up, catching sight in furtive sidelong glances of old friends, Marietta, Pablo and Benito, and unmistakably the young priest Don Xavier Maria Mendoza.

A dozen steps from the top, Don Rafael hesitated. Those near him pressed forward, hands outstretched, thinking he would now retreat. He smiled. He was calm. He continued on his way. The last step brought him to the level of episcopal authority. The Te Deum began, the church doors swung open, incense floated into the rain, photographers discharged their flash bulbs, radio technicians adjusted the bank of microphones that stood to the rear of the Cardinal. The old priest limped to his side and spoke, "The world awaits you. Speak the recantation and then hand the document to the Cardinal and kneel before him." Don Rafael bowed his head in salutation to the Cardinal and moved toward the microphones. There was silence but for the gentle patter of the rain. Don Rafael passed a hand lightly over his forehead and touched his eyes in a gesture of friendship toward himself. He paused and breathed deeply. He began, "I believe in one God, Father Almighty, maker of Heaven and Earth," and he paused, "and . . . and . . . that is what I believe, that is the only belief I share with you." Cries: "No, no." "And the rest that I believe is what I have learned from my father and my father's father and all those in the generations of fathers which stretch back in the history of time to Moses, my first master . . . And so much more, if you would like to hear about it."

Don Rafael paused. He would have continued and told the history of the generations of Israel, but he was not allowed. The microphones went dead, the crowd pushed forward in a mass up the stairs and Don Rafael, shielded by the Cardinal, who stepped forward to protect him (and for his solicitude was slapped in the face by a hysterical woman), retreated to the sanctuary of the cathedral.

Don Rafael surrendered to the darkness of the cathedral. The great doors had shut behind him, the shouts of the crowd had disappeared, even the bishops and Monsignori who had crowded the chancel staring back at him and murmuring in consternation had vanished. He was quite alone. It must be sundown, he thought, for the rose window of the west wall shone purple. His mind was empty of thought or, rather, it was full of so many thoughts he could not settle upon one. The effect was the same—vacuity and apathy.

"It was brilliant," a dry voice crackled from behind him, a voice placed so close to his ear that he felt its breath upon his neck. He had no need to turn. He recognized the ancient priest of the Holy Inquisition, Father Espinosa. "Brilliant, brilliant. The opening of the Credo and no more. I congratulate you." The priest applauded and Don Rafael heard the measured beating of hands behind him.

"Don't mock me, Father. I staged nothing. In fact, Father, I almost went on—the whole Credo, by rote, just as I had learned it from the Sisters when I was a child, but that wasn't possible. I'm sorry, Father."

"You are a trouble, my son. Why couldn't you have been cooperative? Trouble for us, annoyance, irritation, and such an ordeal for you. Oh dear me." The priest was unhappy. "I'm not a young man, you must have gathered. And now all this exertion in my closing years. I had other projects for the end of my life. A visit to the monuments of the East and then retirement to a monastery for some restful meditation, and bleaching of my soul. And now this." The priest sighed. "You won't reconsider, would you?" Don Rafael said no. "I thought not. Well then, what to do? His Holiness telephoned. He was vexed. Do you realize that all of Spain and most of Europe, perhaps even Africa and Asia, heard your ridiculous broadcast? All of Christendom, all of Christendom. Oh dear." The priest cracked his knuckles nervously.

"I am sorry to have been a trouble to you, Father. But it had to be this way. You do understand, I'm sure. I might have signed the paper"—remembering it now, he handed it over his shoulder to the priest—"and gone on as before, masquerading my feelings, but that display you staged out there was intolerable. A humiliation. I just couldn't."

"Yes, yes, to be sure. A little overtheatrical, but then the Church is rather theatrical, don't you think? All our plainsongs and chants, our symbols and allegories, gold braid and lace, liturgical artifacts and mysterious bells, all these devices make the faith a bit spectacular. I find it exhilarating, however. The range is so extraordinary, from austerities that verge on the morbid to such ecstatic opulence. You don't agree. I know. You like your little desert visions, your bleak little vision."

"I'm tired, Father. A trying day, very trying. If you don't mind—and thank you for chatting with me—I'll be going."

Don Rafael rose, nodded distractedly toward the high altar, and went toward a side door at the apse of the cathedral. Three officers were waiting and took him into custody. That Sabbath eve he was flown to Rome. Father Espinosa was on the plane, seated in the tourist cabin, reading his breviary and sipping brandy, while Don Rafael and his captors dozed in the forward cabin.

Don Rafael was taken to Vatican City and turned over to an officer of the Swiss Guard who conducted him to an apartment. A very beautiful suite of rooms, from all reports. A week passed during which Don Rafael saw no one excepting a doctor who certified that his body and mind were sound. He was allowed to think. In the meantime the preparatory secretariats of the Council, those charged with developing its agenda, awaited advice from its listening posts throughout the world as to the effect of Don Rafael's stubbornness. They were not slow in coming. First off, it was headline news everywhere: LAST JEW SAYS "NO" (one paper had it as "No thank you"); JEW BELIEVES ONE GOD ENOUGH; SPANISH JEW DENIES CHRIST; and a thousand variants depending upon whether the paper was a *Le Monde* or an *Osservatore Romano*. By week's end there were reports that a small group of Tibetan Catholics had fled to the mountains to renovate a lamasery, that a former sufi in Cairo had mutilated himself during a trance, that an enclave of Sonora Indians had reinstituted the peyote ceremony, that two missionaries had had their brains eaten by supposedly pacified headhunters in New Guinea, and quite near to home in Abruzzi a shepherd boy claimed to have seen a bearded man with stubby horns coming down a hillock, carrying under his arm two engraved plaster tablets. There were now fifty or more Abruzzians awaiting the reapparition of St. Moses.

It was determined therefore that Don Rafael had to be made an example to the faithful, lest an incident of disease become an unchecked plague.

Eleven days from the evening of Don Rafael's arrival in Vatican City, Don Rafael was accompanied by a papal chamberlain in formal attire and a contingent of Swiss Guards to a chamber buried in the gloom of the Vatican. There an assembly of examining bishops had gathered to query him and hear testimony from others. Three bishops in imperial purple, a deaf Cardinal, and Father Dominic Espinosa.

Don Rafael enters.

PRESIDING BISHOP (*To Don Rafael*) Do be seated. (*Motioning to a fauteuil covered in yellow silk which stands to the side of a long fifteenth-century Spanish mahogany table*) Are you comfortable? Excellent. We would prefer you not to smoke. The Cardinal Archbishop of Turin is deaf, but we will hear for him and (*pausing*) his eyesight tells him more than most of us hear. (*The others smile thin smiles*) Yes, now, what have we here? (*Shuffles some papers, puts on eyeglasses, but peers above them in a curiously affected manner*) Ah yes. You are Don Rafael Arturo Moyse Acosta of Gerona?

DON RAFAEL Yes.

PRESIDING BISHOP Good. Well then. Now what?

FIRST BISHOP (*Pinching his chin*) You are a Catholic?

DON RAFAEL Only in a manner of speaking—

FIRST BISHOP What manner is that?

DON RAFAEL A speaking manner, as I just said. If someone says to me "You are a Catholic?" I say "Most certainly" if it seems likely to end the conversation. I don't enjoy talking about religion. I prefer keeping religion to myself.

SECOND BISHOP To yourself, indeed. My dear man, religion is a matter of public record, like birth, marriage and death.

DON RAFAEL True. For those purposes I am a Catholic. But, otherwise, since God observes the workings of the heart, its intentions, so to speak, I am not.

FIRST BISHOP And for those obscure regardings, what are you?

DON RAFAEL Must I say?

PRESIDING BISHOP Of course you must. Are you embarrassed?

DON RAFAEL Afraid, not embarrassed.

PRESIDING BISHOP What is it then?

DON RAFAEL Jew.

PRESIDING BISHOP Jew what?

DON RAFAEL I am a Jew.

PRESIDING BISHOP How so a Jew?

DON RAFAEL I am a Jew in the flesh. I am circumcised. I am a Jew in the spirit. I await the Messiah. I am a Jew by nature and profession. I am patient.

FIRST BISHOP A Catholic and a Jew. A hippogriff, a gorgon, that's what you are. A bastard, a corruption, that's what you are.

SECOND BISHOP To be blotted out.

PRESIDING BISHOP (*Rapping his episcopal ring upon the table*) Now, now. Please. (*To Don Rafael*) Do you realize the seriousness of the charge against you?

DON RAFAEL What charge? I don't understand. Why am I here? Why do these gentlemen—your colleagues, sir—speak to me in such a strange and insulting manner? I have done nothing to offend them other than—I gather—exist. I endure and my endurance is an offense. Well, then, that's that.

FIRST BISHOP That is not that.

SECOND BISHOP Most certainly not that.

FIRST BISHOP You cannot remain both "this" and "that."

SECOND BISHOP You may become "this."

FIRST BISHOP You cannot remain "that."

PRESIDING BISHOP In other words, to translate these grammarians, you must resume your life as a Catholic and cease to be a Jew.

DON RAFAEL I don't understand at all. One Jew in all the world and you fuss. It's quite foolish. I'm no competition. I don't even want to compete. I wish only to exist. I don't ask anything from you—no charity, no attentions, no favors. I want to be. That's what I am—a being who wishes to be, to continue in his ways, to live out his life. I don't preach. I don't argue. I don't parade my beliefs in public. I am a private man.

FATHER ESPINOSA Not quite. True. You *were* private, but you are no longer.

DON RAFAEL That's your fault.

FATHER ESPINOSA That may be, but fault it is not. You are an impediment. Were you undetected, persistent in your ways, private, as you say, the damage would be no less grievous. Do you imagine the offense is mitigated by privacy? The scandal is to God and it would be enough that He is scandalized, that because of your persistence in unbelief, the

140

belief of others is compromised. No, no. I can see that you are *no* theologian. But we are. We are meticulous theologians. And the precision of our belief demands from us no less pure and undeviating logic. You are the last unbeliever and a Jew unbeliever at that. For that reason you are the first as well. You are unique. You *must* be converted. Do you understand, my dear friend, what your persistence does to this world? It alone prevents us from bringing the Kingship of Christ to the earth.

DON RAFAEL (*Softly*) All by myself?

PRESIDING BISHOP All by yourself.

FIRST BISHOP Does that please you?

DON RAFAEL (*Softly*) No. I am frightened.

SECOND BISHOP As well you might be.

DON RAFAEL No, not pleased at all. What's to be done with me?

FATHER ESPINOSA Recantation as before. But this time very public, exceedingly public. His Holiness will receive your petition in the Sistine Chapel. He will raise you up into redemption.

DON RAFAEL I understand your predicament, but no. I do not wish to rejoin the Church. I decline the privilege of saving the world. Saving the world is your job, not mine. I didn't ask to be a Jew. I didn't ask to be a man, or a Spaniard, or a leather merchant. But I am all of these things. And what I am by providence, I elect to remain. I will be all of these to the end of my life and I will be these faithfully.

PRESIDING BISHOP Well, Fathers, you've heard him?

CARDINAL (*Draws a finger over his throat and gurgles*)

PRESIDING BISHOP Please, your Eminence.

FATHER ESPINOSA We have no choice. He must be punished.

DON RAFAEL Severely?

FATHER ESPINOSA Severely.

DON RAFAEL How? How will I be punished?

FATHER ESPINOSA Humiliation.

The session came to a close. Don Rafael was returned to his rooms. Father Espinosa remained behind and continued to converse with the bishops, who called upon him to describe the implications and consequences of Don Rafael's stubborn refusal.

"My friends," he began, "we are at a curious impasse. It is ironic that now, at this moment in time, as we draw close to the return for which, as believers, we have waited nearly two millennia, our way should be—as Saint Paul previsioned—

141

blocked by the Jew. I shall not fatigue you by reciting the historical miscreancy of that people. To be sure, they did not by their natural proclivity and disposition disdain our Lord or impede the dissemination of His Word. What they opposed, what they denied, they did as if by the implanting of God. He who made hard the heart of Pharaoh that He might rescue His own hardened also the hearts of Israel, that she might wound and slay her savior and remain until the End a people adjudged and condemned.

"We care not that from that time until this the members of that small society of supernatural criminals became the wards, chattels, property of the realm to be fatted or starved, contained or expelled, indulged like children or murdered like men, according to our wishes. We did not count it a certainty throughout that long vigil of time that a day would come—as it has now come—when the sweet air of the End would be in our nostrils. Throughout that vigil we threw down her altars, drove her sons forth, and slew her greybeards. Israel cannot torture forth the last drop of His blood and we cannot destroy Israel. Yet Osiris grows up from his own entrails, dies and returns, forever unto ever again, year by year. We are regenerated and so is she. Ah yes, God hardened her heart and God keeps that hardness resolute, congealed, obdurate, and though we kill, kill, kill, she is there again.

"But now as Saint Paul foretold, the time of the last harvest is come, the gathering in of the gleanings of all our fields. There is one left, one from amid all the peoples of the earth, the last unbeliever, the last Jew.

"The world is reconstituted. The body of the New Adam, until this moment a nervous and puny thing, lying exhausted upon the straw pallet of the world, is healthy and intact, but for this tic in his cheek, this wart upon his thumb, this boil upon his thigh. This last Jew is the sole blemish of the New Adam.

"Having said this, let us counter our own argument. True, we are, in this Holy Church, the vicarage of God, conducting man through the treacherous narrows and shoals of his life, and it is we, with the timbrel of charity and the drum roll of hell, who have brought all dissent to confess its folly before Saint Peter's throne. But we, we, too, are mortal (whatever our virtues and our grace), and though we are already in the forecourt of the Kingdom we are as distant from the supernal throne as infinity and eternity. It is finally up to God. Would we save the world without God? We would not. We cannot.

It is one thing to praise ourselves for having drawn together the appendages of the world, for having made of the disjected members of our species a single body, but without the breath of the spirit, of what value is all this quantity—of what value is it that untouchables and princes, muzhiks and headhunters, Eskimos and pygmies, know a bit of catechism and cross themselves—of what value? No. No. The breath must be kissed into this dumb Adam.

"The Russian theologian A. S. Khomiakov told us in former times of the vitalities of *sobornost*. That noble amateur believed that a congregation of the faithful is numbered not by head count but by heartbeat. Not ten or a hundred or millions but two or three who speak the name of Jesus Christ in purity of heart. There—in that small bedraggled company—is the truth. We, by contrast, are confronted by the reverse of the situation of our Russian friend. We have, not two or three, but one; and this one, in palpable good faith, simplicity, clarity says no. I decline, he says. I confess only the old, wasted inheritance. So there, he says. The New Adam remains blemished. No unanimity to the Visible Body. No concord to the Invisible Body.

"We have a recourse. Let Don Rafael die. Now that would settle everything. A touch of poison, an overdose of pills. Done. An expeditious resolution. (I see some of you like that. Dear me. You do not understand.) Expeditious, but completely misguided. We may deceive men, but we cannot deceive God. No. We cannot be the hand that holds the dagger hilt. We must proceed otherwise. We have already received—did you realize?—a petition from India with more than a million signatures calling for Don Rafael's speedy conversion. In America cenacles of worshipers are dedicating unceasing prayers to the Blessed Sacrament importuning intercession that the heart of our impenitent be melted. And, last but not least, for here is the clue to our decision, the Japanese—remembering well the martyrdom of their own Jesuit missionaries and the veneration they now offer their relics—have asked that Don Rafael be brought to that island for a tour.

"They write and I excerpt the letter of the Bishop of Kyoto: 'Most excellent Fathers,' etcetera, etcetera, etcetera (here note), "unbelievers in the past were employed by us, as living examples to the faithful. By the witness of their materialism, errancy, and sensuality we demonstrated most graphically the virtues of the Faith. The evidence of the unbeliever was good for the believer. Now there are no more unbelievers, but the loss of unbelievers does not make believers perfect. Think not all Christians good Christians. Far from it.' Etcetera and so forth. (Now, pay attention!) 'If, however, you would bring through our land that last unbeliever, parade him as our old lords paraded their captives through all the streets and let the faithful see with their eyes the damnation that awaits unregenerate sinners, it may revivify and cleanse their faith . . .' and so forth.

"You murmur approval. Splendid. Right. Put into the language of theological argument (for we will have to defend our course before the Holy Father), it is this. We are One but for one. We have all power—the power of unanimity. But who knows what power *is* and who *has* power? If one can do everything, one is, insofar as man is concerned, already a god, however much he fails of divinity.

"The predicament of power is that it is mindless. Power has no intelligence of itself. It receives its instruction from outside. Everyone is charmed by the story of Sisyphus and his rock, but no one respects the mountain upon whose surface his heroic folly was dramatized. The mountain was the real power, and were it not for the labors of Sisyphus it would not be known how truly immense, difficult, hazardous its abraded incline really was. The mountain is the raw totality of power, but it is the stubborn stupidity of Sisyphus that gives the power meaning. Our recalcitrant Jew—more than all the believers of Christendom—makes real the power of Christ. Don Rafael is the irritant that makes the Body of Christ move. He, my friends (forgive my ecstasy), perhaps even more than the return in glory which we await, is the harbinger of the Kingdom of God."

It was decided then and there. Don Rafael would be displayed to all the world, toured, paraded, exhibited as a specimen, and at the conclusion of his international tour, returned to Rome, and there, during the hour following the last of the daily masses, brought caged into the square before St. Peter's and left—guarded, to be sure—to be stared at and loathed by deputations of the faithful.

The tour proved miraculous.

In each land of the world a procession was organized, and in imitation of the custom of ancient Rome, the cardinal or bishop of the realm led the procession of penitents through the streets, his vestments gleaming in the sun or sparkling in the rain, and beside him, his hands cuffed, his legs hobbled, hopped the figure of Don Rafael Acosta, his body draped in rags, his face begrimed with ash, upon his head a dunce cap on which was written in the language of that nation: The Last Jew. Somehow, Don Rafael survived. His eyes, blinded by dust, his flesh blistered with the wounds of rocks and the beatings of enthusiasts who broke the ranks of the police to switch him or punch his back, his legs a pulp of sore flesh, he was returned to Rome early in the fall of his captivity. Although he was given little encouragement an energy consecrated by will pressed him constantly back into life.

One morning, the week before Christmas, Don Rafael was brought in his cage into the square of St. Peter's. The bells tolled his appearance, and a crowd of pilgrims surged and heaved to catch sight of him. Children sat upon their fathers' shoulders, nuns trained their binoculars toward him, others stood on camp chairs, straining for a glimpse. Within the cage, his head drooping upon his chest, his black beard falling in snarls, wild and untended, upon his shirt front, Don Rafael shivered from the wind. He was feverish. At a moment before the hour of one, when the guards would return to draw away the cage and bring to an end the appearance of the day, Don Rafael commenced to speak. At first his words were soft, lifting upon the wind and flying upward, unheard and lost but to those few who had commanding positions in front of him. Gradually the crowd grew silent and his voice dropped from the register of birds crying against the elements to the resonant address of one who speaks to his fellow creatures:

"The time of my life comes to an end. I am still a young man, but my life is fulfilled. I did not think it so. I fought against death, but I can restrain it no longer. I have known this for some time now. It is hard to go on telling oneself that there will be a deliverance, waiting, waiting daily for some miraculous hand to reach down and release me from my misery, return me to my beloved Gerona, restore me to my friends and to my livelihood. How could it be, I thought, that God should not pity me and show me mercy? Who am I, I said to myself, but an ordinary man, extraordinarily unfortunate? Why should I be elected for such torment? I was not the first Jew. Why then should I be the last? I suffered all that I have suffered—all indignities and outrages—softly, without public tears (but do not think that I did not cry privately, cry and beg, and call to my mother and father for help—I did), certainly not with temper or anger. What would my anger have brought me? Your contempt, your jeering? I had no need of them. Were I to have railed against you, I

145

would have died long before this, long before I could understand what makes you so hard and cruel, and God so silent.
The two of these must be understood together—your cruelty
and God's silence. Now I understand them.

"I am an ordinary man, I have explained that. But I am an
ordinary man with an unordinary quality. I am a Jew. Now
that fact—being a Jew—could be ordinary, like being a man,
but it would require that you permit it to be so. It cannot be
treated by you as something exceptional, bizarre, suspicious,
uncanny, or else by regarding it as such you oblige us ordinary
men to behave as though we *were* very special. You make us
extraordinary by deciding that you cannot cope with us. So
much for you, but what about God? Why does He not rescue
me? Why did He not rescue all of my brothers who, like me,
have said no to you? Why?

"I shall now tell you. Because He accepts your verdict. No.
More than that. He decided upon it long before you did. He
decided we were extraordinary from the very start, as witness
all our prophets and teachers and visionaries. Why rescue *us*?
Rescue poor people. Rescue ordinary people. They need
rescue. Save them, Lord, before us. To rescue us is to deny
who we are, to make us ordinary.

"And now, do you know why Jesus died on the cross and
was rejected by the Jews? It was because He asked God,
'Lord, why have you forsaken me?' Had He not spoken these
words He might well have died—no less died—but I will tell
you something, all the Jews would have believed in Him. 'He is
surely a Messiah,' they would have said, because He says
nothing, calls for nothing, asks for nothing. He knows that
God is with Him. I know that God is with me, now and forever. You are not yet saved, but I am ready to die."

Don Rafael Acosta closed his mouth and died. He died and
was buried, and in the aftermath of his death, there came
those who believed he was their ransom and redeemer, and
those people, like our beloved Don Rafael, were again called
Jews.

The story was done.

"That's that," said the visitor, relighting his pipe.

"The interpretation?" Simon demanded, pushing away the
blanket, and walking about the room with agitation. "The
interpretation, the interpretation?"

146

The visitor laughed, throwing back his head. "All you scholarly millionaires are the same. You can buy interpretations if you need one so badly. But I won't give you one."

"Then why did you tell me all this, if you won't explain it? Of course I'm not foolish. I understand bits and pieces, but that's not enough."

"Certainly not!"

"Who are you?" Simon asked suddenly.

"That again. No. No. You won't take me unawares. Not me. I'm aware of every move you make."

"You're a devil," Simon retorted, not quite meaning what he said.

"Heh, heh," the visitor began once more to roll with laughter. "How many devils do you know with such good stories? Devils are troublemakers. I'm no troublemaker. What did the Adversary do with Job—boils, and deprivation, and death. I didn't burn your parents. You managed that. And you're as rich and as wise as Solomon despite your bad luck. Me a devil? Much too easy."

" A *malach* then?"

"No angelic messenger either. Not devil, not angel. That's enough for you to chew on."

"So who could you be?" Simon thought aloud.

"You'll have to decide for yourself. Let it be that I tell memorable stories, if one has a will to remember them. But now it's nearly morning. I must be moving along. I'm due at the *mikveh* at daybreak for a chat with an old friend. You don't know him. So don't ask. Stay put, dear Stern. I'll let myself out. Off to bed with you. It's been a long night and you can't afford to catch cold."

Simon looked up and the visitor was gone. The door was closed, barred as before from the inside, but there was tobacco on the floor, charred match ends, and a bit of paper with Simon's name and address written in a neat hand. These remnants of the mysterious visitor Simon put into an envelope which he sealed and dated April 1, 1942.

The days which followed the visitation of the storyteller were predictably unsettled. Simon alternated between lassitude and antic exuberance, languishing in the storage room, reading, lying on his cot and examining the pattern of mildew on the whitewashed ceiling or rushing off to the synagogues of the neighborhood to question the *gabbaim* about any strange, unfamiliar worshipers. There was no trace of his visitor. Simon gradually came to believe that he did not exist, that it was a dream of weariness, projected from fatigue and grief like a magic lantern upon the wall before his bed. But he could not explain the complexity of the story, its forbidding and elusive meaning, and more to the point, the unarguable factuality of the locked door and the contents of the sealed envelope. He forgot his visitor, but not his story. Each night a fragment of the narrative, caught in the webbing of his life, would appear in his dreams and he would awaken, frightened, and look about him, expecting not his visitor but poor Don Rafael Acosta or the spidery Father Espinosa.

Simon Stern never went uptown. Only once, I've said. At the end, with which I began. But that isn't quite so. He went twice (leaving aside, of course, the trip to the cemetery on Staten Island to bury his parents but that was in the other direction), and the first time, in its own way, was as important as the last will be. It was in the late winter of 1943. What did I know of it? I've heard, that's all, but I've heard everything that took place before he saved me.

Simon Stern usually chose to walk. But if the distance was far enough he would take the bus or if it were convenient, motion to a taxi as it slid to a halt before a stoplight. But he rarely took taxis. It was too humiliating, he confided, to be chauffeured. Only if necessity required—dire necessity—would he hail a taxi, and such a necessity was Simon Stern's visit to Madison Square Garden.

It was 1943. And Chaim Weizmann was coming from London to New York. Chaim Weizmann was an Elijah and Jews are famous for Elijahs. He didn't tell the Jews *why* he was coming, but he did have a message for the Jews. The Jews called a meeting. A very Jewish thing to do. A vast Jew comes to town. Call a meeting. In that way everyone is given the opportunity of hearing the news at the same time and no one feels left out of the news. The Jews called a meeting. All the rabbis sponsored it and so did the Zionists, and it appeared as though all the Jews were finally agreeing on something. It was at Madison Square Garden uptown, just north of the garment district and just south of Central Park, where Simon would one day come to sit.

Jews piled into Madison Square Garden. There were so many Jews in Madison Square Garden it was hardly believable so many Jews existed. But the Garden, as it was called, only held twenty-two thousand people, so thousands of Jews had to stay in the streets and there were microphones put in the streets, and Jews by the thousands stayed behind barricades and listened and mounted policemen were about, keeping them orderly. But Jews, coming to hear an Elijah like Chaim Weizmann, are very orderly. They await something.

Simon Stern hadn't wanted to go uptown. At that period of his life going uptown was not yet a decision. It was something he just didn't do. It was only a *meshugas*, an eccentricity which marked him off from others. He was flattered when business-men would come downtown to see him, but of more than that he wasn't aware. He didn't know until the night he went uptown to hear Chaim Weizmann that the reason he didn't go was very serious, that it was something in the nature of a judgment upon the world and a judgment upon himself. And so he saw the placards on the streets in Yiddish and in English and noted the advertisements in the newspapers: Chaim Weiz-mann/Madison Square Garden/March 1, 1943. He had never heard a really great Jew speak, excepting perhaps his father. He was tempted.

Unfortunately the late afternoon of the day Weizmann was to speak, Simon had a business appointment at Ratner's. He was meeting two bankers from Boston to arrange financing for the purchase of a tract of land outside Queens where he thought one day something would have to happen. He thought maybe they'd build another airport or a big housing develop-ment. He wasn't certain, but it was a vast parcel and he wanted it. He was building a ring around the city. Even that he didn't understand. In the Palisades he had land; on Staten Island he had land; in the Bronx he owned land even though he con-sidered it a far-off speculation; and now in Queens beyond La Guardia Airport he wanted land. And so at Ratner's he was meeting the bankers. Usually when bankers came to see Simon at Ratner's or the Café Royale or Rappaport's or Moscowitz and Lupowitz', they were late. It was their habit to be late and they arrived in their tailored coats and striped ties and couldn't believe they were downtown on the Lower East Side selling land to a cranky Jew. But business was business. And so they came and the larger the deal the more punctual they were. For this transaction they were right on time. Simon had reserved a table in the back of the restaurant. He had anticipated problems because he had demanded that the owner—a syndicate of old-time realtors—give him an allowance of $140,000 which he would guarantee to use for draining a flooded section of the tract and for putting in a utility road and electricity. He thought they would argue, but they didn't. It seems they thought it was a good deal, unloading such a faraway strip of semimarshland. At seven o'clock the papers were signed. The four lawyers and two accountants and the bankers put on their grey overcoats, and taxis were called to take them back uptown.

Simon sat dazed and tired. He had forgotten about Chaim Weizmann. He had just given the bankers a check for more than a million dollars and a man is justifiably tired when he's paid real money for a tract of semimarshland. He yawned and rubbed his eyes and tried to think about other things. What came to his mind is not easy to describe, since I have only a third- and fourth-hand version of Simon's elliptical telling of the story. But Simon opened up his mind. Most men close up their minds when they're tired, putting down the flaps of their psyche until nothing foreign, extraneous, perhaps dangerous can penetrate. And then such men feel rested. But not Simon. Simon opens up everything, allowing bits and pieces of the universe to fly in and around, sticking wherever possible, flying out when irrelevant.

Simon began to think about the world. As he told it, he suddenly felt a chill pass over him as though the Angel of Death had come into Ratner's for a cup of coffee and had joined him at his table. Instead of the light and warmth of the old friendly restaurant penetrating him, it suddenly became pitch-black. All right. A diagnostician would say Simon was overtired, more tired than he could know, and was having some manner of hysterical seizure. Instead of letting the world swirl, he was freezing it, and so, instead of life and light all about him, there was the foreboding of death.

It is said that the seizure lasted only a few moments, but in that time Simon had some kind of convulsion, fainted and slid off his chair onto the floor. When he revived, the waiters, who were standing over him, moved aside to give him some air and lift him back to his seat. The first thing Simon saw when his clarity returned—the very first thing, in fact—was a poster on the wall which announced in Yiddish and English that Chaim Weizmann would speak that evening at Madison Square Garden.

Simon Stern regarded everything as a sign. It was not that he was superstitious. It was rather that he expected signs and wonders and was ready for them. Nothing unusual, unplanned, unexpected could occur which Simon failed to ponder. Is it a wonder then, that when such a man awakens from a convulsion in which he has sensed the presence of death and sees straightaway, first thing, that a great Jew is going to speak that very evening—is it any wonder that such a man, particularly if he's Simon Stern, would take it seriously? The next thing (before anyone could stop him and tell him to go home to bed) Simon Stern was in a taxicab, telling the driver to take him to Madison Square Garden to hear Chaim Weizmann, the Elijah of the Jews.

The entrance to the Garden bulged. Long frockcoats and stained hatbands and shirts striped with dirt and perspiration and scuffed shoes and black skullcaps and hundreds of coat sleeves with black mourning bands talked quietly. Vendors shouted beer and frankforts as always, and some people bought candy bars but there was no festive anticipation. No one knew, but all suspected. A woman in a sweater which sagged around her breasts and wearing white sweat socks carried a placard REMEMBER THE ST. LOUIS. Who would forget the *St. Louis*, but after that night—again—who would remember the *St. Louis*?

Nine hundred and seven refugee passengers returned from the sight of Miami to Europe. A bishop in Virginia protested. They were all taken in before the ship reached its final destination in Hamburg by France, Belgium, the Netherlands, and Great Britain. All except those in the last contingent are dead.

Who would remember any of them? Another placard said, WRITE YOUR CONGRESSMAN. Some asked the bearer, "About what?" He answered, "Make a protest."

Simon got out of the taxicab. He handed the driver a few dollars and waved him off. Simon looked around him. *"Yidn"* he muttered to himself. He was not relieved. All his life he was surrounded by *Yidn* but he was not relieved. The Angel of Death had taken a cup of coffee at his table and he remembered that his face was not unfriendly. It was unsettling. It wasn't enough for twenty-two thousand Jews to be gathered at Madison Square Garden. Simon edged his way along the wall toward the entrance. An Irishman was taking tickets. He had to be Irish. He was smiling. Simon hadn't bought a ticket. He thought it was free. All the meetings of his youth were free. He heard Norman Thomas free. He heard Stephen Wise free. He even heard Abe Cahan free and Abe Cahan was a writer with nothing to sell. So why should this cost? It annoyed him until he saw that all the proceeds from tickets went to the Joint Distribution Committee and it was all right. It was a benefit. He paid ten dollars for a seat down front and came back and gave the ticket to the smiling Irishman.

The Garden was vast like the inside of Pharaoh's tomb. He spoke to himself in a whisper and he thought he could hear the echo. There were no signs in the Garden. There was no music in the Garden. There were only silent Jews waiting for the lights to dim in the cavern and lights to illuminate a platform upon which stood an American flag and the blue-and-white flag of the Jewish National Home in Palestine.

The overhead lights dimmed. The stage lights went up. Ten men walked out upon the platform. Their faces were masks, as though bedaubed by common knowledge with a whitewash of pain. One after another they rose and spoke, each more terrible than the last. One reported on Germany; another on France; another on Poland; another on Hungary; another on Rumania; another on Russia. The figures mounted.

The litany of anguish came to an end. A little round man with a grey-white goatee ascended the platform, and the audience rose and shouted to him its greeting. It was Weizmann, the forerunner of the Kingdom. The little man came toward the dais and stepped on a box. He grasped the microphone and in a voice breaking with fatigue began to speak. A word of comfort? None. Absolutely not one word of comfort came from his lips. And indignation? The majesty of indignation fell upon the people as stones fell from the Tower of York upon its besiegers. A stone. What can be done with a stone? What? Tell me, what's a stone? Crack a skull with a stone, but go crack an empty space. Be indignant. My God, Simon told me, be indignant. What's the use? The Angel of Death was having coffee at my table. Tell him to move. The seat's taken. My friend just went to make a phone call to his wife. Angel, he's coming back. That's the point. The Angel sits where there's an empty place and he doesn't care who's coming back. In fact he knows who's coming back. And that's the whole point of being such an Angel. Weizmann telling us that he's angry. Incredible. He's angry. Who's he's angry with? Churchill he's angry at? Cordell Hull? Breckinridge Long? Franklin Roosevelt? What's he angry at? Roosevelt even sent a telegram. The telegram assured twenty-two thousand Jews that the Nazis would not succeed in exterminating their victims. Well said, Mr. President. Simon's head was spinning as Weizmann pounded the lectern softly, pounding with small hands turned palms down so that the sting of polished wood hurt, but the sound of the gesture was hardly audible. Thank you, Mr. Weizmann. What's the total? Give us a number to remember, Mr. Weizmann. Stop being indignant and give us a number. He's getting there. Neutral sources in Switzerland. In contact with the Joint Distribution Committee. Two million Jews have been exterminated. "The Nazis will not succeed in exterminating their victims." So that's it. Two million victims were exterminated. And that's just a beginning.

"We are being destroyed by a conspiracy of silence." Those were the last words Weizmann spoke. He repeated them. Is it a wonder that from that night until this hour Simon Stern became incapable of physical love? Impotent. His manhood had been snatched from him by silence. Silence. There was simply no point saying anything if such magnitudes as these produce telegrams. What could Weizmann do but speak softly and pound the lectern gently and caress tragedy like a woman? There was no point.

The world, it is said, will be saved either when it has become so transparently magnificent that the Messiah appears as a reward or when it aches so from misery that the Messiah comes like a medicine. But there's a third way. The Messiah comes into our midst when men are speechless. That's only my opinion. There's a writer who said the Messiah comes only when he's no longer needed. But that's true only for people who are ironic about Messiahs and suspicious about men. Simon Stern was neither. He wasn't ironic about Messiahs at all and he wasn't suspicious about men. He had come to believe only that men might be ineffectual.

The night which followed his hearing of Chaim Weizmann, Simon Stern had a complex dream, which he noted down the following morning. He is certain it was a dream.

"I lay awake, passing from torpor into something which is neither sleep nor wakefulness. Light from the street slatted through the room, imposing jittery, undulating bars upon the whiteness of the wall and ceiling. I was awake. No, perhaps not quite awake. I dozed. It was a sleep in which I found no rest. As though all the agitated promontories of my life were suddenly exposed to a single gigantic wind which blows them clear of shrubbery and stubble. No protection. Not even roots remained from which to draw strength. Nothing.

"Do I dream this dream? Uncertain. My dreams flit from light to darkness, and wakefulness is no more an inhibition to my dreaming than sleep its precondition . . . I have thought interminably of what it would be like to have had his power, to have been able to lay my equanimity and calm over the troubled to comfort them, and failing of comfort and good advice, to have, at least, saved their lives—their lives, minimally understood, their breathing, their locomotors, their neural-cortical machinery. In short, their lives.

"The Blue Room was creamy blue where he met them—a rich, creamy blue which looked like fired English porcelain. He sat becalmed by his power, sometimes forcing a crippled leg to shift its insensate weight, clasping his hands under his thigh and lifting the leg like a dead member which clung to him but which he did not possess. He had responsibility even to his legs. But when he disposed of those legs, he would wince

154

with pain. Dead members send forth their shocks of pain. Weight shifted, he sat back in his leather chair, spreading himself out until his black naval cape with the high collar—he was already dressed to leave, for a parade would shortly begin down the broad expanse of the avenue that fronted his white house and its porticoes and gardens—made the chair on which he sat invisible. He was power floating in space; only the dead feet, weighted to drown him, held the floor. His guests—a delegation—had come to call. Fifteen minutes was all. His guests had come to plead, even—and before him whose composure was like a stitched quilt—to cry. He was annoyed when he saw an elderly man wipe a tear from his eyes. He was annoyed by tears. He felt the pain in his legs. He no longer cried. He had conquered his pain.

" 'And how do you know?' he asked gracefully, the 'know' arched like a curve.

"A visitor in a faded blue suit replied. 'We have seen the old camps. There we know. One hundred. Two hundred dead a week. But they are German camps. The newer ones, those in occupied Eastern Europe—a score of them built during the past six months—it is much worse. Sir, everyone, old men, women, children.'

" 'The last mission of the International Red Cross'—he pointed to a folder on his desk—'disagrees. They report the camps to be clean, no maltreatment, no disease, and few deaths. Excellent medical facilities. I read to you—' He picked the folder off his desk and read, ' "The camps in Eastern Europe are essentially detention camps while detainees await relocation to newer homes being constructed farther from the battle lines. It would appear the Germans are intent upon resettlement of populations. Talk of liquidation is regarded as irresponsible." '

" 'We have documents, too, your Honor. Many documents.' A small, bespectacled man had raised his voice, and it hovered like the scream of a sea gull over the room. Others turned to silence him.

" 'Tell me of your documents. I will listen.'

"The bespectacled man moved from behind a taller gentleman, whose grey hair was glistening with perspiration. 'Here are fifty letters, fifty, mind you, only fifty out of thousands

that we have, short notes, scribbles, last-minute requests—
these come to us from agencies in Switzerland, Turkey, Spain;
some even reached us from Shanghai and all of these letters
are dated during the last six months. One: "They entered the
town today. We will be dead tomorrow." Another: "They tell
us it's resettlement, but we do not believe it." Yet another:
"They forget us. Did they ever remember us? And now there
is no time." And on and on. Names. Towns. Where. When.
What more do you need to act?'

"'I understand your concern and your government is concerned. I have asked our embassies in neutral countries to pay
particular attention to all information that they receive concerning these alleged murders. Perhaps. No doubt, some murders. They are treacherous, this enemy of ours. Possible.' He
sighed and the pain returned to his legs. I saw him wince. I
was standing at the fringe of the delegation. He continued,
'But my friends, there are *so many* dying.'

"'Yes, sir,' the little man shouted, pounding the air with a
fist bunched like an enraged child, 'we'll die, we'll die gratefully, if we can kill while dying. But those there, they're dying
and killing no one. That's not war. You're talking war, honored
sir, but this isn't war. It's massacre.' He began to cry in his
frustration and I remarked the tears spurting as from a newly
discovered well.

"'What more can be done by us?'

"'More?' Another man spoke. 'A declaration.'

"'An appeal,' another shouted.

"'Go on the radio and tell the world.'

"I spoke at last. I rarely speak, even in my dreams. 'Open
the nation and ransom the captives.'

"'You, sir, what do you mean?' He addressed me. I was now
suddenly alone before him. The others had gone away, receded.
The old man began to pray. It might have been the Afternoon
Service or *Selichot* or Psalms. Another man, I saw but averted
my eyes, had opened his fly and peed on the marble floor of
the Blue Room. I spoke at last.

"'Sir. You alone have power. And you know that. We appreciate your concern and we respect your embassies and we have
all, to a man, voted for you three times, but it is different now.
Here it is not saving the nation and restoring honor and dignity

to labor, of saving the farms, and inspiriting the people to dedication. Oh, sir, not at all. It is simply saving lives. For you, sir, if a plane crashes there are a dozen killed; if a cyclone strikes a town a hundred are homeless, if water floods its breakwater, a village is drowned. You declare, do you not, a disaster area, and you order food and medicine and clothing flown to the rescue of the unfortunate. Indeed, you may even visit them. But here, sir, you cannot visit. And your disaster declarations are meaningless. You can do only one thing. You can buy them off. You can wheedle and cajole and promise and lie and humiliate yourself for them, for they have no other hope. It is not for them more life or less life, it is life or death. And, whatever the Bible says to the contrary, it is not their choice, it is yours. You can save them. They cannot save themselves. You alone, you powerful man.' I stopped speaking for my throat had tightened and become shrill with tension.

" 'Who are you?' he asked, not in anger.

" 'Simon Stern of New York,' I answered.

" 'And you love these kinsmen of yours?'

" 'I do not love those I do not know, but they are my kinsmen and I need their life to love them. How else should I love them if they die? You know, Leader, the dead do not praise the Lord, neither those who go down into the depths. So of course I need them. I demand them.'

" 'Of me?'

" 'Of whom else? Of Him? Of Him above to whom I pray? Of Him I ask nothing than that He let us keep on with our work. He's interfered enough already. It is because I despair of Him who we believe has all power that we come to you who we know is powerful.'

" 'Should I cable the Pope?'

" 'You ask *me* whom to cable?'

" 'What should I do?'

" 'I have told you. We will buy their lives until we have drained ourselves of all our wealth, all the billions we are believed to have, if only to save our kinsmen.'

" 'You wish us to buy lives?'

" 'That is what we wish.'

"A knock came to the door and a military aide bespangled and bemedaled entered the room. He saw that the delegation

157

had not yet departed and came smartly to attention, staring at our raggle-taggle with amazement.

" 'I must go,' he shifted his chair toward the door, the casters turning noiselessly. He winced with pain and massaged his leg.

" 'Your answer?' I approached his desk, above which I could see only the line of objects, a small flag, a glass filled with a replica of his house, a photograph of a dog.

" 'I cannot give you an answer at this moment.'

" 'With whom must power talk?'

" 'There are other interests involved. The nation. Our people. They are dying too. All that money will aid them, will prolong it. It is not easy.'

" 'Interests? What interests? Life and death? Certain death. Possible life. *There are no interests*,' I shrieked at him, and the others around me stopped what they were doing. The old man stopped praying. The other man zipped up his fly. The other man put away his papers. The other man replaced his spectacles. The other man put away his nose tissue.

" 'For you, sir, there are no interests, for you have no power.'

"I had dozed long enough and I awoke, and my pillow was wet and I had cried with rage through my dream. I have no interests. I have no power. And the dead are seeds in the earth awaiting their time."

It all seemed contrived to him, a confluence of events too forced, too driven to be real, as though something deep within him was obliging a conjunction between the events of his singular life and the events of the world, demanding a symmetry, an order. But not in harmony or sweet reasonableness. The conjunction was the pointing of some Plotinian stepladder rising by degrees of mounting abstraction from immersion in the concrete (and its corresponding confusion) to excellent remoteness, where all was lucidity, purity, and perfection. Quite the opposite. No intellectual analogy, this. But rather a series of psychological pulsebeats where the intimacies of personal tragedy enabled him to expand the arc of his rage and his compassion. He did not understand the death of his mother and father; he did not understand the death of two million Jews.

It was nearly summer. Simon Stern was becalmed. He lost interest in finance, in real estate; he visited Lubina Krawicz in the hospital almost daily, out of duty, out of the need to reward his guilt with fresh accusation. She would not talk to him, although she allowed him to hold her hand and to offer her a tissue when she cried, as she did frequently, noiselessly and without warning. The doctors had already performed four skin-graft operations, taking tissue from her thighs and hips and placing it like strips of fat upon the gutted sections of her face and neck. Gradually a face emerged, puffed and red, a new face designed not for beauty but utility, the skin drawing away from lips in the pinched anguish of a scream when she opened her mouth to speak and relaxing into uncontrollable motility when she closed her eyes to sleep. Her face was an image of rescue, not restoration, a gesture toward civility, not grace. And she knew it. And Simon knew it. She had loved Simon as her only friend, but now she was left with no connection to life except in hating him.

Late in an afternoon in early March, more than a year after his parents' death, Simon Stern received another visitor, a stocky man, with a pressed beard and pink fingernails, whose silk jacket and twisted *gartel* and round black hat identified him as a Hasid of some importance.

"My name is Blutstein, Reb Leib Blutstein. I'm sorry. I am very late. I have a letter for you from your father."

"My father's dead," Simon replied, disbelieving, fancying the introduction as an insinuation for charity.

"I know. A saintly man. His memory for a blessing," he replied gravely.

"So. How come a letter?" Simon was rude.

"Many years ago. Many, many years ago. To be precise—for it is written on the front of the letter—the Hebrew date would make it 1899, on the evening of your birth, your father wrote this letter. He gave it to my predecessor—Reb Pincas was a good man, may he rest in peace—with instructions that the letter be given to you in the event he and your mother were to perish in a disaster in which you were in any way involved. That has come to pass, may God have mercy upon us. And I, as the new *gabbai* of the sainted Klausenberger Rebbe, have the responsibility of delivering it to you."

And with that Reb Blutstein took the letter from a pocket in his *kapota* and handed it to Simon, nodded to him, and left. Simon rested the letter on his lap and stared at it. The envelope was yellow and the ink had faded, but the writing was that of his father, Abram ben Belim Stern.

Simon's eyes danced as he read the notation—the Hebrew year and date, the first day of Elul, 1899. "To be delivered to my son, Shimen ben Abram Stern in the event of the death of myself and my beloved wife in any accident in which my son may have been involved. If such does not occur, or if either myself or my wife die separately and of natural causes, this letter is to be destroyed. May it be Thy will!"

"It was not His will," Simon said and struck a fist against his heart. He could not bring himself to break the seal of the envelope, to pick clean the wax and withdraw the letter. For several hours he sat, huddled against fear, the letter still upon his lap. At last, as is often the recourse against such paralysis, he seized the letter and tore it open, not caring for the precious envelope or its seal.

My beloved son,

You are not yet born. Your mother labors at this moment. But you are a son to me. Of that much I am certain without even the instruction of which I must tell you now.

It was a winter's night in Warsaw when I was still a young man, the evening of the festival of Purim. It happened that I came into the presence of an indescribable woman. She was, I have never disbelieved, a prophet, who like Hulda of old could read out the future without understanding it. Not like Jeremiah and Isaiah, to be sure, but a prophet no less, a visionary, to be more precise, and a visionary in our fallen times.

The prophet told me that I would meet your mother. She told me that I would marry her. She told me that your mother would be revealed to me in a strange and wondrous fashion. She told me that we would have one child, a son. All that—in splendor, but natural wonder—has come to pass. At this moment, perhaps, dear son, you are being born.

But (and it is here that my heart breaks in the telling) she told me as well of two other prodigies, one in the miracle of redemption and the other the price which we, your mother and myself, must pay, that the redemption come to pass.

You are, dear son, no less than the Messiah, the Messiah for whom Israel has waited, the Messiah of Joseph or David, no matter, for if the former you announce the latter and if the latter, may it be His will, the former shall come assuredly in our time. That is the glory and it is to this point that your mother knows. She wishes only you and no Messiah, but I am prepared to have our son become whatever God wishes, even if it should be the case—as the visionary warned—that we, your blessed mother and myself, should die in an accident in which you are involved. (Why is it always so, that good should come out of evil? I do not understand God's ways and He knows best how to break our hearts that we might learn. But to perish before you are revealed will be hard. At all events, so be it.)

If you are the Messiah we shall have already died. Should I wish this? I do not know. Should I wish to die by your devising that all men might live into His glory? How can I decide? If this letter remains undelivered, I will carry the false prophecy to my grave, and shall love you no less for being simply a good son to us. But if it should be His will that we die that you might be revealed, I assure you of our love, that we bear you no anger in death, that I will comfort your mother in Gan Eden, awaiting your return to us in glory.

Your loving father,
Abram ben Belim Stern

The tears which Simon cried that afternoon were immense —tears which rose from the center of the universe and flowed down upon him like a bower of willows, until all of him was covered by the water of his tears. It came together—all—in that hour of disclosure.

It was time, he determined, to begin the work of redemption.

Book 2

Prologue

A blind man sees nothing but the ecstasy of form. The blackness is undifferentiated.

A real color, black is textured and valued no less than others.
It is not the negation of light. It is that, to be sure, but light
is no more an affirmation than darkness its denial, nor light
the presence of which darkness is privation. How much more
is this true of me? I live an entire universe in my imagination.
And now I must inhabit not only my own but Simon Stern's
as well.

The quills are sharpened and the roll of skin, thinned and
beaten, is tied with ribbon, the ink a fluency of berries and
gall.

I must go uptown to greet him. He called for me. A messenger came before daybreak.

I have lived since the fire in the house of strangers. They saw my face, a river of lines, a birch forest of beard, thin and penetrable as I conceive my beard to be. They observed me walking disconsolately around and around the square block where the buildings of our compound had stood. The smoke caused my eyes to cry and the smells of disuse and destruction made me cough, and once, on that first morning, I retched my misery into the street, and a young man, who spoke in the Italian language, took pity upon me, perceiving me no derelict, befriended me and, as others in the neighborhood had done, remembering the many kindnesses and benefactions which our master had bestowed upon them, had gathered me to his home to await a decision for the future, a decision for me and a decision for them.

I have lived with the family of this young man for two days now, numbering the hours until he would call me to him. He had fled the fire and disappeared. Where is not known. Wandered in the underground of the city, sleeping in subways or in the holes opened by the diggers of the city, disappeared, and today, three days later, a messenger came to me, asking that I join him in the large park, the theater of the city, where trees and lakes raise a flaccid hand against the noise and debris of all these devisings of men. (I am very tired but like him I have no despair. Born into the light, plucked out, and given over to darkness, I am one whom no new terror can terrify. I have seen the work which men can do and I am not afraid.)

I must go.

A blind man mocks the walking of men. Stately indecision, the blind man walks as one whose pride is his defect, his cane, his dog, all these artifacts which prop his pride are as nothing before the will to see through a fog that never goes out to sea. I have made walking a defiance. I greet the challenge of that simple maneuver of maturity as though once again learning to walk as I did so many years ago, when, crawling the floor toward my father's outstretched hands, a sliver of wood pierced the soft flesh of my knee and I rose up to flee the pain and fled upon two feet into my father's arms. Even then I walked in flight, and as the years advanced, dignity supplanted flight as blindness replaced sight, and I step into the street, under my arm the velvet sack in which the tools of my calling are arranged, my beard combed and clean, my cold head covered by a black hat and my overcoat tied around me with a leather belt from which I hang my cane when I come to rest.

In all the years of my habitation with Simon Stern I had not ventured far from our settlement. I had come to know every turn, every step, every doorway of the compound, the location of closets and culs-de-sac, disused rooms and secret passageways, but of the street where the life of man is conducted among the poor (of which the blind are psychological members) I knew nothing. And to adventure northward into the land from which none return, out of the sanctuary of my familiars, I was genuinely afraid. Simon had told me so often of the lures and dangers of that other world, the world outside our fortress, that I believed him, without questioning his judgment. He had saved me and I believed him. I was ready to believe him—the world of the Americans, speaking so many different tongues, collecting so much injustice and tying it off with the tissue and bows of good will, hearing from visitors of the anger and cursing and rage in which strangers conducted their salutations, reading of the disputes, the arguments, the fighting that occupied them in the hopes of redress and compensation, these alarmed me. Not unlike Simon I chose to stay put. As a blind man, moreover, I chose to stay behind when others in our community went abroad on missions of compassion and regeneration. I knew Europe and had no further interest in her future.

Going uptown was therefore a more prodigious adventure than returning to Hungary, in which I had passed so many years, or venturing to the sands of the Negev in which I had spent my youth.

My name, Gaza, derives, as you might suspect, from the city of Gaza. When I was a boy, Gaza was an outpost for Jewish settlers and Bedouin. My family had come from Hungary much earlier than my birth in 1905, during the eighties of the past century when Jews went to the Land like weary travelers to the provender of an oasis, water and dates, oranges and palm fronds, beating sun, relieving cool at nightfall, spring dew and autumn rain, temperate joy, inclement risk.

What did my parents know of desert life? Ah, nothing, but the wonder of being near to the source of it all: rocky clefts and undulant sands, houses of baked dung, and waterholes, gushing up out of nowhere and dying out like a limp member, moving in small congregations of the Lovers of Zion, visiting Safed to see the white-robed followers of the dead Ari, singing his hymns in Meron, putting messages upon the graves of the great decedents of our past, all those fabled sages and saints—skulls and bones in shrouds and prayer shawls—coming to the sites and sanctuaries of our lovely past and sojourning there while recounting the prodigies of our heroes. I know the place where Saul put the sword into his gut and where Absalom hung dead, where Ruth wept, where Abraham lies buried in his beard, the mount where Elijah dismayed the idol worshipers, and the hillock from which Moses revered the land he would never reach.

I know all these places and more. Do I have to see? I know so much, for I walked with my father through all the land of ancient Israel. We, hand in my hand. He sustained me and pushed me forward, shielded me behind, caressed me above. I know all of that land. I have no need to see more.

It is true that I wish I might see the face of Simon Stern. Seeing is more than touch. To touch without sight is only the reading of one's self, blindness conditions vulnerability, and what I know by touch is only my bovine dependence upon the legibility of the world, that the lines are there to be deciphered.

I am in the street now. Simon calls for me to come.

I am coming.

Simon Stern's anger accumulated slowly.

He had put away the letter of his father under the mattress of his bed, but he could not forget that he was lying upon it. There, among other documents of his life, his birth certificate, the naturalization papers of his parents, a lock of his mother's hair which she had cut from her head in his childhood and pasted to a birthday card, a letter of embarrassed tenderness which Lubina Krawicz had handed him one afternoon several years before when he visited with her—important documents, these documents of involvement with the world he kept beneath his body while he slept. And among these was the letter from his father telling Simon of his prodigious destiny.

The first night Simon awakened and cried out and remembered the letter. Upon his knees before his bed, he scrounged among the documents, withdrew it, reread it and gasped. But he did not return the letter to its place. This time he hid it in the cabinet above the wash basin, folding it up and concealing it behind bottles of medicine. But he did not forget the letter, and the next day, in the early afternoon, it came into his mind and he read it before his closed eyes and he knew that it was ineffaceable, that even if he destroyed it he would still remember it. It was then, he recalled to me, that he despaired.

It was a bright day. A March sun was frozen in the sky. The windowpanes of Simon's storage room were begrimed and frosted. The sun broke into the room at crazy angles, diffused and smashed upon the packing boxes, the books, the piles of magazines, the tattered sofa on which Simon lay sleeping, curled up, a finger on his lips.

Simon started and a voice he thought he recognized said to him, "What are you doing about it?" Simon awoke and looked about, but saw nothing. He smelled tobacco, but in the mustiness of the room, the dankness of a century, the flavors of disuse gathered up the tobacco, and blended with peeling walls, ceiling stains, shredding bindings, the atmospheric suspension of dust trapped in sunlight, it lost its distinctiveness, disappeared. "What are you doing about it?" clangored, however, like an echo, and though he drowned it with whistled tunes of his childhood, he remembered that he was doing nothing.

There was no one with whom to speak. No one. That thought

struck him in the late evening of the second day. Who was there? Not a single person. Rubino from the library. What could Rubino say or the Pintele Rebbe, what could he understand? Or the lady who sold halvah and dried fruit at the corner or the newspaper man whom he visited every morning? He was alone. Everything in his life had been constructed as an offering or an amen to Abram and Ruth and now they were gone. But there *was* the money. Simon thought of those tens upon tens of millions of dollars spiraling like the floors of the Babel tower, rising up in a confusion of promise and invitation.

The knowledge of his aloneness and the companionship of the historical officers of the nation gazing at him gave him some relief until he realized that a thousand Jacksons, a thousand Hamiltons did not make a single living man. The second evening he had rummaged among the cartons and boxes about the sofa and found the envelopes that he had hidden there. He withdrew the bank notes and arranged them in a checkerboard before him and turned on the radio and listened to tone poems and cantatas until early morning; however, when the checkerboard surrendered to the thudding blackness of the night and the sheltered lamplight which stood behind the sofa no longer reached the squares of green before him, the greyness of it all repelled him. He got down upon the floor, and seated upon his legs (the habits of his diminutive days would never desert him), he dealt the bank notes as cards, winning every hand, for he and his opponent were himself and he owned the deck of those three thousand dollars (three thousand two hundred and sixty dollars, exactly, as Simon remembered the sum). From cards, to building trees of dollars, to making magic circles about himself. By morning, when he heard a neighbor's dog begin her bitch moan and heard the milk truck pass down the street, he had exhausted the fantasia of pictorial wealth, for those little symbols and devices were no more than what they seemed—unspent energy, unused power, neutral, neuter as he felt himself to be.

When the shops opened on Rivington Street Simon Stern was there. He bought a dressing gown of Italian silk, covered with black and red diamonds. He bought slippers lined with fuzzy wool. He bought two boxes of Havana cigars. He bought a stopwatch. He bought a chocolate cake. He bought a jar of sweet cherries in liquored syrup. He bought a dozen magazines filled with photographs of current beauties and the atrocities of the day. He bought thirty, forty items. It took two trips to bring back to the storage room all the presents and gifts he had given himself. He sat down on the third day and looked at all the boxes, all the festooning ribbon and tissue, all the debris of his luxury, and of the sum with which he had decorated his nocturnal somnolence he had consumed only two hundred and sixty-five dollars. He began to laugh. He screamed with laughter, and the tears fell upon the black and red diamonds and he blew his nose on the Italian silk and cried out, "What am I going to do about it?" Simon ate a cherry, chewing the stem until it vanished. He sat around during the afternoon, lounging in his stained silk dressing gown. He smoked two cigars and even thought of lighting a cigar with a bank note. It all came to nothing. By himself it was hopeless. At the rate of two hundred and sixty-five dollars a day he would never catch up to his wealth. It could never be consumed.

Early on the evening of that third day he dressed. He put on a suit. He brushed off a spot on the lapel and he picked a drop of tallow from the sleeve. A blue suit. A suit too light for winter. He put on a white shirt and a black tie. He brushed his hair and flecked a dried sleeper from the corner of his eye. He was ready for the night. He went out, but when he came to the corner he had no idea what to do. The street lights were on, and people were shuttering their shops and others were sitting about their dimly lit stalls, drinking tea. He visited a synagogue, but did not stay. The *shul* was humid and nearly empty. Evening services were over and two old men, their hats tipped back on their heads, gestured to each other. It did not seem that they were speaking. Simon walked the streets. No one recognized him. He was famous, but no one knew him. A woman passed him and her face burst into a smile, but she had mistaken him for another, and the smile was extinguished and she disappeared into the streaming crowds leaving a subway station. A newspaper headline about the Americans stalled at Salerno. The Yiddish press was discussing a conference. It was Fourth Avenue.

"Take me to supper, will you, sir?" a voice whispered. Simon did not know the voice and continued to walk. "Take me to supper. I mean it. I'm hungry," the voice touched his elbow lightly and he stopped. A young woman, Simon thought. It was a young woman talking Yiddish to him, a gentle Yiddish.

Why me? Simon's eyes asked and he shrugged his shoulders, dismayed.

"But why not, sir?" she continued. "Why not you, for all the world, why not you?" She was a small woman and her face was young, but her body had seen a different time, for her breasts were full and about them black crepe clung like a basket enfolding a tithe offering. "Give me a meal," he heard the voice ask again.

"Yes, yes," he resolved suddenly. "But where? I don't know restaurants."

"I'll take you to a good place. A really good place."

The young woman took the hand of Simon Stern and held it gently. Simon could not make it out. Did she know him? Was she even remotely aware that she had accosted the richest man of the Lower East Side? He smiled to himself, smugly perhaps. One doesn't know, but he smiled upon this accident and thought momentarily about the bending of light. The bending of time, the bending of circumstance. What else was accident? The girl smiled at him. Looking up at him she seemed content.

"You're so much taller than I am," she said, holding his arm more firmly.

"Not much," Simon replied. Her face was white under the street light, and Simon could see the powdered whiteness of her face, univocal and undifferentiated, an even mask of white, with only the faintest shadow of paint beneath her eyes and lips of brilliant red, lips of immoderate sensuality, like waves cresting in a summer wind.

"Herta. That's my name. My name is Herta."

Simon received this information and nodded. Her chestnut hair, cut short, closed about her neck like a choker. Simon held her still for a moment as she was about to lead him across the avenue. "Let me see you, Herta," he said quietly. "Only one moment. Still," he said in his own warm Yiddish. She stopped and put her arms to her side and stood before him. She smiled then and waited for his opinion. "You are very beautiful, Herta." Simon shuddered.

170

Geltmann's, the kosher Jewish night club, was nearly full. Each of the small tables was outfitted with a white gardenia floating in a dish of water and an electric light, muted by a colored shade on which was emblazoned, *Geltmann's The Finest in International Jewish Entertainment.* And what, after all, is a Jewish nightclub but international?

Simon Stern and Herta were shown to a table near the dance floor. The captain (his name was Fritzel, as the little name plate above the breast pocket of his blue dinner jacket announced) nodded familiarly to Herta. Simon realized that she came often to Geltmann's. No sooner were they seated than the champagne arrived, unbidden. A waiter with hooded eyes and thin lips slowly eased out the cork, the champagne oozed and a napkin caught the dribble as he poured the first offering into Simon's glass.

"Sample," Herta said, for Simon did not understand the ritual. Simon tasted the wine and smiled, which the waiter took for approval and completed the ritual. Fritzel returned and slid the menus under the little light. And not a moment too soon, for the entertainment was about to begin.

"The nine o'clock show," Herta whispered.

It was endless. The Master of Ceremonies, as he was called, appeared in tails and top hat with a red rose in his buttonhole and told humor, that is, recounted tales and fables in Yiddish each of which ended in some consummating line of abusive resolution, humiliating himself, the gentiles, the Jews, or even God Himself. Humor, he seemed to believe, consisted in discerning a flaw in the operation of a piece or the whole of the universe. It was difficult for Simon to laugh. His eyes squinted in disbelief and he kept asking Herta to explain to him the point of each of his sallies. Simon did not comprehend humor of this order, but at last the jokester returned to his proper task, introducing the artists, as they were called: Mischa and Trude, direct from an engagement in Brazil, who performed a combination of flamenco dances and ballroom tangos, with *brio* and panache, although Trude tripped once on the train of her flowing gown and nearly slid under a table. Mischa and Trude were followed by The Great Boris, naturally a magician, who produced rabbits out of oversized *Kiddush* cups; Flora Herzlieb, the inevitable chanteuse who once sang under a different

171

name in a cabaret in the Bois de Boulogne, how long ago one could only imagine, but who nonetheless managed a medley of songs from the great days of the Austro-Hungarian Empire; two guitarists with gypsy names, who obviously had done their act throughout the Pale at local inns and spas which once had called for Yiddish-speaking entertainers; and at the end a Palestinian folk singer, Mordecai Zindel, who had worked on a kibbutz when he was very young but still spoke of the pioneering days of the Labor Zionists in the swampland of Galilee and how it was blooming (a blooming song he would sing) and how the young children were becoming strong and beautiful (a strong and beautiful young-child song would follow) and he concluded with the national anthem of the Jewish people in Palestine and out of nowhere an American and a Jewish flag began to flutter on either side of the stage in a breeze of forced air. The Master of Ceremonies returned, told more jokes, praised President Roosevelt, cursed Hitler and ground him into the dance flooor with his metal-tipped dance pumps and departed. It was dancing time. It was dinner time. It was conversation, drinking, spending time. The next show was at one o'clock in the morning.

The second bottle of champagne arrived. Simon didn't realize that throughout the entertainment he had been drinking steadily. He began with sips and tastes, and as the fever mounted in his head and he took to tapping his toes and bouncing on his seat, he would consume whole glasses of champagne in one gulp. Herta was unaware. She was amused but unaware. She never inquired who he was, who this eccentric, patently unworldly and bizarre man really was.

The menus were consulted and they ate. She began with chopped liver and worked her way through soup with gizzards, cutlets with peas, cucumber and tomato salad, strudel with coffee. She smacked her lips and lifted her peas with her knife. Simon was bored by food. He didn't eat. He looked around him and smiled gaily. He began to walk around the room, stopping at tables and chatting with strangers, tugging at the elbows of waiters and inquiring about their families. He found Mr. Geltmann in his office behind the men's room. Geltmann was a fat man with a black toupee, who sat before an adding machine totaling receipts.

172

"You're Geltmann?" Simon asked. Geltmann nodded. "I've never met a night-club impresario. I'm Stern. Pleasure to know you, Geltmann." Geltmann was quizzical, but extended his hand, shook Stern's and then turned back to his bills and bank notes. But Stern did not leave. He pulled up a chair next to Geltmann and sat down. "I'm very good with figures, Geltmann," Stern said, watching closely.

"What good's that to me, Stern," Geltmann replied lugubriously. "What good? You saw the acts. Lousy, weren't they. If they're good they're with the *goyim*, if they're lousy they're at Geltmann's. Why is it almost full? Who knows. Last night we had seven tables. Tomorrow we could have five or ten. So tonight we have forty. Who can figure? A convention uptown. The *landslayt* in Queens take out-of-town customers to the *shtetl* for a visit, eat a rib steak, throw up, drink our rotten champagne, and laugh at these dumb entertainers who haven't had a real laugh since they were orphaned. What a business. What to do? Close it maybe."

"No, no,'" Stern protested. "Make it authentic. That's the trick. Make it authentic."

"*Vos meynt dos?*" Geltmann looked up, undistracted. The lever of the adding machine was depressed. Geltmann peered at the figures and nodded approval.

"Authentic. You know. Make it a real Jewish night club. What you have is imitation. The only thing Jewish about this place is that the entertainers speak a rotten Yiddish—Yiddish they learned in the street. Ach. Lousy. Have Yiddish poets and troubadours. Have a maggid give a *derashah*. Do the handkerchief dance. Have singers chant *Kol Nidre*. Now, that's Jewish entertainment. What you have here is make-believe. Make believe we're *goyim*, that's what. Who wants it? Jewish entertainment. *Vey iz mir.* Jewish entertainment is a commandment. When Jews are entertained, they're instructed. They stroke their chins, they wrinkle foreheads, they laugh bitter laughs. They don't slap their sides. They don't double over in hysterical fits of laughter. That kind of nonsense is for the crazies everywhere else in the world, who fight wars, and kill people, and then go to museums and concerts to admire beauty. Jews are integrated. Even the entertainment's integrated. I'll show you," Simon concluded triumphantly, pounding Geltmann's back.

"Stern, *ir zayt meshuge*. You're out of your skull."

"So what's wrong. So I'm crazy. All of our ancestors were crazy and we held on for centuries. A toe hold, but a hold. So I'm crazy. Let me entertain, Geltmann. Let me. One o'clock, how many tables? Ten by that hour. Who will I embarrass? No one. Absolutely no one, Geltmann. And I'll pay you for the privilege." Simon reached into his hip pocket and drew out a neatly folded hundred-dollar bill and put it into Geltmann's chubby hand.

"Okay. You'll entertain. It's midnight now. Calm down, will you. You're perspiring. Your hand is trembling. Stern, what's going on up there, something loose," he said laughingly, pointing the hundred-dollar bill at Stern's head.

Stern went back to his table, but Herta had gone. There were only some crumbs from her strudel and rose lip marks left behind on her demitasse cup.

"Where's Herta, Fritzel?" Fritzel had passed by his table to say goodbye to customers and shrugged. When he returned, Simon grabbed his arm.

"Fritzel, dear Fritzel, my captain, tell me where has Herta gone?"

"I should know. I seat people. I say goodbye to them, but I don't ask where they're going. You want some champagne, maybe?"

"Yes, more champagne."

The night club emptied. The little orchestra of violins, clarinet, and accordion played on. Couples danced. Fat men looking like sleek gigolos, their little feet together, their little feet sliding and dancing. Stately women with capacious breasts shuddered their way through waltzes. The night club was down to twenty occupied tables. Simon counted them dizzily. At the back of the room he saw three men sitting at a table casting dice from leather cups onto a tablecloth. He stood behind the men and watched. They didn't speak. They didn't notice him. He stood behind a stocky man with eyebrows thick like uncut hedges. He stood for five minutes and the stocky man lost. He lost lots of money and then noticed Simon and pointed to him with an enraged index finger. Simon didn't understand the gesture, but moved away and stood behind the second of the three gamblers. The stocky man began to win.

The young man behind whom he stood now had a pasty complexion, corpselike in the light of the little table lamp. The young man lost three games in a row and snorted disgustedly. He looked up and noticed Simon. 'You make me lose," he said. "You made Max lose and now you're making me lose. Get the hell away, will ya?" Simon smiled and moved away from the table. He was bringing them bad luck. They should know he could buy and sell them, the night club, the whole block. It didn't matter. Simon wasn't worried about buying and selling. He was going to be an entertainer.

It was nearly one o'clock now. The dance music had stopped and the musicians rested, lounging near their instruments, smoking cigarettes and talking. The lights dimmed. The Master of Ceremonies reappeared. His rose boutonniere drooped. He was tired. There were only fourteen tables with customers. Exactly thirty-seven patrons—nineteen women, eighteen men. There were no children. The Master of Ceremonies was brief. Simon Stern was indifferent. He drank champagne without considering the consequence. His arm would reach out, miss the bottle in the cooler which stood upon the table, and fall to one side, regain himself,, then aim for the other side. Miss the bottle, gain the bottle, pour the drink, splatter the tablecloth. He was very drunk.

"And now, from the sidewalks of our own *shtetl*, from the Lower East Side, we bring you a special attraction, the one, the only, the unique master of stories, Simon Stern."

They had introduced him. A blue spotlight picked up his table. Simon Stern had fallen asleep, but not really, dozed more likely, the sensorium still humming, the words reaching the parched desert of the unconscious and lodging there like meteorites. Simon started up, rose up like an extinct breed, hulked up from the table, lurched to the raised dance floor, took the microphone in his arms, cradled it like a mother, and lullabied a yawn which screeched and broke upon the distant wall.

"And so I am. The one, the only, the unique. Now, tell me, friends of humor, is there anyone here who is not one, only, unique. I ask you that in all drunken seriousness. You, madame, your face muddy with disbelief—you don't believe me. You don't think I'm an attraction. I think you're very attractive, a veritable attraction. Perhaps the one real attraction, because I see seven of you, fanning out like a book with rapidly turning pages. I riffle your face like the pages of a book and what do I see?

"Now, madame, forgive me, seeing your face in succession, what do I see? Not the same face, but different faces. I know what you're thinking. Wait a minute. Let me think. I know you're wondering to yourself whether your husband can afford to pay the check. Don't worry—what's your name?—yes, yes, wait a minute, your name is Weltbild from Cincinnati (wherever that is?). Of course, he can't, but don't worry, I'll pay it. I'll pay for your dinner, your corsage, your anniversary entertainment. Tenth anniversary. A little round of *mazel tovs* for the Weltbilds of Cincinnati. Fine. Enough.

"You now, you're the gambler from the back of the room. I made you lose, didn't I? Cast lots and throw me overboard. You did. I went. And now I'm in the belly of the deep and I speak deeply and low as if from the belly of the deep. Watch it, Mr. Gambler. They don't like you making book in this neighborhood. Good clean-living people here. They don't like you taking money off of innocents and fools. As a matter of fact, take my advice and leave through the window in the men's room. They're waiting for you out front. And for heaven's sake, swallow the sheet of bets you have in your lapel pocket. Good. Right. Good. Tear. Chew well. Swallow. No evidence. Now the bathroom window. Fine. That makes three people gone. We're down to thirty-four. Soon there will be none.

"Now. Let's take a different view of it all. Not so direct and personal. A general vision. The gentile view of reality. Gentiles didn't exist without Jews. There would be no gentiles— *goyim* to you, but I'm speaking gentiles, because there are eleven slumming gentiles with us this evening and I want they should understand what it's all about—if there were no Jews. Jews created gentiles in order to make it difficult to be Jews. Jews never rest up. They never take it slow and easy. When it's going slow and easy they whip up a sandstorm of reprobation and reproof. *Oi vey.* All those prophets. Why? To make it difficult. Who needed them? Not the gentiles. Do you think for one moment that Nebuchadnezzar, the great Persian of Persians, really gave a damn about capturing Jerusalem—a

176

little city by city standards, a little country by country standards, a little people by people standards? Why? Because a voice said, Nebuchadnezzarele, go up, get up, get you up and give a slap to the Jews, give them a hit, a knock, in a word, an honest-to-goodness chastisement and then burn them, knock down walls, break up their cisterns, and march them off to your country. What the hell for? To make it difficult. For whom? For the Jews? Not really. They made do in Babylon. They stuck around. They *davent*. They made music. They wrote a whole Talmud, they had so much time on their hands. Do you think Nebuchadnezzar enjoyed it? He did not. Centuries later they tried to knock off the whole kingdom, and Haman, the scoundrel, read it right and tried to get them all killed, but the good God, the biggest conniver of them all, turned around and with a *geshrey* got Haman hanged and lots of Persians killed for their trouble. The *goyim* (pardon, the gentiles) couldn't stand it, being used by God to batter and then be battered by the Jews. Such a lot of trouble. The Jews. So. We got it coming to us: anti-Semites. You eleven slumming *goyim* are all anti-Semites. Don't get angry. Sit down. Pay your check, but sit down. That's right. Hold on. Don't hit me. I'm an entertainer, mister. It's all in fun. Right.

"But the truth is, you are. You're all poor gentiles from Queens. Some of you are Greeks, some Italians, some Germans. Okay. But you're still anti-Semites and with reason. *With reason*, mind you. You all have a fantasy of reasonable anti-Semitism and I don't object. It's only that, for a change, please get it right. Once upon a time God was a big show-off, an actor, an attraction like I am. He'd send a prophet. He'd send a general. He'd send a punisher. He'd send voices and wonders and plagues. He'd cut up like hell. But for two thousand years, gentiles, He's been quiet as a mouse. Not a peep. Not a murmur. But because you're dumb gentiles, you don't even know the difference. God doesn't give a damn about the Jews. I don't know what he's doing, but he doesn't give a damn. So, change over. Don't be anti-Semites. Don't be Jew lovers. Just get it through your heads that if it goes wrong—life, that is—if life goes wrong, it's not God's fault because He doesn't give a damn and it's not the Jews' fault, because God doesn't give a damn about the Jews. And so goodnight to you, gentiles.

"We're down to twenty-three *unzere layte*. Good. I'll be intimate now. I'm sitting down on the floor and taking the microphone with me and I'll tell you a story.

"Once upon a time, there was a very rich Jew, a Jew as rich as Croesus, the King of Lydia and as powerful as Alexander the Great General, who ruled over a small kingdom. The boundaries of the kingdom were uptown, downtown, east side, west side, and the rich Jew lived in the midtown of his small kingdom, surrounded by an outer ring of synagogues, a middle ring of shops and stores, and an inner ring of packing boxes and books. One day a man came to him in the middle of the night and said, 'Rich man, what good is your money?' The rich man said, 'I can buy anything I want.' And the visitor exclaimed, 'How much can a rich man eat? how much can a rich man wear? how much can a rich man love?' 'Not very much,' the rich man answered because the rich man knew he would die. And then the night visitor said, 'So what good is tens upon tens of millions of dollars?' And the rich man answered, 'It's not the money that matters and it's not what the money can buy, it's only that the money holds off the world, money keeps the world at bay, money protects me.' It was then that the night visitor got up and came near the rich man and hit him in the face. 'Why did you do that?' the rich man said crying. 'It didn't keep me off, because I'm not afraid of money.'

"Now, *Yidn*, what's the point of the story? You can all afford to come to Geltmann's, The Finest in International Jewish Entertainment. You can buy off the world with an evening of frolic and fun. But here I am to slap you in the face and to tell you, even here, when you should be laughing at me and be mystified by my mind reading, that I'm not afraid of you. You can't buy me off. You can't buy me off."

It was then that a voice from somewhere in the cavern of the room, a hollow voice that was of nowhere and no place was heard by Simon Stern to say: "Simon Stern, so what are you doing about it?"

Simon Stern, seated upon the floor of the night club, wept, and as he fell unconscious from the champagne, the Master of Ceremonies, laughing, said into the microphone, "Simon

Stern has finished his act. His last gag was 'Next year in Nineveh.' Goodnight, folks, from Geltmann's."

An office in a loft in the forties of the city—peeling desks, wooden chairs on steel casters, and telephones ringing, always ringing.

They tried to rescue Jews from such an office. Lovers of the Jewish people in shirt sleeves, with hysterical chins and big eyes. They read the New York *Times* in the morning, understood that the news was already old, and organized a protest. They sent out postcards telling people to send out postcards. They met powerful men in order to persuade them to meet other powerful men. They came in busloads to rally and protest, but always ended by capitulating to tears of helplessness. What did they think they were doing? They hardly knew. It was out of their hands. Like praying mantises, they raised their arms and waved against the air.

The telephone rang. "The Committee of Rescue?" a voice asked.

"The Committee of Rescue," a voice replied.

"May I speak, please, with the head?" the voice demanded.

"*Avineu sh'bashamayim,*" a voice answered, laughing.

"Not Him. I don't expect to find Him in."

"He's the head, you know," the voice replied in a Viennese accent.

"*Flesh and blood. Flesh and blood.*"

"Who is this?"

"Simon Stern from the East Side, downtown."

"Well, Simon Stern. Think of me as the Chief Jew and tell me what you want?"

"Two million Jews are dead. Right?"

"Two million two hundred and eighty thousand."

"More than last month."

"They've been dead for more than three months. We just learned of it from the New York *Times.*"

"I read the Yiddish press first. I'm always behind on the New York *Times.*"

"The Yiddish press will have it next week when they copy the New York *Times.* By then they'll be out of date. The New

York *Times* is out of date. Ten thousand Jews we don't even know about are being killed right now and the news will go to Switzerland and from Switzerland to London and from London to New York. They prepare memoranda. Civil servants at hospitals and refugee centers in Switzerland take down information, write it up, mail it to the International Red Cross, and the International Red Cross speaks to London and says, 'By the way, another ten thousand gone in Mauthausen and Treblinka. Tell New York, will you?'

"Who is this? I don't even know you. What's your name?"

"Simon Stern. You can trust me."

"Why? I don't know you."

"Trust someone you don't know."

"So, Simon Stern from the East Side. What do you want?"

"I want to give you five million dollars to rescue Jews."

Silence.

"Are you still there?"

"Yes, I'm counting."

"What are you counting?"

"Jews. I think, with all respect, Simon Stern, you're *meshuga*."

"And you, too," Simon laughed.

"What are we talking like this on the phone. Let's meet. The Belmore cafeteria. That's where worried Jews meet these days."

"Is that uptown?"

"Yes, it is," he replied, amusement rippling his voice.

"I don't come uptown."

"Well, where then?"

"Ratner's. You know it?"

"Who doesn't know Ratner's."

"Tomorrow morning. Eleven o'clock. Wait a minute. To whom am I speaking, Chief Jew?"

"Klay. My name is Klay. Dr. Klay, Ph.D., first name Fisher."

"A Jew with a name like that."

"I'll tell you when I see you. I'm thin and tall and I wear a mourning band."

"Someone died?"

"You need to ask that, Simon Stern? Until tomorrow morning, then."

How many messiahs does it take to save the world? The need for more is a consequence of having too many and tiring of them.

Can you imagine that ancient Palestine had at one time— early in the first century of ordinary time—more than one hundred spiritual gymnasts competing with each other to save the Jews.

Contemplatives with eyes turned like milk glass toward the sun, saw visions and reported confusions; conventicles of messiahs encamped by the Jordan, telling the mysteries, interpreting the portents, clawing at each other to see the falling asteroid and describe its passage through the heavens, and all those sinners—unsatisfied onanists or louche vintners— who at the hour of death recovered their souls and rose up restored to health, gave praise to God and went off into the desert to spend the remainder of their lives in thanksgiving, ascetic self-criticism, and the organization of prophetic hail-storms upon the loose-living. The gaggling of untalented saviors—like all saviors, I sometimes think, who imagine that the means by which they restore themselves are for that fact alone useful to everyone. If for no other reason than this— the overabundance of Jewish gnostics who had little else to do in the wastes of Palestine than to feel the heat of heaven on their shoulders by day and the dew of God's tears at nightfall. They weren't wrong. Don't confuse my sentiments. They were fools, but their folly was not disingenuous. They took it seri-ously. Their imprudence was that they demanded that others take it seriously as well. And others did. The unfortunate con-sequence was that the Romans (not yet the Latins of our day) meticulous in their sense of rectitude, couldn't bear such con-fusion and hung them upside down or right side up until their souls dropped on the ground or were plucked out by birds and carried to the skies.

Messiahs and murderers alternated with uncommon fre-quency. The sensible messiah was one who kept quiet or spoke in glossalalia.

"Stern?"

"Klay?"

They were unmistakable. Their greeting, simple though it

was, passed as a formality. They could not have missed each other. Dr. Fisher Klay was as he had described himself—tall and thin, he wore a mourning band. Simon Stern was recognized, however, not from his self-description, for he had not described himself, but from his agitated face.

Klay had arrived before their appointment and was seated at the front of the restaurant at one of the tables near the display window filled with varieties of cheese cakes and schnecken. Klay looked over a cheese cake, ebullient with strawberries, and saw Simon walk toward the revolving door. A large man was exiting. Simon was nearly pushed over. That must be the man with five million dollars to rescue Jews, Klay thought, without amusement.

"Stern?" Klay rose and extended a tapered hand, fingernails clipped and rosy.

"Klay?" Stern grasped the hand, and held it for a moment, feeling its coolness and calm. He trusted Klay's hand.

They sat down and a waiter brought them coffee without asking. "I am not surprised that it is you," Klay said abstractedly, looking down upon the man who sat before him, muffled in silence and embarrassment.

"I feel helpless, Dr. Klay. Very helpless. I asked you to visit with me in this—the crystal palace of my diaspora"—he motioned about him to the eating faces and the hovering waiters and the baskets filled with rolls flecked with bits of onion—"to speak of dying kinsmen and my helplessness."

"*Our* helplessness."

"Yes, ours, but before that, may I ask you to tell me about yourself? You do not strike me as a fund-raising man, Dr. Klay, or even as a man of charities and organizations. How do you come to the Committee of Rescue? Your charcoal suit, your silk tie, your soft grey shirt. You are a very elegant man to be in such a miserable business."

"It is miserable," Klay admitted lugubriously, pulling at his cheek, and then spiritedly, "but I am attracted by misery. It does not please me. Misery, that is. But it is irresistibly attractive."

"An exaggeration?"

"Not really. You see, it is quite true. Literally quite true." Klay began to play his fingers upon his chin, as though it were a keyboard. "Do you know anything about the great Vienna where I grew up—the Vienna of reality, not the Vienna of her poets, musicians, painters? The real Vienna. For Jews, that is. I can tell you it's no wonder that Hitler was Austrian. A claustrophobic people, baroque, farcical, ridiculous with their waltzes, Franz Josef mustaches, dashing operetta uniforms. Underneath, the Austrians are absolutely outraged that finally they're nothing.

"The very distance between their fantasy and their real condition permitted the excellence of Vienna in the early part of the century and the horror of Vienna today. Vienna suspended reality and made possible the orchidean rarefaction in which genius flourished. It was bourgeois, on the one hand, with excellent concerts, opera, restaurants, ballrooms, whore-houses, and on the other, it was wealthy, aristocratic, refined. In the middle, like swans in an artificial pond, the artists floated. I, however, was no artist. Nor, for that matter, was I born into a family of stolid tradesmen. Nor, still again, was I an aristocrat.

"I was the only son of a Jewish millionaire. And not even a millionaire who smoked cigars and went to the clubs of the liberal Jews and the spas of Badgastein. My father was a hard-working, coarse—some would say vulgar—millionaire and his millions came quite simply from exploitation. He bought up bankrupt estates of Polish, Hungarian, Croatian nobility; he advanced monies to idle sons awaiting their inheritance; he bought commodity futures in timber and grain; he owned serfs, he even owned Jews (though he never admitted to this). But my father never went near his lands, never visited his forests or sifted a handful of grain. He was quite simply a merchant banker—more correctly, a usurer. He was a gross man and I despised him. But I valued his life very much."

"I would not have valued it."

"You didn't know him. He was a lesson and I studied him the way Hieronymus Bosch studied his nightmares. I knew that he had no knowledge of evil, not the slightest recognition of his pathological corruption. He was often benign, often gentle, always in control. And I regarded him as demonic and fought him from the earliest days of my life."

"You've already told me a great deal. Do you want to continue?"

"I had no intention of telling you even this much." That was true. Klay had no intention of telling anyone the events of his life. It was irrelevant to others. But the telephone call from Stern the day before had released a flood of memory. The voice, nearly the diction, the acquired tongue coated with the deprecatory sadness of natal Yiddish, all these were transmitted through the whine and hum of the telephone. But not alone the similitude, for similitude would have elicited despair (that another might live, exactly the same), without curiosity. Klay was not depressed by the prospect of Stern. There were audible differences. For one thing, Stern was offering of his own wealth to save others. The gesture was spontaneous, unguarded, without the covers and evasions commonplace to millionaires who wish to be generous, but invariably resort to manipulation and self-congratulation and spoiliative self-righteousness. There was none of that in Stern's voice. Klay was encouraged. Like, but then unlike. The magnitude of the similarity promised, however much it could not guarantee, the magnitude of dissimilarity. He was unafraid to talk to Stern. Quite the contrary. He needed to talk to Stern, to disburden himself of the load of history which he had carried solitary and unshared for nearly three decades. "I'm not afraid."

"There is no reason to be afraid of me, Dr. Klay." Simon reached across the table and patted Klay's hand. "None at all. It's not that I'm harmless. It is only that I would do you no harm. Your face I respect. What you say I believe."

Simon Stern was completely absorbed. He sat there without condescension or discomfort, his eyes scanning the face of the tall man before him, playing his eyes over the other's handsome face like the feelers of insects, otherwise immobile, committed.

"Yes, for the critical point is still to come. How I became a Jew."

"But you're a Jew anyway, isn't that so?"

"You're more astute than that, Mr. Stern. In the past, being Jewish was eternal being. No longer. It's an option of knowledge or an option of stupidity. Do you think most of those two million two hundred and eighty thousand dead Jews knew why they were being killed? They did not. My father would have understood. He wasn't a good Jew, but his Jewishness was a legacy of anger. It's one way. Not the only way. My way was different. I came to be who I am because of my father's death. He was murdered, you see."

"Murdered!" Simon's hands trembled and he lifted his coffee cup, holding it cradled in both hands to steady the tremor.

"Yes, precisely so."

"By whom?"

"By a clerk in his office. A Jewish clerk."

"Extraordinary."

"Is it? Let me tell you." The fingers played again, an arpeggio of recollection. "Lefkin was his name. Ilya Lefkin. A revolutionary, but an accountant. He came from Lodz, where his father was foreman of a small timber-processing plant, cutting the wood, cleaning and treating it for use by furniture makers. A simple business. My father owned the forests that supplied the plant and shortly before his death he bought the plant. He met Ilya's father, and old Lefkin, proud of his son—'the educated one,' he called him—asked my father to take him to Vienna as an accountant.

"It worked out. One of the three accountants my father employed had just left, and young Lefkin seemed bright, educated, with a wispy mustache cultivated by latter-day *narodniki,* and with smart eyes. What Ilya Lefkin did not know was that my father had loaned his own father several thousand dollars to pay for an operation for his mother. Not only did my father charge him his usually exorbitant interest, but demanded as well that old Lefkin repay the money in full within eighteen months. Not unreasonable, except that it was already 1929. By 1930 no one was working, least of all small lumber-processing plants. The plant collapsed. Old Lefkin was out of work. My father demanded his money. Old Lefkin tried to drown himself, was saved, and succumbed to double pneumonia instead. The following week while my father was at his desk Ilya Lefkin entered his office, his smart eyes brimming with tears, and choked my father to death, smothering him in a mass of accounts papers which he stuffed down his throat. At the autopsy—mandatory in murder cases—they even found a scrap of paper covered with numbers at the base of his windpipe. My father literally choked to death on his money. Oh well. Not undeserved, I think. Except what happened afterwards."

"Ilya Lefkin?"

"He became a hero. The Communists thought his gesture martydrom of the proletariat and the grinding boot of usurious There were Ilya Lefkin rallies. Great speeches about the martyrdom of the proletariat and the grinding boot of usurious capitalism. But all this Communist enthusiasm was combined with an unsightly resurgence of popular Viennese anti-Semitism. The right loathed my father for being a millionaire exploitative Jew. And so did the left. The right loathed Lefkin for being a Communist Jew, and his own supporters despised him for having personal motives for his crime. A sordid business. Lefkin was found guilty of manslaughter and sent to prison. But it didn't end there. I was alive. I was alive and well and indifferent. My mother had died years before. I was eighteen at the time. I was as handsome as you see me now, more so, because I was younger. I was a splendidly formed young man—chiseled to aristocracy, but still a Jew. I studied law and philosophy at the university. I led a quiet life. I had a gentile mistress of quite common looks but extraordinary tenderness. What was wrong with me? Absolutely nothing. Except. Except that I had inherited all my father's wealth—the not inconsiderable sum of four million dollars in unaudited assets. It was not enough that a Jew had cleansed the world of a Jew. More blood was called for. Mine. Rallies were held in the street before my apartment, first by the young Catholic reactionaries who wanted me destroyed for their reasons and then broken up and driven away by the young Communists who rallied to exorcise me for their own. I became an innocent celebrity.

"It was in all the newspapers. The trial had created a sensation, and interest was no less frenzied when my father's estate was probated. The headlines in one paper—a scurrilous journal, but not unusual—read: USURY MAKES JEW RICH and then goes on to tell how I inherited my father's wealth.

"But I achieved a kind of pride and a clarification of rage. I liquidated my father's assets at a fraction of their worth.

It was 1932 and the depression was upon us. It was difficult but not impossible. When it was all done, I was left with less than a million dollars and that diminished quickly from inflation. I was once more what I wanted to be—a man of modest means, independent, honoring no one but myself. My income was about fifteen thousand dollars a year and a bachelor of refined taste could succeed quite admirably. It continued that way for more than five years. In 1938 I was twenty-six years old. I was a lawyer, although I never practiced law. And I was a philosopher who philosophized, an uncommon practice for someone who studies philosophy.

"I felt stripped, Stern. Stripped naked. All my family was gone. Fisher Klay was alone in the universe. Modest Fisher, on modest means, with an independent brain filled with law and metaphysics had to make do in a collapsing Vienna. There were riots daily. Jews were being assaulted, humiliated, harassed. The National Socialists were upon us. The imminent moment. The imminent moment. The moment for the right act."

"And what act could that be?" Simon asked.

"I had no idea but I listened."

"Listened?"

"Precisely. Each morning I got up, dressed neatly, not differently than you see me now. Very Viennese. And went out into the streets and walked. I walked and walked. A coffee and a roll. My gloves folded upon my knee. A newspaper, perhaps. A book on rare occasions. Mostly, however, I listened, awaiting that rustling of reality which would condense decision."

"And?" Simon questioned. It seemed to him unmistakably correct that he should be sitting with this astounding Viennese, listening to such intimate revelations.

"It came."

"When?"

"Not very long ago. I left, you see, two days after *Anschluss.* That would be a little more than five years ago."

"Go on."

"The Nazis entered Vienna in early March. The streets were lined with cheering Viennese who put aside their cakes and excellent coffee long enough to shout '*Heil* Hitler.' (You should have seen them. You would not have believed it, Mr. Stern.) Imagine the morning the Germans entered Vienna. They had ringed the city with tanks and artillery, although no one believed there would be any opposition. And they organized a parade. All the local Gauleiters were out in their polished jackboots and the Hitler Jugend were commandeered as cheerleaders and traffic marshals. But the Viennese, the Jews among them (however much they quaked), maintained their decorum, taking their coffee in the cafés, reading their newspapers and magazines, even talking about literature and the arts. The great Dr. Freud saw his patients. But I was ready for something quite different. It was clear to me that the end had come. I was well aware that my passport (which I always kept in order like every reasonably intelligent European and like every Jew since the first century) was of no value. The Nazis would keep you if they wanted you and release you only if your fame made your imprisonment a liability. Very few Jews were famous enough. The same Dr. Freud was one. He was permitted to go to England, but there were very few like him. With the memory of the Lefkin trial reasonably fresh and vivid, I had no illusions. My dossier was current and up-to-date. I would not have been permitted to leave. The cheering and the shouting continued. As the parade passed down the center of the city, first one café would rise and shout '*Heil* Hitler,' and then another. It was funny and pathetic. I continued my daily walk.

"I came to the railway station. It was uncommonly quiet. A few passengers awaiting local trains to Linz and Salzburg, but little other movement. No international travel. No hamper baskets awaiting the Orient Express. There were a few German soldiers about. Most had come by truck convoy or plane. The trains were not useful for great displays of power.

I began to walk along the tracks which fanned out from the station. About a hundred yards from the cavern of the station where the train yard and roundhouses are located there is a catwalk suspended about fifty feet above the tracks, built no doubt for trainmen and traffic control. A woman had begun to climb the iron ladder to the catwalk. I ran toward her.

"It was clear to me what she was intending. It was the first thing that came to mind those days. There were already so

188

many suicides. (In the hundreds daily, well over a thousand for a week's count. Jews mostly, but also despondent Communists, an occasional liberal professor at the university, one pastor.) I could see her. I was nearly beneath her. She was fair, her hair bunned at the back of her head, and her face was white even in that sun, and she carried a bundle in her arms. I did not call to her. I could not have dissuaded her. Why should I have dissuaded her? In another world, at another time, elsewhere, I would have spoken with her, calling up to her small words of comfort and concern, but then, at that moment. Who could understand her reasons? And why not? (In the camps, Stern, what would you think if the Nazis were to find all the Jews dead by their own hand, like York in the eleventh century or Masada even earlier. A proud death. The last freedom for men who have no other.)

"She stood there high above me. I had to shield my eyes from the sun so that I could see her. She saw me and held up the bundle above her head and released it. It began to fall to me and I reached out my arms and caught it. Like a large ball, but no different from a ball. I caught it, thank God. It was alive. I ran away. I did not stay to see her death. Minutes later I heard her cry. At the edge of the train yard, near a shallow embankment, I turned back. A dozen men converged on her broken body. I stopped running. The bundle had come open in my flight and I saw an infant child in my arms.

"It was not compromising to return to my rooms. The maid had gone. She was a Nazi and would not return. She told me that it would be her last day. She had no intention of working for Jews. And so the apartment was quite empty. I put the infant in my bed. It was soon asleep. I imagined that it was her child, that at the last moment, seeing me beneath her, she had taken pity on it. That would have been too much freedom. Suicide is one thing, murder quite another. A Jewish view, I realize. It did not cross my mind that it was not to be my child. In those days, Stern, if one had the courage to be responsible, one took any responsibility that became one's own. We didn't look for responsibilities. I'm not saying that! But those that were shoved forward, pointing at us, those we shouldered. They were ours. This was the rustle of reality for which I had been waiting. It commanded and gave no out.

The infant was mine. Everything seemed more urgent now.

"I had to leave Austria immediately. I turned up the volume on the radio. We kept the radio on incessantly during that fitful period. There was no news. Only *Die Walküre*. I sat down to think. Smoked a cigarette. I listened to the music. Wagner had given way to the overture to *Der Freischütz*. The news came on. The great liberation was extolled. The reorganization of the government. The pacific parade, the triumphant entry into Vienna. The hundreds of thousands of cheering cake eaters. Toward the end of the news the relevant item was announced. The infant son of the General Secretary of the National Socialist Party of Vienna had been kidnaped. An embittered Jewish woman. The suicide. The disappearance of the child. The search for the child. Toward evening I went out and bought some milk. At the druggist in a neighborhood where I was not known I bought the bottles, the diapers, the few oddments that I recognized would be useful in caring for an infant. Some were totally irrelevant. I was quite ignorant. The druggist helped me, amused, I confess, by my story of my wife's early delivery and our lack of preparedness. No matter. On the way home I bought all the evening newspapers, trusting the story would be elaborated. It was and in considerable detail.

"The woman's name was Goretz. She was not a native-born Viennese, but had come with her own child from Prague several months before. Her husband had deserted her. She was, as the newspaper put it, with familiar objectivity, 'a wandering Jewess of which the nation already has too many.' Apparently her own child, a girl of six, had contracted scarlet fever and she had tried to bring her to the hospital. She was refused. Told there were no beds. Given the names of Jewish doctors and sent home. The little girl died. Clear. No question about it. It was a matter of indifference whether one more Jew lived or died. It was evident even then, Stern. We should have known then. We should have known that what is happening now on such a gigantic scale was being prepared by a multitude of small but no less consummate tragedies. The Goretz woman, her first name was Lotte, had decided to take revenge. She followed the wife of the General Secretary to the butcher earlier that morning. The woman's pram was left outside. She took the baby and walked to the stationyard, where she passed the baby to me and killed herself.

"I began to look upon the infant differently. Little Kurt Mannheim, little son of the party I began to call him. I fed him well and put him to sleep. He was no more than four months old, a quite pretty little child. But now he ceased to be a child of the suicide and became for me a thing of use, a means of barter. About eight o'clock that evening I sent a special delivery letter to the General Secretary of the Party. I stated quite clearly that I had the baby. I described him in minute detail. I certified his good health and excellent looks. And then I stated my demand. I wanted the first hundred prisoners who had been taken in that day (their names were given in long lists of detainees which had been published in the press—they were all described as political prisoners, or else as degenerates, or malfeasant Jews) to be given exit visas. I specified that the forward car of the first train leaving Austria for Switzerland at eleven o'clock the next night be set aside for their transport. At the exact time of departure I would appear, introduce myself, receive my own valid papers and board the train with an appropriate government official. I warned them not to try to apprehend me, as I would kill myself immediately. I feigned desperateness. At the border post, when the other detainees had crossed over into Switzerland, I would transmit to my companion the name of the rooming house where the child would be found comfortably asleep. I had no idea whether it would work. It seemed so direct, so public, so arrogant that I could not imagine it would work, but as it turned out it was precisely its clarity, its humiliating directness that worked to its advantage.

"At seven o'clock the following evening I rented a room in a boarding house located over a bakery in a working-class section of the city, unpacked my infant hostage, fed him and put him to sleep in an open bureau drawer where there would be no chance of his rolling out and hurting himself. The boarding house—it was called Der Arme Groschen—was one of thousands in the city. They could never search them all, and the child was small enough and well enough fed that he would sleep quietly for a number of hours. I left the room, locked the door and went to the railway station. At exactly ten-thirty there was a commotion. Sirens sounded and three trucks rolled up in front of the station. The doors opened and my hundred descended. They were lined up. An official spoke to them in loud and contemptuous terms, reminding them of the spontaneous munificence of the government, cautioning them to speak gently of the regime lest those they leave behind suffer for their good fortune. Men and women. There were a dozen or so women. They all wept. Clearly they had not been given the opportunity to notify their families. Three men begged to be allowed to stay behind, but were forcibly restrained from fleeing. The line-up moved toward the train. They had no belongings. They boarded the train. The car behind the engine.

"At the last moment as the trainmen called out their warning alerts and blew upon their copper whistles, I stepped forward and addressed a gentleman whom I took to be the General Secretary. 'Herr Mannheim,' I said, my voice low and pleasant, 'your infant son is in excellent health. He is sleeping quite soundly. At the border you shall discover where. Shall you be joining me? Or another. I see, I shall be accompanied by this young officer. Very good. Shall we be off?' Mannheim wanted to question me, his red face, generously fattened, puffed. He thanked me. I waved off his gratitude and thanked *him*, motioning to my carload of refugees. We departed. I sat in a small compartment reserved for first-class travelers. The officer sat across from me, smoking attentively, looking at me every once in a while, but saying nothing. He was astounded by my daring. I was no less astounded. It was not that long a trip and it went off smoothly. I had converted most of my wealth in the previous weeks into diamonds and gold coins. I was carrying a suitcase with some few books (my Spinoza and Grotius in re-bound student editions, two copies of my doctoral dissertation, a lovely edition of Schelling and a small leather-bound edition of Kant's *Kritik der reinen Vernunft* which I particularly cherished since I had annotated it with all my confusions about the nature and optimism of reason). I guaranteed to the officials at the border that all my charges would be given $100 in Swiss currency to begin their livelihood and allayed their anxiety that they would become paupers and dependents. At the precise moment called

192

for, as the last of the detainees crossed over, I turned back to the lieutenant who nervously paced at my side and handed him a key, clearly marked with the name Der Arme Groschen, and a piece of paper on which I had written the room's precise location. He phoned Vienna. Fifteen minutes later, word came back that the child had been found. I did not choose to say goodbye. I passed over the border into Switzerland. Indeed, a child had ransomed us."

It was late afternoon by the time Klay had completed his story. Simon had not interrupted him. He sat still, immobile. He kept thinking throughout the narrative that he had found the first, the first of very many. It seemed to him confirmed. "You must be completely exhausted?" Klay nodded. "And I would imagine not a little depressed?"

"Dispirited is more like it. Dispirited."

"And of the hundred? What became of them?"

"Most I never saw again. In the weeks that followed I occasionally saw one or another in the street or at a café. Several actually crossed back into Austria to find their families. They are gone. Others—obsessional agitators—were interned by the Swiss. They wanted to make a revolution in Switzerland and lost no time setting about it."

"You saved one hundred people, Dr. Klay. That's a nobility."

"Not so. I don't believe it for a minute. Saved, yes. A nobility, no. Merely an elaborate gesture."

"And so? What's wrong with gestures? That's all we have left. More or less grand and eloquent gestures. I read in the newspaper this morning a very small item, that Spanish Republicans—you remember their cause, dead four years now—blew up a train carrying military equipment to the gendarmerie of Bilbao. No one was hurt. The police have taken prisoners. I laughed when I read this item. The world is quite mad. Here you and I sit exchanging stories about our life (or rather, you telling me stories of yours) and sharing with each other the tales of tragedy of which modern history consists. Over there" —Stern motioned toward Europe—"the Allies are advancing against the Nazis, caring not one bit about the millions who are dying behind the enemy lines, and in Spain, as if oblivious to all this, the remnants of another cause are making gestures."

"It is dispiriting."

"Not at all," Stern replied, clapping his hands together and then entwining them. "Not at all. The gestures are for men. It is what keeps them going. Do you think most men attend to history, think about it? No. They do not. The killers and the victims. None of them have any notion of history. A slogan or two. That's all. But not history. What they know, all they know and register, are gestures. And I tell you, the life of man is more profoundly affected by gestures than by great designs and programs. The insignificant lieutenant who was abashed by your arrogance and your courage is altered. He may become more cruel and ruthless as a result, but as well he may be more tentative and uncertain. You have added to the universe a gesture of contrast."

"But, Stern, gestures while million perish."

"I have said nothing of quantity. I can't think of quantity. The moment I think of quantity all my conviction vanishes." (Simon had visited Lubina that morning and observed what he thought to be the return of light to her eyes. She had been brushing her hair. She had not yet spoken to Simon, but he was encouraged by the light.) "I can only focus upon faces. At night when I cannot sleep I count faces. I think of the faces going to the crematoria. They die no less assuredly for that, but they die described in my imagination and they are remembered as a flickering of my imagination. It is my gesture toward them. To make them alive by thinking of them as human beings."

"We are diseased. For the Nazis our life is a malignancy and for us it is a disease. There is a kind of confluence."

"Not really. One dies of malignancies, but there are pertinacious diseases that neither kill nor depart. Only dispirit."

"Quite so. It's been a curious interview. As the Americans say, I have been selling myself, I suppose, justifying to you the reasonableness of my nature, legitimating your confidence in me. You see, Stern, I want that five million dollars."

"And you shall have it. Five million and millions more. But we must think together about their employment. It is not a simple matter disposing of millions of dollars. We would like our gestures to be observed. I am not interested in the question put by that eighteenth-century English bishop: If the tree falls in the forest and there is none to hear it, does the tree fall noiselessly? Undoubtedly not. But even as a speculation the question mocks us. Our gestures must be to a point, to an end. We must identify the pieces in order to gather them. But first we must decide what is the goal."

"Isn't that absolutely clear? To rescue Jews, surely. Any kind, in any way."

"Superficially. Superficially speaking, that is the goal. But not actually. You see, we shall have no opportunity to rescue Jews. You know as do I what is happening. This government is unwilling, no less the English, to trade money and goods for Jews. Why should they? Why should they risk lives for lives? What's the moral percentage? No, Klay. We must begin by recognizing one fact: Jews are dispensable. There is no moral appeal possible for Jews. None. I daresay there would be none for Frenchmen if English and Americans had to make the identical choice—if others had to risk their lives for them. Morality is the domain of history, and as I've said (and I believe it), only dreamers and historians think about history. Mass murder is a victorious crime precisely because its scale makes it unimaginable. No, my friend, ours must be a different program—a program of gestures. We must address ourselves to persons, for only persons can be addressed. History never."

"Two million are gone. Tens of thousands each month. Several million a year. The machine is efficient. We have no time."

"All we have is time. The Allies will destroy the enemy within the next two years. Two years will cost us three, four, perhaps five million more Jews. But at the end we must be ready to take over the work of the remnant."

They sat in silence for a time. It was evening. The restaurant had filled with early diners. Bowls of steaming potato soup and plates heaped with groats and mushrooms and vegetarian cutlets garnished with sprigs of parsley. Around them faces opened and closed, teeth appeared and disappeared once more. The energy of eating. Perspiration beads. Handkerchiefs wiped away the remnants of digestion. Water and milk. Coffee and buns covered with butter. But Simon Stern and Dr. Fisher Klay sat with their stale coffee, thinking silently of each other, of their meeting, and of its portent.

"I intend," Simon said at last, interrupting the silence, "to put at the disposal of a foundation, let it be called The Society

195

for the Rescue and Resurrection of the Jews, all of my wealth, many tens of millions of dollars. The few years that remain before the conclusion of this war must be given to preparation, the establishment of centers and domiciles where the broken and neglected of those who survive may come to repair themselves, to study if they study, to work if they work, to think if they think, to paint or to sing or to play instruments if that is the restorer of their soul, and to learn again and ever again the nourishments of self-protection and the pride of survival."

The Ratner's Conference—as it came to be known in the oral tradition of the Society—lasted until the restaurant closed early in the morning of the following day. The conversation which followed Dr. Klay's confessional was a refinement, an elaboration, a spinning of details and considerations, but at its conclusion a declaration had been written—a declaration, later recended as the Ratner's Declaration of Conscience, which both Simon Stern and Dr. Klay had composed, their faces flushed, dizzy with excitement.

THE RATNER'S DECLARATION OF CONSCIENCE

1. The modern history of the Jews is not recreative. It is an undiverting chronicle of hard work and martyrs.
2. *Axiom*: Too many martyrs make martyrdom ordinary, uninstructive, and hence superfluous.
3. Whether one survives cruelties in fact or endures their spectacle in the imagination, the psychological effect is the same: Jews throughout the world, from the death camps to New York City, can no longer believe in good will.

There is no good will. It is a fantasy, a self-contradiction, and therefore nonexistent.

Good will is a practical means of disengagement in the state of nature, but even in the state of nature the beasts only temporize if they fall to the ground and bare their necks to their enemies.

Good will is a rationalization. It is a purchase of time. It is a patina to ferocity. As the Psalmist has said: "Do not trust in men. . . . All men are liars."
4. It does not matter whether Jews resist their enemies or sub-

mit, whether they fight back or remain passive, whether they claw and stamp their feet, whether they die nobly or abjectly, whether they snivel, grovel, or cry, whether they ask for mercy or rain down curses, whether they sing songs or defecate in terror, whether they commit suicide or succumb to cardiac arrest.

The fact is that more than two million are dead and many more millions will die.

The pride of the living may not be salvaged from the conduct of the dead.

5. Not normalcy but derangement is the future condition of man.

This is the case for those who are only alone. How much more so is it the case with Jewish human beings who, not only alone, are as well like the leopard, who cannot dissimulate his spots (or like the black cannot change his color or like the Oriental cannot grow body hair).

The predicament of persons who are not only alone, but odd, is that they are not free to be objective and reasonable. They are by definition abnormal, and their abnormality is a fact and the precondition of their destiny.

6. The abnormal are always paranoid about their abnormality.

Therefore, *be it resolved*: make paranoia a way of life. Make it livable, habitable, bearable, even funny and enjoyable. The paranoid will never be comfortable with their paranoia, but they will be far more uncomfortable if they attempt to conceal their paranoia because it is socially disagreeable and makes friendships with strangers difficult.

Let every man be paranoid. In this way, by making the abnormal into principled behavior, it is possible for human beings to endure the horror of other human beings. This is a corollary of the foregoing. It is not an assertion of whim. It is a realistic concession to the hopeless condition of man.

7. Trust no one but one's fellow paranoids. Associate with paranoids of one's own culture, but try not to belabor it.

Mistrust and enmity, suspicion and its consequential neurasthenia, however much they may be the estate of modern man, cannot be overindulged, because they make survival impossible.

It is true, as the Stagirite said, that man is forced to make community with his fellow-man unless he be a god or a beast. Clearly no man would wish to be a god and no man chooses to be a beast. The former is as lonely as the latter, and our principle of association—that is, the paranoid condition—is social. COROLLARY: it is not thought by us that the mass murder now in progress is the work of a god nor the work of beasts. It is the work of decent paranoids who failed to socialize their paranoia.

8. The virtue of the Jews is the same as the murderousness of their enemies. They are of the same coin and coinage: God the designer, the human metal identical in both. Two sides, two images—same substance, same imagination.

The Jews are virtuous in the aggregation of their moral conscience because they lack the opportunity to be vile. They are too few in number and, as we behold, their number dwindles daily.

Their enemies are consciously organized as enemies (the National Socialists, the Soviet Communists), and those who are anti-Nazi and anti-Communist are no less anti-Jewish, which makes opposition to the murder of the Jews casual and inconsequential.

Therefore, the righteousness and wrath of Jews who are not presently murdered and the apparent passivity of those who are is not to be ascribed to virtue, but rather to the pain of flesh into whose undifferentiated softness the red tooth is indifferently plunged.

9. It follows that if Jews wish to endure—not because of the magnificence of their Mosaic inheritance nor for the excellence of their moral vision nor because sufferings past make them deserving of life—they, alone, in their paranoid self-possession must be responsible.

No man will help them to survive and no nation may be trusted. They must go it alone.

10. BE IT DECLARED, therefore, that a community within the community of Israel be established, an enclave in which to cultivate the resources of stubbornness, a remnant whose strength shall be in mutual love and helpfulness and disdainful removal and estrangement from all others.

11. And in the hope of the Messiah, the light and ransom of Israel, let all this work be done.

198

"Do you believe these hysterical formulations, Simon Stern?"
I asked him when he showed me, several years later, the
original draft of the Ratner's Declaration. Simon nodded, but
the nod, like all nods, was vague and indefinite. (I never
believe the asseverativeness of nods, pouts, bunched shoulders,
rubbing palms, raised eyebrows. They tell us only what speech
is unwilling to confirm or deny. They are virtual speech, but
remaining unspoken they are inadequate.) The point is that
neither Simon Stern nor Dr. Fisher Klay believed literally in
the principles of the Declaration.

"They are similitudes of feeling, not representations of
thought," Simon replied, smiling indifferently. "Our condition
then, not now," Simon added, turning back to the pile of
papers on his desk. But I realized Simon was being disingenuous. He might not have believed the syntax and diction
of the Declaration, its unstately organization, its tendency to
repetition. But he believed in its uncompromising ferocity. It
would not have been possible—all his numerous works on our
behalf—had not the ferocity been genuine. Stern was the
flame and Klay the steel. The Declaration did not stand by
itself. There was a course of action as well.

During the months that followed the Ratner's Conference,
Klay and Stern were inseparable. They walked together
through the Lower East Side, examining the area, marking out
possible locations, determining the availability of sites—incon-
spicuous and undramatic in appearance, but solid brick and
stone, without obvious hazards. They walked and they planned,
imagination detailing what reality had not yet disclosed. They
traversed the streets from Delancey southward to Canal like
the spies surveying Jericho, westward to the Bowery and east
to Seward Park where it becomes East Broadway like Moses
from the mount of the desert searching out the promised land.
They met every weekday morning at exactly nine o'clock in
Stern's office. Occasionally Klay would be obliged to wait while
Simon was in synagogue—Simon went to synagogue only for
Rosh Hodesh and festivals, the reading of the Torah on Mon-
days, Thursdays, Sabbaths, and, clearly, to honor the birth
and death days of his parents. Otherwise, when Klay arrived
Simon would be folding his prayer shawl and unwinding the
thongs of his *teffilin* before returning them to the velvet case

his mother had made for him when he was *bar mitzvah*. They sat down before their maps and surveys and shortly a waiter from a café around the corner brought them steaming coffee and buttered rolls.

The question of maps will seem amusingly pretentious for an area so small and self-contained as was the so-called Lower East Side, but there are maps and there are maps. The question for Simon Stern's and Dr. Klay's consideration was not merely the location of streets and numbers but, more particularly, building plans, elevation studies, sewage and electrical conduits beneath the city, access to tunnels and egress to the city streets through the channels of Consolidated Edison, underground streams and rivers, the suitability of existing foundations for expansion and reconstruction. They wanted the ideal square block—a block upon which existing buildings were either so horrendously fragile and debauched that they could be torn down at modest expense or else so solid and well constructed that they lent themselves to expansion and enlargement without major structural alterations. The vision of the project was of strength disguised by disuse and neglect, to the casual eye a sheathing of rot and mildew, dangling buzzers, broken steps, desiccated paint, buckling doorjambs, corroded fire escapes, but within the possibility of a fortress.

They wanted the architecture of poverty to hide from the inquisitive world their true intention.

Simon Stern besieged? Then Simon builds a fortress. Identify the enemy, lay waste his forage, burn the fields beyond the fort, post sentinels to watch from the crenelation, boil oil, fire faggots to hurl upon the unwary, gather boulders and raise them up so that they can be cast down, prepare, prepare, and if the preparation is impressive and word goes abroad in the land that the work is done and done well, let the enemy beware, let the ordinary and simple enemy beware.

The vast enemy, of course, remains unconcerned. What is one fort against his might, one castle against his depredation. He does not seek a domain *within* the world, but the world itself. The mighty are simply mighty in number. Not by power, but by etc., etc., etc. Yes and so? It's all well and good if you have power, for then you can enjoy the luxury of despising it and discourse instead about duty, honor, right, spirit—but it is consoling to have power first.

Look then, as Simon Stern has done, at a map of this city. It is shaped like a virile member, an uncircumcised member at that, shrinking to a tubular aperture, but perfect in its way.

Look at the map again and think aloud. Where would you hide if you were besieged? Up there, where the city, callpypigean, swells and broadens to become top-heavy as it joins the northeast of the nation? Absolutely not.

If besieged, the question is not, Can you win? but Can you survive the siege and will the enemy withdraw, leaving burned-out pasture beyond your walls? Can you grow enough inside? Can you manure your own kind, shepherd your own flock, harvest your own fruit and grain? Do you need the enemy so much that even if they were to retire from your walls you would have to give in, go among them, mix your grain with theirs, commingle your flocks, share your blood. That depends. It depends upon how you see yourself. If you see yourself utterly solitary and independent, you can actually starve to death and never know it. Pride will juice the stomach and secrete its stoic enzymes to feed nothing, to stoke fantastical and unreal energies. If you are used to the idea of the siege you will automatically congregate where a siege is best withstood.

The besieged desire only to withstand the siege, to have the enemy go away, to see their tents consumed by fire or blown away. The besieged never expect victory, unless they're more numerous than the enemy, or if they have allies or superior tactical and technical expertness. The besieged can never win. They can, however, survive. And if they're fortunate they can actually win, convert the enemy to their banner, and join them, not as conquered, but as conquerer, and conquer (subvert?) others.

If you were to come then to this country, to enter through its aperture, to land upon that island which is only a dot in the mouth of the sea, and to march out from its barracks waterfront through the swarms of agents and officials, carrying your bundles and your cardboard cases, wearing your fur hats and your black kerchiefs, would you go north to the fingers of the city or would you stay down there where the wrist funnels the arteries of the heart, where the muscle pulses its energy to the praeputium of the nation? Of course, stay where weariness drops you, where angry faces speak your own tongue, where people tear the same loaf, where there's a chance of dying or enduring among the familiar.

They stayed down there because it was more safe. They had their back to the sea, and the enemy was not a sea power. They had their front to the city and their flanks to a no man's land of other miserable enclaves of depressed and self-preoccupied immigrants. They stayed there.

It was left to Simon Stern, founder of the Society for the Rescue and Resurrection of the Jews, and his director, Dr. Fisher Klay, philosopher and legist of the University of Vienna, to recognize that it was insufficient to congregate for body warmth. It was not enough to live in voluntary self-enclosure. Huddling is no protection. Holding hands no defense. How much more so now.

While they searched out blocks and buildings, Stern and Klay harassed the nation, printing announcements in the Yiddish press each month of the mounting death figures, preparing advertisements to be inserted next to the obituary notices of the New York *Times* in the Friday edition when that distinguished newspaper also carried news of synagogue sermons for the coming Sabbath. Their insertions read—appropriately coded to the portion of the Torah read that week—

> Go Forth (*Lech Lecha*)
>> How?
> Three million Jews are in Nazi
> prisons and cannot *go forth*
> (except to mass graves and lime pits)
>> UNLESS
> the Allies bomb the camps
>> NOW

or, no less startling, given the pedestrian recitation of tribal families with which the Book of Numbers begins—

> In the wilderness (*B'midbar*)
> Millions are dead
>> But

Even *in the wilderness*
There are Jews who will read today of
The redemption of the first-born.
You will read and will not understand.
They will read and be dead tonight.

The advertisements—all written by Simon Stern and de-livered by Dr. Klay to the various newspapers of the city—were signed, "The Society for the Rescue and Resurrection of the Jews, Simon Stern, Founder, Dr. Fisher Klay, Director." No address. No telephone. Paid for in advance. Discreet and discomforting death notices and reminders.

What to say to this now? The advertisements were registra-tions of feeling, nothing more, keeping the hand in, putting a lighted cigarette to sleeping flesh. The dying died no less. The numbers mounted. The New York *Times* often questioned the authority of Simon's statistics, his political contentions, his recommendations, but it was an underling in the advertising office who regarded his text with incredulity while taking Klay's check unhesitantly.

The idealism of wealth, no less than its romanticism, were so many agitations of the mind and little more. They mattered not at all in the country to which Simon had come, for the fruit of doctrine and the issue of passion was the giving of a speech at election time, the enunciation of a principle, and finally—at the long end of injustice—the passing of a law. The issues of life and death were hardly recognized. One cavils at this less because the action which results is so banal than because the promise was so great.

But now, Europe occupied, Russia invaded, the Pacific over-run, America became engaged.

I, of course, was not available at that time to observe the nation at war. I was doing other things. I suppose that I was getting ready, pulling myself together for the time to come, making certain that I could endure.

I have told you of my wandering childhood, my holy vag-rancy in the Land of Israel. But it was not all stealing honey from the bees and gathering manna in the desert. I, too, not unlike my master, was given to understand an appointment.

As I have told you, my father was a scribe—the profession into which he inducted me, the eldest of his sons—but my uncle, my father's brother, the esteemed but hardly popular Rabbi Moses Abishag was (forgive me for calling you this) a rabbinic dervish.

Uncle Abishag was an enormous man. He weighed, for one thing, more than two hundred and twenty pounds, but there was no fat on his body. His strength was like that of Samson and his red hair was long and abundant, but his strength was not in his hair, nor his vulnerability in any Philistine temptress. Quite the contrary, strength, and no less his vulnerability, was his memory.

Moses Abishag saw and remembered. He knew the entire Talmud, Babylonian and Palestinian, by heart and his mind was like a palimpsest. Describe a dispute among the Palestinian *amoraim* and immediately there would come to his mind the right passage in the Babylonian recension to which it was parallel or identical. He was the source of disputation and its resolution, but, alas, memory is not judgment. He knew the source, but could not assess its value. All disputes were the same, all examples equal, all truth one and undifferentiated. In short, his mind was a morass of information.

It proved to be his downfall and it carried me into exile from my home.

It happened once that my family had gathered to celebrate Passover at our mud-and-brick house in the dirt city of Gaza. It was many years ago (shall we agree on 1932, when I was then a young man of twenty-seven?). Uncle Moses had returned to Gaza with two of his nephews with whom he had traveled to Safed in the north to celebrate the birthday of the Holy Ari—may his memory remain with us uneffaced—and to pay his respects to fellow Talmudic scholars. He arrived at our house the day before the leaven is gathered to be burned, and was greeted by a young woman in tears who informed him that her husband to whom she had been betrothed earlier that month had disappeared into the desert the week before and his mangled remains found earlier that day, pecked and clawed by beasts, but with a bullet in his neck. Her question to Uncle Moses was this: Could it be presumed that it was indeed her husband who had been murdered, since he carried no identification, his body marks were gone and his face was already indistinguishable from that of any other mutilated corpse? The young woman was in the law of Israel an *agunah* —an abandoned woman, married incontrovertibly, and not released from her vows by incontestable confirmation of her husband's death. My uncle correctly saw her plight. He could not bring to mind any rendering of the law which would release her.

Now, Uncle was a wild man, I have asserted. He appeared a settled genius, a granary of knowledge, stuffed full with all the wisdom of our fathers. But that knowledge was also his frustration. Because he could forget nothing, he saw the consequence of human action. He could watch Jews and know in an instant what law they broke, what admonition they ignored, what council they denied. He would watch a Jew at prayer and know the passage he could not speak in truth. He was a monster for that fact, but his monstrosity was offset by the largeness of his body and the maniacal enthusiasm with which he fought the abundance of his information. Because he knew so much he often chose not to think, and because he was burdened by his knowledge he was continually tempted by the wish to throw it all out, to feel the world instinctively, to love creatures because they were beautiful or oppressed rather than because they were Jews or Bedouins, transgressors or devout. And when this girl, her face furrowed with rivulets of grief, dropped to her knees and clutched his feet, wiping his slippers with her hair, he said simply, "He is dead and you are free. Have my brother prepare the document and I will witness it." It was done.

The girl gradually recovered. She had, remember, been married but a month. Some time later—two years, let us believe—four months after her marriage to a young scholar with long and musical hands, a knock came to her parents' home and the husband of her bereavement appeared, his body covered with burns and blisters, his tongue black with the sun, and quite simply out of his mind. He had wandered off in a seizure, and since that time had roamed throughout the country until by some instinct of light he had returned to his source.

The young woman, already bearing the seed of her new

husband, could not contain the magnitude of her transgression and cast herself into a brackish desert well and died.

It was the custom of my uncle, Rabbi Moses Abishag, to begin his studies of the day at that hour of the afternoon when the desert sun is highest, burning the face of the land, when everything is still and all reasonable creatures hide away in the shadows of their dwelling places to rest. Uncle Moses would seat himself upon the covered porch of our home, and there, a pitcher of tepid tea at hand, would move from Talmud to *Tosefot,* to Holy Zohar, until evening. He would open a folio, and removing from his pocket a silver pointer surmounted by a ball and tapering to an articulated hand, its index finger elongated to a blunted point, would begin to trace the passage of his eyes and his voice would rise and fall while he sang the text in the style of the teachers in whose yeshivot he had studied in the days of his youth, when all our family were still pensioners of the diapora.

The afternoon following the madman's return and the desperate suicide of his transgressing wife, the father of the unfortunate young woman came to Uncle Moses, and placing his hands upon the folio, stopped the movement of the pointing finger. In a voice low and constrained, as though about to scream, he told my uncle what had transpired and cursed his wisdom.

I cannot guess the logic of his guilt and punishment, but at evening when it was my custom to interrupt my uncle's studies and bring him to meet my father and my brothers and go to synagogue for the concluding prayers of the day, I found him slumped upon the folio. I sought to rouse him with my voice, thinking him asleep. I nudged his arm, but there was no movement, and then it was that I saw edging through the tangle of his hair, which covered the folio, blood, matted and sticky, purpled from the heat. I lifted his head and blood poured once more from the vacancy of his left eye and in his right hand he held the menacing finger, whose point, tipped with blood, had served him as his own avengement.

A month later Moses Abishag, his left eye healed but blind, took up a staff, and with a leathern pouch at his side and his little monies tied in handkerchiefs, a book of Psalms and his prayer shawl and *teffilin,* set off to do a penitential journey for his sins. He vowed to return to his birthplace in Hungary, the village of X, and there to pray for forgiveness at the graves of his father and mother. Since he was weak from his mutilation I was deputed as the oldest of my father's sons to accompany and give comfort to his beloved brother. I kissed my parents and promised to send them word of my travels. I spoke of my return but knew in my heart that I was bidding my family and my youth farewell forever.

It was fifteen months before we reached the village of X, twenty miles from the Hungarian railway junction of Tonaj. There, weakened from his travels, his lungs breaking with cough, my Uncle Moses prayed at the graveside of his parents and died, his body put to rest in the earth beside them. I was alone. I had traveled with him northward to Turkey and through Macedonia into Rumania and from there to Hungary. The stories of our travels are not of moment to this narrative. It became clear to me, however, from their curious fortuities, from the lost opportunities which were presented and ignored to return to my father's house, that it was not my destiny. After remaining in the village for thirty days until the period of mourning had passed and my own sadness lifted I made my way to Debrecen, south of Tonaj, and I came to the attention of a distinguished Hasidic rebbe, a disciple of Schneur Zalman of Liadi, who took me as his secretary and scribe and undertook to complete my education, mottled as it was by the lost time of my adventures. When I was not serving him, copying out his rabbinic decisions or transcribing his dicta or preparing marriage contracts or writs of divorce, I would bury myself in his own library, supplemented by furtive excursions to the library of the provincial university situated in that principal city. It is no surprise then that, alongside the knowledge of our own tradition, I should have filled myself with history and philosophy, and it is from those days that I trace my considerable knowledge of the history of European peoples, my familiarity with Gregorovius, Ranke, Mommsen, Droysen, Leitzmann and other theoretical restorers of the secular and sacred history of the West.

I was not aware that a war had broken out. Of course I read the newspapers in my own language and in Hungarian as well, but in that corner of the world, hard by Rumania to the west and the Ukrainian north it could not be imagined that I would give much time to the movements of German ranters and Anglo-French diplomatists. In those days it was all still terribly far away. Its proximity became plausible to me only when I would read of an excavation which had uncovered Roman fortifications on the Bosporus or the horde of marauding Indo-European tribesmen in the fourth century along our own intimate riverbeds. I wondered to myself how these ancient peoples had come such a long distance to Hungary, but it did not seem possible that Germany in our times would be much interested in the small city of Debrecen. How very wrong I was.

It was early in the morning when I heard the bombers overhead and by evening I learned that German parachutists were securing the outskirts of Budapest. What wonder then that three months later I was on my way to a detention camp which funneled Hungarian Jews to Auschwitz?

There is little point in recounting my years in Auschwitz. They were ordinary. I shall only recall that it was in the autumn of 1943 that I escaped what I was certain would be my death.

It was customary for the efficient commandant of Auschwitz to prefer selecting for death those who could no longer work.

It had been my stupidity to overeat one day. Overeating is not what you imagine. We were starving to death most assuredly. To overeat was little more than finding a cache of food and eating it all at once. An elderly Jew from Posen died in the bunk next to mine. I watched him die. It was in the middle of the night. Under his pillow I found three boiled potatoes, the stump of a carrot, and a crust of bread. I ate them immediately, fearing that in the morning others might ransack his belongings looking for his food and strip me if they suspected I had hidden it.

It happened that way no less inexorably. In the morning I was beaten by two of my fellow prisoners, but I had no food. I had eaten it. It was a bitterly cold day, and by nightfall I was not only exhausted, but tormented by stomach pains accompanied by spasms of diarrhea which I feared to be dysentery from their violence and frequency. The following morning I could hardly get from my straw-covered bunk to make roll call, and the following day I knew that I could not get up. I was terrified of being reported sick. Automatically if you became sick you came to the attention of the block officer, and from there your name made its way to a selection list. I did not wish to die there. I managed it. My diarrhea was subsiding but I was still weak and needed one more day to rest. Sometimes it was three or four days before the corpses were collected in wheelbarrows from each block and taken away to be burned. The collection had taken place the day before, and in the morning there were already two fresh corpses. At the moment when all the inmates of our block stumbled to the muddy ground for roll call I hid myself beneath the two corpses which had been stacked at the front of the block, and there I rested and slept throughout that day. I was missed, but when I turned up the following morning straining to appear eager and well, my absence was noted but not reported, and for three cigarettes which I had preserved for such an emergency the Kapo who called the roll dismissed his observation and I survived.

It was on the day of my escape from death, which I remembered long after as the festival of the Great Hosanna, that Simon Stern, many thousands of miles from Auschwitz, was informed by a seedy rabbinic functionary in one of the synagogues that abounded on the Lower East Side that a shopkeeper on Orchard Street had been told by his landlord that the building in which his store was located and two others on that block were going to be sold.

The seedy functionary, Solomon Gorodetsky, had approached Simon in the vestry of the Rumanian-American synagogue on Rivington Street and tugged at his prayer shawl.

"You're buying, the crow tells me, Mr. Stern?" The upward inflection indicated that not a crow was telling but a fish was nibbling. Simon looked away. He disliked discussing business in synagogue, and even though services had concluded and he was about to fold away his prayer shawl and leave, he was indifferent. "You're looking to buy buildings? You're always looking, aren't you?"

Gorodetsky knew nothing. He was talking to the earlier

Simon Stern, the Simon Stern who bought everything. "So? What are you telling me, Gorodetsky?"

"A bit of news. Do you like to hear it? don't you? It doesn't matter one way or another."

Simon smiled at him. He knew Gorodetsky's reputation. A functionary with an ear for gossip, a nose for scandal, a sense for indiscretion. He made little bits of money for his household by inventing suspicion and then effacing it. "So tell me then. I'll do you a favor if it's good information," Simon encouraged.

"It's the corner house on Orchard and Broome, the wonderful building like a mausoleum—the one with the French fire escapes."

Simon recalled the building. The corner one and the two next to it on Broome were witty inventions—stone and brick, solid, with marble staircases and turned iron landing posts, and fire escapes (what fire escapes!) with delicately rounded turns instead of the familiar vertical iron stays, a complexity of floral whorls painted blue-green. Simon listened. "It's for sale, Mr. Stern, that building (it's residential, you know) and the two buildings up from it on Orchard going towards Rivington. I have the figures and telephone numbers to call. Do you want them? They're right here. I wrote them down when I heard."

Simon took the paper. "You'll hear from me. Maybe I'm interested. Maybe I'm not. A hundred dollars for you if I am. But listen, Solomon Gorodetsky, tonight is *Shemini Atzeret,* and the day after is the joyous festival. Don't come asking me what I've done." Gorodetsky helped Simon fold his prayer shawl and held open the door of the synagogue.

Dr. Klay investigated. It wasn't easy. There were three buildings for sale, but there would be twenty-nine more to buy. The corner buildings made it easier. The landlord sold quickly. He wanted the money. It pleased him moreover that the indescribably wealthy Mr. Stern was the buyer. But he held his tongue. He wanted to call up his friends and tell them the news but it was a condition of sale that for three months the buyer be kept secret. The three buildings cost Simon sixty thousand dollars with a discount for cash without mortgage. Simon was very willing. The beauty of the buildings was that they shared a common backyard, and a shaft of light from the unobstructed sky made its way into the miasma of garbage and broken bottles that filled the little courtyard. Once a year an old Jew who lived on the top floor of the corner building cleaned it out and constructed a tiny *succah*. The festival past, the courtyard would fill again, the rats would return from exile and the nights would sound to their chatter. But the little courtyard was for Simon the promise of other possibilities. It could be expanded. The other buildings could be altered. A shed attached to a wooden building further down the block could be removed and the protuberant glass-enclosed second floor, which a Russian family had rented for thirty years as a social hall, could be dismantled. That would add another six hundred square feet. Simon wanted an inner courtyard of no less than four thousand square feet. He had almost one thousand. He dreamed already of that distant time, although he discussed his dream with no one, not with Dr. Klay, not even with me. His councils were silent, swaddled in his dreams, described only in the clumsy sketches and diagrams which were found later. But in the time of these negotiations all that Simon spoke which alluded to that time to come was, "Where is free space? I want open space in the center, in the midst of it all, space where they can breathe, where they can enjoy the sun and walk in the rain, where they will be unobserved, where the clouds will cover them, and they will be unafraid. More space. At least four thousand. The minimum for our freedom."

It wasn't all as easy as the first purchase. It took sixty days, secrecy, agents, surreptitious dealing and negotiation, left hand ignoring right, to buy eighteen more buildings for about three hundred thousand. Sixteen hundred square feet of light. Twelve more buildings to buy. Three from the bank. If the bank sold, the robbers and holdouts, the slow pokes and sharpies, would sell the remaining nine and the square block would be his.

The three houses owned by the Pierson Bank were the major problem. The original owners had defaulted on their mortgages in the early thirties and the bank took them over. The properties were shambles, but the bank was indifferent. It wanted what it asked. Simon was annoyed. He had offered thirty thousand for the buildings. A package and more than they were worth. The bank wanted a little more. The interest it had lost, a representative explained. One day therefore a sign went up on the front of one of the buildings already purchased, which was adjacent to those owned by the bank. A discreet sign, not imposing, unthreatening. It read simply: "The Simon Stern Home for Delinquent and Derelict Children." Not an untruth at all. What would the remnant be but delinquents and derelicts—those who have lost time and place, those who were late at dying and survived, those forsaken and abandoned? But the bank had no knowledge of the real meaning of words. For them it meant trouble and troublemakers. They called Simon very unkind names, not the least of which was "blackmailer." He acknowledged the truth. He didn't care about their property. He knew they would be scared. Tenants would move out. Simon even arranged for a few tenants to complain to the bank that "good-for-nothings" were invading the area and that they were thinking of moving.

It worked. A week later a gentleman with brushed grey hair and a pink face approached Simon as he was leaving his office and introduced himself. "So. It's pleasant to meet a banker on Essex Street. Have a coffee with me. There's a nice dairy restaurant around the corner." Simon led him by the hand. They had a coffee and a cheese Danish, which the banker ate with a knife and fork. A crumb stuck to the banker's chin. He couldn't find it. Simon indicated it with his finger, but the banker's white handkerchief dabbed frantically and only on the fourth try succeeded in removing the piece of flaky crust. The banker was unnerved.

"You've won, Stern. It's yours. Thirty thousand."

"Yes, it is mine, isn't it? I could even have it for less now, couldn't I?"

"Not a penny, Stern. Don't Jew me, Stern. We don't need your money nor your blackmail," the banker said, forgetting himself in his anger.

"I see. Well, then, in that case. I'm patient. My little project is moving nicely. I have two young bandits ready for the reforming atmosphere of the Lower East Side, regular little cutthroats they are. I know I can help them with my little home, decent food, an education, spending money, daily worship. Now, don't you think that's a good idea?"

The banker was in a rage. The old man who took the money at the counter had heard the conversation and reached for a baseball bat he kept near the register. He would have hit the banker. "Not a penny, Stern. Not more than a thousand off. Twenty-nine thousand. That's it."

"I don't think it's enough, my friend. Not for all the trouble and embarrassment of waiting upon your word."

"We're fighting the whole goddamned world to save you gougers," he fumed, crashing his fist upon the white linoleum. "Not a penny less than twenty-seven eight."

"You need to sell, don't you, Mr. Uptown Banker? Don't you? Well, taking into consideration how you're insulting me, and the waiters, and old Mr. Shimkes at the counter, let's hold out for a good figure, say, twenty-six thousand."

The banker shouted, "Jews, goddamned Jews," and Simon reconsidered, announcing, "Twenty-five thousand in that case," while the banker pulled his hat on his head and counteroffered in desperation, but Simon remained adamant, resting his head upon his folded hands, like a bored child, a child-man in an attitude of disgraceful mockery. The banker spat "Jew" and Simon lowered the price. Minutes passed. The banker was near tears. Simon was near joy. At last there was quiet. Old Shimkes drank tea to quiet his nerves and belched. The waitress with hennaed hair sat in the back reading a magazine.

"We've come to rest. The exhaustion of anger. Dear banker, don't you understand? I have no wish to 'Jew' you, as your expression implies, not to gouge you, not to suck on your blood. Not at all. All I demand from you is respect, and failing that, I will behave as you compelled me. I wil bargain, gouge, suck. I will humiliate you." Simon spoke very quietly, his voice barely audible to the banker, who leaned across the table to catch his words. "And since I have been honored by your rage and capitulation—for you are a banker in need and I am a multimillionaire without needs, I will give you what you asked —the price I offered and about which your associates first sulked so ungraciously for the past weeks. The original thirty thousand. The original price."

The banker began to laugh. Virtually hysterical, his laughter broke with sobs, his chest heaved with the pangs of euphoria, his eyes poured forth torrents of exaltation. He had won. He had lost. He got his price. He was abased. Simon was quiet again, his small feet clutched together beneath the table. "I don't understand. I don't understand," the banker said at last, wiping his eyes.

"There is need for you to understand. You *should* understand, but you must work, my friend, to understand. For the moment, draft your papers. I'll notify my lawyer. You'll hear from him. He's a nice man. A little hard of hearing and very slow to anger."

The banker fixed his homburg and reached for some change to pay the bill.

"No, my friend, this is my world, not yours. I'm delighted to pay for your visit to the neighborhood." The banker put a quarter on the table and Simon lifted it and carried it to the front where he inserted it in the blue collection box of the Jewish National Fund.

"Thank you on behalf of the trees and the salt marshes of Galilee. It will count in your favor at the Last Judgment."

With the fall of the Pierson Bank, that is, its capitulation to Simon Stern, its accession to the whimsicality and devastation of that remarkable man, the procedure of assembling the block, its total rectangularity, its motley of tenements and storefronts, its rats' warrens and its cesspools, its filth and smells, its desuetude and neglect proceeded to consummation. On the first of the year 1944 the entire block from Orchard and Broome southward to Grand Street and bounded by mild-mannered wholesalers of Ludlow Street to the east passed from the hands of eleven incredulous landlords to Simon Stern. And with it forty-seven hundred square feet of unobstructed interior space. A celebration was held, attended by Simon Stern and Dr. Fisher Klay, and the deeds tied with red ribbon were bundled into Simon's office safe.

By the spring of the year the Anglo-American army had resumed its drive up Italy and the clouds of the end of conflict gathered, the fleets assembling, the convoys mounting, the troops marshaling for the assault that was to come. Simon Stern had relocated the tenants of his buildings, emptied them of living persons, and begun the work of reconstruction.

214

Client and Contractor: The Letters of Simon Stern to Gerson & Ostrovsky, Inc.

1.   March 20, 1944

Dear Gerson and Friend Ostrovsky,

I appoint you. You shall build my fortress.

You have never built a fortress. That is quite evident from the almost casual imprecision with which your estimate of the work has been presented. I grant you that the plans upon which your calculations are based are no less imprecise. It is clearly unprofessional for architectural measurements to be offered in cubits. As you observed, the cubit is not up-to-date. True enough, but it served the needs of Solomon admirably and I tend to think in Solomonic modes. However, you may translate freely into inches and feet if that makes the work proceed more expeditiously.

The architect of record is like myself a casual gentleman, more familiar with the construction of ancient cities than with modern ones. Dr. Setzer is no ordinary architect. He is an archaeological architect and, for that reason alone, completed his education in architecture. He spends his time reconstructing in scale model the ancient city of Carthage; the baths and water conduits of Sidon are more his specialty than the plumbing requirements of the City of New York; the battlements of Acre and the visionary gardens of Babylon more to his liking than our own centers of urban peace and recreation. His plans are marvelously drawn, you will admit, his penmanship splendid, his straight lines utterly straight and clean. It is unfortunate, therefore, that he has forgotten what he once knew about electrification, and his ability to read, much less comprehend, the plumbing catalogs issued by the manufacturers is deficient. He called me this morning and blustered in a rage that these sales manuals were written in a commercial English which he found incomprehensible. By all means, then, translate his little remarks about light, air, and sanitation into the requirements of electricity, skylights, fire escapes, plumbing and sewage. It will cost me extra, but the pleasures of working with Setzer outweigh any consideration of cost.

I am signing the formal document which you enclosed. I am returning this document by the hand of my personal emissary and courier, Dr. Klay. He will also transmit to you a small earnest of my seriousness. I should think a deposit of $50,000 is quite enough for this project of nearly a million dollars. I

doubt you will abscond to Argentina. I laugh as I write this.
I am beginning to be a happy man.

Yours,
Simon Stern

2.   April 10, 1944
Dear Gerson and Friend Ostrovsky,

I have not communicated with you for several weeks.
Each morning I have walked about the buildings that comprise
our project looking for evidence of your attention. As yet there
is nothing. Not even a sign bearing the code name by which
we designate this undertaking. I should like to see such a sign
made and affixed to the fancy building at Orchard and Broome
which is the "cornerstone" to the block. It should bear the
legend:

SHEARITH HOUSING CENTER
Architect: Haim Setzer, Ph.D., Oriental Institute
Contractors: Gerson & Ostrovsky, Inc.
Date of Completion: Undetermined

There is no completion date. Correct. Then why mention it,
you may ask? The answer is that I have not determined one.
You must work like lightning, searing the block with your diligence, but without a definite time for completion.

Let the right date emerge rather than be affixed.

Yours,
Simon Stern

3.   April 18, 1944
Gentlemen Gerson and Ostrovsky,

I appreciate your alacrity. The blue lettering is regular
and I prefer sans serif.

There is already comment in the neighborhood. The mnemonic, Shearith Housing Center, strikes some of my friends
as ironic, others as typically metaphysical. One reminded me
that Isaiah named a son Mahershalalhashbaz. A metaphysical
mouthful. But Isaiah had his reasons and I have mine. I
allude, as I do in all things, to the remembrance of death and
the passion for life and regeneration.

I am pleased that your trucks are at last in evidence, that
workmen in steel hats are gamboling through my buildings,
ripping and destroying. The street is silted with dust and the
debris clatters into the troughs of disused doors which you
have constructed around the block.

You have permits, don't you? Of course, you do. In all events, the work of evisceration must be done.

What is our time schedule? I am looking at it now. Demolition takes three months. Can that be? Three months. The Allies are north of Rome already. I think we must begin to think with more urgency. Lightning, I said, searing, destructive, wild-mannered.

I observe that your workers on occasion laugh and drink beer. Some eat sandwiches and drop bits of ham onto the rotten floor boards. As our sages have noted, ordinary workers are allowed into the innermost sanctuary of the ancient temple, into the most sacred Holy of Holies where the High Priest could enter only after multiple ablutions and prayer, without so much as washing their hands. Repair precedes redemption. Let them eat ham sandwiches if they're hard workers. By the way, are any of them Jewish?

Yours with many questions,
Simon Stern

4.   April 30, 1944

Dear Gerson and Friend Ostrovsky,

I am glad that you have taken to writing me. I do not like the telephone. I prefer not to use the instrument. My speech is frantic, my diction agglutinated. I sent you a secretary this week who will be on permanent loan to your company to make certain that my letters are answered with promptness.

My letter confused you? It confused me. I have never had, until this moment, much intimate contact with the world. You know of my millions upon millions, but let me assure you that all this money was amassed without contact with the world. Money is an abstraction and is made abstractly. I have not made money, as you have, by the turning of earth and the labor of hands. I made money by enacting fantasy, by dreaming a situation and finding it. What does it mean to say that one has assets of more than one hundred and three million dollars, that each year one's income from interest, dividends, rents, etc, is roughly nine million, that capital appreciation is more than twelve million, that I would be able to become a billionaire if I put my energy to the task, that I can leverage, multiply, weight money until the dollars turn somersaults. Nothing. An abstraction. An abstraction.

The executioner may be poor, but he can kill with a blunt sword.

You misunderstood the intention of my question. I hope the

workers are *not* Jewish. I would appreciate moreover if you would dismiss any Jewish workers presently involved in the Shearith Housing Center. Give them a generous bonus and send them away. I want only non-Jews to build my housing center. There will be work enough for Jews when the times are full. The nations of the world will build my center. All men will build my center. Let it be founded on the languages of many men. If they laugh at the frockcoated greybeards who ogle their labors, pulling incredulously at their *peot,* so much the better.

Let the Jews stand and wonder. Let the nations laugh.

Let it be done, good friends.

Yours in trust,
Simon Stern

5.   June 16, 1944

Dear Friends Gerson, Ostrovsky,

Ten days ago the return of fraternal madness to the shores of Europe began.

The buildings are like blasted wastes. It was last night that I walked with Dr. Klay around the compound. Three times we circuited the blocks, and in the moonlight, quiet at three o'clock in the morning, it appeared to me an unearthly spectacle. From one street it was possible to see through the open windows of many walls to the sleeping houses several hundred yards away. It was as though looking through an enlarged kaleidoscope in which the broken pieces of colored glass were replaced by the skeletal remains of beams and girders, the piles of broken glass, slivered disorder, a dizzying window frame hanging loose from the center of the building at Ludlow Street moving rhythmically in a gentle warm breeze, the doors that opened and closed to so many decades of Jewish men and women squalling to get away, now arrayed in panels of blue and cream and brown to receive the shards of their residence. It dismayed me to understand that I had forced all this world, so long contained and hidden, to be unearthed. The crowbars pulled at *me.* The hammers pounded at *my* past.

A domestic surreality. Forgotten *mezzuzot* like disused appendages, hanging useless from emptied doorposts. Bedrooms with the rotogravure supplement of a Yiddish newspaper—probably talismanic photographs of the heroes of our past—and decals of other harmless watchmen to the night. Popeye and Mickey Mouse.

And tomorrow the trucks will be filled for the last time and the loads of twisted rods and plaster, the banisters and slats, the door troughs themselves will be taken away.

The demolition will be done and in a week's time new workers will arrive. The heavy men with arms and legs as thick and weighty as I am myself in my entirety will depart. Builders will come. Carpenters with their toolboxes. New fittings will cover the sidewalk. That is beautiful. Four hundred toilets. Five hundred and fifty white and metal sinks. The kitchen equipment of aluminum. Brass fittings for the plumbing. Thousands upon thousands of light bulbs. It makes me shudder to think of all this newness.

Pray for the Allies, gentlemen. They are advancing.

Yours,
Simon Stern

6.   August 7, 1944
Dear Gerson and Friend Ostrovsky,

Do you understand the urgency of your work? Four million are already dead. This complex of housing is for survivors.

Gentlemen, do you understand what it is to survive?

Yours,
Simon Stern

7.   August 11, 1944
Dear Gerson, Ostrovsky,

Survivors cannot endure vulgar colors. We must renounce the familiar palette of the building trade. I am well aware that our painting contract calls for the application of easily applied, washable color, two coats beyond the primer, but when I saw the booklet of the color range I was horrified.

We cannot paint these domiciles in eggshell blue, oatmeal beige, desert grey, marble pink. Those colors are not colors of survival, but carry with their palpable indecision and tastelessness an invitation to lasting depression. Those are colors without conviction. They are colors for those who refuse to see around them, who cannot see color, and accept minimal visual demand in order to confirm their blindness. On the other hand, as I have said, the rooms cannot be violent.

There is in France an architect all of whose buildings are white, whose walls are white, whose vistas and horizons are white. Needless to say, he paints walls white. His theory is that whiteness repels the human propensity to lay off upon the environment the ills within, to displace into others what a man cannot bring himself to remember and accept. White is a baffle to the soul, a color which is no color and for that fact the principal color, since it is an echo chamber to rumblings within. For this reason I should like every interior apartment, those for single men and women as well as those for families (if there are any) and orphaned children, to be white.

Let the humanity of the environment arise from the decision of the occupant. Halls, public spaces, stairwells—there, let us introduce color to relieve their anonymity. Porcelain blue, the purple black of evening, rose scarlet of dawn, yellow of birds, the green of emeralds—panels of color, a discovery amid the white, an oasis of color at landings when our guests ascend, winded and tired from forays into the city. Let them pause and be greeted by a cheer and welcome to counterpoint their mood of disconsolateness. Do you understand? Human color, the color of emotions, but no color must be allowed to intrude upon or, for that matter to humiliate the already unhappy consciousness of the survivors.   Yours,
Simon Stern

8.   August 17, 1944
Dear Gerson and Friend Ostrovsky:

It's ridiculous, I know, but I have to make an addition. So much of my life is an afterthought anyways that it is no surprise to you that I should discover the meaning of a decision months after it was made.

You will notice on the plans that provision was made for an apartment to rise above my own, connected not to the appropriate landing, as are other apartments in the compound, but linked to my own by an interior staircase. I told Dr. Setzer to provide thus for a triplex, but it was unclear to me why. I know why now. A friend of mine will occupy that upper apartment. Not just a friend, a most particular friend—is my meaning clear? Must I be more explicit? I think not. I must be tactful, but you will accept my circumlocution and behave accordingly.

Enclosed find, therefore, a small tracing which Dr. Setzer has prepared diagramming the division of the space already allocated. Need I explain to you gentlemen how to employ it? Lay it over the unspecified area which rises from the interior stairs in the hidden passageway and there will emerge the lineaments of a commodious and attractive apartment in which my friend will pass the remainder of her days.

Cordially and confidentially,
Simon Stern

9.   September 1, 1944
Dear Friends,

It is late in the year and time is quickening, don't you think? You read the newspapers. Our friends in Europe are driving towards Paris, pincers are closing upon the enemy in the Lowlands. Slowed in Italy they are crushing the demons on the Eastern Front.

It is not customary for clients to address their contractors in terms of world history, but everything speaks to everything, all things are one despite their fissures and cracks.

Have you received Dr. Setzer's shopping list for the storage basement? Very important. N. B.

                                              Yours,
                                              Simon Stern

10.   September 11, 1944
Gerson & Ostrovsky,

I write this letter without cordiality. You have misread Dr. Setzer's drawing. Why have you begun to reface the exterior of the compound? No. No. Within, the buildings must be of steel and concrete, but to the innocent eye their visible skin must be wrinkled and creased with age. The fortress must deceive.

Have you never seen pictures of ancient cities? Dr. Setzer has shown me nineteenth-century steel-plate renderings of Troy and Herculaneum, of the townships of Etruria. The enemy would pass through verdant fields, gardens, rivers, sport fields, sacred groves, their horses would slow to nibble at the grass. The enemy would think themselves already victorious. Such lazy, unwarlike people, they would imagine. But the defenders of the town would count upon the ruses of nature, the succulence of their vineyards, the sultry brightness of their sun, the cool refreshment of their streams—all the skin of deception. Behind the brightly colored walls, recessed within the sacred niches and groves, the warriors would wait, and when the enemy approached drunk and sated, ready to the plunder, their arrows would be unleashed, their chargers plunge, swords ablaze. Don't you see?

The project is a deception. We, in this city encampment, have none of the devices of nature to dull suspicion. We are not the visible warriors of Greece and Rome. We are warlike Jews who cloak their rage in self-deprecation and apolgia. Our "skin"—your technical word for the sheathing of a building—must be mottled and grey, begrimed and humble, with-

221

out airs of pride. But behind, behind, let all be steel, hard, enduring. They shall not enter our fortress. We shall deceive them.

Whatever you thought, whatever you imagined Dr. Setzer's intentions to be, you were wrong. The marble which you placed upon the outside should be inside, fronting the court-yard which we have scooped out of our reconstruction. It is the courtyard which is the statement of our glory and our honor. Let the world believe us to be crushed.

I apologize to you for my anger. I am not angry.

Simon Stern

11.   September 12, 1944

Dear Gerson and Friend Ostrovsky,

I am over my anger of yesterday. It is completely passed.

You inform me that the requisition list of Dr. Setzer is confusing. For what, you ask, does he wish to have one thousand planks of the finest cedar wood, cut to the length of one foot in thickness of an inch and a half, notched in equal measures to allow for the joining of male and female? It is a confusion, isn't it? But it is critical that his instructions be followed meticulously. The planks must be exactly measured and cut. Moreover, each must be wrapped and numbered. The cut stones, one foot in thickness and height? Well, that's another matter. More difficult, but I should think the quarries of Alabama or Vermont would be able to accommodate our curious request. Yes, precisely! The stones must be cut as the ancients cut theirs—with other stones. Definitely not with iron or any other substance out of which men make war. No, again, each stone must be wrapped in cloth and numbered according to Dr. Setzer's description. The archstones, the cornice stones, and of course the particularly monstrous cornerstone must all be clearly marked and indicated. The delivery and sequestration of these items, along with the numerous decorative smaller pieces of wood and stone, the burl wood counters and cubes, the teak doors and window frames, the sheet glass, all these must be properly marked and annotated, checked against Dr. Setzer's list and specifications, and placed in the storage room in exactly the order which he has specified—the last shall be the first and the first shall be the last.

The storage room and the chamber adjacent to it—the one we call the Chamber of Hewn Stones—must, of course, be air-conditioned and heat-controlled. At the very last moment when

Dr. Setzer's needs have been satisfied, the steel doors will be closed and the storage room completely sealed off, but free access to the Chamber must be assured. (Note our instructions for ingress and egress through the false wall to be introduced into the corner store at the southern face of the compound). It is not as logical as the labyrinth of King Argos, but no less complex.

Yours,
Simon Stern

12.   September 16, 1944
Dear Gerson and Friend Ostrovsky,
    Why is it illegal? Illegal to whom? What is this law that forbids it? What is this code about which you write me so elaborately? I am aware that the state is empowered to protect its citizens against its exploiters, against cheaters, deceivers, miscreants who trade in shortcuts and compromises. I agree. The bathrooms should have ventilation, plumbing should be fluent and sanitary, electricity should be insulated, the buildings should be fireproof, and to forestall catastrophe, sprinklers, alarms, buckets of water, extinguishers. Fine. No objection. But what is the right of the law to know all my secrets, to know of that hidden storage room or of the network of tunnelings which we have constructed, like the bulkheads of submarines, to communicate underground, each building with its fellow, each neighbor with his neighbor? I see no reason. Moreover, friends, I cannot comply. You know our storage room is beautifully safe—neither fetid and damp, nor dense and unventilated. It is totally controlled. The glass room which governs the interior of the cavern, and in which the panels for controlling heat, humidity, air conditioning, water flooding, any and all possible underground dangers, also controls lights which enable us to see into, without entering (except in desperate emergency), the vault itself. There is no danger. No. I demand my secret. Destroy this letter.
    Get me a Christian inspector—an Adventist, a Witness, a Mormon—and bribe the hell out of him. Also promise him paradise and the Kingdom of God. Anything. I will deliver my promises.
    Do you understand? I am frantic when I hear about the law and its codes.

Yours, frantically
Simon Stern

Dear G and O,

It is particularly gratifying to know that my own quarters
are nearing completion. I shall be the first of the remnant to
be gathered in and domiciled. This morning I inspected the
arrangements with Drs. Klay and Setzer. They were exuberant
as well. My bedroom is just right—small and unpretentious.
The passageway which leads from the bedroom to my study
is as dark and airless as I specified and the stairs which lead
from that gloom to the lovely apartment above are just
right.

I have discussed with Dr. Klay the appointments for both
quarters, my own and the guest quarters above, and we have
reached agreement. I shall be high Gothic and Renaissance,
and the guest quarters shall be warm, luminous, modern. Dr.
Klay purchased for me at an auction house uptown the first
of what I imagine will be many contributions to the lightening
and elevation of my spirit. I would rather my heart were carried in the mouth of doves than in the talons of eagles. It was
good then to have the Matisse still life (who is this Matisse?
he has a serene vision)—those oranges, those lemons, the wall
paper. What extraordinary color. There is no color in the
world like the colors of the imagination. For me Klay found
in the shop of an antic little Italian, Pozzi, the most extraordinary carving of a prophet—a head of stone, with a beard
whose curls seem like a bunch of grapes, and as well, for a not
inconsiderable sum, a late fifteenth-century tapestry from
Burgundy that depicts the animals of the forest secluded in
sunlit arbors and peacocks and birds of radiant plumage peering from fruit trees and in the distance, seeking entrance to
the charmed maze of nature, a band of royal hunters. (They
had such an orderly universe. The hierarchy of their vision
made possible the containment of all things, the arrangement
of pains and pleasures, the exegesis of all which came to pass.
They had from the ancients the idea of entelechy and from
their religion the ideas of justification and salvation. So easy
then to think that everything which came to pass was an
augury and an instruction, nothing meaningless, everything
symbolic, nothing out-of-place.)

We, dear builders, we have no such conviction. For us
everything is a mortal leap. Everything that we do is a venture of risk predicated upon incertitude, facultated by wonder
and unbelief.

The little beauty that we buy costumes our disarray. It is

our cosmetic unrealism. So much for the necessity of beauty. When will my quarters be ready? The date, please?

Yours with appreciation for listening,
Simon Stern

14.   October 4, 1944

Dear G and Friend O,

November 1. Excellent. My apartment including the guest rooms? And Dr. Klay's? I will plan accordingly.

Many thanks.
S. Stern

Technically the compound of the Society for the Rescue and Resurrection of the Jews was a renovation. Not a new creation, but a renovation. The multiple houses which composed the compound were simply sheathed with a new skin of disguise, steel and concrete beneath, brick and board without. It was Simon's explicit wish that the face of the buildings to the street be indistinguishable from its neighbors, that the compound assume the worn and tired aspect of the neighborhood. Simon wanted to be nondescript in order to remain aloof and hidden. He did not wish his guests to be fingered by the gaze of strangers, to be handled, touched, abused by stares and looks, by tour groups and visitors, singled out on bus tours of the region, observed by guides in visored hats speaking corruptly into megaphones. He required the concentration of all his strength and intelligence without distraction. His was a monumental task. But in those days he scarcely knew its extent, its vastness, its totality.

Messiahs never know their vocation. They are always looking over the shoulder. They believe in the fact of their power, but not its fantasy. That is one of the critical marks of the true prophet. For example, there can be no question that Elijah saw with his own eyes that the rains came when he demanded them to put out the idolatrous fires, that, at his command, Dagon toppled to his knees. But this did nothing more than shout aloud the already vouchsafed answer of divinity. The prophet knows that he has the power to bring forth the succorous attention of God. But such men, such Elijahs, such Jeremiahs, and all the other dead-raisers, rainmakers, water walkers—

what do they know? only that when they need something God answers. The greater the power they incarnate, the less do they rely upon it. Not one of these would retire to bed at night and in the moments before sleep descended would, as we do, speculate upon the deeds of tomorrow. Not one would say, "Tomorrow I'll put a blight upon the rich man's fields and see him come begging for forgiveness," or better still, "I'll shoot up the council hall with lightning, start a fire in the file cabinets, and burn up the secret code."

Prophets don't fantasize. They don't play around with the imagination, concocting ways and means of showing off. The key thing is that they don't, for a moment, know that they're saving the universe. Saving a universe. And yet that is precisely what Simon Stern is doing. Saving the universe? Of course, the salvation of the universe—a universe made up of more than two billion people—by an ordinary Jew of a man who has never yet gone out of the neighborhood is a little hard to take. I don't blame disbelievers at all. They're absolutely right to disbelieve. But the fact is that Simon is doing just that.

There is an assumption hidden in the logic of the narrative which you might as well know now. There's nothing to hide and you'll catch on anyway. The Messiah is a Jew. No two ways about it. That's settled. I'm not talking about illuminated men, serene wise men, perfectly integrated men. Other people have them. I wouldn't sniff my nose at a Buddha, ever. They are genuinely extraordinary human models, pneumatic personalities, spitting the fire of their peace. Buddha, from the Sanskrit budh, perceives, is aware. A cleared spirit. Confucius, K'ung Fu-tzu, the master of humane wisdom, who indeed lived it. And then saints upon saints, unraveling the consequence of their holy anger, their sacramental hatred of the world in order to mend a fence, lance a boil, speak a simple word. They're all right and the world is absolutely better for them, marking time through millennia until the right moment fills up and in its plenitude is ready to overflow.

Simon is anything but peace. He is anything but serenity and calm, wholeness and integration. He shakes with the anguish of the world. He stutters and splutters. A calm Messiah? Even the last messiah, the one whom God tried upon the world some thousands of years ago (to our shame and tor-

ment), even he is not witnessed in peace, an uncontorted countenance, but green and grey, pallid and dying, falling down upon his cross, with mothers weeping and wise men grieving, and men of the world, stricken with arrogance and confusion, muttering about him.

We are a civilization fed upon history and nervousness. Unavoidable throughout all our times upon the earth. And no different now. Except that Simon Stern will come for us, particularly, at this juncture, when everything seems in bondage to the unforgettable, to the vivacity of our memory, to the ineffaceable burn.

Many months were to pass before the war ended. The formal war, the public war, which newspapers report and historians annotate. The other war, that of the survivors, would go on. Indeed, it is not over even now, many years after the treaties of cessation have been signed. It continues now. It will continue for many years, for many decades, perhaps centuries. The war of the survivor. The combat, no less mortal than that conducted with guns and bullets, is one of explication, the inculpation of the innocent and the exculpation of the guilty, the torment of broken hearts, moans in the night, visits to the cemetery of remembrance.

Another generation, in fact, will arise who have no reason to know of the horrors which in but a few short months will be opened to the scrutiny of the world, but even that new generation will know and be taught. We are obligated to look backward to what has been done. How shall we learn to look forward to what is not yet? And with what trust, what hope, what spirit of generativity?

November the first was not a bright day. The sun rested listless upon the grey palette of the sky, and cold and dampness made each ray of light shudder in the morning. It was not a bright day.

Dr. Klay arrived at Simon's office, where he had lived since the death of his parents. He did not find Simon immediately.

In the months which had elapsed since the death of his parents, the office had ceased to be an office. A hutch perhaps, a warren, a hive—no, not that at all—a cave like to that described in the ancient metaphor, but not a cave in which the

227

light of lanterns threw images of images upon the wall to deceive the chained perceiver—a cave in which piles upon piles of books, papers, reports, memoranda overflowed cabinets, replaced broken chair legs, stuffed burst pillows, supplanted the springs of broken couches. It would be possible—indeed, it happened—that strangers, not even strangers, Dr. Fisher Klay himself, would enter the office, a bell would sound, and call out for Simon and there would be no answer and beneath a cascade of books—toppling over, falling on his head, knocking him out, cutting his forehead, causing him to bleed and have a black eye—he would find Simon, there, passed out in a corner under a mound of literature and statistics of Jewish dead.

"Simon, where are you?" Dr. Klay called. There was no answer. "I call for you, Simon. Where are you? The hour is now. The movers have arrived. Come, now. I know that you're here."

Dr. Klay thought it some kind of a game. Simon sometimes played at hiding from his face, mocking him by building around himself a playhouse of Talmudic folios and crouching beneath them, torts as walls, *Mesechet Kiddushin* as ceiling and before him as a movable flap through which he would peek, the laws of the Sabbath. A remarkable game, but then possible for Simon Stern. You remember that he was once a midget. A midget, to be sure, but not minute. That is, not grotesque, or rather, not quite grotesque. He was, you will recall, four feet and eleven inches; he grew to be five feet six and one quarter inches, but he retained the habits and delicacies of small men. Simon had transformed remembered speckness into a nobility. The girth of a man most generally is modeled to his height. If either is unrestrained, proportions yield to exaggeration (a giant is that—a giant, and giants must be cruel and ugly like Goliath, for in no other way can we assimilate the unfitness of their size, and dwarfs must be gnomes and goblins in their infinitesimal smallness—fat and jolly and unserious). But Simon Stern was not a dwarf. Seated. Not very much taller than the Biedermeier desk that will inhabit his new study nor much smaller than the Thuringian candelabra which stand in the council room. He has size, but it is moderated. More impressive even than his size is his extreme thinness, an elegant waste of form, small bones pieced like the skeleton of fowl—nibbly, cracking bones—over which a thin felt of veined skin is wrapped. But on this particular morning, clearly Simon was not simply playing. There was no reply to the calls of Dr. Klay, no muffled cough, no constricted laughter. Where was Simon? Hidden in the garden of literature, lost among the detritus of Yiddish newspapers and the rich humus of Talmudic literature which gathered around the stumps and sticks of his furniture.

"Where are you?" Klay called again and stamped upon the floor as if mocking the tracking steps of hunters. Dr. Klay turned slowly around a blocked desk and called out once more. No word. He got down onto his knees and put his eye level to the floor hoping to catch in the morning light the sight of a hiding Simon Stern. Dr. Klay then became frightened and he got up and walked quickly around the small front office, moving aside cartons already packed, pulling open cupboards and closets. He entered the storage room in the rear where Simon slept. And then he understood.

Simon Stern lay fully dressed upon his bed. His prayer shawl wrapped around him, covering the soles of his sneakers, masking his head, his face a pattern of black stripes, the single capsule of Torah protuberant upon his forehead. His lips moved, and tears gathered like small pools in the declivation of his eye cups. He was motionless. Dr. Klay came nearer and knelt down beside him and whispered into his ear. "Dear Simon, where are you?"

"I am saying goodbye, friend. I am saying goodbye to my father Abram and my mother Ruth."

Klay could scarcely hear his words. It was as though Simon had struggled through the night to endure, and now, wrested free of the dead, was returning slowly to life, the first survivor of the fire, the first to come back from the pit. He had dressed to die and lain down upon the bed expecting then to give himself over to death. But however he had prepared, it was not the time. It was a gesture of complaisance, an offering of himself to the God who lives, a gentle offering of himself as an exchange, no, not even that, a saying that "if you want me at this point I am ready as I have always been, in the past when I was born and when I lived and they died." Simon Stern had tried to offer God an exchange. He made it convenient for God to say, "All right, Simon, now's as good a time as any. No need for the messiah yet. They can get along a bit more without him. They can manage. I'll take you back and hold you for another day."

"Simon, my friend, it's time to leave. You have survived." Dr. Klay lifted Simon and drew a dampened cloth over his forehead and Simon Stern returned to the living. He rose up and put off his prayer shawl and his phylacteries and tore up a letter of instruction he had addressed to Dr. Fisher Klay.

They were alone by early afternoon. It was less complicated than Simon had imagined. During the preceding days Simon had complained: "It's not ready," he kept repeating. But Dr. Klay had been firm. "Everything is ready," he reported. "Inspect again," Simon had demanded and Dr. Klay would leave him and walk the four blocks to the compound. Workmen were putting the last touches to the building, checking to make certain light switches worked, ventilation functioned. Gerson, who chain-smoked and dropped ashes into his cupped hand, went through the buildings with a checklist and noted the minor complaints which Setzer had raised. Everything had been done that needed to be done before the first occupants arrived.

Dr. Klay clearly understood Simon Stern. Dr. Klay was a completed man. Simon Stern was still upon his way. It is for this reason that Dr. Klay is always Doctor. I could think of him in no other way. Nor could Simon. At most, Simon would sometimes address him as Dr. Fisher, girding warmth with the ice belt of formality. And Dr. Klay was precisely that: Doctor. A doctor of information, a doctor of theorems and postulations, a doctor of our mental physick.

When he first met Simon Stern he was but recently become a Doctor. He had collected his degree in philosophy and law only three months before his eccentric flight to Switzerland. His interests were useless to the administration of survivors—the idea of the state of nature in the *De Jure Belli et Pacis* (1625) of Hugo Grotius, Spinoza's *Tractatus Theologico-Politicus* (1670). The essay had been published by an academic press which served the University of Vienna—five hundred copies bound in blue buckram with gold stamping.

230

Ten copies went to the university. They have undoubtedly been removed and destroyed. Several copies found their way to Paris and Bologna where humanist-renaissance studies enjoyed a parsimonious existence even during the war, and to Bamberger and Wahrman, booksellers in Jerusalem, which had a standing order for all publications of the university. Dr. Klay purchased four of their extant copies at the end of the war.

When Dr. Klay made the acquaintance of Simon Stern he offered him an inscribed edition. Simon read the work patiently, but confessed to not understanding it. Dr. Klay was not offended. He did not find the work inspiring. He was proud of it, but no less than Simon, regarded it as unreadable. Alone among the argument of the work he cherished its preface, and it was about the preface that Simon and he passed many hours of conversation.

DER NATURZUSTAND BEI GROTIUS UND SPINOZA
Einleitung

It is not my intention to revolutionize the interpretation of seventeenth-century thought or even, more modestly, to astound the interpreters of those thinkers about whom my discussion turns.

The dissertations which are mandatory for emerging academics are circumscribed by youth and inexperience, and, not infrequently, inadequacy of knowledge (for the more remote from one's own time the subject of interest, the less intense one's passion and the greater one's freedom from subjective bias, but quite equally the more numerous the antecedents of one's scholarship and the greater the quantity of resources, languages, literatures and civilizations upon which one's understanding must depend). There is always loss and compensation. But more to the point is that for me the task is not without its relevance. I do not think myself the friend of Grotius and Spinoza, nor of Valla, Erasmus, Luther (the progenitive humanists to whom I make frequent reference), nor of Goethe, F.H. Jacobi, Thomas Hobbes, Rachel von Varnhagen, Schelling, Schopenhauer to whose recapitulation of aspects of the problem I make ardent reference. They are as distant from me as their death and as

231

contemporary to me as the life which endures in their thought and my recollection of it.

Not these—not even Grotius and Spinoza themselves—but the issue which occupies me makes them live. The state of nature and the origin of human community and law is the issue. The thinkers of the seventeenth century knew much of the civilization of antiquity, but little of the prehistory of man. The sciences of geology and paleontology—related as they are to our understanding of prehistoric man—were in their naïve infancy. The seventeenth century had little but the intellect (and a feeling for the inordinate complexity of the civilization with which it had to deal) to guide it in searching out the hoary origins of its own unhappiness. It is no wonder that the humanist renaissance of that century should have survived a hundred years of religious warfare and, burnt out and exhausted, imagined a more hopeful occupation for man than ideological mass destruction. Not being able to look forward—for looking forward is always regarded by politicians as revolutionary and by theologians as apocalyptic—it looked backward. If man cannot hope to be perfect in the future let him at least believe that he was perfect in the past. The state of nature is the dream of the unencumbered directness and immediacy of human meeting, when men were not yet reconciled to being schooled beasts or self-deluded gods.

By turning then to the idea of man's primordial state, as understood by the humanist Grotius and the critical deophile Spinoza, our interest is less in the turns and weavings of their doctrine than in the transfigured vision of man's past which is not less than the dream of man's future.

"This is the state of nature, isn't it, Dr. Fisher?" Simon asked, smiling, looking about him at the debris the movers had left behind.

"Those," Dr. Klay replied, pointing to the half-opened carton.

"No, this," Simon replied, indicating the blackboard which he had begun to pull from a packing case.

"Yes," Dr. Klay acknowledged.

The slate was divided into a grid of rectangles. The first column bore the names of the principal centers of extermina-

232

tion stenciled in white paint; the second, the third, the fourth continued to change as Dr. Klay supplied current figures. Previous month, present month, cumulative total and in the center of the board THE TOTAL. The figures—all unreliable, sometimes merely assumed and averaged—were chalked in for the month of October, and the slate hung behind Simon's desk.

It was late in the year. More than four million were dead.

Each evening Dr. Klay would return from the offices of the Committee of Rescue, which he continued to administer, and report the day's events in the large world. He knew of all the hands that wrung, all the proclamations of dismay, all the notes and conferences and telephone calls that passed between the very great and the very great, and daily he learned of the mounting figures. Each day the recitation concluded, the report delivered, Simon Stern and Dr. Klay said the prayer for the dead.

It was at the end of November that a letter arrived at the Society which transformed Simon Stern and Dr. Klay from theorists and helpless bystanders. The letter was covered with seals and stamps. It was postmarked Cairo and had been given to an American official—perhaps it had been carried about for months by Ira Hirschmann who had been sent with confused authority to spy out the reputation of its writer (but that had come to nothing, for higher than his good will had been the communications and signals exchanged by the warring allies to disregard his information).

July 11, 1944

Gentlemen of the Society for the Rescue and Resurrection of the Jews:

I do not know who you are and it doesn't matter.

It's so late that trust is given by me with the speed and desperation of a drowning man thrown a twig. It doesn't matter if I drown, but if I have a moment longer, that is enough. I offer you a moment longer and you may choose to offer me one in return. It is all that hopeless.

I shall put the matter simply. I do this well, for I have told my story so many hundreds of times now, to so many officials, to so many governments, to so many emissaries, that with each telling the story is condensed as the hope shrivels.

233

It is the case that during the early part of April, while acting as a leader of the Jewish community of Hungary, I was approached by a high Nazi official, Adolf Eichmann, who was responsible for organizing the extermination of the Jews of Poland and Czechoslovakia. He offered to sell me the lives of one million Hungarian Jews. He demanded in return a quantity of foodstuffs, trucks, one truck for every ten Jews (ten thousand trucks), and as earnest of his seriousness he offered immediately upon confirmation that the transaction would take place to move one hundred thousand Jews to the border for passage into a neutral country.

You may think saving lives is easy. It is not so. I flew to Turkey and negotiated with the appropriate agencies, but that was not sufficient. I met with Moshe Shertok, but that was not sufficient. I have spoken with American representatives, but that was not sufficient. Now, my friends, I am a prisoner in Cairo, held by the British, who doubt my authenticity, who will not even release me to return to Hungary, where at least I can be of some good in continuing the negotiations while others, like yourself, plead and cajole on behalf of a million Jews, now a half-million, and shortly none at all.

If you are not simply tasters of tears, then I urge you to do the following:
1. Transfer substantial funds to that good man of whom I have heard, Saly Mayer, who is acting like myself in Switzerland.
2. Find the means of getting funds to Raoul Wallenberg, a Swede who is saving our people in Budapest.
3. Contact John McCloy, Cordell Hull, Anthony Eden, Winston Churchill, Ira Hirschmann, John Pehle, Angelo Roncalli, (a nuncio in Turkey), the Pope, Franklin Roosevelt. These men are all very powerful and they can help.

(Signed) Joel Brand

The letter arrived in November. It was also postmarked in Washington. It had been delayed and delivered by ordinary carrier. The Jews of Hungary were all gone. The bits and pieces that remained were to be ravaged by that other race of madmen, the Russians, who occupied Budapest a few weeks later. It hardly matters now.

When the banks opened the following morning Simon Stern alerted the astonished manager that he wished to transfer immediately to the Swiss account of Saly Mayer of the Joint Distribution Committee the sum of six million dollars and cabled him that instant to confirm acknowledgment and communicate any further request for funds. It was not necessary to return to the bank to complete the transaction. There was no reply to his telegram, but in the mail he received from the New York office of the Joint a formal acknowledgment of his interest and a request that he renew his contribution of the previous year. The only successful contact that he made was a gift to the government of Sweden of one million dollars in gold which undoubtedly found its way to the Third Secretary of the Swedish Legation in Budapest and managed to save a Jew or two at the very end, if not from the Nazis, then from the Soviets. It goes on and on, you see.

On the eve of the newest year, the year 1945 which saw the end of the war, Simon Stern and Dr. Klay decided it was time. Bergen-Belsen, Dachau, Buchenwald, Mauthausen, Auschwitz, Oranienburg, Ravensbrück, Birkenau were almost free. It was clearly time.

Out of the question to fly to London. Simon refused to go to the airport. It was outside his limits. He held fast. Ship then. Dr. Klay boarded the vessel at its customary pier, and at the Ambrose Lighthouse a fast launch which had collected Simon Stern from a launch near the Brooklyn Bridge transferred him to the vessel. He was resolved never to go beyond the precincts of his fort. His papers were in order. A dispensation had been granted him. He did not appear at the passport office in the center of the city. A notary and an official from the Department of State had visited him at the request of the mayor, who was already familiar with his eccentric ways and his generous contributions to the neighborhood. It cost Simon a great deal of money to be so curiously principled. He was right, of course. That is, if you wage an offensive war.

Blackout. A submarine scare. Fire drills.

Simon never left his cabin. They arrived in London at the beginning of March. He did meet Dr. Weizmann, however, whose hand he shook politely, but they did not converse at length. Simon Stern and Dr. Fisher Klay were now at the disposal of the Joint Distribution Committee, which regarded them both as strange, querulous, mysteriously powerful and extremely rich. They were benefactors who could bear to see with their own eyes.

235

Book 3

Prologue

The devastation of my blindness is not that I cannot see. It resides in something more fragile. It is a contribution to misunderstanding.

Other men shelter their vulnerability, covering it with wisps of beard or soft sibilants, wearing crusts of grumpiness or snappish hostility. They glide and slither across the surface of the world, not touching, remaining untouched. And they mature, in time, a facility of communication in which all the necessary words are spoken and so few of those which are optional to feeling. But I, carrying a velvet bag packed with the instruments of my calling, my cane (like an extension of my arm) tapping against the enmity of the world, must circulate through seeing men, and with my clumsy dignity, my unconfident sureness, bring them up short, compel them against their will to recognize in my naked vulnerability the vulnerability they do not admit.

How many times have I been told to watch where I'm going, to mind how I walk and how many times have I answered, no less firmly (and not without irritation), "I'm doing the best I can without eyes" or no less testily, "Keep *your* eyes open if *you* can see" and then they recognize the equipment of the blind man, the grey milkiness of my eyes, the vacancy and slight indefiniteness of my attention, and my cane.

Tap. Tap. I stood for many moments and waited for an arm to reach out and take mine to guide me across the broad avenue which leads me beyond the confines of our burnt-out habitation upon these shores.

An arm came forward and led me to the other side. And the voice thanked me, as happens many times when the blind are aided by the sighted—such an assuagement to the guilt of completeness, but I understand its source and respond to it, doubling the mood of thanksgiving by thanking more vigorously than I have been thanked. How many are those whom God remembers at the last for such a simple gesture. And so the streets were traversed, one after another, crossing over and being left, tapping the length of the street, four minutes, five, my cane sweeping the terrain before me, spying out the land, avoiding subterranean elevators and listening for the opening of doors, the lifting of metal covers, the shouting of pedestrians who could (and have) flattened me to the pavement.

It took more than an hour, with waiting and crossing and conversation and greetings and dead-still reflections and tapping upon the land, until I reached the subway which would carry me up the avenue into the bowels of a large department store from which I would come forth and make my way to the large park where Simon sits.

Down into the subway I descended and put a nickel in the turnstile and moved carefully toward the track until my cane touched air soundlessly and I stopped. The train arrived. A hand took mine and guided me into the car. It was crowded. I could feel the pressure of bodies, number coughs, hear the wheezings. I extended my hand to excavate an opening, for I wished to walk until I came to a clearing where I could stop and engage a body to help me. My hand reached out, and to my horror I found a quarter inserted between my fingers. I replied foolishly—I don't know why—"Thank you, but not for me," and turned the quarter in my palm, shifting it to my thumb and index finger and gesturing vaguely toward the person who had mistaken me for one seeking alms. I pressed forward between the bodies and nearly collided with another man who was passing from the other end of the car. I heard him shaking coins in a cup and I put my quarter into it and he shouted, "Jesus be praised and God bless you, friend. He who helps the blind will see forever."

I shuddered and passed the blind man.

You may think it is easy rescuing people?

I remember hearing many years after the events that I recollect and set forth here that the President, the same one who had, at the time of this narration, commanded the armies of the invasion (he was called Supreme Commander, mirabile dictu) invited to his home in the capital city ten citizens to whom he presented citations and medals for having rescued people. I found the event extraordinary. One young man had thrown himself into icy waters to save a drowning child. Another had fought off a bear that threatened to maul an elderly woman in a national park. A third had climbed out upon the escarpment of a building to retrieve an infant wanderer. And so on. I saluted them in my heart and congratulated the Supreme Commander on the fitness of his choices. Single human beings laying their own lives over the abyss. A saved child. A retrieved woman. An elderly cripple. One of the rescued was blind. From which of the myriad pits into which one day all of us will plunge had he been snatched? I marveled. I sang of their heroism. Had these been ancient days, a song of victory would have been sung and poets would have competed to extol their deeds. It seems so neat and uncomplicated. If it were only so. If only simple will, uncomplicated decision, straightforward action made the difference between the living and the dead.

They don't. The single man confronts his task like a woodsman with an ax. One man, one instrument of iron, one obduracy of centuries. The tree speaks a language of resiliency. It grows while it dies. The mouth excavated in its flesh becomes its own mouth, and until the last when the tree tumbles into the forest the cells of growth, however shocked by the assault, continue to multiply dumbly. But Simon Stern is no courageous youth nor woodsman in laced boots and mackinaw.

It has no poetry. What Simon did has no poetry.

London was all confusion in those days before the war's end. The knowledge of the end was in the late winter's air. The news was all good at last. But ending a war is much more complex than beginning it or, in this case, even fighting it. The English, no less the Americans, suffered from the sportsman's view of combat. When the conflict ends the combatants pack up their gear and leave the field. That's the simple view. It held during the Great War of 1914–1918. The Germans left their trenches, the French and English and Americans left theirs, shouted hurrah, shook hands, abandoned the lacerated earth, and turned over the making of peace to diplomats.

It didn't work. The new war that came a generation later was nothing like the first. The difference was understood in London. They knew perfectly well that with each bombing civilians died. They buried them daily and the hospitals were filled with the hysterical, the wounded, the crippled. But even then they imagined that when the bombs dropped no more the war would be over. They couldn't conceive that for years to come—for one, two, three years, more—many tens of thousands would die, that Europe would be a continent without boundaries and borders and the homeless and the stateless and the displaced would wander to and fro, murdering each other, continuing the conflict that would shortly come only to an official end.

It was good that Dr. Klay was a European. He knew how to wait in line; he understood the delicate evasions of courtesy and the decibel stridency of English arrogance. It was helpless enough to sit becalmed in the faded luxury of the Savoy, surrounded by officers conversing in hushed tones, hands folded over their pressed pinks; to know as well that virtually no one in all of England had any notion of what calamities awaited them when the final whistle blew was provocation to despair.

One morning, a week after he arrived, Simon was sitting in a pool of sunlight in the breakfast room. (Dr. Klay had an early meeting with officials of the United Nations Relief and Rehabilitation Administration to discuss the minimum daily caloric requirements for survivors. Professional dieticians, an Anglican theologian, a physiologist and a doctor were to present papers.) Simon dissolved a lump of sugar he had saved from the previous night in a second cup of tea and, preoccupied, looked out the window.

The gentleman approached him quietly and waited, anticipating Simon's return from his thoughts. A few minutes passed. The gentleman, his rotundity draped loosely with blue cloth of a distinct age and shine, stroked his beard and studied Simon's abstracted face. Aware no doubt that the others in the

241

breakfast room were observing his patient examination with curiosity he cleared his throat, but Simon paid no attention. Softly, "Mr. Stern," but no reply. Again, somewhat more confident, "Mr. Stern, may I sit down?" Simon retrieved himself from the distance of his reverie and motioned uncomprehending to the chair. "I'm seated, but may I talk to you?"

"To me?" Simon replied.

"To you, Mr. Stern. May I talk to you?"

"If you wish. Have we something to say to each other?" Simon asked, not irritably as his words suggest, but with that quizzical uncertainty and self-deprecatory indifference with which he covered his pride.

"Do I know you, sir?" Simon asked, looking up at the grey-green eyes sparkling above the beard.

"I don't think so, sir, but I know you or at least I know something about you."

"Yes. What do you know?"

"You are a praying Jew."

"You know that. That's true. I am a Jew who prays. No, that's not exact. I am a Jew who salutes God. That's more to the point. But how do you know that?"

"I have watched you pray every morning. My room is directly across the courtyard from your own. Each morning I pray. So do you. But you never look up. It is very moving. You have helped me to pray at least twice. Particularly, earlier in the week, when it was *Rosh Hodesh*. You spread out your hands as though inviting God to descend and then you clasped your own body and burst into a smile. It was quite extraordinary. I determined to find out more about you."

"Have you?" Simon asked, attracted.

"Bits and pieces. American. That's obvious. I don't need to establish that by independent authority. But more. Exceedingly rich. And, moreover, you are here in London on a mission involving the survivors. Is that correct so far?"

"Completely. Completely correct."

"I offer you my services."

"Your services? And what are they?"

"Let me say this. It is an introduction I always use. It delights and provokes. I am a Jew who has been on the losing side of every major conflict of the century."

"That *is* provocative. Do you take me for another lost cause?"

"Yes. Most assuredly. Yours is a lost cause and I support it wholeheartedly."

"More. Tell me more. Start back and tell me. What is this record of lost causes?"

"Moscow. July, 1917. The Kerensky government. I was a Minister of Supply. A radical socialist, an old-time radical, although in those days I was only a young man, not even thirty. But even then a praying Jew. I studied at Voloshin in Lithuania. My father was a haberdasher who owned a large store in St. Petersburg and had forty traveling Jews who sold clothing throughout the Pale. We had police permission to live in St. Petersburg.

"At the time of the Beylis blood libel, members of the Black Hundred set a fire in the packing and storage room of my father's warehouse and it was burned out. A telegram called me home from Voloshin, and when I arrived it was all over."

Simon was sitting in his familiar position of absorbed attention, his splayed fingers cupping his face like the petals of a half-open rose, nearly covered, his eyes—a watching lion peering above the shrubbery. He didn't move, but his mind, one suspects, was recording the mood and gesture of the speaker's words even more perhaps than their content. Simon was always a believer in physiognomic truths.

A waiter approached on squeaking shoes, set down the pots of hot water and tea and placed a cup before the bearded gentleman. The speaker stopped and poured the tea over the strainer, swishing the leaves with his discolored index finger.

"All over? Your parents weren't burned, were they?"

"No. They were very much alive and enraged."

"Well then, friend, not all over by any means."

"Quite so. I exaggerate. They wrote to the Czar, but naturally he never saw their letter. The office of the Holy Procurator received it as it did all letters from Jews. In time my father was visited by the secret police and told politely it would be best if he left the country. He did. He packed up everything that remained and shipped it to Berlin, but not before he did a damage of his own, a ridiculous damage, wrong-headed and muddled as he often was. I inherited that quality.

"One night he entered the small church of St. Stephen in a quiet quarter of the city, and there, while pretending to pray, before a venerated icon of the Holy Family, he paid it back, setting it afire with a match and gasoline-soaked wadding. He left as quietly as he came. The newspapers reported it as arson and unfortunately assumed that it must be the work of either a subversionary atheist or a Jewish incendiary. Since the newspapers had allowed for both possibilities, public reaction was uncertain, although some windows were broken in one synagogue and the Orthodox Youth League beat up a few old men leaving evening service. The point is, Stern, it was a wasted gesture, a gesture of rage. Foolish and unavailing, but it allowed my father to leave the Russia in which he and his ancestors had lived for centuries in relative calm at quits with her.

"It wasn't as easy for me. I didn't hold with my father all the way. I was a Voloshiner and you know what that means, Mr. Stern? A severe believer and a classic rationalist, which means no reason at all, only faith in the reasonableness of God. What condensed and acidulous minds they produced at Voloshin! With my hat pushed back on my head and my full beard, large as it now, but cut square, fingers stained yellow from three packs a day, I could dance the study of the Talmud with the same sinuous whine you must know from the Lower East Side where you live. (I know that, too, you see.) In all events my rage took a different form. I made contact with the radical socialists, subversive, but still not fanatical. My parents left and I went underground. I loved the complex indeterminacy of my life. By day I studied Talmud and did odd jobs for the various scholars of the city, and by night I met with other young revolutionaries and cranked out leaflets and distributed them in working quarters. Once I got picked up, but was released because my papers (by then all falsified) were in order.

"I met Kerensky in 1913 and became his secretary dealing with Jewish propaganda—my Yiddish was as good as my Russian and I had English, German, and French as well, because I had handled correspondence for my father when he dealt with his overseas agents and suppliers. I was full of dreams and ambitions for Russia and for Russian Jews. I believed so much that Russia would bear the Messiah into the twentieth century and that he would be raised aloft with giant hurrahs by good Jews who loved Torah and Russia. As you can see, it didn't happen. I'm here. It didn't happen." He paused and scratched his lip. "You know, I haven't told you my name."

"I know. I was waiting for you to remember that. It isn't important. I knew I'd find out eventually if I waited for it."

"I'll tell you in a minute," he said, his face crinkling into a smile. "My first mistake comes now. You'll see why my name is so beautiful to me. As I said, I joined Kerensky. I really thought the Communists would destroy Russia—destroy all the energy and spontaneity and youthful populism which was so much the joy of the intelligentsia. Was I wrong? Not wrong to oppose Lenin, whom I knew well. But I really thought the Russians were reasonable people. They aren't. Their intelligentsia isn't intellectual, and their peasants are cruel dreamers. In any event, you know what happened. Kerensky came to power and didn't last. It was over before it began, and I got thrown in prison by Lenin. I prayed in prison like a good Voloshiner and Lenin let me out because I knew a thing or two that was useful. What was more, I knew a lot about goods and services and distribution, and in the early days of the Red Revolution Moscow was a complete mess. My second mistake was Trotsky, who was as great a theorist as Lenin, but a real intellectual. Even though he had no Jewish education he could have been a product of Voloshin. I attached myself to him. Bet wrong again and fled in the twenties. I should have been dead twice by now. But I wasn't even touched. They were afraid of killing me in prison because I wore my *teffilin* all day and they were frightened of them—'black eyes,' the guards called them. Yes, indeed, I got away with my life. So then you can understand the pleasure my name gives me: Lazare Steinmann. The resurrected stone man."

"You know why I've come to London, Lazare Steinmann? You know, don't you?" Simon said, removing his fingers from his face and pushing his head forward across the table, almost lifting himself out of his chair.

"I do know. Of course I know."

"What is it then? Why have you come to me?"

"To help you, Simon Stern."

The pool of sunlight had disappeared. The breakfast room was empty. Outside, generals and their adjutants fidgeted before the dining room waiting for the first luncheon service. A few ladies in weary furs and large hats spoke into attentive ears and sipped pink gin. Lazare Steinmann and Simon Stern fell into an appalling silence from which each struggled to escape.

"I don't want to know what you think of me," Simon said at last. "I am only a very unimportant Jew with a vast amount of wealth who must do something. Now that's enough, isn't it?"

"Enough. Surely. Shall I continue with my story? It will tell you more. You need to know as much as you can about me."

"Another time, my friend."

Simon began to gather up his papers. He looked at his watch and pushed away the teacup. "We can't go on now. I have another appointment."

"Yes, I imagine you do, Mr. Stern. Dr. Klay, isn't it? The marvelous Dr. Klay."

"Indeed. You know all about him, too, I suppose."

"Of course," Steinmann answered, smiling. "Of course I do. I was in Vienna for several months after *Anschluss*. I know all about Dr. Klay. I know about his escape. I met some of his charges in Switzerland. Dr. Klay is quite redoubtable."

"You get around," Simon mocked.

"What with all my mistakes, I keep moving. One step ahead of the executioner. But I've survived. Mr. Stern, look at *me* tomorrow morning when I pray. I shall be praying for you as well."

Simon Stern slid from his chair and reached under the table to retrieve his grey homburg which he patted down upon his head. "Yes. I will do that, Mr. Steinmann."

"Rabbi, Mr. Stern, Rabbi," Steinmann called after him.

"Rabbi, yes. He must be a rabbi after all that," Simon muttered to himself as he approached the elevator. It was not until the doors opened on the seventh floor and he stepped out into the corridor that he realized that Dr. Klay was in the elevator as well, indeed standing quietly beside him, and now grasping him under the elbow, steadying him as they walked slowly toward their suite.

"You won't believe it. You won't believe it. They don't expect any survivors. The meeting was only a moral obligation. Would you believe that? There was an incredible lady present—a dietician from a provincial children's clinic—with the most remarkable set of capped teeth, who said at one point: 'My dear Dr. Klay, do you realize that this little conference of ours is *only* a Christian duty?' There was a round of 'Hear, Hear.' A parliamentary discretion. I very nearly turned over the table on the Anglican theologian Canon Whitebait. My God, my God."

"Dr. Klay, please don't cry," Simon said, putting a hand on his shoulder. "Don't cry or I will cry, and we will both be sitting here only a thousand miles from our suffering friends crying. They need us for better than that." Simon poured Dr. Klay a glass of water, and as an afterthought added a generous lacing of brandy.

"Of course, but I'm very tired. I will try to tell you what happened calmly. Ten officials of UNRRA, mostly American, energetic, concerned, pragmatic and completely naïve. Several rabbis in uniform—young men with curly black hair, using Hebrew expressions like quotations from Cicero. The English —we know that already—are all splendid personages, incredibly correct, even right-headed, but stuffed with a kind of punctiliousness that makes even the Pharisees models of flexibility. And the agenda? 'Assuming that there will be survivors, how to feed, clothe, and house them.' I interrupted the moment the chairman, an English colonel in the medical corps, finished reading his little statement. His ruddy cheeks flushed even more when I began, I confess sarcastically, to question the assumption. 'Who are *you*?' he asked, peering through his half-spectacles to a sheet of paper on which the names of the conference delegates were typed. I continued, ignoring him. He persisted, ignoring me. 'I am Dr. Fisher Klay.' 'I don't find your name on this list, Dr. Klay. Do be good enough to tell us who you are?' 'Fisher Klay, director, but not founder, of the Society for the Rescue and Resurrection of the Jews, New York City.' 'Well, I do hope, Dr. Klay, that we find some of your Jews to rescue.' Everybody chuckled. 'And now shall we get on with it?' I held my ground, Simon Stern. I held my ground. 'One moment, please. What is the source that leads you to this assumption, and if your assumption is correct, why bother with this exercise?' I heard a gruff harrumpf from the rear and a face vaulted with a mustache replied, 'I think I can help the American representative of whatever the name his organization for the Jews is called. I'm with Anglo-American intelligence and I'm quite qualified to speak to the question. We have reason to believe that the Germans in their retreat into the center of Germany from the brunt of our advance and that of the Russkies are scorching earth, putting all their nastiness to the torch. Rotten lot, these Nazis. No evidence to be left behind. Everything up in a poof. And with the flames goes the evidence. You see what I mean, sir, I mean, Doctor.' 'We're talking about people, Major, not evidence. I don't give a damn for evidence. Leave that to the War Crimes Commission. I'm looking for people, whole or broken.' 'Quite right, old man, I do agree, but that's the whole point, surely—there won't be any. No people at all. A lot of unburied corpses, I should think. What? Right?' Could he be right, Simon? Could he be?"

"I haven't any idea. I haven't any," Simon said sadly and fell back on the couch. "But of course I do," he shouted, slapping his forehead, "Of course I do, damn it. *Ha Shearith.* The remnant. There's always a remnant. A piece of a piece of a piece."

Slowly they revived. It was only later that Simon Stern told Dr. Klay about the curious Rabbi Lazare Steinmann. The following morning—it was April 7, 1945—they observed him praying. Simon Stern prayed in motion, every bone in his body convulsed by feeling—weaving and waving like a blade of grass before the wind, rocking and swaying, turning and bowing—his prayer was so much a rapture and an appeal that God might not ignore so ordinary a man who spoke to him so tremendously. Stern had finished before Steinmann began, and Klay, whose morning devotion was to say the *Shema Yisrael* with prolongation and complete attention followed by a reading of Psalms or Job or Ecclesiastes—whichever book of the Scripture seemed right to his daily intention. But Rabbi Steinmann was quite a mysterious Jew at prayer. Where most Jews cover their eyes—speaking the high confession of faith—

248

Steinmann was open-eyed and naked, but at all other moments he covered his face in his *tallit* and did not move at all. While others would rise and sit, as tradition or the honor of the Name required, he remained standing continuously. It seemed that everything that he did was in apposition, a mistake, if you will, but perhaps moved by another and more obscure incentive. They both watched him pray—and he prayed for nearly an hour. When he was finished they opened the window of their suite and called out over the courtyard to him. He saw them and smiled and they invited him to join them for breakfast.

"You pray impressively," Simon Stern acknowledged, taking Steinmann's hand and shaking it with warmth.

"No eyes, you observed. No eyes. Only *Innerlichkeit*." Steinmann spoke gaily, without pomposity, although it is hardly imaginable that such self-congratulation could be spoken without at least a trace. But it was so. He meant it with a kind of disingenuous pleasure as if to say, Behold. I have spent much time thinking about how to talk best with God and have come up with this. (It is only thought pompous and vain to speak about one's habit of prayer because God is thought so unapproachable that no man can imagine Him his equal. It isn't so, of course. All men are His equal and for that reason embarrassed. Steinmann wasn't embarrassed. Ever.)

"And you must be Dr. Klay," Steinmann said, confidently walking toward Fisher Klay, who was pouring their morning tea. "It's a pleasure to meet you. I have some news for you."

"So?" Klay replied. He shook Steinmann's hand and then motioned with a brisk snap of his wrist for both of them to come to the breakfast table.

"Ilya Lefkin is dead," Steinmann said before breaking a piece of toast and blessing it quietly.

Dr. Klay gasped and dropped his cup. "Dead?"

"Dead, and if the logic of our sages can be believed, dead as he caused others to die."

"Murdered then?"

"Yes. You see, I saw Lefkin briefly when I was in Austria. The same time as yourself, although I left several months after you, somewhat less dramatically—smuggled into Switzerland in a false compartment of a truck under two hundred sackfuls of potatoes. Heh! Heh! "Mr. Stern, here, knows something of my past. Through 1917. But after that there were many other mistakes. Weimar. Territorialism against the Zionists. Dubnow against Ahad Ha'am. Politics and ideology. In all things pragmatic I have been wrong. But I don't think I have ever been morally wrong. Foolish, benighted, romantic, but never against my conscience. In any event I was sent to Vienna by the German B'nai B'rith to see what was happening to the Jews in the weeks before the takeover. An observer, I was called. I observed, but I also stirred things up. I brought in false passports and identity papers that a little organization I ran in Berlin had produced. Fortunately I kept one for myself.

"You remember that Austria was beginning to behave with good National Socialist fervor several months before it was actually taken over. There were three staged trials against Communists and other political agitators. I went to one of them. I was curious to see whether they would be like the Soviet trials of '36. More a question of comparative totalitarianism. Well, of course, they were. The same quality of cruelty and the same elevation of patriotic rhetoric. Lefkin testified for the prosecution at one of these. He was no longer the young man who had gone to prison a hero.

"No hair at all! Absolutely bald, and his face was taut with vengeance. He swore that a certain Professor Langsam had been one of the most ferocious Communist agitators in the gymnasia system of Vienna. (What was happening clearly was that the Nazis wanted the credibility of the middle class smashed, wanted the school system which sustained the humanism of old Vienna demoralized.) Lefkin certainly helped. Professor Langsam—a decent man, a socialist assuredly, never a gangster of either right or left—was discredited. He cut his wrists in the jail and they let him bleed to death. Lefkin, however, had made a deal. If he did his part he would be amnestied. And so he was. A week after *Anschluss* I saw him getting drunk in a cheap night club where I had a meeting with one of our underground contacts to whom I was passing some false papers. I couldn't resist the impulse, as I left the club, to knock a glass of brandy all over him. An accident. I apologized. A good gesture. No?"

"But you say he's dead. How do you know?"

"I can tell you now. A few months back I would have held my tongue, but it's almost over, so I can tell you. There's a Jewish communications network—not large, not even official (nevertheless countenanced and tolerated by the Allies)—but widespread. For more than sixteen months we've been monitoring broadcasts from underground and partisan groups in occupied Europe, single-mindedly collecting, sifting, collating scraps of information on every Nazi criminal. Lefkin was among them. Yes, Lefkin. He turned himself inside out, from Communist to Nazi, from Jew into anti-Semite. Not a remarkable conversion. In any event, as our information indicates, Lefkin was picked up by the Nazis in 1941 or 1942. It didn't matter that he had helped them in the Vienna show trials. Off he went with other Austrian Jews to Mauthausen. He became a trustee—they call them Kapos—and had a good hand in beating Jews, and killing a few. Is it any wonder that one day he was found with his face smashed in with a shovel? About eight months ago that was. The French partisans operating in eastern France near Colmar relayed the information. We struck Lefkin from our list."

"There's life then in the camps—resistance, even?" Simon queried intently.

"Of course there's life—whole communities of life, worlds of life, but not life as we know it. The life of tundras and taigas. Life cut back to the bone, pared down to the rudiments of consanguinity.

"The imprisoned aren't behind bars. That's the curious fact. For one thing, the Nazis aren't as efficient as everyone imagines. The hell they've created isn't the hell of technocracy, efficiency, *blitzkrieg*, the genius of the machine. To think of it that way is foolishness. They're not at all efficient. They're mad and they have the efficiency of madmen, which is none too efficient. In any event the camps are cheap, dispensable, unhuman. The only thing they understand is that murdering can be done cheaply. Fire is cheaper than bullets. Gas cheaper than fire. It's that simple. The living aren't imprisoned by judgment. There is no conspiracy of guilt except in a few psychotics who had already condemned themselves before they even got there. What is involved is that the prisoners think of death like feces and urine—filthy and routine and inexorable. Even if they weren't taken daily to be killed they would all in time succumb to self-corruption. The fact that thousands die every day keeps other thousands alive. I'm not talking about those who die from dysentery, typhus, and other camp diseases. Actually if the camps were utterly pristine and clean, but empty of all human contact, all noise, all exchange, virtually everyone would kill himself or go mad and die. It would take longer, but the work would be done as efficiently.

"The combination is cheapness and madness—the Nazis are cheap and they enjoy killing. The result is that not everyone will be killed. There will be survivors because for every one they kill there's someone else who fights to stay alive, who refuses to go easily.

"Yes, Mr. Stern. Yes, Fisher Klay, there will be survivors. Most assuredly. And it's coming soon. Maybe next week. The Allies are almost to Buchenwald and Bergen-Belsen. We'll know shortly. And so what do we do?"

"You'll join us?" Dr. Klay asked.

"Of course. Why do you think I contacted Mr. Stern? Of course. Of course. I have to do something after it's over."

"A lost cause, though?" Simon persisted ironically.

"Of course a lost cause. What are you doing? Tell me and I'll tell you why it's a lost cause."

"You want a policy statement. A Rescue and Resurrection manifesto. Well." Simon got up from his chair and walked back and forth before the windows, looking out across the shattered city. Several times he began to speak, but wiped the forming word from his lips. He came to rest before the table, and his words began slowly like the pebbles of the seashore feeling the first tremor of a large wave forming out in the deeps.

"We want to gather a symbolic remnant—a remnant of a remnant. Few in numbers but mighty. These few—these several hundreds, several thousands—we shall bring together to live and work and think and pray.

"A small Bene Brak as in the days after the destruction of the ancient Temple. Rabbis, teachers, musicians, poets, mothers, electricians, carpenters, engineers, lawyers, doctors— all professions, all capacities—and to do nothing but rebuild each other's flesh and spirit. The unwinding of their flesh—

252

their life and presence, their productivity and confraternity—shall be a witness that despite all, everything, Jews will endure. That is the visible spectacle of the Society for the Rescue and Resurrection of the Jews.

"The interior landscape shall be different. Do you remember the tales told of the Greek convert, Aquila of Pontus, who studied with Akiba in Bene Brak while awaiting instruction from Emperor Hadrian to do the work of rebuilding Jerusalem from the ruins of Titus's desecration? Recall then that Jerusalem was a waste, that its earth was charred and stained, that nothing lived, no grass grew, no tree stood in that once verdant valley. Nothing. And yet throughout the world Jews continued to smile upon Greeks, Egyptians, Spaniards, Romans, speaking thoughtfully to them, showing them courtesy and manners, but despising them in their hearts for the desolation they had worked upon them. They were gentle to the world—no less than they are today, not thanking the world for having murdered them, but neither cursing it for having allowed it to come to pass.

"Our witnesses shall enact what the world has compelled them to be. We will testify to the world that it is a monstrous place. We shall not do as did our ancient forebears, smile upon the world while loathing it. We shall loathe it and we shall do works of genius and renovation while loathing it. We shall despise the world and work to bring it down and be ready to usurp it when it cries like the jackals cried in the hills around Jerusalem.

"We shall do differently than did others in the lineage of our past. We shall not make the world worse that *we* might be saved; nor shall we make it better that *they* might be saved. We shall hold up to the world the mirror of its desecration. We shall become the death's head of the world, the skull through whose eyes and apertures the world will see itself.

"It is not that I wish revenge upon the world—like your lists of criminals, Steinmann (that is to accept the conventions of justice and expect justice—neither of which I acknowledge). I wish merely to unfold a logical demonstration to God, that this and this is the way of the world, thus and so is the way of your creatures, choose then who you wish to be. Choose, dear God, if you wish to remain our God!"

253

Steinmann reacted with joy. No sooner had Simon finished than Steinmann rose and began to shuffle across the room in an unabashed parody of dance, singing loud the seven psalms of ascent (called the psalms of Hallelujah), which conclude with the repetition of a string of exuberances:

"I will give thanks to thee, for you have answered me and become my deliverance."
"The stone which the builders rejected is become my cornerstone."
"This was the Lord's doing; it is marvelous in our eyes."
"This is the day which the Lord has made; we will be glad and rejoice thereon."

and to these he added

"We are the builders who shall place the cornerstone."
"We shall spark fire from the rock."
"We shall draw water from the sand."
"We will transmit life with a straw."
"We will be the bellows of the universe."
"We will be the bivalve of the deeps and from the grit in our shell will grow the pearl of the people."

He sang and laughed. A telephone rang and Dr. Klay answered it. An irate voice pierced and Dr. Klay put a finger to his lips and motioned to Steinmann to subside. "A colonel with a fever begs our silence." Klay smiled and led Steinmann back to the table. Steinmann was exhausted from euphoria. Dr. Klay was calm and orderly. But Simon Stern was depressed.

"Is it lost, Rabbi Steinmann?" Simon asked.

"I have no doubt. I believe it is lost. But it is, I must add, a loss of glory, an exalted loss."

"We have enough of those, Rabbi," Klay observed sadly.

"Never enough and not of the same quality. Don't you see the difference? The generations before you were not able to put the case as clearly. Do you think it was thought sufficient by our ancestors to point to the deserted city and the desolated sanctuary and say 'Exhibit One in the case of the People versus God'? Nonsense! They knew it wouldn't hold up. Almost immediately, therefore, the writers of the nation produced learned works and pious exhortations condemning the mis-

254

creancy and vice of the people, defending divine immaculacy against human condemnation. There were a million exhibits for God against the people and the people lost. Exile. Dispersion. Depredation. The victory of Christendom and Islam. The triumph of the nations. God let us have it. Stiff-necked, arrogant, all the prophetic nastiness trotted out for millennia to prove again and again that the people should shut up and be good, pray, do the commandments, love their neighbors and hope. Oh yes. Hope and hope and hope. Now it's different. No temple. No sanctuary. Dispersion for centuries. We did keep quiet. Good and quiet and poor and oppressed. And did it help? You'll find out in a few weeks. Absolutely not at all. One exhibit against God? We have millions. Don't talk to me about trying God. No need for a trial. If that were all, He'd be condemned in a trice." Steinmann began to weep. "But you see, friends, what makes me weep is the confident knowledge that God couldn't help it. Not at all. Our life is a blink of the eye, the green flash, a summer storm, a rainbow. Our day is already His yesterday and His millennia and His eons of pastness. God is in fact no past, no present, no future. He is the rapture of desire—eternity and incompletion, without justice, incapable of politics and practicalities, but a dreamer of impassable visions, wanting to feel, but not feeling, desiring humanity, but unhuman. He is suffering perfection.

"And I do not weep for us but for Him, that He wants so much and can affect us so little. We can condemn Him and what will it get us? Nothing. Not even His anger. Because He knows nothing of justice. His kingdom is not one of justice. Abraham asked whether He who makes justice can do injustice. What a magnificent complaint. How irrelevant! How sentimental! He is neither just nor unjust. Justice has no portion of eternity.

"Mercy, feeling sorry, sadness, the weeping of angels, the hair of saints turning white, the beards of sages wet with lament—that's the extent of the feeling of the divine and the blessed, that they can see it all and cannot help. There is no justice. Justice is a human convention, a covenant of the fallible. The only justice to men is the knowledge that there is a God who weeps. And I weep for Him, for I would have him glad and joyful with creation. We will fail, dear friends,

255

not because our anger is not just, but only because it cannot be eternal. A God who knows so much and is so helpless, is either not God or He *must* weep. And I, I confess, that I (I who have been wrong in all the causes of the world's justice) I, I understand the glory and the weeping of God."

They talked immensely. They did not imagine, not for an instant, that their words shook the foundations of the universe. Not like Abulafia's kabbalistic permutations which could blow up kingdoms and ignite the parchment of Papal decrees, they did not believe that the shifting of syllables amid saliva, pushing language against teeth and bridgework were as *logoi* spoken in the no-time of God and from them creating worlds.

When the talk was done they rose from their seats, and paced their rooms. They had no desire to see London. Steinmann knew the city well and volunteered to show them its wreckage, the Houses of Parliament with shrapnel wounds, the East End, a decimation of flame, and the zoo, but they did not need the city and in fact Steinmann was not enthusiastic to show it to them. They were traveling other regions and seeing other ruins than those which were definite.

Simon left the living room and returned shortly, fully dressed as though ready to leave immediately, his overcoat buttoned, his hat firmly clamped upon his head. "I am ready."

Not an hour passed and word came from the desk that an official wished to speak with them. The following evening they were to fly to an airstrip forty miles from Buchenwald, which it was expected the Allies would reach and take on or about the tenth of April. There, behind the lines, they would be attached to the medical corps of the American army to make preparations for bringing relief trucks into the camp when it was liberated.

I was one of the first to be liberated.

Liberated. A humane euphemism. An American euphemism. A captain, who accompanied Simon Stern, walked briskly toward me as I hobbled forward, dragging one bandaged leg behind me—I had been bitten by the wolfhound which the camp commandant had also liberated when he fled the camp—and saluted me, saying, "The Americans have liberated you."

I was the first prisoner liberated at Buchenwald (which

only means that because I was blind I didn't move much after Simon found me, and was standing by myself in the assembly area of the camp waiting for Simon to return and a line of American trucks which had entered the camp stopped right in front of me, the bread and soup lines formed, and I was the first in line).

The captain said "We have liberated you." And I said, not thinking, "Thank you for liberating me," and the few thousand prisoners who had survived said "Thank you for liberating us" and waited for the captain to stop congratulating us for being liberated so that we could begin to eat. The captain then introduced a lieutenant general who brought us Greetings from the General and the President of the United States and congratulated us again. We were then encouraged to eat. At the first swallow I vomited.

I came to Buchenwald by accident. In the same way that I got to Auschwitz. Simply a question of being in the wrong place at the wrong time. It's a long story which can be briefly told.

During the fall of 1944, shipments of the lethal gas by which we were exterminated slowed up—some shipments in fact were apparently sabotaged. Other plans had to be made for doing away with us. Mass firing squads were reintroduced to take up the slack. But most explicitly, it was thought prudent to increase recruitment of the able-bodied for use as forced labor in Germany and Austria. The program didn't last long. Fifteen hundred of us were rounded up and began the long walk across Poland to southeastern Germany, where we were to be used for making the Bavarian Alps impregnable for the last stand.

One night we slept in a field near the German city of Gleiwitz, which junctured the Polish, Czechoslovakian and German borders. The following day we were supposed to march south across Bohemia toward Munich. Housing accommodations were at Dachau. I took the occasion on this night to fall into a cow pit, a not unconventional field trough in which sedentary cows make themselves comfortable during long days at pasture. The hole, not large by cow standards, was overlaid with rush and stubble, since it was near a virtually stagnant pond. By morning I had covered myself in mud, and there, chilled though I was, I remained hidden until my brother prisoners had moved off.

Roll call was not quite efficient on open marches, guarded as we were by relatively few soldiers, all of whom found the duty as disagreeable as we found it painful. They were content to have a few accounted dead in their tracks and misplaced or, if escaped, then surely to be recaptured or die (which was our ultimate fate in any event). I dared not say, after the fact, that I was free. No hugs and huzzahs. Not even a muffled smile. I stayed put until nightfall. I was by then weak from hunger and cold. However—and here I condense— I survived in this way, hidden by day, stealing forth by night, making vaguely for where—Switzerland (across Austria?), France (across Germany?). Making vaguely for some place to put myself away for a few months—a deep forest with a glen, a mountain eyrie. It didn't come to that.

I managed to stay alive and provisionally free until the middle of January 1945, some three weeks after I had detached myself. Long enough, as it turned out. I was picked up by three soldiers—their combined age was scarcely a half-century and it was I who was obliged, with affectionate consideration, to persuade them that their carbines were loaded and dangerous and that I was properly terrified of their invincible might and that of the Reich. They shook with terror and pride as they delivered me, thank God, to the sergeant on night duty at the barracks outside the city of Meissen, rather than to the Gestapo who would surely have cracked and broken me as any other defective crockery cast away in that famous city. I was sent to Buchenwald, which was less than fifty miles distant.

My blindness—the condition which has become the seal of my life—was well advanced by the time of my rearrest. My eyes have never been splendid. They were worked too hard. Frequently I would awaken in the mornings of my youth and, after a night of absorbed study, could not open my eyes, dried shut by a protective emission. Colds afflicted my eyes. Pink eye and swellings. My eyes were unsightly, discolored and watery. During the three weeks of my wanderings through eastern Germany I developed acute conjunctivitis, flaky and itching at first, raw from cold and unprotected, and by the time of capture my eyes were full of pus. It should not be imagined that such a simple ailment, far advanced though the abrasion of the conjunctiva had become, could not have been reversed. But it was not. No solutions. No bathings. No rest. By the time of my arrival at Buchenwald in early February, my head ached from the strain, and my vision was blurred and indistinct. A few weeks later, as the camp began to dissolve with the approach of the American army—guards disappearing, food stores mysteriously vanishing in the night, prisoners gradually assuming control from the imprisoners—my sight went. Cold water was scarcely a remedy. Perhaps an emergency operation, an excavation of the troughs of pus which irritated the vital membrane, would have saved them, but by April 13th when Simon Stern found me it was already too late.

On that morning I was standing before the gates of the camp absorbed in reading a prayer book (which had been thrust into my hands some days before by another prisoner, imagining as he did that I needed to see in order to represent the congregation in prayer, and I, succumbing to the fantasy, had taken those foxed and brittle leaves and kept them, drawing them forth each morning as I said my prayers, although I could not see the page) when a voice addressed me.

"You are at prayer but you cannot see."

"No differently than Him to whom I pray."

"You have strength to laugh? That's good. What's your name?"

"My name is Nathan Gaza. Who are you? You speak quietly. It's been a very long time since anyone has spoken to me quietly or, for that matter, asked my name."

"Mine is Simon Stern. Will you come with me to New York?"

I confess that I laughed. It was so ridiculous. "And after New York we will visit the moon and Venus."

"In time, if you wish, but for the moment let us say New York. You see, I am a citizen of the United States who works for the rescue of the Jewish people. It's simple. I'd like to rescue you."

It was like a proposal of marriage. May I marry you? he seemed to say, I can show you a good life and honest love. Or perhaps: I can reform you and restore you. It didn't matter.

The voice was quiet and there I stood in my prison rags, holding my prayer book, and my blind eyes began to cry.

It was easy rescuing me. I was simply there, standing still, waiting—so to speak—to be rescued. Moreover, I was perfect for rescue, or by definition so patently imperfect that I demanded rescue, evoked rescue without having even to request it.

It was not so easy rescuing others. At the time of our liberation by the Americans on April 13, 1945, there were at Buchenwald approximately fifteen thousand Jews in various states of dying, and numberless Poles and Slavs, Communists, gypsies, several score or more of habitual criminals and various homicidal maniacs. If not quite the cream of selection (for there were many other camps in Germany and Austria liberated during the following weeks), my fellow prisoners provided Simon Stern with explicit indication of the difficulties. In fact, recollecting the extraordinary events of that first week, the rescuer and the rescued entered into a relationship no less mortal than that which had existed between murderer and murdered.

The dying continued to die. The process of mortification is not speedily reversed. Food does not feed; medicine does not cure; freedom does not liberate. The starving, sick, and imprisoned have first to acclimate themselves to the reversal. The apocalypse does not take place in the twinkling of an eye. Messiahs are not annunciated by simple proclamation. We are conditioned creatures, and when we have made a covenant (however entered) to die, it is not enough to announce its abrogation. Learning must take place.

I threw up the first mouthful of that nourishing vegetable soup. It gratifies me that my body behaved so intelligently in the matter of food (it relieved me of having to condemn it out of hand for the special foolishness of my eyes). Had my body not behaved so prudently I might well have died from the gastric explosion which overtook others more gluttonous. Buchenwald lost thousands of survivors in the first months. Other camps did likewise. Indeed more than one hundred and fifty thousand survivors died before the end of 1945. Not all of them from gluttony.

In those first weeks of "liberation," the camps were riven by the confusions of victory. Victory over whom? The victims were now victorious and yet they had won no battles. They had merely endured longer. They claimed to themselves no special strength, no extraordinary fortitude. They had simply outlasted the murderer. But now it became necessary to ascribe to them something more than the numeral identity stitched into their skin. As flesh was renewed, so names, histories, nationalities asseverated their claims. And let the confusion multiply: not all victims were the same—some were more victim than others.

At war's end the camps of extermination and subsequently the way-station camps of the displaced, homeless, and stateless were crowded with a multiplicity of moral and political simplisms. A Jew might be a Polish national and a non-Communist nationalities asseverated their claims. And lest the confusion when he was returned to Poland (thereby relieving him of his statelessness) only to find in the convoy of repatriation a Polish nationalist who had served as voluntary labor in a war factory in Düsseldorf. They return together. The village of their birth receives them. The home of the Jew is occupied by a Catholic family which despises Jews. The Polish nationalist kills the Jew, and Poland is rid of one more Jew. It happened hundreds of times. Jews refused therefore to be considered Poles. They did not wish to be returned to Communism which despaired of Jews as Zionists, or to Catholicism, which loathed them as Jews. They returned to the camps.

We are what we are—Jews. That was enough reason to deliver us to Hitler and kill us if we survived. Favored victims have no other politics than to get out.

On the fourth day of our liberation, at dusk, roll call was taken. The liberated gathered before their cell blocks in the compound square, and faces and numbers were matched. It was not otherwise now than it had been before.

"Would you like to come to New York?" a voice addressed me and fingers dug into my arm.

"Simon Stern?" I replied uncertainly, for the voice was not his.

"Simon Stern, of course, Simon Stern, who else but he?" the

voice continued. "Yes, indeed, Simon Stern, the great liberator, the Bolivar of Bavaria, of course, none else. And what will you do there, blind Jew."

"Where?"

"In New York. What will you do there? Weave baskets? Ha Ha. Why aren't you dead, like the others. Why don't I go in your place?"

"What do you want. You're not Simon Stern at all."

"Of course not, who do you think I am?" the voice persisted, the nails dug at my skin, and an arm encircled my neck and pulled tight until I could not breathe. "Don't shout at all. Not a word. Now I will see for you. The prisoners are gathering, the survivors—heh heh—they are coming to order before the hangman's platform where I used to call the roll. Ah, now you know. Yes, quite right, Obersturmbannführer Linz—correct— dressed now in prisoners' rags (I don't want to step up and demand new clothes like all the other Yids—I'll wait my turn until the Americans catch on). The others fled. Not Linz. I'll go out in style. To America I'll go dressed as a Yid." His voice became louder and his grip tightened about my neck. "I'll go up to Simon Stern and tell him, 'Stern, dear Stern, Nathan the blind Jew couldn't make it. He left us too soon. He asked that I take his place. I'm a Hungarian Yid like he was and I'm healthy. I can see.' And he'll take me, blind Jew. You wait and see. Simon Stern will take me to America—to America."

Suddenly, as unexpectedly as he had seized me, his grip loosened. I dropped to my knees, gasping for breath, and retched upon him. Who saved me? I have no idea to this day. One as murderous as the other laughed—"I've killed seven so far." I began to vomit again, and the saving guttural voice moved away, screaming, "Seven. Where's eight?"

I called out, "Simon, where are you? Take me *now* to America."

"To America, is it?" a voice took up. "To America, blind Nathan." And that voice shouted, "To America. Let's all go to America. Let's all go." His voice shook with laughter.

"Where's this Simon, where's this new Moses. Ha ha ha ha," a voice screamed. "Where is he? Let him lead us out of this shithouse to the Promised Land."

"Yes, yes," other voices shouted. "Stern. Where's Stern?

Where's Moses Stern? Where's Moses?" Other voices took up the cry and soon thousands of voices stamped and shouted and screamed like madmen. "Stern Stern Stern Stern Stern Stern." A rhythmic insanity chorusing that single name. Behind the crowd a truck stopped, and army soldiers, I understand now, must have taken up positions ringing the crowd and converged upon it like riot police. A squad of soldiers rushed past me and I could hear one say, "Sorry, Stern. No time to be nice. Up with you." Forcing a passage through the crowd they lifted Simon to the hangman's platform. "Up with you, Stern," I heard him shout above the subsiding cry of his name, and at last silence came and Simon began to speak in halting Yiddish: "Jews. Survivors. I'm the Simon Stern you want." Simon halted, his voice died away, as though he had lost—before the multitudes of the remnant he had sought—the power to speak. "There are so many of you to save and so few of us to serve you," he continued, abashed, and his voice rose, wet with his tears, for he had begun to cry. "How shall we honor you?" he started again, questioning the falling night, and then, renewed, he spoke, almost prosaically, "Some will come with us to America. Others will go to France or Italy or England. Most of you will go to the Land."

Murmuring began among the listeners.

"The Land?"

"America."

"I want America."

"I want our Land."

"Those of you who wish to come with us to America—" Simon intervened, "to New York City," he particularized, "to New York City, a vast city within America where I live, and am making plans, should tell us of your wish. We will speak with you. Some will want to go and cannot. Others will not want to go and I will persuade you to come. Those of you who want to join me in America go to the left of this—what is it?—this platform."

Simon became aware that above him rose the inverted L of the scaffold and a knotted noose moved in the wind. There was momentary silence as the assembly considered his invitation and then a cry went up: "To America. To America." And others replied, "To the Land. To the Land. *Eretz Yisrael.*"

Fists hit against the air and arms struck out against others.

The fight began near the platform, and before long, with shouting and cries of America and Palestine, Jews fought against Jews. Shots sounded and bullets spent themselves in the darkness, and the noise of terror brought the fighting to an end, and not cries of anger but the wailing of frustration broke from the congregation of elderly men who had already formed at the back of the crowd to say the evening prayers and the weeping ended and the Doxology could be heard distinctly, "Magnified, and sanctified be his Holy Name."

"Where's Simon Stern?" a voice shouted. "Where is he now?" He was not to be seen. The trap door had sprung beneath his feet and he had fallen into the void under the hangman's noose. The sounds of prayer—"May he who makes peace in the high places"—and mocking laughter welcomed his face, its reddish-brown eyes still moist with tears, as it emerged from beneath the platform, and Simon Stern, selector of the living, disappeared into the night.

On that fourth day of our release from bondage, we became aware—all of the prisoners and I, those who continued to walk about in their striped costumes, ludicrous, humiliating drabs of white cotton streaked with black, now gone grey with mud —that nothing had changed, that nothing would change for some time to come. The liberators had replaced the captors, but chaos had replaced order. A horrible nervousness settled upon us, a nervousness so unfamiliar that none could trace its source or meaning.

My only friend—he has since died an ordinary death—used to stand beside me on the muddy assembly grounds, his hand at my elbow and repeat, "We're not used to living, Nathan." And indeed that was the case. All of us, those of us at Buchenwald and the millions of other captives elsewhere throughout Europe, had grown accustomed to struggle each day for a bit of bread, a minute of rest, a moment in a quiet place, the sight of a bird or a clean, unsplattered blade of grass. A little thing would keep us going. A very little thing. You cannot imagine how little was our connection to life and how very little things managed to sustain that connection. The struggle was not against ideas, or people, or nations—that would return later. The struggle was against growing faint, losing weight, getting the runs, not being able to work. Those things meant death. Death was the enemy. And death was such an enemy that the meaning of life was bound up in the struggle against death. The struggle was every moment. A day over, we would all mark it against a calendar that had no dates, no beginnings, no ends. We did not understand therefore what it meant to be liberated. We had no idea of freedom. Freedom to choose to die? Perhaps that is why many of us died so quickly after it was all over. At least the choice had become our own once more. You might think that this is a contradiction. How strange, how mocking, how ironic you may think it is that someone who has waged a war against death for so many months and years should within days of being liberated succumb to death. That would be wrong! At such a moment dying was a free decision once more.

One had an alternative, of course. Stay on at the camps, join an action committee, distribute clothing, work in the kitchen, organize records and inventories, seek relatives. There were many who did, and those managed not only to pass through the ennui of freedom but to repair their lives and eventually make their way back into the world of the living. But for others of us, the days after liberation were days without air, the air we had come to know and breathe—fetid, stinking, death-heavy—was nonetheless familiar. It was full with the expectations of dying, and though we breathed that air it was with a ferocity that signified our refusal to die. The new air of surcease and rescue was flaccid and purposeless. Most of my comrades sat in the sun smoking cigarettes. The stupefaction of release, dumb, leaden, preserved us in inaction. We were suspended in a formaldehyde of freedom; dead, but alive, arrested in the prolonged agonies of dying, we were preserved in that estate.

The word of Simon Stern had gone through the camp. But for those first days only I had been chosen to follow him into the new land. His presence was known. It was rumored that Simon Stern was forming an army of survivors to retake the homes of the imprisoned from their alien occupants. It was rumored that Simon was actually a secret emissary of the Zionists, that Simon Stern was simply a civilian official of an international relief agency, that Simon was a neutral observer, a spy, a friendly, charitable millionaire. All these rumors, like bits of paper in a wind, bore a message, but the message could not be deciphered, for the wind of confusion was too strong and the bits needed to be reassembled in calm, flattened out upon a steady board until the reconstructed message could be interpreted.

Simon was obviously not interested, at that moment, in encouraging such clarity. Instead, working with Dr. Klay and Rabbi Steinmann, they dispensed medicines and clothing and food and information. One would pour soup into the tin cup, and the other would start a conversation. "Where did you come from? What did you do before the war? You taught languages in a commercial academy in Vilna, you say? You were an agronomist? Do you want to learn more or are you tired of all that? You want revenge? Upon whom? The world? Not particular enough. You want peace? In this life, do you expect peace? You do—and what is peace? life without agitation? And what did you do, little mother? You took care of small babies—you were a wet-nurse? Do you still love children? You believe then that children can grow? You believe in the living? That's good, a commendable belief. Take her name and block number, Dr. Klay."

At the end of those early days Simon Stern departed. He had not spoken to me again, but in the meantime, Dr. Klay had approached me on the assembly ground and we had talked.

"Nathan Gaza. That's your name, isn't it?" Dr. Klay had begun. I nodded and he continued. "May I put my hand upon your shoulder? It will make it easier, I suspect, for you to talk with me." A firm hand, not large, but bony and tapered, long fingers that were deft and confident, rested upon my shoulder and an index finger occasionally tapped upon my neck. "You were the first he chose. He said to me before he left that he found in you a resource of strength, deep as a well of cold water and as dark. He told me you were a scribe by profession and a learned man. You will stay behind here until the rest of our company has been gathered. We have chosen thirty-seven from Buchenwald. They do not know each other, but during the coming days they will identify themselves to you. It is you whom we ask to be their temporary leader, to deal with their difficulties, calm their fears, give them the assurance they need. But most important, Simon Stern and our community, the Society for the Rescue and Resurrection of the Jews, should be discussed as little as possible. We should like a minimum of conjecture and speculation. They were chosen, and that choice is firm and irrevocable. But they will have difficulty if they try to guess what was in our minds in choosing them. Some of them are ignorant, some skilled, some crippled—like yourself—some in need of psychiatric care. But what they have in common is a passion for renewal. That is the passion that will make it work."

It was more than a month before Simon Stern returned to Buchenwald to collect the thirty-seven Jews who had been left in my charge. Fisher Klay, in the meantime, had interviewed survivors of Dachau, Bergen-Belsen, Mauthausen, and aggregated for the journey two hundred and seventy more, and Steinmann, departing from Buchenwald, joined Simon Stern for travel to Berlin and, with permission from Soviet authorities, went on to Oranienburg, Auschwitz, Grodno, and other camps, where they accumulated four hundred and eight additional survivors. There were now more than seven hundred, and each day by hearsay and word of mouth others would join themselves to the congregation of the remnant.

During the first weeks of June 1945 the trains which arrived in Paris from the north and east bore families and elders, sons and widows for embarkation at Le Havre, Marseilles, Naples for the journey to New York. A number, contacted by the agents of the underground in Palestine, stayed behind— not without Simon's blessing and endorsement—to assist others to make the illegal journey to the Land. These, in turn, would, within the years which followed, establish communities within the Land to protect and inure the generality of migrant Jews from enemies not even yet discerned or detected.

There will be by the commencement of the year 1946 at the Society for the Rescue and Resurrection of the Jews in New York City more than one thousand survivor Jews (1,037 to be precise). In London, domiciled through the efforts of Rabbi Steinmann, who later joined us in New York, another three hundred affiliates and in Marseilles, although still agents of the *Brichah*, another three score and eighteen, attending to the ideology of our founder—perseverance in study, prayer, and physical restoration. There were, in sum, fifteen hundred members of our community throughout the world, and with sympathizers, friends, affiliates, collaborators, nearly two thousand.

BERLIN, May 12, 1945

A woman, young in age but already marked by age, her hair loose and snarled, her face a map of grief, stood beside a lamppost which was all that remained amidst the ruins. Down the street coming from the east a troop of Russian cavalry trotted, six troopers and a young officer. The officer saw the weeping woman and halted his troopers. Addressing her in German, he asked why she wept. "Three years I hid in a basement, two years I was in forced labor, two years I was in prison awaiting death. And now that I am free and have returned to the land of my birth, there is nothing."

The officer—he was not only young but immaculate, his uniform clean, his medals bright, his boots sparkling in the sunlight—withdrew a pistol from his holster and pointed to a German who scavenged in the rubble. The German held up a pot. The officer looked at the woman and she nodded. The officer fired and the German fell. Turning to the woman once more he saluted her; he raised his hand into the air and the troopers trotted off.

This woman, Rochel, is now the chief cook of the compound of the Society for the Rescue and Resurrection of the Jews.

LODZ, June 1945

Rabbi Steinmann encountered a Jewish poet—one who wrote in Yiddish and had not published a single volume, even a volume of thirty-two pages, during the whole of his youth. This poet—his name was Halil Kantor—had escaped from the ghetto of Lodz before its sealing and destruction and taken refuge in a Christian cemetery. He lived in the crypt of a mausoleum and each night went to sleep in a stone coffin whose rightful occupant had not yet appeared.

One night he heard a low moan from the adjacent mausoleum and crept out. There was no light but that of a half-moon which, obstructed, nonetheless cut a sliver of silver in the interior of the crypt.

A woman was suffering in childbirth, and from her cries and moans, her softly spoken plaints and her tiny calls to her own mother, Sarah, he realized her to be a Jewish woman giving birth. He thought to himself that the child must surely be the Messiah for whom he waited, since none but the Messiah could be born in the tomb of dead people. And he continued to watch and in his head he began to compose a poem of annunciation which would show this baby's glory to the world. The hours passed. The child was delivered and the mother fell back exhausted. With the morning light he knew that he must return to his own coffin but he continued to watch. The child had rested upon the mother's breast for many hours when suddenly hungered by its own ordeal it began to draw upon her nipple, but she was without milk.

The mother began to cry and the child wept. The poet, Halil, knew then that the baby was not the Messiah. But that was good, for in the days that followed, the poet became the comforter of the woman and the child and, thereafter, their protector and father, and at last at the end when Rabbi Steinmann met him, he was in love with the woman and the child and they accompanied him to New York.

PRAGUE, June 1945

Rabbi Steinmann met through the friendship of the poet, Halil Kantor, another woman—Lotte Schon, a half-Jew, a whole Jew, a Jew by descent of maternity, kept in ignorance by the caution of her father.

It happened shortly after the assassination of Reinhard Heydrich that at eleven o'clock in the morning Lotte Schon was shopping in a quiet square of the city of Prague when its single thoroughfare was blocked by a detachment of the S.S.

Speaking through a bullhorn a young lieutenant instructed everyone in the square to stop in their tracks (there were perhaps sixty people in all, milling and chatting in the light spring rain—each drop enclosing a ray of dispassionate sun). The people froze as they had been instructed, and a middle-aged sergeant accompanied by soldiers with machine guns counted off every third person— No No Yes No No Yes No No Yes— until twenty people, men women children, Jews Christians, were separated and assembled. By then every window upon the square was crowded with eyes peering beneath shades hastily drawn.

The lieutenant shouted out the decree: "In all the squares of the city of Prague at this moment every third person of wanderers and passers-by will be shot to remind you all that the criminal murder of Reich's Protector Heydrich will not go unpunished. A thousand today. A thousand tomorrow. It will go on until the murderers are delivered to us." And with a motion of his gloved hand a detachment of riflemen arranged themselves in order before a stone wall. The twenty persons were lined before the wall. Lotte Schon was among them. The lieutenant ordered the detachment to attention. There were cries and screams. There were curses and heroic "Long live" to this and that. But only Lotte Schon, her face pressed like the others against the cold stone, did not cry out nor did she weep. As the lieutenant called for the detachment to become ready she turned and with a deliberate step walked into the midst of the detachment. A half-minute passed during which the lieutenant might well have shot her down, but he did not. No one stopped her. As she disappeared out of the square she heard the gunfire. She did not turn back but continued to walk. At each step she expected to be dead. But she remained alive until the hour of her coming to us.

VILNA, May 1945

An engineer by profession, Erich Saft was obliged to leave his young wife one evening in the ghetto and steal out to find a doctor who could assist him in the abortion of the child which his wife was carrying, for he was resolved that he would not leave yet another to die. It was moreover known that women who were pregnant would be selected and deported to their death more speedily than those not requiring special attention.

They had lived for several months in the basement of the building which they owned, and their superintendent, a warm-hearted gentile, had allowed them to encamp in their own cellar. As he passed through the darkened streets at the hour of curfew he heard the sounds of a piano playing. It was one of the *Gnossiennes* of the French composer Erik Satie. He was familiar with the music of Satie. He came closer to the window.

He saw a living room, bright with candlelight and a young boy —a boy of perhaps fourteen—playing the music of Erik Satie.

He did not summon the doctor after all, but returned to the cellar. Six months later his wife gave birth to a son. She died in childbirth, but the child was taken by the warm-hearted gentile. He survived, and father and son were reunited and came forth to the Society.

DACHAU, May 1945

Dr. Klay told us of this story (he had observed its unfolding —in fact, participated in its denouement): it concerned Pieter, an eight-year-old boy, who had come late to the camp because he was born in a mountainous region of Austria where only two Jewish families lived. Peasants had sheltered him until they were denounced toward the end of 1944. His parents were already dead, but he had been preserved not because of his age but because he seemed to the officialdom of the camp to be so strikingly fair that his racial contamination was thought questionable.

When Dr. Klay arrived at Dachau—more than a week after its capture by the Allies—he found Pieter playing in the field before the camp. He had dug a shallow hole, scooping out the dirt with a tin cup, arranging flowers—field daisies and buttercups—around its edge and forcing himself to lie in sepulchral estate, hands crossed and at rest. After a moment he would laugh, jump up, dig the hole a little deeper, augment the arrangement of the flowers and repeat the ritual. Dr. Fisher observed the repetition of the game for many minutes and then interrupted its third performance at the finale of repose.

"Who has died?" Dr. Klay asked.

"Hitler," the boy replied, smiling.

"But don't you know, child, that Hitler is *really* dead?"

"No, that is not true," the child responded gravely.

"But it is. I tell you that he is dead. I will show it to you in a newspaper."

"He cannot be dead," the child protested. "I am still alive."

The common ingredient of these tales is not alone to celebrate the victory of survival. What is implicit in all of them is a turning upon the delicate hinge of life and death.

271

I recall reading during the time of my scholastic enterprise in the city of Debrecen many works of psychoanalytic theory. There was one which broached the question of infant suicide. The Viennese doctor, Sigmund Freud, had already persuaded me of the existence of sexual fantasy and enactment in children —and bizarre as such a notion was (so totally at odds with the naïvetés of purity and perfection in which my childhood was passed)—it was even more strange for me to encounter the idea of child suicide.

The deprivation and despair to which a little one must be brought that it would not alone fantasize and later recollect but, in fact, execute the project of suicide struck me as so horrendous as to shred my vision of a universe ruled by a just and forbearing God. I had read in those same days of my life all of the works of Fyodor Mikhailovich Dostoevsky and recalled not alone Dostoevsky's fictional account of such events (but I ascribed those to imaginative extremity) but his narration of the desolated child who actually jumped to her death, crucifix in hand. That seemed a confirmation from life, but then her despair was well advanced and her misery and morbidity seemed amply justified, supported by the drunkenness, beatings, foul poverty which surrounded her life. In those days I said to myself—over and over again—life, life, didn't that child see any other prospect for life? She did not. She saw less the prospect of life than she did the release of death. Death was life, a richer, more complete, more peaceful alternative to a life which was barren and empty as death should be. The child reversed the realities.

What incredulity, therefore, when I encountered many years later the description of orphaned children in the clinic of a South American city, their parents dead from quake and fire which had devastated their homes and left them abandoned (they were already hungry and ill). In the months that followed, many died, not for lack of food, nor for lack of medical attention, not for want of formal succor, but for the lack of a tender voice, a gentle and consistent hand, an open window with bright sunlight. The reporter and interpreter of this phenomenon makes it clear that they starved themselves out of the world for lack of human food. It was then that I came to conceive of human love and divine compassion as a sub-

stance—a quite material substance—without which men would will themselves to death. And how much more so the disaster of little ones who have not yet learned to ignore the odors of death which abound in the world. Not having addressed themselves as "I"—still fists of need and grasping hands beating upon humid air—how can it be imagined that they would be able to endure the indifference, no, the brutal flight of the world from the cries of their deprived existence? Those orphaned babes had no alternative but to die, to starve themselves to death, to strangle on their cries, to constrict and condense themselves out of the world in the same manner as they were condensed and pressed into it. They had no mother to which to return and no world to enter. They perished by aboriginal will.

Now if you allow the extension of my theory.

Each of us carries about within us an unperished infant and me that will never mature. We molt into life and we grow toward normal death, but we reserve to ourselves, deep inside, buried under the deposit of the world, filtered through dreams and nightmares, covered by the blue and pink swaddlings of memory the unmatured infant. The motor infant is gone, transposed into willed movements and skilled manipulations; the rosy abundance of childish flesh is trimmed to the utility of the world; emotions are habituated to expectations and defeats; and healthy intelligence instructs the self and discriminates among the opportunities of creaturehood—but with all this learned sophistication, all this trained and conditioned optimism and frustration there remains hidden in our breast an altar to the ageless child. At the feet of this altar, shimmering with the gold film of memory and bowered with flowers and sweetmeat offerings picked out of the everyday of our lives, we preserve the idyll of what we were (or perhaps of what we never were for quite long enough) and which we never wanted to leave behind.

It is not that we choose to return to that childhood, to slough off the tasks of our world, to give up the semblance of our growth and maturity; rather it is that we keep this altar cleaned and ready for our visitation of worship, and there, refreshed by the deathless image of our beatific dependency (the days when all was done for us, the time of our exquisite passivity), we are strengthened to return, to come out again into the world of men. All men have these altars, and their images of the little god upon that altar are as varied as the selves they become, but of the magic power of their infancy I have no doubt. It is as an infant god that we first come to understand the divine narcissism from which all creation and life proceeds.

There are times such as ours (and there are always those times, whether in the imagination of a novelist or in the grim episodes of single children dying away from the loveless air they breathe) when vast communities of men are pressed against the wall of their secret altar and forced to choose— old men who would have died shortly, young men and women who had before them all the expectation of life and again small children—these who had passed out of infancy, receding from the altar of their infant godhead, lengthening in the perspective of time the distance which separates their outward eyes from the altar of their refreshment and reparation— whether it is worthwhile, much less possible, to endure such a world.

There have been millions upon millions of deaths in our time in which there was no choice, and there were others, countless thousands, who determined to enter into death as a better way than that of life patient before death. But there were still those others who retired to their secret altar and willed to die and cursed not the enemy nor screamed out wrath, but cursed God, smashed the altar, and cried, starved, sickened, throttled themselves into death. And not even of these can we speak of ignobility.

There is never ignoble death—who is to say that the sniveler, the cringer, the whiner, the pleader dies ignobly? He is a dead man, and the living judge only against the secrecy of their own altar, the fantasy of their own invulnerability and the imagination of their own heroism.

The company of our survivors (myself among them) was formed from those who were able to grow and continue to worship at their secret altars. We managed somehow to trip the hinge to life. We might all of us have died and there would be none for Simon to bear off on his eagle wings.

The decision of the bullet or the gas is not within our con-

274

trol. What each of us controlled was the vision of that altar, for I have known since the earliest time of my life that I had eaten well of the fruit and condiments of love.

Paris at the end of the war had lost its lucidity. It was no longer the city of clarity and discrimination, the virtues which, by extrapolation, one applies not alone to the ideas of Frenchmen but to their cities and civilities as well. Of course, I could not see when I arrived at the Gare de l'Est, but Simon held my hand and described the dirty stone and the begrimed glass through which we passed out into the boulevards. The air was fresh but voices were sharp. I did not know French, nor did Simon Stern. We were somewhat at a loss, therefore, leading our raggle-taggle of survivors to the Rothschild mansion outside the city where we were to assemble and encamp until transportation to the United States was arranged.

There were two hundred of us wearing army greatcoats over skirts of tattered fabric and pants grey and green. Our languages were a confusion of tongues, German suppressed, Yiddish abashed, Polish growled, Russian exuberant, and tatters of intimacies from other dialects and Hebrew. We had gathered the nucleus of our fevered vision, for there were among us skilled surgeons, engineers, poets, historians and archivists, cobblers and electricians, as well as partisan fighters (Jews who had vanished into the forests of Poland, Byelorussia, the Ukraine, Bavaria to forage the land and harass the enemy). We did not question their reasons for joining our society. The living determined to live. That was all. That was enough.

To the "Rothschild château." The very phrase stretched upon our tongues, elongated into a whisper of wonder.

The heat of late day slid away to evening cool. We tramped down the highway from the last train station toward the château, sequestered behind trees. We marched in our fashion down the long winding road which continued more than a mile from the highway to the château, past the gatekeeper's house, past the stables, past the greenhouse, past the arbor of fruit trees, and there before us, spreading out as though an asylum had been hidden from public view, were our mad comrades, talking to themselves, walking in discourse, lying upon the ground, disporting upon stone benches, chattering like birds who had no care but to sing until dusk.

We came upon them, our two abreast of survivors, our Simon Stern remnant, to take up lodgings until our transport was ready. And it was there, amidst that assembly, that our eyes turned toward a moaning figure, slithering across the grass, his hands sliding down upon his drawn-up legs, his hands pressing down the legs and stretching upward, shimmying upon the ground, foot by foot, dragging himself at first and, moments later, pushing himself methodically and, at the end of some minutes, angling and turning his body like a man become serpent. As we came near to the spectacle, he saw us, that shaven head with sunken eyes, and he rose up, a beast of the ages, and bowed to us: "I am Janos Baltar, a survivor. Let me welcome you to the château of the Rothschilds and invite you to our performance tomorrow of the play of Job for which you see I am rehearsing."

The tableau was in progress upon the unmannered lawn which flowed around copies of Roman statuary and stone benches, fountains with urinating cupids and bunches of pruned dwarf trees. Here and there groups of refugees sat, staring into the sunlight or face down embracing the living earth, looking perhaps at colonies of orderly ants.

A thousand survivors, to which ours were the most recent addition, greeted each other and excavated common names and birthplaces, countries of origin and friendly dynasties. There were those who had nothing left in the world but the fellowship of being rationalists from Lithuania or having once visited the yeshiva at Slobotka. Others, however, could speak Russian or Hungarian together and recall summertimes in the countryside near Budapest.

The tableau was in progress and the actors gestured without speaking.

Simon Stern had received a private room in what had been servants' quarters in the northwest annex of the château. The night had been restless, and cicadas clacked until morning

276

and birds had replaced their repetitive insistence with a spirited chorus to a hoot owl. I closed my eyes but I did not sleep. Simon paced the room. The morning came, and after we had said our prayers and eaten our breakfast of bread and coffee we had gone outside to rest in the sunlight.

The actors were assembling upon a terraced enclosure, a semicircle of stone dotted with urns, surrounded by geranium bushes in bloom. A hand came into mine and lifted me from the warmth of the sun and led me toward the open theater. I sat among unknown bodies and dared not feel around me, but after a moment the hand returned to mine and sat down beside me. It was a woman's hand, the clasp was thin, the bones small, the skin rough but without aggression, confident and calm. I did not dare to ask who held my hand.

The players began to enact, and a voice, the voice of the narrator, opulent and vast like an actor's, the voice of the Speaker (he who had introduced himself as Baltar) spoke the words, his words, I now realize.

"Our players here, all amateurs at acting, as they were amateurs at surviving, will present for you this morning the heartrending and lamentable tragedy of the patriarch Job, millionaire of Uz, who (unlike our benefactors here, the good Rothschilds who had the wisdom to parcel and sequester their wealth in many places, in furniture and goods, in banks and houses, jewels and vineyards) had it all tied up, as did we, in lives and tangible substance, and the tragedy wrought upon him by a vain divinity unsure of his power and a clever willful ironist, Satan, the adversary (called by the book 'a Son of God'), who had the fruitful insight to use poor Job to test God.

"Job is dressed in one of Madame Rothschild's afghan coverlets, his head poking through the pistil of a rosette. He isn't even thirty years, our Job, but he plays with the gravity of a man of eighty. You must see him. Look up, straight ahead, and I'll describe everything to you. Friend, what is your name?"

"Nathan," I answered her.

"A gentle name, Nathan. I will be gentle," she said, and I

felt her smile warmly and she lifted my hand and held it to her cheek.

Job sat upon the stone bench, his tapestry robe gathered about him. He sat stroking his beard with contentment and gazed about the lawn with smiles and satisfaction when, of a sudden, there rushed onto the scene a young girl, her tunic skirt cut from the fabric of a prisoner's drab, her short wooden sword miming the retainers of Job's flocks and properties. She gesticulated mournfully. Another entered from behind the trees, this time a boy, similarly robed in classical costume, tearing upon his hair and rending his garments, and then, another and another until the four bringers of the tidings of depredation were all before Job, gesticulating the tragedy which the Speaker of the drama declaimed: "O Master, beloved of God, you, good saint of forbearance and peace, opulent and content, sitting here gazing upon your green lawns and thinking of the good fortune with which God has heaped you for your virtue, let me inform you that your flocks are gone, stolen and plundered, your houses are buckled and collapsed, and your properties seared with fire, your vineyards blown away, and your daughters, all three, and your seven sons, dining in the luxury of your eldest's house are all dead, their skulls cracked like wheat kernels, their brains and hearts spilled upon the ground like chaff. All that you own is gone. All that you love is dead. Is it you, Job, who asked of your sons that they be certain to make the benediction lest there be evil in them that is not atoned? O Job, dear Job, poor Job, how you have mistaken the order of the universe."

"And Job is rending his garments, Nathan. He tears upon the cloth and splits the rosette and his undergarments show. They are dirty, Nathan."

Job rises and leaves the semicircle of stone and urns. The first scene of the tableau is completed, and now God the Father enters upon the stage, a tall man, his face caked with white flour, an unearthly God, whose eyes seem like the orbs of planets winking through the whiteness of space. He stands in lonely contemplation. Upon the stage four messengers come, without wings, though they have staffs and wear pouches on their sides for the keeping of messages and the collection of alms.

278

The messengers bow down before the white divinity and brush their hair upon the stone floor of the stage, but one angel rises before the others and puts forth his hand to touch the fold of the divine garment. Bestirred, the God withdraws from him, shrinking from the touch. The angel now smiles and circles the God, surveying his height and his depth, remarking his menacing aspect and then beside him, begins to address him in a whisper, cupping his hand to his mouth.

"O divine Father," the Speaker hissed, "I have done what you permitted. I have taken from Job all his possessions and power, but what are these if he is alive and strong. Who would deny your power and grace if they are well? There is no fatality in money. Only fools would curse your dominion losing all but having still the energy and strength of life. Let me, I beg you, test him in the flesh. Let me afflict him and I will show you his worth. Men are liars and this one no less than all others will deny you." The God raises his hands to his face and draws down lines upon the whiteness of his countenance, marking the flow of his tears, for when God thinks he cries.

"He wags his head, our player. It is a mysterious art, to play this God. Do you think he will give Satan permission? Do you think so, Nathan?"

The God weeps again, and the Speaker of the drama calls out, his head rising from behind an urn. "You see, you children of the living God, that your Father weeps for you. That is a comfort, isn't it?" The divinity raises up the fallen angel from his abasement and puts his hand upon his head.

"He comforts him, Nathan," the voice said, warm with excitement. "And now the Lord stretches forth his hand to comfort the beseeching of the Adversary, a child of his no less than all of you (and that's the trouble with the universe, isn't it—God's sympathy is so general). The divinity opens his arms to the universe beneath and about him and a smile comes to the face of Satan. The God has agreed that Satan may proceed to test the steadfastness of the upright Job. 'You may try him, son and adversary. Try him to the marrow of his life, but let him live. I tell you that Job will not desert or abandon me.' A marvel, isn't it? God is concerned lest

Job abandon him. No thought about the trial to which Job has been subjected. Very much like our brother Isaac under the knife of Abraham. All glory to God, all hail to the patriarch. Abraham is acquitted of the thought of murder, not because he repents the iniquity of his imagination but because God rewards his steadfastness with an unblemished ram summoned from the thicket to die in Isaac's stead. Children of God, sons of Israel, who is the savior and who the saved? Who the sinner and who the sinned against? Who innocent and who guilty? Job, the sons and daughters of Job, the Son of God and his adversary, or the divine arranger, the courtesan of the heavens. Forgive me. This scene is over. I have talked too long."

Job returns to the stage, his face and body now shrouded by his tapestry of Empire luxury. He stands erect and un-bowed and slowly uncovers his flesh—nakedness to the loin-cloth that conceals his privates—his flesh like a speckled cur, dots of color drawn over his flesh, lesions of blue and yellow staining his thighs and markings of brown and black making his face a confusion—is that eye or boil? both are red, and water spouts from both. Job steps from the stage and slowly circles the audience, and as he passes around he plucks grass from the earth and shreds it upon his head and takes up the mouldering manure which lies beneath the bushes and rubs it upon his forehead and stains his red garment with its filth.

Job mourns his condition with the green and brown of growth and putrescence. He completes the circuit of the viewers, and they, sensing his tragic condition, fix their eyes to the darting figure of the Speaker who lies now curled like a serpent at the perimeter of the stony stage and exclaims: "Look and see what it is that God does to Job who had nothing but love and affection for him. First, depredation and death—all his property burned and his children slain—and now even to the crown and soles of Job the boils multiply and Job, in pain, sits down to wonder at such a universe. Intermission and I will address you." But the serpent does not rise and assume the form of men—rather, he inches his way like a cripple, slithering to the center of the stage, and there like a snake with the head of a man, a man-serpent, he discourses reasonably to us about the nature of the universe:

"You watch a tragedy. An unfinished tragedy. Tragic so far, but an incomplete tableau. And all of you say in your hearts: There is no tragedy in the Holy Word. How is there tragedy when the word of God is true and trustworthy? There is no tragedy in Israel, you say. But *you* know so much better, do you not? We know all about tragedy. We believed well, did we not? Women sang to their children before the open pits, and fathers held the hands of their sons, but the finger pulled the trigger and we toppled over into our graves. Untragic! Who was there to have pity and fear? All those who watched were not spectators. There were no actors nor audience. How can there be tragedy even here in the sad story of Job the millionaire of the East, for Job will know the answer. They will try him, those scrupulous moralists who will come to dissect his heart and his motives, but Job will outlast them. We have neglected to show you the advice of Job's wife. 'Curse God and die,' she says. But that is no advice. Job might well have plunged a knife into his breast and given out a curse, but a curse is no reproach to God nor any vindication of Job. Job does not trivialize. He holds on instead. He holds on and makes the righteousness of his comforters vulgar and cheap. He holds on and humiliates Satan. He holds on and embarrasses God. And so, like Job, we have held on. We must be proud and humiliate the world.

"And now let us proceed to the conclusion of the play."

While the Speaker of the play would speak I sat very still. Nearby a voice buzzed, explaining to another, perhaps a child, the movements of the players, but when the Speaker crawled upon his belly to the center of the stage and spoke out his rage all were as silent as I. The woman's hand took up my own and pressed it to her lips and bit upon my flesh, but I did not cry out, for her terror was like my own and the pain of her terror before the Speaker's vision of our world bit into my own. The Speaker was the figure of death around whose hand we twisted as in the medieval metaphor which conceives the capitulation of Eve to the serpent as the bringing of death into the community of men. But we Jews have no redeemer who releases us from death, no Virgin

281

the answer to Eve. We are simply Job naked and covered with boils.

The Speaker persuaded me at that hour and I drew close to my companion. She whispered into my ear. "Later you will love me." I shuddered, for I had never known a woman and I was a man grown, with a beard, and a history of misery behind me. What can come forth from a blind man?

The tableau began once more and the figure of Job was seated now upon a broken marble column and about him figures of the comforters, arranged in quiet confidence, gestured slowly, explaining and admonishing, expostulating with pointed fingers and raised eyebrows. Then there arose the similitude of thunder as cymbals clattered and corrugated metal was rattled in the summer air, and though the sun did not darken and birds continued to twitter in the trees of the Rothschild garden, gloom lowered upon the assembly. And suddenly Job lifted his head and bestirred himself, hearing with an ear (by which men could scarcely hear) the noise of the world, and though the comforters continued to mime their studied instruction and expand upon their moralisms, Job stood up in transport and heard from amid the vast clatter a spectral voice—as out of the cleavage of the earth or conducted humming from the center of a speeding meteor —the voice of existence. And after hearing that voice, Job bent down before the world and opened his arms wide and into the center where his arms stood open there came three daughters and seven sons and messengers (who had earlier brought to Job the news of his disasters), one with crook and the other with stave and a third with length of halter rope and yet another with scythe in hand to symbolize that to Job had been restored asses and camels and flocks of sheep and wheat and granaries laden with the goods of the earth. And Job wiped from his face the boils of his affliction and covered his nakedness once more and sat down again upon the stool of stone and retired to the contemplation of God and his gracious bestowals.

"It all ends well, sons and daughters of men," the Speaker rasped, stepping forward and closing the imaginary curtains upon the players, who froze in the positions of their final enactment. "Job is relieved by God and Satan is discomfited

and the sons and daughters of Job are come alive and twofold
are the cattle and produce of Job. But sons and daughters of
men, not to you is this? Yours are buried beneath the earth
of Europe, and your sons and daughters, issue of your loins,
are not restored to you. And there is no less righteousness in
you. Our only sin, children of men, is that we are not God
but know well how true Gods should behave towards us.

"Conclude, then, this tableau of the life and sorrow and
regeneration of Job by joining with me in my closing hymn
to our Lord God, protector and sustainer of Israel.

"Let us rise and listen well, with eyes closed and heads
bowed down.

> "We do not curse you
> We will carry your boils forever
> Ashes and manure are upon us
> We are not crushed and never will be.
> There is no tragedy in us.
> And we believe in you
> But yours is a foolish regency
> The crown of your dominion is askew
> Your scepter broken
> Your face blinded
> And though we honor you
> We shall never trust you again."

The young woman led me away from the lawn. The audience
dissolved and small groups congregated about the stone stage
awaiting the next event, the next distraction in the festivity
of survival. She drew me toward her, and as if leaning upon
her breast she bore my weight leading me more rapidly than
I could have known to sightless walk and we began to descend, feeling our way along stone walls into the basement
of the château.

We stopped and I heard her say, "Here. Here. Stop." She
pressed her hands upon my shoulders and I gave way, sinking down to a bed of leaves. "The leaves of last autumn.
They came through that window above you," and I could
feel the summer heat slide into our cul-de-sac. Before us was
the entrance to the wine cellar of the château, barred by an
iron gate secured with lock and chain behind which stood

yet another oak door. There was no light but that panel of sun through which our autumnal bed had blown. She opened me to my nakedness and I could feel my restless member arise within her hands. My cheeks rose heavy with blood and flushed, I poured out upon her breasts which had come forth like choice fruits from their cupboard shelter a thousand kisses. And my kisses upon her neck and upon her soft cheeks and upon her breasts, and then lower still, touching my tongue to her watered garden I gave out my love to all those whom all those years in solitariness and pain I had longed to kiss, but kissing air, kissing fantasy, kissing dreams I had not kissed a woman.

It is never to late to give up the solitude of one's virginity. I would not be rescued from death by a quintessential virgin, and if it be desire under the eaves of Rothschild opulence, the eve of my growing into maturity—however, blind, with suffering behind me (let me be done with the pain of what I knew before I had experienced the pleasure which can be found in this world)—then this Eve of mine may tempt me many times and I will give over and know nakedness in darkness. We loved and held each other loving and I cried and she cried at my crying and wished that I might see her tenderness, but I claimed no need for seeing, feeling all within the nerve ends of her touch, moving over my body like pebbles in a stream, touching, darting, flowing over my still-youthful flesh.

"Who are you?" I asked her late in the day and she did not answer me. "Will you speak?" And there was no voice. I had awakened from a wearied sleep. We had loved three times and leaves covered my face. "Who are you?" I must have asked out of my sleep and I neither heard the answer, for there was none, but I imagined hearing a voice comforting my abandon and a young girl I had known in my youth in Gaza had given me a bright orange to suck and I asked once more "Who are you," and a grown woman who sat in the market of Safed where I had smiled upon her long braided hair, wild-faced like a gypsy from India, extended to me a palm covered with powdered cinnamon and blown its sweetness into my nostrils.

"Who are you?" I asked again, awake, and felt about me,

but there was no one. The woman was gone. She had loved me in my blindness and both of us were fulfilled, she and I, knowing not the other, but having renewed the tenderness of our flesh, it was valuable to be alive.

It took me a long time to pass out of my underground bower, but at last I came up out of the dark place into day setting to dusk and heard voices and nearby was the voice of the Speaker talking more of the tableau of Job and accepting the uncomprehending appreciation of the survivors. I had been blind for more than four months, but it was still exceptionally difficult for me to discriminate between wakefulness and sleep. To be sure, in the day when I was about and ambulating through the obstacles of the world I could not afford to examine the luxurious pathology of my difficulty, but at night when I put myself away to rest, the difficulty became monumental. And on that day—the day of the play of Job in the recension of Baltar, the Speaker, and my discovery of enraptured flesh—I could not sleep at all, I could not stay awake at all, my eyes wandered in my head, and lights from other worlds, colors and sensations moved through my sensorium like the optics of paradise. Asleep, awake, how should I know?

Simon had gathered me in at some late hour. I had sat alone in the vast reception hall of the château where beddings and cushions were arranged like the clumped seating of picnics and grating voices swirled about me like winds of dust. She had not come forward again? My hand lay before me like a palate awaiting another offering of grape and almond, but it grew heavy with anxiety and my palm perspired. I withdrew it.

"It is very late," Simon whispered to me. "Aren't you tired, Nathan?"

I was and I rose like a child who is only too willing to be led away to rest, already beslumbered and past the recall of the day's events which he would nonetheless wish to have go on and on, endlessly, beyond pleasure and satisfaction, until tears of weariness and joy break forth. Simon led me by the hand, walking near me, his head occasionally brushing my chest as he leaned forward to open a door and guide me through its way. In our quarters he undressed slowly, talking slowly of his plans for the gathering of his community, of the loyalty of philosopher Klay and the intelligent wit of Steinmann. I was already his ears. I sat, I recollect, crumpled upon the cot awaiting Simon to tell me that it was time to sleep.

"Should I turn out the light?" he asked finally, and our game proceeded. The question was already his distracted custom and I, like many other species, saw better at night when all lights were extinguished and my darkness, commingled with the darkness of all things, enabled me to make discriminations which colors of the day forbade. There are many shades of black. How long it was, how many hours later I do not know, but the door opened.

"It is Janos Baltar," the voice announced.

In the day, from the distance of the sunlit stage, Baltar had been a voice, succulent and insinuating. His quaquaversal movement, described to me and perceived by the darting quality of his voice, its distance and nearness, its alternation of resonance, suggested a body, motile as quicksilver. When he entered the room he surveyed it rapidly, and though it was dark (only a night light burning in the corner where Simon had been reading before lying down to sleep) he seemed to engorge everything. Those eyes, like a raven, black and unsettling, swiveled in their sockets, pecking at the surface of the objects of the room, people and things together, but while the eyes moved, his head remained stationary, fixed like a pylon sunk in a block of concrete. It was massiveness and strength which struck everyone who came to know him with premonitory foreboding. His presence suggested a cumbersome immensity at first reassuring until one observed his way of moving. Then the anxiety would begin, for his movement was not that of a large and encumbered mastodon as one might have imagined—and hoped. He moved his enormous body with meticulous care, as though each foray into space had been studied and estimated, circumspect, his feet feeling out the terrain before he stepped, sliding out to check the surface before committing his weight. And yet his care did not obstruct rapidity of movement, for he could (as we had learned) wind and swivel, slither and careen as one who had

286

a serpentine physique. He moved therefore little. He had no need to move except as adjunct to his voice, which like a ventriloquist, he cast and threw.

"I thought you might come to visit," Simon answered. He too had been awake. "I saw you—how shall I say—lurking in the corridor. You could have asked and I would have invited you."

"I wasn't certain that you would," Baltar answered, momentarily distracted.

"Why not? I am always available."

"I thought the play might have offended you."

"Not at all. It was fierce, perhaps too theatrical, but not at all offensive. More often than not I agreed with your commentary."

"So. Good. May I come in?"

"You have already," Simon mocked. "But enter further. Sit down. That rattan chair, our only one."

Baltar descended upon the chair as in times to come he would descend upon a thousand chairs until arms, rest, seat disappeared, and he seemed to float free, only his feet placed together having contact with something firm and immovable. He was not obese, for such massiveness is not obesity. Strength perhaps, yes, strength, muscles of strength rose like a collar from his neck. He seemed of iron. Arms swelled out the black gabardine he wore winter and summer, and his chest was so impressive that one felt that if he breathed deeply or shouted, the buttons on his jacket would fly off. His face, unlined, without the scars of maturation, was impassive and ageless, though he was not much older than forty years. His face was as if carved in glacial stone or like the plaster of a death mask.

"Do I disturb your friend?"

"Nathan. I don't think so. Nathan, does Baltar disturb you?"

I should have answered that he did. "Not at all, Simon Stern. I'll listen and not speak, if you don't mind."

"As you wish, Nathan. Go to sleep if we tire you. And now"—turning once more to Baltar who sat quietly, his hands resting asplay upon his knees—"what is it that I can do for you?"

"Simply this. I wish to continue on to New York with you."

"You wish me to rescue you?" Simon asked, incredulously. "You seem quite rescued, quite in control. I doubt that we can do anything for you."

"That's true, perhaps that's true. But I can do something for you."

"Surprising," Simon mused, not without irony.

"You shouldn't be surprised. I am, as you have observed, a powerful man. My physique is no accident. I wasn't always powerful. Nor for that matter was I always theatrical. Both are accomplishments. I have been called for the past few years—*ein Grenze Mensch*. You know German. 'A limit-man.' That's what they called me at Ravensbrück and before that in the labor camps in Austria—I was in quite a few, from 1942 until now. I stayed alive by keeping at the limits, by dancing along the narrow ridge. It's no accident. I was a tightrope man. My balance is beautiful. These little feet. They have names, each of them. When I was on the high wire I used to speak to them as I'd slide them along the wire. I'm Rumanian. A Rumanian Jew who fled home and lived with gypsies, carnivals, circuses until my early twenties. That was a few years ago.

"And then something happened to me. It's not important. A personal matter. I gave up the circus and became a Hasid of the Belzer Rebbe. I was ignorant then. Not a speck of Jewish information. But I began to put weight in my head, build it the same way I had built my body. By the time I was through learning, I had picked up a lot. I knew Bible, the Psalms by heart, backwards and forwards (literally, you can test me—my memory is prodigious), *Shulhan Aruch*— all the useful laws and ways and means of interpreting them in good, solid style. I made myself helpful to small communities in Poland and Hungary, traveling around doing circus tricks, preaching like a *maggid* and answering questions of law. I wasn't a rabbi, but lots of these little communities didn't have a rabbi. Ignorant Jews, poor and ignorant, who wanted to be upright and learned. I helped them. I showed them how to walk the rope—not literally that, but you understand what I mean, how to steer a course between good and evil, how to tell whether a chicken egg has a speck of blood

288

in the white and what to do if you had to trade it to a gentile for a kosher egg. I was useful and I made my way in the world."

Simon listened to Baltar in a curious way. I had not known him long, but I was already familiar with his predictable mannerisms. He was behaving unusually. It was his ordinary custom to follow conversation like a child jumping across rocks in a pool. He would follow a conversation, his throat pushing along sounds and grunts, helping his interlocutor to speak by sharing with him the effort of speech. Talk was always committed action, transitive, a gesture of joy and play and whether or not he actually spoke, all the words were his, for they were spoken so totally to him, that they were somehow his alone. Conversation with Simon was therefore enthusiastic and abandoned, and the many who spoke with him made stupendous efforts to say everything, to open themselves to him with a complete trust. But all that I could hear that night was the voice of Baltar raised to the stone ceiling, absorbed and softened in the wooden beams, bouncing from the walls and muted in the hollows in which the faceted vitrails were set. His voice played the room and I could not determine whether he had sat upon the chair offered to him or was moving silently about the room. Simon was absolutely still.

"You are a very gifted man, Baltar," Simon said slowly.

"But will you have me?"

"No. I don't think so. I don't think so." Simon spoke deliberately, offering nothing more.

"But you need me," Baltar boomed, and his voice rose and dropped like a leaden plummet, aloft and then plunging with rage.

"That's precisely the point, dear Baltar. I am certain that we need you. But you must need us as well. There is no community without mutual need. I fear that you shall demand, and whatever your inestimable value to us—your strength and deftness—our community cannot bear new demands. All of us, no less myself than those I wish to help, are creatures who cannot support new demands. We cannot be belabored. We are already beset." Simon stopped. He had spoken with taut control, and his voice, sounding like the steady firmness of a cello muted in the minor mode. "But also, my friend, you must learn again to speak the truth."

"What is truth? I spoke as much as you need to know."

"Not nearly enough. Not enough by far. You spoke glitter and show, silver and gold dust thrown in my face. I cannot have this."

"You will have me. You wait and see."

"Perhaps. I am willing, but I must wait. Good night, Baltar."

A cock crowed. Morning was not far away. "Has he gone, Simon?"

"Yes. I thought you were asleep."

"I was frightened of him," I laughed nervously.

"You must not be afraid, Nathan. No harm will come to you."

"Not for myself, Simon Stern. For you. I was afraid for you."

"Yes. I understand that. He is a man of whom one can be afraid. It is not the last of him."

We did not sleep much that night. In the morning when the tower bell sounded, the noise of wakening flooded over us. It was good to drown in such sounds.

"Did you see my billfold, Nathan?" Simon asked. "I may have lost it. Perhaps it will turn up. Not much money though, and the papers are of no value. Sentimental documents mostly." Both of us knew that the billfold had not been lost. Later in the day when we returned to our room to rest before supper, the billfold was found under Simon's pillow. The money was gone—more than a hundred dollars—but all the letters including the annunciatory letter of his father, had been returned.

The population of our château shifted and settled during the days which followed, rising to nearly twelve hundred and falling off again, as wanderers and the displaced came and went, swelling our number by day for classes of orientation and study, declining by evening as many departed.

"When do we leave?" Simon asked Dr. Klay six days after our arrival.

"We have booked a ship sailing from Le Havre in three weeks' time. I've taken over the whole freighter. It's stripped down to carry refugees and the hold is being fitted with cots

290

and bedding. When our people are on board we can outfit them, distribute clothing, documents, information. Headquarters in New York is behaving very well. Much of the material we need has already arrived and is in warehouses dockside."

"And you, Steinmann? Are you tending to our friends?"

"They're doing well. There will be problems most certainly when they arrive in New York. Virtually no English at all and many of them are sick, but fortunately no contagious diseases. Mostly malnutrition of body and soul."

"Feed them both."

The weeks before the sailing were languorous and desultory. The heat was moderated by the breezes of the countryside, although the château was not very far from Paris. Visitors came and went. Baltar would appear in the morning, sometimes before the sun was up and we could not ascertain whether he had returned to Paris after supper or slept in the garden or by the side of the road. It wouldn't have mattered. It was not even three months since the war had ended, although France had been liberated earlier in the year. The roads were bloated with wanderers making their way back and forth. Thirty million people were on the roads of Europe. Everyone had lost his place. Baltar seemed never to have had one to lose.

During those weeks Baltar had presented another tableau, this time the story of Jonah come up from the belly of the whale to do reluctantly the work of the Lord at Nineveh. Baltar's comments had been no less acidulous than they had been about Job. God was a fool. Jonah was a fool. Job was a fool. He was tremendously persuasive. The Fast of the Ninth Day of Av was not far off and Baltar drew appropriate analogies between the ransoming of the penitent pagans of Nineveh and the destruction of pious Jerusalem—and lest his audience forget, the savaging of their own generation. Besides his theatrical productions, Baltar gave popular lectures on the history of the Jews in Biblical times, a pastiche of quotations from the Bible, occasional references to Rashi, and enactments of dramatic episodes—Moses and Pharaoh, Moses and Aaron, David and Absalom, with Baltar always taking both roles, delivering the lines of the Bible like dramatic dialogues. He was very popular. He received food and the offering of lodging which, to the best of our knowledge, he did not accept.

Baltar made several further efforts to win the friendship of Simon Stern, but he was politely rebuffed. Dr. Klay he sought to bribe—ridiculous—and Rabbi Steinmann he threatened, but both were unfamiliar with his earlier meetings with Simon Stern and were shocked and confused more than frightened. They discussed Baltar's insinuations and importunings with Simon, but Simon was reluctant to speak of Baltar. Dr. Klay, more than Rabbi Steinmann, had sensed the indefinable contagion of Baltar and whenever he came into his presence he would shrink to let him pass.

"There is something overwhelmingly physical about my fear of him," he explained one evening to Simon. "It's as though he were an enlarged slug or a giant mole—that vast body upon such delicate and graceful legs."

"You are not wrong, Philosopher, but what you say isn't enough. You need my view to make it complete," Simon replied with unusual aggressiveness, as though he had thought long about Baltar and had reached a conclusion. "How shall I put it? I too sense something unclean, but I sense no less something desperate and needful. You know, Dr. Fisher, that the universe is a tension. God makes alive and kills. What does Isaiah mean by that? Nothing less than that God contains within Himself the possibility of good and evil. He is creator. He is the unique creator. The Fathers of the Roman Church, our own medieval sages, undervalued the wholeness of Creation and restricted God to being good. They made evil an absence and a lack. I don't agree. I think evil is real, as real as the good and as constant in the universe. We can admire the diversity of evil no less than we applaud the achievement of the good. Both are from God. Evil men are highly imaginative, and perhaps it is the imagination from which the projects of evil come.

"Do you know the Talmudic controversy (reported baldly and with incomparable brevity) in which our Sages debated endless years whether it was good or not that God created the universe? At the conclusion they resolved that it were

292

better had not God created the universe, but since He did we have no choice but to make the best of it. What a daring controversy (unfortunately we know nothing of the argument, only its premise and its conclusion). They seem to admit that Creation is faulty. Now that is where I take issue with them. It is not faulty. It is simply complex, and its complexity consists in the fact that all men do evil, but desire the good. The self-righteous demand the punishment of the evildoers, but evildoers are never consistent. Even evildoers, on occasion, act with nobility and heroism. The remarkable fact is that Creation is mixed, as God is mixed. God contains and reconciles, what we—little things of His hand—must pull apart and examine, element by element, parsing reality into packets of virtue and vice. It isn't so.

"Baltar, now, this Baltar, whom we suspect. He comes to *us*—not to any other. He comes to us, not because he expects wealth or comfort or glory, but because he senses in us the counter to himself. He is right, and we will have him, but not until the time is right."

It was I who received the final overture and it was I who succumbed. I am not certain (although Simon is) long after the event, whether I was in fact saved by Baltar or tricked by him.

A few days before our community was to depart for Le Havre several detectives from the Sûreté appeared at the château and asked to see a refugee by the name of Sholom Lansky. It seemed that a number of homes in Paris had been burglarized during the past week, and jewels and silver of modest value had been stolen. The thefts had not been cleverly executed. The thief appeared more interested in the publicity of the theft than the value of the items stolen. Desks were pried open, books scattered, paintings scarred, and at each home—casually sealed during the crisis of war and still virtually unoccupied—objects of trivial value had been removed. The police were less baffled than annoyed by these thefts, for though the owners of these houses on Boulevard Raspail and Faubourg Saint-Honoré were prominent Parisians, they complained more out of a spirit of bourgeois violation than from any concern for the items lost. The evening before, a tip had been received at the Sûreté that one of the refugee Jews at the Rothschild château was responsible and a name was given.

My involvement, I believed, was a fortuity.

It was my evening custom to sit in the reception hall of the château where many of the refugees passed the night. Despite my blindness I was a man of physical presence, acute hearing, and a gift for languages. I was therefore the appointed guardian of the community, and very often refugees would approach and ask that I guard their meager belongings, handing me a cardboard suitcase tied with rope or a woman's purse belonging to a dead wife or sister containing a few photographs, letters, a gold watch, a wedding ring wrapped and sealed in oilcloth. To each I would promise the watchfulness of my blind eyes and off they would go sometimes to the neighboring village for a pastis or into Paris or simply for a walk in the fields. One man, the man in question, was a shifty fellow, an old furniture dealer from Cracow who had survived three years in Mauthausen and was passing through the way station of the château before leaving for Marseilles and Palestine. He kept a shoe box under his pillow, tied like a chest of Houdini's, with ropes and thongs and a thin chain. Lansky always asked me to keep his shoe box for him. Even if he was only going to the bathroom down the hall or out of doors to catch a bit of air, he would say "Nathan, watch my box for me," and place it in my hands. He was my most constant petitioner. Baltar observed this and said to me, "He trusts you a lot, doesn't he?"

"They all do," I think I answered. I was not aware that Baltar was so often nearby.

I was sitting in my accustomed place on a window bench near Lansky's floor bedding when the officers entered the room. Someone pointed out Lansky to them and they approached him. A nervous silence fell upon the twenty or so people in the room.

"Sholom Lansky?" they asked.

"Me?"

"Are you Sholom Lansky?" the Frenchmen said.

"Yes. What do they want?" Lansky called out in Yiddish.

Baltar came forward and began to translate. "The police have a warrant to search your belongings."

"Me? Why?" Lansky screamed, snatching the shoe box from under his pillow, and holding it crushed tight like a doll beneath his chin. "It's private. It's all I have left. It's private."

One of the officers bent down and wrested it from him and began to open it. With a cry Lansky jumped up and rushed toward me, screaming, "You bastard! You bastard! You told them. You looked. You told them." He struck me in the face with his fists, all the while screaming obscenities at me. It was when he pulled a knife and was about to stab me that Baltar intervened, striking Lansky's arm with such force that the knife flew across the room and Lansky doubled over in pain.

The police were uninterested in the violence. Baltar wasn't quick enough to stop the beating, but he saved me from a wound, perhaps even a fatal wound. I was full of gratitude.

The policeman opened the box and Lansky collapsed to the floor, weeping hysterically. In the box they found some jewels and silver. They also found ashes and bits of charred bone. The officers spilled out the ashes and Lansky fainted. When he was revived they took him away.

I was so overwhelmed by the episode I did not think clearly when Baltar said to me minutes later: "I saved your life, Nathan Gaza. Now save mine. Speak to Simon Stern. Beg him to take me to America."

I did. I spoke with Simon Stern. I left the reception hall as Lansky was being led away, handcuffed to an officer. I felt Baltar about me. I went to Simon in our quarters and began to speak with him, hesitantly, for I knew his reservations about Baltar and was aware of the magnitude of the decision which I had been charged—by fear, by implicit threat, by ambivalent gratitude—to force upon my friend and leader. I described the circumstances, the person of Sholom Lansky, his secret box and its contents, the police, his cursing and his assault. Simon listened to my story and then began to write in my open palm, over and over again, with the nail of his index finger, the word NO. I did not understand and my confusion settled into anguish, for I feared to give Baltar yet another refusal.

"I do not believe the story," Simon said emphatically. "It

295

is not true," he repeated, continuing all the while to indent his refusal into my perspiring palm. "It is not true, but there is now a new truth. Our friend, Janos Baltar, is dangerous. I have no doubt but that poor Lansky is innocent and I will make certain the restitutions are done and that Dr. Klay sees to his release, whatever the cost. But I ask myself, Why should Baltar confect such an intricate deceit? All to elicit the rage and terror he had observed in poor Lansky? All to turn that rage against you? All to save you in order that I might save him? What is this secret of Baltar? What is his past? Other men, more prudent and circumspect than I, would begin to investigate, would send emissaries and inquiries to spy out the secret reason for his extraordinary passion to join our small and select community. But I think otherwise.

"You know, Nathan, what I believe. I believe what we are taught. Were it not for the evil imagination of men there would not be houses and homes, granaries and fields, wives and progeny. The evil imagination—that men wish to survive their own death—ensures that life goes on; that, in fact, life does survive beyond death. The very heart of the struggle between good and evil, between Baltar and ourselves, is that we are not all good and he could not be wholly evil. Repentance. Turning. Turning away. Turning back. Returning. These motions of regeneration are what the Jewish people must always stand for. I admit, Nathan, that I suspect Baltar. Baltar is danger. But I shall accept him.

"Know only this, friend, Baltar no less than ourselves enjoys a conditional existence. He must live up and I shall watch out for him, even though it may appear, from time to time, that he deceives me."

Janos Baltar was the last survivor to be selected. I am horrified, but I use the verb nonetheless. Selected. Selected by an officer deputed to strike off names against a list. To one side. Step to one side. All those whose names are called step to one side. And the names would be called. Those names would die. The rest, not looking behind them, would break rank to despair and hope. "Not today," they would sigh with relief.

And what is it for Simon Stern to select to life. Any different for us who had battled death like the seven plagues, beat-

ing our arms against the locusts of death, scratching against the murrain of death, feeling against its darkness? No difference. Were there any in all the camps who had counted upon the selection of Simon Stern and, disappointed, died of hope lost? Not really. The selection was random and for no explicit reason as was theirs. They chose the sick, but some were not that sick. They chose the insane but some were not so mad. They ended choosing the ugly but even they were not that ugly. And Simon Stern? He chose from a logic no less obscure —the whim of life, the ember of passion, these were what he judged. There would have been tens of thousands that he might have chosen. Hundreds of thousands. Millions. All who survived should have been chosen, but he could choose only a remnant.

Why then Janos Baltar? No different from the others. Random. Chance. Fortuitous. And I say that was right. Any reason, any logic, any public philosophy of selection would have been an unbearable parody. It would have been right for someone to assassinate Simon Stern (or crucify him) had he examined teeth, or listened to heartbeats, or stethoscoped the lungs of his selected—physical or spiritual. He did not. He chose from feeling.

There were only two days more before our contingent was to depart for Le Havre. Baltar was already making himself invaluable. He had learned the names of all of the members of our community. He would approach them singly and in groups, questioning them, ascertaining their condition, their hopes and expectations, making note of their specific needs and requests and forwarding them to Dr. Klay or to Rabbi Steinmann, depending upon whether the request was speculative or practical. Those questions which he could presume to answer himself he did, and although I think some of his notions eccentric and perverse, he seemed to satisfy most curiosities. Simon Stern was beginning, tentatively, to be sure, to reconsider his judgment of Baltar.

The first I learned of Simon Stern's decision to go on pilgrimage was the night before the departure. Throughout that day Simon had remained hidden away in our quarters. He took a light breakfast in his room and lay down upon his cot, his face split by sunlight which shafted through the high window cutting his forehead in two, one half to dance in radiance, the other ashen with gloom.

"Have I ever told you of my night visitor?" Simon asked when I returned from my customary visit to the reception hall. He had not, but the narrative of the last Jew on earth is already known to you, emplaced as a cornerstone in the events of his annunciation. He told that story many times in the years to come, the years before the end and the time of his emancipation which followed, but that afternoon the encounter with the traveling storyteller was invested with a single question: Was it dream or reality?

Dream or reality? I have virtually nothing new to say about this complexity which has not often enough been said. Dreams are not simply fabrications, nor is reality unballasted by the air of fantasy. The skein laid over events by the imagination is woven of both: obdurate fact and the breezes of fantasy. Dreams—those night-time fantasies in which all of the underworld of consciousness (like the enchanted creatures of the forest who come out in the moonlight to disport themselves) emerge and play their delicious and their grotesque games unchastised by waking control, unhesitant, unchecked—those dreams in which glory and abasement exchange clasps of recognition are not more unreal than the platitudes of everyday life, which lumber through time more slowly, curtailed by direct language, clothing, costume, rouge and mascara. Are they more real?—those plodding vehicles of masquerade than the fast synapses, the yawning bites and truncations, the shorting of the neural circuitry which produce the fantasies of the unconscious, the word plays, the confusions of gender, the disjunct scenes, the coarse and cruel humor, the gaieties and horrifics of restless dream. There is nothing of life, in sleep or wakefulness, which is not splattered with the blood of dishonesty and untruth or spread with the jam and honey of generosity. We are no more the stuff of which dreams are made than we are the dreams from which stuff condenses: the retort is fired by the burner and whatever is put there to heat condenses its product, powder into crystals, solid into gas, vapor into solid—the whole chemistry of agitation depends upon the flux of dream and materiality—from one to the other and back again, like the predicament of visionaries who take for granted, unquestioningly, the existence of what they see, despite the fact that the goblins and ghosts with whom they converse so amiably are not visible to the generality of men.

Who then should know? It may well be that Simon Stern hallucinated on that night, that like the ancient Etruscan haruspices he saw his own living entrails, in the mirror of the imagination, and discerned their needs and requirements, projecting the constellation of liver and intestines—their agitated pulsation and constriction—to signify a demand upon the world. His father immolated, his mother smoked alive, young Lubina scarred and tormented with pain, what were these to him? So many lesions of the world, drawn and tight, calling for him, like the blood soaked into the earth, for justification and meaning.

The great energies of talented men, the fantastic enterprise of genius, the impassioned exercise of leaders seem to ordinary men so prodigious as to be inexplicable. But, reflecting now, I think not. They arise no less occasioned and ordered by the delights and tragedies which leave simple men with mouth agape, face muscles flaccid with amazement, or chins sour with the contagion of meaninglessness.

His parents burned to death—a tragedy? Undoubtedly. But I, a simple Jew from Gaza, would have said contentedly in my youth that it was the handiwork of a disorderly divinity, who cannot attend to all things, particularly not to worn-out and inadequate electrical wiring. I would not have called that event tragedy for long. "Tragedy" is intoned only by sophisticated people who have forgotten how to feel the event. The Greeks at the annual plays suffered indescribable anguish and commiseration with the doomed Antigone and the beset Oedipus, but did not leave the ampitheater and speak of the excellent acting or the painted masks or even of the play's event and detail. The upper-class Athenian, perhaps already supercilious and indifferent, saw the performance of the tragic cycles as useful means of control, as weapons of political manipulation, abasing the helots, flattering the freed middle class and tradesmen by exhibiting to them their happy exclusion from tragic destiny and obliging only themselves, the rich and powerful, to come to terms with the irrational order of the universe to which they were subjected and to which, therefore, they alone had need to come to terms. But to speak of tragedy as a reality out there, distant, enacted in the masks and mimes of other people's lives is to make it cold and lifeless. Our contemporaries cannot bear such tragic dramaturgy, can feel for it no empathy nor terror, for they know so much more than did the ancients about the loveless actuality of the world. The play is no mirror of the order of the universe. It has no justice and no reproof to teach us, for the play is everywhere and what transpires now and at every moment is more grand, more total theater than ever the ancients imagined. Everything is split off from everything, all connections severed, every mirror cracked. Let the gods look upon us with pity and fear; let the tragedians give us their masks; and let all the tyrants of the stage and all the harrowed mothers and distraught children of those didactic spectacles look at us, their audience of old, and acknowledge that we are taught so well what it is they play that we invent our own dramas and play out their lines without having even to memorize them.

It would have been unexceptionable had Simon Stern buried and mourned the misfortune (for untimely and foolish deaths are always a misfortune—street accidents, falling in bathtubs, drownings are stupid deaths and never tragic unless the dead seem to us disproportionately judged, and who is the judge and who is judged if you care to answer that with certainty?) of his parents' death and gone on to add yet another fortune to his first.

Most men are not interrupted by life to inquire of its meaning. They are few who hold a fist of dry clay in their hands and wonder at the universe as they pulverize it. But Simon Stern, responding to something else in the detail of his life, descending into the basement of his past finds there the ruins and disjected members of earlier days that acclaim him and denounce his treachery, that force him to bring into a unity of tears and horror all that was in the miniature of his life and the magnitudes of events that we repeated over and over again, in giant majuscules, throughout the world.

Everything suffers from faulty wiring, does it not?

300

"If it was a dream, then it was as true as any story made up out of the material of the world is true, and if it was not a dream the story is no different."

"It doesn't matter whether it was a dream or not. The story is true."

"It does matter, you see. If that Jew existed, if he really sat there in my locked storage room and told me the legend, he was telling it to *me*, only to *me*, because the legend *was* for *me*."

That was incontestable. The question had shifted. Not general truth or falsehood. Men think that's important. Whether God exists or doesn't? Whether men are good or not? But such questions don't matter as general questions. They only matter if one is singled out for a special benefice.

Some gods of India have many hands and upon those hands are a full complement of fingers and the gods turn on the axis of the universe and those myriad fingers point up and down. It doesn't matter, you see, if they are mythic creatures or not. It only matters if they happen to point at you. If they point at you, their existence is presumed. If they don't you can slip in and out of life without being noticed (and without having to notice). But let them point, and you feel their finger on your tongue, scratching at your brain, pressing your eyeballs. You know if you are fingered by the universe.

"I ask only one question of my night visitor. Was he telling that story to me because that story existed only for me? If he made up the story it was still for me. If I dreamed the story it was my story. If the story was made up ages ago and never told until it was told to me it is my story. And even if it has been told once in every generation, then it is my story for this generation.

"Will you go with me to Gerona, Nathan? A train leaves for Barcelona this evening. We will be there by midday tomorrow. We shall see what we shall see. It may be nothing, but perhaps we will discover in Gerona some trace of Don Rafael Acosta, some reminder that he existed and that his existence was part of my own. What I want is some reason to continue to the end what I have now begun."

301

The sun of lemon trees and the breezes of the sea stroked my sleepless eyes as the train descended from the border down through the brave coast of Spain, weaving through villages of white and blue and yellow wash and small factories made of corrugated tin, passing hurriedly through Gerona to which we would return, and two hours from then, drawing slowly, in spasms of movement and retreat into the glass-covered festival station of Barcelona.

He was already looking for Jews, for furtive eyes, averted stares, for pale faces, for replications of images of conformity that he, as all people, had buried away in the album of recollection, stored to the turning of occasioned need. A gypsy, he thought, a Catalan businessman carrying a worn leather briefcase from which a loaf of bread protruded, a fat mother with thick grey hair bunched like a *bubba*, covering her children in a spume of Basque affection. He looked for Jews in Spain like a bird looking for forage in a desert. There were none to be found, none that could be recognized. Those there were, who had surely endured until now the fourteen centuries which had elapsed since the first synagogue was burned on the desolated island of Minorca in the sixth century, were now silted over by catechism and forgetfulness, although their names (how many names, Vives, Mendoza, Vidal, Lopez, Colon and our own Acosta) were all Jewish names with glorious ancestries and broken gravestones.

The Ritz, we were informed by the nervous concierge, was unchanged since earlier decades, unchanged, that is, immobile under the weight of dust which clung to the draperies in the breakfast room, which clustered in tiers of grey elegance on the necklaced glass that made up chandeliers of the hallways and the *art nouveau* leaves that cupped the naked bulbs of the bedroom lights; no help, no servants, ancient cleaning women in starched white, supporting faces like dowager aunts and the dwarfs of El Greco, feather dusters tucked in their leather belts and wearing filthy scapulars like nuns from a convent that despised the body. The small driveway, the small doorway, the small desk, the containment of Catalonia elaborated by arabesques and turn-of-the-century gargoyles awaited us, diminutive pilgrim and his blind companion.

The concierge, a man of fifty in shiny grey twill with green piping and the medallion of his office around his neck bowed us into the lobby. We had not reserved, but we had luggage, which was unusual for travelers of this time, and we asked for and received a double room and a bottle of lukewarm mineral water. We had arrived in Spain, where the destruction of all that was worthy in Europe had begun. The watermark of high culture was all that remained—the smudge of Toledo and Córdoba, the Alhambra, the shards of the Almohades. Down the waters had come. What burbled still were flamencos singing in night clubs; weary bulls from Andalusia, starved from the neglect of a decade of war, bellowing on Sunday in the Plaza de Torros; grim, sullen Catalonians sunning themselves on the Ramblas and waiting for someone, anyone, to arrive in Barcelona.

It was easy in that city of no movement to find a car and driver to take us to Gerona the following morning. No English, no other European language but Spanish and Catalan. Sufficient. We had little more to say than "Gerona, *por favor*," and that much we knew, that little we knew and a hundred words more. We had only two days. The day after tomorrow at eight in the morning a ship due from Gibraltar, from Naples, and Athens before, would collect us and sail on to New York, burdened with other refugees.

A Citroen idled before the Ritz attended by an elderly chauffeur in a creased black suit who was lazily stroking its chrome with a feather duster when Simon and I appeared. The feather duster vanished up his sleeve, his visored hat swept down before him, and we, like royalty incognito, were enfolded by his large gestures.

The Citroen moved between trees and kiosks down the broad boulevards of the city in the direction of the Plaza de Torros out of the city by the coast road and north. It would be a lengthy drive, perhaps three hours, perhaps more. Simon embraced his body, his arms crossed, his hands gripping at his shoulders, one foot drawn beneath him in a position one would have thought cumbersome. Not for him. He sat as a child become comfortable for a long journey and he melted into his thoughts.

The sea glistened like burred steel, undulant and cold, and receding beyond the imagination of the eye. Where was I? I was no longer there, not in Spain, not seated in my blindness in the luxurious declivation of a Citroen moving toward a city of which I knew scarcely anything in order to discover the verisimilitude of a dream. I had put this away. I was vanished into the desert of southern Palestine, bouncing through the sand on the bony promontories of a donkey's back, holding fast to the hips of my father who kicked against his indifferent flanks; "*Yalah, yalah,*" he called to the Arab mule, who knew no Hebrew and cared not a bit for the going down of day, and but occasionally, as the car slowed for a turn, I would raise my chin to the angle of the wind and catch the smell of rotted fish or the freshness of cow dung steaming at the side of the road. All things came together for me, crystallized time, all those stalagmites of memory pressing up their shafts against my passage and touching (like the fingers of God and Adam) the stalactites of immediate sensation which descended to join them. Tissues and overlays, the bleedings of the margins of my life, speeds and movements, the jog of child days in the desert and humming movement toward an unsecured future. Who spoke of fear the first? Was it I? Did I cry out or moan? Was it I who took his hand? He took mine and held it. Mine he took and held it in both his hands.

"It's sometimes beyond bearing, Nathan. I feel myself bunched into a fist. I'm suddenly afraid. It is sunny, Nathan. There is sun out there and the road is clear and nothing keeps us from speeding to Gerona, but I feel a cold, a wind out of nowhere which cuts through the heat to me. I have been away too long.

"For the others the old neighborhood, there, on the Lower East Side, is the childhood to which they will never return. Surrounded by the fence slats of their memory, they put the eye of sentiment to the light that slides through and they remember. And they remember, quite understandably, what they wish to remember. I have heard from others (since I have no children of my own) that a child of six or seven, an intelligent and percipient child, will survey his small past and say, 'When I was very, very young'—and even add, 'so long ago that I can hardly remember it—I went on a picnic with my aunts and uncles,' the child will run on, words tumbling, and the child will say I cannot remember Aunt so-and-so whom

304

I know is gone away forever and then quite as openly recall Aunt so-and-so giving him a toy cart and stroking his head. What the child cannot do is conjure her ghost, cannot frame off the world, for he has no wish to divide and subdivide as we do.

"There is a German philosopher who tried to work out a way of understanding how we experience the world and instructed us that we should bracket experience, put about it the blinders and curtailments which disentangle it from the riot of connections which implicate it in the existence of everything else. In that way he imagined we could begin to intuit clearly what it is we really see when we open our eyes and know when we put our minds to something. But such errors! We should not want to reduce down to the essence, but to build up toward everything, to embrace and hug as much as we can, to make our eyes wide-angled apertures extending the horizontal breadth of our sight, however much it foreshortens our vertical vision (and that's right too, for the vertical vision is inside a man and what really counts is that he have a broad sight to support his vision).

Try to look out now through your slit-eyes, you Chinaman Jew, and what do you see out of your window, Oh God, what do you see out there, dirty grey houses bulging like a paunchy reeling drunk, your smokestack hat widening and enormous, perched precariously on a flat terrace of tar and tin sheeting, and above you the arc of the misty sky and curving downwards descending to the corners of the horizon which you have never seen before, at the edges where the tears drip out of your eyes and run down your cheeks, there, at the right a woman sits before her street cart on the next block and sells red apples and an old man sweeps the street before his shop, and out of your left eye you see down there where spots of dirt make the retina smart and bruise your pupil a knot of people standing before the Iglesia Del Rey Cristo, which was once a *shul* of the Jews of Tarnapol. With this broad-angle vision of the world, curved to the minuscule of our life, everything is encompassed in a sweep of the passage of generations and time and history and the impulsion of particles which pushes the future out of the way to make the path straight for the present.

"But the others of the old neighborhood I long to see will

305

remain only a fiction. Sometimes of a Sunday, Nathan, I used to leave my office and walk by myself through the streets. I would thread between the carts and go into shops and sample the endless boxes of candies the wholesalers put out to sell by the pound and quarter-pound and ten cents' worth and eat a pickle at Gus's stand, selecting one from the brine of dill and vinegar, and then I would sometimes find myself beside a family from where? New Jersey, from towns named Englewood and Passaic, and once I heard the voices of New England clipping through the fog of their own past in short nasal gasps of recognition—'Your grandfather told me about the great delicatessen you can get down here' and 'See, they still have pushcarts like when Cousin Yella was a girl'—and I will know that families have come to call on their past, pay a visit out of their nostalgia to find something, anything, that tugs at them a bit, puts them out of joint with their velvet lawns of green and their barbecue pits soiled with suckling ambition. They've come back to the old neighborhood of their general past and they reminisce over soda pop at the corner stands about those who came through here and got away. I listen to them and love them, too. Sometimes, of course, I hate them when they smoke very long and powerful cigars and look around the streets uncomprehending and wrinkle their noses at the smells of the *medina*, but that passes. What I know is that they're out there (even with their divagations and trap doors evading it all), out there and alarmed and confused, waiting for something they can't even mention any more, whose name they have even forgotten, but still in my mind, I know, waiting.

"I continue my walk. Most people don't know me by sight, so it's easy. They don't consider such an unobtrusive man like myself. They rush by me, sometimes almost knocking me over or flood around me when they observe this ordinary man in his homburg.

"I note that the paint is peeling from the green columns supporting the *bimah* of the Minkatcher *shul*, that the tiles of the public bath are stained with rust indicating the rotting of nineteenth-century pipes, that the Educational Alliance needs a new bulletin board, and noting these items in my notebook I dispatch cashier's checks in the morning (they will never know that it comes from me; not yet the perfection of the

way of the Rambam but close, for I do not observe their
abashment, for sometimes those who receive my benefactions
do not understand them—why should the columns be painted?
why should the broken mane of the rampant Lion of Judah be
restored? why should the stained-glass windows through which
light roses the congregation be rejuvenated? Why? Why? Of
course, no reason other than that I want it that way, that I am
the hidden king of the *medina*, the wealthiest man of the
medina, the multimillionaire of the *medina* who walks through
its streets, tentative like a hunchback, surveying it for disrepair, for the unraveling, loose threads of pride, and must
restore it, all, everything to the beginnings from which it did
proceed.

"They do not know me. When I stop to observe the walk
before me, the shops on Essex Street, the old tinsmiths, the
yarmulke makers, the herring wholesalers, the tatters and torns
of furniture stores, fabric and remnant houses, I see back into
my memory and I remember the old neighborhood screaming
with life, with women throwing themselves at the pike and
carp minstrels who sang out on Thursday mornings that the
fish was fresh and ready to swim in bathtubs until nightfall
for the grinding and dawn for the boiling and the blessed eve
for the delectation of Israel, and men with muscles of iron and
beards as long as their frock coats jousting with uptown
merchants and the slaughterers in bowler hats offering chickens, and more and more I can remember of those days when
we lived like *fellahin* in Djerba, and we laughed in the streets
and we wept when the Balfour Declaration was proclaimed
and the wireless told us in our tongue that one day soon there
would be ours *there* as well as *there* on velvet lawns of green
and so much more than Kishinev and Bialystok in older days
and a German Foreign Minister who was ours assassinated by
one of the enemy who had a country but denied him a portion
of it and the German Ambassador shot dead in Paris by an
enraged patriot with no country.

"We wept in the open and we prayed down the walls of the
hundreds of *shuls* and synagogues of our *medina*. Yet, no walls
kept me there and I stayed. Even the shops of the *medina* are
now run by travelers, who take off their jackets mixed of forbidden cloth and put on their pure coats of white cotton to

carve meat and hide away their soft hats and as of old put on white straw boaters or black skullcaps and do their trade, and at nightfall if they have time to say their prayers, if they remember to say their prayers, if they still know those prayers, they crunch themselves into a corner of the past and summon twilight before they rush to the ends of the line, to Coney Island and beyond, to Forest Hills, even some—those prosperous appliance dealers—to small houses on Long Island or across the uptown bridge to New Jersey.

"Would one have imagined years ago in my youth that a day would come when people would conduct their lives in the suburbs beyond and daily return to the *medina* to earn their livelihood? Unthinkable and still not quite thinkable. They choose to return. They panic to flee and having escaped they return. But not quite. There is something cynical about their election. I am not naïve after all. I know what Shmuel is thinking standing there among his ten thousand boxes upon boxes of shoes. Don't I know? Didn't I sell him fifteen years ago two-hundred-dozen overshoes for left feet only for 12¢ @—the old kind, you know, canvas with little metal prongs that you forced through a hook eye and folded over and sometimes cut yourself on the stamped-out metal—2,400 left shoes. *Vey iz mir.* Who would have thought Shmuel knew what he was doing. And did anyone think I knew. But I did and so did he. A company out there had written me and told me they had an overstock of left shoes in a model they had discontinued for the Army and offered them to me at 4¢ @ and so I bought them, bought everything in sight fifteen years ago—left-foot overshoes, mackinaw hoods without the mackinaw, fittings from bankrupt restaurants, you name it, on and on I could go with crazy items everyone thought unsalable—they'd come down to Star Enterprises, where I had my office, and I'd bargain out the prices with them, treating all of them—Jew and gentile alike—with equal toughness or fairness and the merchandise would go to the warehouse in Brooklyn to be resold. Sold Shmuel the left-foot overshoes and what does he do? Latin American comes in a month later from some place in Peru and starts looking for cheap raincoats and Shmuel tells him he doesn't have coats, only shoes, and the Peruvian tells him that he's got hundreds of Indians working on his plantation high up in the mountains and that they're not as hardy as they used to be before the Spanish came (and Shmuel reminds him that that was five hundred years ago, but the Peruvian doesn't care when it was, and keeps saying '*Muy frío*' and wraps his arms around himself and shakes to show how cold it gets when the rains come). So Shmuel starts telling him about overshoes and that colds come from the cold ground and pains in the legs begin from the emanations of the earth and from the cold people get rheumatism, arthritis, lumbago and that Peruvian Indians have small feet and could easily put on left-foot overshoes over their bare feet and that feet are more important to protect than heads which are already covered with hair. The Peruvian buys all his left overshoes for 21¢ @ and Shmuel comes to me and says '*Mamzerle*, you thought you had me, didn't you, you sweet *mamzer*!! and so, look, I made a couple a hundred and we're all happy. So what have you got for me, Shimen—slippers without heels, sandals without straps, shoes for people with six toes, what *meshugas* have you got.' I thank him for his praise and note down his enthusiasm to remind myself when the time comes, if it ever comes again, that I have some foot oddity to call upon Shmuel the Shoe Wholesaler.

"But *now* Shmuel stands there in front of his shop, the shoe boxes piled up inside like unsteady skyscrapers and he waits for customers. Shmuel is comfortable now. He lives in Bayside and his son goes to a college near Boston and his daughter wants to be an actress and his wife, she has arthritis and not from the cold of the Andes either. They're all comfortable. Shmuel commutes and, when he sees me, he looks away and nods to me even though he doesn't want to see me and it is not possible to ignore me. I upset him. I am an embarrassment to him. He doesn't even cover his head any more. He keeps his shop open on the second day of *yom tovim* but not on Rosh Hashanah. He goes to a Reform *shul* with an organ and a choir borrowed from the Methodists.

"Shmuel, dear customer Shmuel, remember the days of your youth. I never forget them and now they are all that I seek to recall, the days of my youth and the extraordinary future when all Israel will be young again.

"I believe in the coming of the Messiah with a perfect faith, and even though he is slow about it I am sure he will come and implant monkey glands in the children of Zion and we will be young once more—and what does Solomon sing in *Shir ha-Shirim* about our faces and our bodies and the golden down upon our cheeks when God will have girdled the universe in an eternal rainbow. Shmuel, don't forget me, for I am a herald, a shofar *blozzer* who begins to practice his horn-blowing on the first day of the month of Elul and never stops throughout the month and keeps on blowing throughout the year, sharp clear notes, so that all the inhabitants of the *medina* will know and report that Shimen is keeping the ancient faith still. But I, too, am beginning to age and the sound within me becomes more anxious and strident, for the old neighborhood is really changing, really changing and vanishing. I'm no sentimentalist, you know. I don't really care all that much about the dying of Yiddish or the disappearance of Jewish theater or the coming of Spaniards and artists and young men with disorderly beards and coarse blue pants to the neighborhood. Why shouldn't the old neighborhood change? Time passes, you know. We can't always lounge around the parlors of our past, as though the past were a game room to which we can retire for recreation whenever we choose. I call the old neighborhood a miniature Bet Ha-Mikdash, a tabernacle, a holy place, not a game room. I can't leave it because that's desertion—no, worse, a kind of treason against the past, no, not even that, for the stress falls on the wrong word. It's treason against the People, against the whole of the People, its *corpus animata*, its corpse, its living and dead body, for which I am responsible."

Simon had talked for some time, his voice fluting and falling to the rhythm of his recollections, unaware of what passed outside, continuing, inflected and passionate, though the car had passed through two road blocks administered by the Guardia, although we had shown passports and our driver had conversed casually with the soldiers. Simon had paused or become silent, but had continued his reflections without interruption.

It was early afternoon, nearly one o'clock, that our car entered through the outskirts of the city of Gerona, passed through the grey buildings of the business and administrative quarter of the city to the banks of the Ter on the other side of which rose the old city, its congestion of Gothic and

Baroque, its churches and hospices and palaces, and its cathedral.

I had prepared in my mind how we should proceed and had formulated a question for our driver which might have assisted our inquiry, but as the car drew to a stop in the square behind the Calle de la Plateria and the Avenida de Generalissimo, Simon returned from his meditation.

The car stopped and the driver addressed us, "*Señores? Y ahora qué?*"

Simon Stern understood and, with an exhausted sign, answered: "*Volveremos a Barcelona. Esta nada y nadie.* It isn't necessary any more. It isn't necessary, Nathan."

It was midafternoon before we stopped again. The sun had passed through the center of the sky, burning once more the gnarled olive and almond trees; the sun fell to its side, exhausted from the day, languishing and parched, waiting for the night to come. Both sun and earth were weary.

Our driver pulled off the road and stopped in the shade. He was tired. He had driven for nearly five hours. He disappeared for some minutes and returned with a goatskin of wine which he poured into thimble cups produced from a hamper that had rested on the floor of the car. We had a small lunch from the hotel—boiled eggs and coarse bread with olive oil—which we shared with him. The shade was meaningless. It gave no cool. Dry heat covered everything.

We heard a voice singing a short distance away, behind us, to the right and behind us. The voice sang, small bursts of exuberance, spinning into webs of nasal lament and dying away, returning, thin, delicate, sad. Simon followed the sound of the voice drawing me after him. It was then we realized that our car had stopped in a small grove of trees at the side of a deserted cemetery. A cemetery amid olive trees forgotten by everyone, memorial stones green with moss, their iron crosses snapped like dried wood, an ageless cemetery, a cemetery beyond age and the counting of the years. The voice sang and we caught the name of God thrown into the heavy air.

A small house stood in the center of the cemetery surmounted by a marble angel. Before it, seated on its steps was a young man. He was dressed in black monk's robes and his hands hid his face. Our driver came up behind us, a cigarette in his mouth, and looking at the youth, snapped with contempt: "*Uno hermano de los muertos. A brother of the dead.*"

Simon called to the young man, "*Ola, hermano,*" and after some moments the young man removed his fingers from his face and addressed us, and the gravity of his face was frightening in its beauty and in its sadness. Simon had asked him nothing, but he answered as though to explain immediately. "*Yo vivo con los muertos.*"

"*Digame, hermano, porqué?*"

He did not answer, but threw open his arms to the olive trees and the hills behind him covered with fir trees and the sun and the dry earth beneath our feet and I realized then that he was speaking of all of the world, of the whole of the creation, "*por ellos y por tuyos y por El Señor, creator del mundo.*"

"*Pero los muertos?*" Simon said pointing to the graves, for he could not understand why it was that one would live in a cemetery as did all of the members of his brotherhood, why he would spend his life among the dead in order to celebrate creation.

"*Nadie muerten. Todos, todos, todos los muertos viven en Dio y en me.*"

"Nothing dies," Simon repeated, "nothing at all."

It was no surprise to me that, following these remarkable affirmations, Simon should have confirmed what was already virtual in our relationship, that I should become his ears, his eyes, and his voice to future generations of those who hope.

It was so good the following day to leave Europe and to sail forth upon the ocean to meet the destiny that even then was gathering to receive us.

312

Book 4

Prologue

I had never been uptown, emerged to light. It was not a matter of principle, an exegesis of doctrine as it was with Simon, which had constrained me, but rather a function of my indifference. It didn't matter to me that there was an uptown, a midtown, a side to the sun and a side to the night. Those considerations animate tourists and adventurers. I was neither. I was a sojourner, but not a tourist. I passed by but I had no intention of stopping.

There had been, before the fire, nothing beyond the cubits of my room, the compass of my daily ambulation from room to room, the expanse of my peregrination through four blocks of the compound, holding on to railings, greeting shopkeepers, smiling upon unfingered and unfelt smiles, tapping out the signals of my progress through the enclave, calling hellos to the watchmen in the upper windows of our preserve who kept note of my movements and guarded me in my return.

Come up to light. Up to light.

"Come up to the light," the voice that trembled in the hand that guided my elbow spoke. A soft and even voice. Was it man? Was it woman? It was a voice specified to succor and without origin, in that toneless evenness of speech which is any order of the heart, any dimension of the genitalia. What did it matter, for all the way, all the route of ascent—climbing the degrees from the lowest bowel of the city to the aorta of the city—I was rising out of the depths to visit you, becalmed and lost in the world uptown.

"Come up to the light," sweetly and even. "I will follow. Hold my arm," and the hand slid along my gabardine to my wrist, tapping it when I should step up and pressing it down when I should halt. I counted more than twenty steps. I do not remember exactly.

A news vendor cried the papers and the news. "One dead—" but no more, for a train screamed into the station on the other side and his hawking voice, strangled, drowned within the noise.

"One dead."

What is that one that is dead? And where? No matter. Not my dead. Perhaps my dead? No matter. Up to the light. And what is light for my blackness has grown blacker. (You think, as Goethe believed, that black is a muddy, dirty color, which spatters clarity and cheapens distinction. A clean German. Not I. Black is the color of my life and what I see I invent. Black is the only color. All others are the corpuscles of dreaming.) Up to the light.

"May I leave you?"—the solicitude of indefinition.

"Leave me? Yes. I am well. You may leave me."

"Thank you," the voice called, the cry like a kite in love with a cloud. Thank me. I laughed. "One dead . . ." and a car sounded its horn and a siren wailed.

"Lexington Avenue?" I spoke to the wall of the department store.

"This way," and a hand spun me about, for I was walking

316

into a window. "This way." I was confused. No wonder. Yes, it was the Avenue.

"Which way?"

"Towards the park."

"I will point you. Are you confident?"

"Of what?"

"Forgive me. Of yourself?"

"If not of myself then whom?"

"And if not now, when?" We laughed.

"You know the text?"

"I am the text." The old man laughed. A bony finger with a long nail like an incisor bit into my shoulder. "To the park? To visit Simon Stern?"

"You know?"

"Of course. Who does not?"

"One dead," the voice spoke at the crossing of the avenue toward the newsstand. A voice declaimed, an intonation, a litany: "One dead in East Side fire."

"Aaaagh. One dead. Who?" I stopped and called out. "One dead? Who is dead?" I turned around and my white cane beat air, touching no one.

"Old man, stop! Old man, calm down! Hold it." I was not old, but blind men seem old. A strong arm circled my neck and held me, stilling a dancing vein. "Hold on. What is it? You're all right. Friend. I'm a friend. Calm down." I quieted and fell against the building at my back. I gathered myself, collecting the parts of my body that had fallen like the appendages of a marionette, their strings loose, their conductor sleeping, together and ready, attentive, wishing to move, awaiting the blowing in of spirit, inspiration, prepared.

"Who has died?"

Each word clear, separate from the whole. Each word. "Who?" They don't know. Burned to carbon. Only gold teeth. Only a cleavage in the skull. They don't know. Has? Is. Most definitely. Seventy-three hours ago. "In the compound? You know of the compound?" In the compound. Whatever a compound is, whatever a compound is doing in this city, among them, there? I don't understand. And dead? That's the crucial word. He's dead, whoever he is, but he did not die. *He* did not die. But he *is* dead. The dying of the dead is normally a con-

317

volution of will and action, the action replacing will, the will becoming action. Here—in all such situations, involuntary, unwanted (wanted?) the dead do not die, but were died, were deaded. It should read: One deaded, for he was not killed, but impelled to die. He succumbed to death. He gave in to death, but he did not die.

I said to myself at last that it was true. Janos Baltar did not die. He was suffocated by death. Death at last deaded Baltar.

Simon Stern, my redeemer, the pure act of these occurrences,
ACTUS almost PURUS. He does and I conserve. My conserva-
tion guarantees the perduration of his acts. He is without me; I
am not without him. He does without me; I do not without him.
He acts, but I write the history of his action, and to that extent
the generations to come must believe upon him in the redaction
of his amanuensis. They must believe me as much as they think
it is he whom they believe. It is in this way that men come to
share in the destiny of their heroes. The concession of the intel-
lect in belief, the giving of trust, the offering of loyalty and com-
mitment, these gestures of freedom, however ordered by the
evidence and the argument of history, are the generous gifts
which each man bestows upon the fatum *of the historical. With-*
out such co-participation, there would be no freedom. Fatality
would roll over us like lava and bury us beneath molten earth.
By the willingness to record and transmit (that is, to select
and order to the ends of posterity what it is we hear and
observe) we provide men with the opportunity of making over
fate into destiny, transforming grinding weight into the iri-
descent translucency of butterfly wings, the despairing agony
of the ineluctable into the choices of free men.

The community is gathered; the people are settled. The
bunting shudders in the warm spring breeze, flags of blue and
white, flags of red, blue, and white, flags with inscriptions and
phrases. "Do not forget," the flags catechize. "Hallelujah," the
flags exult. The flags wave above the raised platform erected
before the entrance to the compound, that modest door of
peeling paint, behind which is hidden a vast door of teak and
ebony controlled by an electric eye. Any date? It does not
matter. It was a day in spring, the spring of the year following
our release from bondage. It would have to be 1946.

The crowds began to gather early in the streets around the
compound. Light filtered through the grid of night, and
already at that hour old women, holding fast the fat fists of
little boys, congregated. They stamped their feet against the
chilly night and awaited dawn. A tub of tea stood on a wooden
table, and faithful Rochel, whom we had gathered to us from
the rubble of Berlin, bundled in four army sweaters of faded
green, was ladling the steaming brew into paper cups.

319

It was to be a vast celebration. The newspapers had heralded it. Even the uptown newspapers, which are written in the English tongue, had described Simon Stern and his Society, and a small advertisement had appeared in the press, situated, as earlier advertisements we have described, on the obituary page where religious items (and this was construed to be a religious item) infrequently appear, announcing the inauguration of the Society and its domicile.

The announcement was not even necessary. It was a confirming gesture, setting forth in ineffaceable print what was already transmitted by the gossiping tomtoms of the neighborhood until its reverberations were heard in Coney Island and the Bronx, requests for tickets of admission being received from holy congregations twenty, thirty miles away, from admiring fund raisers on Eastern Parkway, from state assemblymen and senators, from Italian and Irish politicians who were elected in part by Jews and supported in the main by them, from leaders of fraternal organizations and the Jewish War Veterans.

An all-day celebration.

Sodalities of Hasidim, carrying banners and sacred scrolls coddled in velvet, would cross the bridge from Brooklyn, and singing Yiddish songs embedded in Russian rhythms, were expected to chorus greetings from Ger, Klausenberg, Lubavitch (the Hasidim of Satmar—as in all things, being sulky— were ordered by Rebbe Joel to stay home), and one of their number was to deliver an allocution of welcome which Simon had been told would be a salute from Scripture and Talmud, good phrases culled and bent to the occasion. The staff assistant of a United States senator—which one I do not recall —was to bring personal greetings from the President of the United States in Washington, several hundred miles away, and the Mayor was expected in person, in the company of various of his commissioners, notably, Fire and Sanitation, to commingle their praises with those of religious and secular leadership.

The crowd had swelled to nearly a thousand by nine in the morning, and the small band which had been hired from the local social hall two blocks away was tuning on the dais—two violins, a drum, a horn player, and strangely out of place, a bass violist, cadaverously thin, but incredibly tall, nearly seven feet in his sweat socks and black slippers. Several notes. Tuning. The cry of the untamed violin. Silence.

The microphones were placed along the dais, which ran forty feet before the entrance to the compound; forty feet of wooden platform and tiers of green benches from the Department of Parks, enough to seat about two hundred and twenty persons. At noon the microphones would be turned on and the symphonic orchestra, a collection of instruments borrowed from a Hebrew high school, would arrive and perform selections from Handel's *Israel in Egypt,* followed by the chorus of dedication from the triumphant *Judas Maccabeus.* And as well folk songs and sonorities from the Polish-Austrian school of post-orthodox, pre-reform cantorial idiom would be presented.

A policeman walked by, swinging his night stick—small tricks of wit and domination. What for a policeman? We police ourselves. What need of them? He stopped and chatted with an old woman who blocked the sidewalk, her folding chair leaning against a lamppost. "You'll have to move it, grandmother." "Who you calling grandmother?" She said nothing else. He waited a moment. She looked away. He tapped the chair with the night stick. "Cossack!" she shouted, and heads turned toward them. "All right, grandmother. Stay where you are. You're a nuisance, but not a lawbreaker."

It was approaching noon. I was still in my room. I had been sitting at the window since daybreak. I listened to the noises. I heard the voices, constructed the day from the bits and pieces of information that were carried on wind. I knew the plan, the order of events. Occasionally someone would enter my room and visit a minute. I would calm them and reassure them of success. "What's going on out there," I would ask as they turned to leave and they would tell me. "A cop got after Klatzkin's *bubba.* I'm told she hasn't missed a parade in sixty years—she's been out there on her camp stool since seventhirty." From that I construct. You've read it already. Not distortion, but fulfilling a historic secretarial function—drawing together the lines of argument and improving their syntax. *The world about me is always saying, "Nathan, take a letter." I prepare myself, of course, sit back, unroll my* tabula rasa *and flatten it, focus my dead eyes against their sockets, crease my forehead and wait. What comes is more like this—"Tell the world to get off my corns, they hurt." I reconstruct this simple instruction into formal prose. "Dear Sir, It has come to my attention that you have for some time now—clearly without my permission—come to rest upon my corns. Certainly, kind sir, you have freedom of mobility, considerably greater than my own. Won't you be good enough to choose some other place to stand? Another place, another set of corns." I continue on like this for some time, but then my solicitousness and good will give way. My corns hurt ferociously and at last I become enraged. I threaten action, legal action, and I conclude the letter, once more with politeness and gentility in the French manner, "Pease be assured of my most devoted feeling."*

Ah, the letter is written, but the world has yet to get off my corns. The ineffectualness of my letter writing results not from my failures as a secretary—for I can invent letters as well as any secretarial-school graduate with modest intelligence—but from the fact that my secretarial skills are linked to my scribal function. I invent, but I also transcribe. I am imaginative, analogic, hieratic in my scribal vocation; flat, literal, bound by the visible horizon of my transcribal vocation. As scribe I make history for ritual, as secretary I transmit ritual to history. It is all very different, but in me they are one and the same, not confused but undifferentiated.

The people had gathered, the celebrants were present, but the principals, the recipients, the benefactors and the bestowed were absent. The crowd was a single body with many heads and numberless feet. Seen, if one were of a mind, from the eye level of the pavement, thousands of shoed feet squirm and stamp, tap to the music of the minstrel players, shuffle to the beat and, from the eye level of the dais (if one were of an estimating mind), hats and wigs, children with close-cropped hair, with braids and bangs. Black faces, a delegation of Ethiopians from the upper ghetto, their skullcaps invisible, smiled. Our people had come, all of them, out of the desert to the oasis of their dreams. To celebrate, to rejoice, to eat of the ten thousand cakes we had baked, the nougats and chocolate-covered cherries we had confected, the wine and fruit punches we had stirred in vast vats which we would spigot upon them like open water hydrants. They had come to celebrate us. But despite their numbers, 4000, 5000, 6000, who could estimate such a throng, all that received their expectant faces was the sawing of two violins, an exuberant but ungifted trumpeter, the pounding of drums, a meaningless percussion, a thumping bass viol, flitting sounds like the idle buzz of honeybees.

I was not yet dressed. I knew the others would be languishing, reading, writing, nibbling buns and stirring coffee. Simon Stern, of course, grave and thoughtful man, was undoubtedly sitting in his robe putting turns to his address. Not even he was dressed and it was already past the eleventh hour. At noon the processional, and half past midday, the addresses and musical offerings, addresses and the children's threnody, and by three, the dances, the refreshments, and the breakup of the crowd.

Earlier I had visited with Rabbi Steinmann. He had knocked at my door, entered, and sat down in my easy chair, for I was still in bed, tapping out messages with my fingernail, humming tunes and distracting myself with memories I could see. "To think of it, Nathan. We are really here." He began to laugh. Whenever Steinmann was overwhelmed with an emotion he burst out laughing. I joined him. I am a cooperative man.

"Why are you laughing, Reb Steinmann?"

"I didn't think it possible—I, the master of lost causes. This one seems to be winning."

"It's too soon to tell," I replied, not with pessimism or with fear. It was only that I thought success as premature as failure. But Steinmann wanted to believe that it would work. He left the compound every morning and traveled to ladies' luncheons in Woodmere and Hebrew day schools in Long Beach and Hadassah gatherings in Larchmont to describe the wonders of single-minded conviction and the passionate undertaking of the Society. He did not foreclose the hope of Zion *redivivus*, always speaking lustily of the *halutzim* and *aliyot*, the collectives and the Histadrut. He loved unabashedly all the signs of life, freely construing from the rabbinic interpretations of the love song of King Solomon the intimacies that took place between God and the Jewish people, discoursing with unconcealed eroticism about the furtive fingers which played beneath the sheets of history, feeling, touching, caressing the body of the people despite the march of predatory red ants crisscrossing the woolen blanket of time above. For him there was no difference between Simon Stern and David Ben-Gurion. He drew none of the haughty distinctions between those who build castles in the sky and those who build castles in the sand. Both were, from any reasonable point of view, shaky and unstable, but the former were the constructions of visionaries and the latter the constructions of unskilled engineers. The fact that the visionaries had kept the People alive for thousands of years was proof enough that the engineers would in time learn their trade. Simon Stern was like the builders of whom the exalted Chief Rabbi of Palestine, dead of cancer, thanking God for the pains given to him in his extremity—"pains of love" he called them—spoke kindly, those unbelieving pioneers who were the rebuilders of the *sanctum sanctorum,* building, making, doing, enduring for the sake of the Lord they did not know but would one day come to know intimately, for *His* work they were doing. Ultimately it was all His work. Ultimately, but most immediately, it was a filthy job cleaning out the sanctuary, removing the sludge of centuries from its walls, irrigating the temple, sluicing it of the excremental mire of pagan generations who had crapped in its corners and the turds of braying donkeys who had slept beneath its eaves. That task was not given (or assumed, I might add) by little pietists. It was done by peasant pioneers who left it to Chief Rabbis to fancy their hard work into a mystical vision.

Simon Stern had no mystical vision, but he suffered to the end from great impulsion, from the interior bleeding of past ages, and he knew that the only way to stop its flow, its continuous leakage of pure red blood, was to do a monumental action. But Steinmann, on the other hand, a passive sufferer, had been so desperate to discover in the clefts of the world even the smallest of small hopes that he had come to us, and of that desperation and its conquest he had planned to speak explicitly that day in his short address of welcome to his comrades in desperation and victory. I let Steinmann rhapsodize and rehearse, wagging his head from side to side in disbelief of the miracle of the hour. But I was not dressed, and at last wearied of Steinmann's exuberance, excused myself, and went to the bathroom to wash my teeth.

When I returned to the room he had gone. I had had enough of his ecstasy, for I knew of other omens. That morning, early, before the dawn, having listened to the auguries of the night before, I had gone to Baltar's room. The experience had kept me awake. No wonder that at this advanced hour, nearly a quarter until noon, I was still in my room, undressed. I was, you will understand, quite shaken.

I had felt Baltar asleep.

Earlier, before the day of celebration, it would not have been a justified intrusion, but even then I had come to understand certain things by entering his room (one floor above mine at the front of the compound, adjacent to the rooms which Simon inhabited) and feeling the dullness of the atmosphere. (Baltar never opened his windows, never, whether in winter, when fresh air might cool and evaporate the steam heat which hissed continuously from the radiators of the reconstruction, or summer—the end of the summer of our arrival—when the rooms were already clogged with waves of heat, stacked with weights of air, smelling fetid with odors contained for decades and now insulated with new plasters and paints.) Fresh air never entered that room, a room lean and undecorated, as though architecture had made way for light and life and all Baltar's efforts had been turned to obliterating its suggestion—the unadorned whiteness which Simon had specified remained untextured by optional colors or by prints and drawings, which we all had the privilege of selecting from the treasury of graphics which Dr. Klay had been assembling for our delectation. The room was bare. His bed, a tangle of sheets and blankets (and depite his refusal of ventilation, two blankets, smelling from the perspiration of his body) as though nightly contest ended before dawn with sheets wound about him and blankets shrugged to the floor. (Once Baltar tripped as he got out of bed and sprained his ankle, a sheet having somehow wound itself about him during sleep and held fast against his weight at morning.)

I sometimes opened his door at daybreak and inserted my head to see his room, which meant to feel its presence, that is, his presence, his weight within the weight of the room's rancidity. The smells were disgusting smells, smells of all the apertures, smells of unclean linen, smells of simple unhealth, but I accounted it to nothing and Simon, indifferent to such matters, had no difficulty conferring for hours with Baltar in his quarters, and not once mentioned their insalubrious stench. To be sure, Simon had on one occasion asked the housekeeper who oversaw the cleaning women of the compound to clean up his quarters, but he had mentioned specifically the stuffed trashcan, bulging with papers, and piles of books scattered on the floor, under his bed, in disarray upon his desk. Since normally it was the custom of the members of the community to attend to the arrangement of their own effects—books being such among others—it may well have been Simon's discreet way of suggesting that his staff fumigate and air the quarters to ask that they enter Baltar's room and arrange the books and dispose of his refuse. It was done, but Baltar's outrage was so disproportionate—he even threatened (an idle threat, since he was incapable of acting upon it) to leave the community if his privacy was ever again compromised—that it was decided to forgo such cleaning expeditions for Baltar's sake.

Everything was permitted to Janos Baltar. Everything was permitted to him, as everything was expected of Simon Stern. When the bus had arrived from the docks, depositing the first contingents of our survivors before the doors of the compound, a small collation had been prepared, schnapps and bits of herring. It was early in the afternoon in the fall of 1945, months before the events I recount now. Baltar became drunk. Everyone else was nervous, excited, joyous, sad. Europe was really over for them. But for Baltar, the arrival was more than a banishment of the past. While the others talked quietly among themselves, downing thimbles of refreshment, Baltar drank whole tumblers, and after a bit began to sing in a loud voice, gypsy songs punctuated with cries of diminutive intimacy with God, a not uncommon manner of singing among Hasidim of all varieties and persuasions, who convert threnodies of the mundane into hymns of celebration.

It was the first time, however, that we learned that Baltar could sing. We knew he could act, interpret, dance, do acrobatics, but sing? We had no idea. I was told that while aboard the refugee ship, he had maintained a scrupulous quiet, playing chess by himself in the lounge, or greeting the survivors, inquiring of their needs, making arrangements more comfortable if such were possible, keeping the insolent crew and condescending stewards in line. Baltar became our intermediary with the world. He seemed to know how to negotiate the business of the world, how to address its gnashing teeth and mean jaws with an implacable calm and strength which reduced the emotional Greeks and Italians who manned the vessel to subdued service. But on the day of the arrival he seemed wholly transformed by raucous song and exaltation. He had made it out of Europe and yet he sang of Europe all the while, its vast women, its rivers and mountains, its winter fires, its peasant joy and mischief, all hugged and kissed by the little diminutives of holy Yiddish, embracing God in *tateles* and *tatenyus*, small fathers, and small, ever smaller, infinitely small fathers, in whose arms minuscule men might hide. Oh Baltar, how you wanted to believe what you sang. Your voice in song was a heaving of breath that could not be contained. Breath that should have given your blood faith become oxygen was blasted out in song. We heard you. We were happy in your drunken enthusiasm. God heard you, but nothing remained inside to be hummed or whistled in solitude.

They all marched into the compound that afternoon in smiles and happiness, Baltar leading them with his song. He had a tremendous hangover and for two days after we did not see him, but when he appeared again, he was the familiar Baltar, vast and forbidding. But we allowed him everything. He was our rock and he guarded us. To every request he replied: "I will see to it." To every complaint he responded: "Don't be afraid. I know the world."

Even Simon Stern began to confide in Baltar. The Simon Stern who returned from the monstrosity that was Europe was sad and preoccupied. He would say to me, recalling the words of the monk of the cemetery: "So nothing dies, nothing, ever—well, what do you think of that, Nathan? He's a fool, Nathan." I would argue with Simon Stern, but to no avail. He knew that the monk was somehow right, but he was still obsessed with the display of the world's repulsiveness. He wanted to believe the monk. That was clear. He had already believed him even before we met him or else he would not have turned back from Gerona without seeking out the origins of the tale of Don Rafael Acosta. The young brother of the dead had only confirmed what Simon had learned, there in Europe, in the camps

—that life endured, that men have a passion to endure, that nothing perishes ultimately. But Simon Stern was back from Europe. He was once again amid loud voices, screams in the streets, people tearing at worn-out clothing on bargain tables, jostling, pushing, nagging, hitting out for little advantages and trivial victories. It seemed so ludicrous. Once, in fact, several weeks after our return, he almost struck the woman we called Shrieking Peshele, a fat girl in her early thirties, who had taken to shrieking everything—even the smallest word was shrieked; "good morning" sounded like a siren in the mouth of Shrieking Peshele. Simon was passing her in the hallway after morning services and Peshele shrieked a greeting. Simon, abroad in his mind, was startled and raised his hand to slap her. Peshele ran away and hid (we found her an hour later wailing in a broom closet on the other side of the compound). I remonstrated with Simon and had almost persuaded him to apologize to Peshele at lunchtime when Baltar interjected: "Never apologize, Simon Stern. It's done. It's finished. But never apologize. No one apologizes to us. What begins with apologies ends with a corpse."

"But Peshele is one of us," I added, sensing the argument. "Train anger on our own, master it, and then use it on the enemy," he had replied.

"What a doctrine," I snapped, irritated by Baltar's undertaker gravity. He did not respond immediately, but when we had reached Simon's rooms, and seated ourselves, Baltar took up my implied challenge.

"Do you really think it a strange doctrine, Nathan Gaza? I do not. It is true that the life lived by ordinary creatures in the world is never absolute. It is conditional life, involving partial thought, incomplete reasoning, sketchy emotion, dumb and uninstructed feeling. The behavior of men is always a grey—sometimes light as the cast of the sky in early morning or dark, most often, as the waters in a well. But grey. Not white, not black. And men carry on their lives with a single practical ethical doctrine: 'We're grey, our lives are grey, our thoughts are grey, our actions and passions, they, most of all, are grey.' And the greyness of it all rationalizes the most incomprehensible horrors. If it's all grey, then no love is pure and no malevolence complete. We see nothing for what it is, we are so content with greyness. But I do differently. I agree with the practical ethics of the world. Greyness makes it possible for the world to get on with its business. A grey morality of adjustment makes it easy for murderers to hide out. The world can be counted on to forget. The victims will eventually end up doing business with their tormentors. It's all grey, grey, grey, they will insist when called to account. So what does it matter.

"But Baltar does not hold with such a view. I acknowledge the greyness, but I examine the colors I am offered and I make absolute what predominates. And my friend (and I hope, Nathan Gaza, you will decide to become my friend), black always predominates (with the possible exception of our benefactor, Simon Stern, whose purity is, I find, excuse me, Mr. Stern, more often innocent than moral). And so I find the world black, and if black, black as pitch, black as the face of hell, then the task of confronting those who wish to endure a blackness such as this—black themselves—is to set themselves decisively, without reservation against it. My blackness is different from yours, Nathan Gaza, and ours is different from the blackness of the nations. Obliterate distinction, pretend to be loving and merciful, and we commingle our blackness with theirs, and theirs—vast, uncompassable, limitless—will envelop us. No. No. Train anger, I said. Equip it, discipline it, make it ready."

Baltar finished and I did not reply. Simon, however, chuckled, which struck me as inappropriate.

And so Baltar was permitted his unsocial habits. They offended no one but those who were obliged for one or another reason to confer with him, and since everyone in our community had some curious behavior, if anyone took it into his head to bestow normalcy upon us, they would have neither standard nor criterion, they themselves being eccentric. Moralities we acknowledged, but the incipient thrust of personal behavior which, had we the sophistication and knowledge to discern, would have provided us with a harvest of symptoms of all the perversities of mankind, we managed to ignore: some to remain unclean, others to leave boils and sores exposed, others to wear galoshes and heavy boots at all times, yet others never to brush their teeth, others to allow their hair to grow like weeds, others their nails to be mired with filth.

Defective images of the flesh, but not alone these. Faulty and impaired images of the spirit—associality and disdain, hostility and aggression, anger and suspicion, fantasy and delusion —our community was the exemplification of all these disorders and confusions, fabricated in the environments of Europe, confirmed in hell, and resurrected in our small paradise. What wonder that some of our community never spoke, others hissed their words (one member, who had lost nearly all his teeth from neglect, spoke as though his tongue were the brush of the world, for after each word it flailed about his mouth and hung out between his closed lips when he was silent, a pink-green stick of flesh—I am grateful I could not see it, but my imagination more than made up for my blindness—I avoided his company); yet others only shouted, their voices pitched like cats in the night; and among habits of eating—can you bear this description of incivility and madness? It was so grotesque that Simon was ultimately obliged to post in the compound's dining room, where single people and families who had no wish to cook in their quarters might come to eat in assembly, simple rules that would have seemed to ordinary society sufficient exhibition of our depravity, our deprivation and ravagement. The raucity of voices—hoarse, loud, grating, scraping, strident voices—the grabbing of hands, the pushing and tugging at plates of bread and tureens of soup, the refusal to use implements of dining other than knives to cut off hunks or pare vegetables, the wiping of hands on chairs and clothing, nose-picking, ear-cleaning, eructing, farting. We were of the peasant company of Brueghel folk, cut back to the earth from which we had come, standing naked before the advent of the devils and demons. But it was a working of rage, rage against the unforgotten past and rage against good Simon, who sat at a table by himself or with me or sometimes with Klay, Steinmann, or Baltar and others who had, by invitation, come to join him for a meal. He was careful, always neatly dressed, with tie and jacket, and he drank wine from a carafe with his meals, a single tumbler, and always used his knife and fork casually and undemonstratively. He never looked up when food was being thrown or plates tipped over, when a fight would break out and embittered voices swirl above the tables. His very ease and detachment eventually restored equable calm, low voices conversing as voices at table should, and meals would conclude in the civility of tea and coffee and the guests leave after having spoke their benedictions or thanked their stars for being there.

Gradually, although it took months of such unruffled temperateness and the advice of Simon's rules about sociality in the public spaces of the community, a semblance of civility returned and hopeless finger-eaters and food-grabbers returned to the disciplines of their childhood, and meals became once again agreeable occasions for conversation and exchange. But Baltar's behavior, if one takes the evidence of his rooms, was unregenerate, or, more accurately, *status quo ante*, neither improved nor further retarded, for Baltar was an itinerant from childhood, grown up as he told us among gypsies and circus people, and had none of the ancestral memories of courtesy which it was customary to find in even the poorest Jewish homes.

Baltar did not appear to know the gestures of sociality. That is not to say that he was boorish and coarse. Not at all. That would miss the whole point of Baltar, to imagine him a simple wild man, an animal. Most definitely not at all. I thought at the outset that he might be likened to the animal child who returned out of the estate of nature to the artifice of society and was instructed in its habits and findings, periodically rebelling with the pathos of any overindoctrinated organism, falling apart into despair and tears. No. Not at all Baltar. Baltar was no child of nature. He despised nature. Nature was not his home. Nor the conventicles of men.

Baltar's apposition to human society was not, however, easy to detect. His manners were flawless when he chose, his bows exaggerated, his warmth palpable, his correctness impeccable. There was no fear, ever, that Baltar would betray his crudity. In fact, if one did not know Baltar's room, if one had not examined Baltar asleep, one would not have known the Baltar that I knew. He was a monolith before the world, but at night —moreover the particular night when I felt him asleep—he revealed his disgusting symptom.

An additional word about Baltar's room. Disarray, filth, confusion. That is established. But amid the disorder there was a center of clarity: a small table upon which stood his chess set.

Where he had acquired that chess set and how he had preserved it is unknown to me, but it was a remarkable achievement of craftsmanship, made undoubtedly in Germany in the
latter part of the sixteenth century. It was a *Totentanz*, for all
the figures were apocalyptic: the bishops mitred skeletons with
scythes, the pawns dwarf corpses covered with pocked flesh,
the knights all Quixotes on skeletal Rosinantes, the rooks towers
of Babel in disrepair, and the Kings and Queens imperial
crowns and robes, through whose open folds glistened unresur-
rected flesh. The set, splendidly carved in white and black
ivory, was always in readiness at the table, and although Baltar
never played with anyone, however often Rabbi Steinmann
had offered him a game, he referred many times to having
beaten his opponent, taken him in six moves, worked upon
him some modification of a Ruy Lopez or other exotic opening
and dismantled him speedily. He spoke animatedly of his
chess combat as though, in fact, the activity of the game was
coeval with the symbolism of the pieces. No wonder, then,
that the day before the celebration of the inauguration of the
Society it was noted that Baltar had become preoccupied during the late afternoon and by suppertime black as a night
without stars. Not sullen, not pouty or irascible. Nothing.
Blackness. At last, after more than two hours of ceaseless
prodding by Simon Stern and the others at our table, for the
conversation had been occupied with the joyful anticipation
of the celebration to come and the details of its preparation,
he muttered grimly as he left the dining room, "It's simple.
This morning I lost. The first game since I learned to play."
We immediately understood. Naturally. He had lost at chess.
But to himself? He had beaten himself. It would appear simple
in the telling, but obviously it was not. The involuntary will
had bested the controlling will, for even in the solution of
chess puzzles, beyond the point that the moves are spelled
out and the positions consolidated in the printed directions,
the ability to force "white" or "black" to win or lose in the
appointed number of moves requires excellent play and powerful control. And Baltar had lost.

In the hours before dawn of the day of our festal inauguration I came to Baltar's room and felt him asleep.

The door to his room opened soundlessly and I entered. The

smell was rank, but not alone the humidity of airlessness and the secretions of sweat ducts rose to my nostrils. There was something else, a nauseating smell, which, like a puddle, situated in one place, not aerated and generalized, nevertheless emits, from its swamp of breeding, missioners of disgust into all the surrounding atmosphere. A single horsefly came to rest on my forehead and walked the terrain. I did not kill it, and it flew off, buzzing vertiginously throughout the room. I approached the bed and the smell rose like a fog. I placed my hands, all fingers, attenuated like the microscopic feet of centipedes and crept over the face of Baltar, a face stretched and taut as catgut, virtually hairless, and I discerned a contraction even in sleep which held together against the night all the throbbings of the body within. The heart sounded like a bass voice in its lower reaches, hollow in the cavity of his chest, which was a forest of hair on which his breasts were situated like the rounded acclivities of burial mounds.

My hands worked over his body like a pickpocket, penetrating from the hair stubble (a field burned clear of weeds and stumps) down to the hooded eyes whose proscenium of brows and lashes were but fringe to the hidden treasure of his gaze, to the nose—to all reports his most perfect feature, but to my fingers, touching their pulse and motion, like the flared sensitivity of stallions. My hands stopped above his lips and cupped the immensity of his jaw, tapering but slightly to the chin and curving like a crooning voice to meet the cranial cap which, descending, joined it. Oh Baltar! What a face you have to my fingers. Your mouth, I have spoken already of your mouth, that aperture of lips thin, and without generosity, held clamped even in sleep, the molars grinding unspoken words until by morning you will spit out the chaff of rejected dreams and your jaw will ache from the exertion of restless sleep. Down, down, the neck of iron, the neck of granite, in which ribbons of texture would have to be as in stone the gesture of color, for to touch, all was evenness, undifferentiated orotundity and hard, hard as the muscles of your biceps.

The smell, bitter, rose as his body moved. He was sleeping on his back, his legs raised like a drawbridge, and my hands continued to play, down his neck, his chest, his stomach; they lay upon his hips a second and then Baltar turned, a moan escaped his mouth, and a small stream of water pressed from his loins broke upon my hand. The nauseating smell, that smell of the night which I had not identified, was clear. Baltar wet his bed. The sheets were sticky when I entered and now they were soiled again.

I returned to my room at daybreak. A garbage truck clangored through the streets and a Hasidic muezzin, not unlike the door-knockers of any Eastern European *shtetl*, cried out to the Jews, "Awake and greet your Maker." It was approaching the hour of seven. Old Reuben was never late. He beat upon a tin cup and shouted out, "*Yidn*, pay attention. It's morning. Rise and greet your Maker." "Who loves you, your Maker who loves you." "Lovessss yooooooooou" drifted down the street, like a mist. Some voices from the multitudes already gathered below laughed back, "You, maybe you, old Reuben," but then a congregation formed, and ten Jews, twenty, perhaps more, collected before the grandstand vested in *tallit* and *tefillin* and began to call out joyously the ancient salutations of Good morning, dear God, Your tents are gracious, You're full of abundant kindness, we are not afraid because You are with us.

It was then that I almost cried out against my destiny, dressed as I was in gloom, the smell of piss lingering on my scrubbed hands, my cubbyholes of remembrance affixed to forehead and arm. I was strong, but I was becoming afraid.

The terror passed and behind it came the serenity of acceptance, for could I fear more than death? What else was there to fear in this life? All had been done and I had done all. Blow by blow, I had exchanged equal with life. Blind. Indeed, and sometimes full of pity for myself, blind, but not broken, and that's what life tries out on all of us, to break us. A fair test. Pass it and endure. Give over and nothing but the open pit, the same pit, the same blackness, only earlier and unremembered. The dead do not praise the Lord, neither they who go down into silence, but then neither do the living unless they set themselves to such a task, to praise and be thankful for the chance to hit back. That's all a real man can demand for himself, not give up, not give over. Damn my blind eyes, but I do not blame God for that. He sets it up, but he doesn't run the detail. We're in charge of the detail. And we're all interconnected, meshed to each other, like an endless train of coupled cars. He starts the Creation, ends gathering up the dead. I am beyond blaming. I blame no one, not even the Germans, because, after all, they were coupled to me and I to them and they learned something of my ways and I learned something of theirs. Beasts and giants of the field, titmice and sparrows, scale and dimension only, but in the end not size and power but only intention orders the universe. And I'm as much tied to that as I am to the self-pity of rage and the guilt of my blind ineffectualness. Calm yourself, Nathan. It is still permitted to praise God.

How long I sat in my introspected nudity, exposing my body while covering it with artifacts of prayer I do not know. I know the prurience of my ancestors and at one moment felt my body and shivered. But it was a liberty I took from blindness. I would not follow my eyes into sin nor could my body delight and terrify my eyes. How much, I realized at that instant, was dependent upon sight, not alone the seeing of the world, the seeing of oneself, but more than that the moral order depended upon sight. The hair of the bride is shorn, the dress rises to neck and descends to knee, head covered, arms concealed—all precaution lest the eyes behold. But do the eyes need sight to know? To that question our ancient had no answer. In one sense they knew that such questions were beside the point, for the intention of their embarrassment before the body (before nature) was a further prohibition against idolatry, lest the body be worshiped, lest the stars be worshiped, lest a bundle of sticks and stones be called divinity. True it was that none but He who made the universe deserved our worship. Could it be denied that in seeing perfected form, we adumbrate divinity and divinity runs like a vein through all things?

It must be more, this terror of mine, this imagined vision of the incongruity between my nakedness and my covering of shawl and phylacteries. I stood up and drew the shawl about me for warmth (there, that's one indication, for the shawl of prayer became a comfort against the early morning cold), and I scratched my leg with a fingernail and the thongs that

335

bound my arm rubbed up my leg and the skin bristled and rose. What then? Nothing. For my eyes could not conjoin the sensation of the body to the devisings of the imagination. The faculties connect. Nothing more. They supply the nexus between the factitiousness of reality and the spectral dreams by which we protect ourselves from the world. The eyes oblige us to connect the real and the imagined. But all this speculation was intended, I know now, to compose myself against the suggestions of terror and collapse which clotted the casual unfolding of time. About me, about us all, were palpable dangers, hints and bodings of what was to come. Had I known to read them? Had I known? Answer: Nothing could have been avoided.

A whistle sounded at the construction site a few blocks away and I knew the hour of eleven had come. The workers would come down from the scaffolding and another shift would ascend. They would take coffee, ogle the passers-by, crush beer cans in heavy fists. Eleven, and I sat still. I must dress. I undid the thong that bound my fingers into the ineffable Name and unraveled the connection which tied my heart and intelligence to other spheres. I was returned once more to pre-nuptial nakedness. I rubbed my face with my hands, and the smell of Baltar clung now to my beard. I could smell it. No one else would be aware, but my nostrils—now like those of horses, who smell what they cannot see—were revolted.

Left shoe. Where was my left shoe?

It was my custom to undress by ritual. Shirt upon straight-back chair. Tie in collar (a single tie of nondescript design and color). Pants, durable pants of corduroy, laid upon the chair seat, their unpressed legs languishing upon the floor. Socks crumpled. Shoes. A blind man's obsession. Things in place. What does a blind man do when age chips at memory, when he can no longer recollect the detail of the rhythm he enforces upon himself; he falls apart. Quite simply falls apart. I was whole, but, sometimes, at this moment, anxious to be dressed and before the multitudes, I sat down on the floor, my hand having swept a dozen times the linoleum beneath my bed, and I wept for my lost shoe. I cried out, "Oh left shoe. Oh left black, cracked shoe. Why have you deserted Nathan?"

"Not at all," a voice answered, a low and vast voice, a voice, shall I say, like a rumble in a cavern, a voice which I had to believe was that of Balter. "Behold. I give you this day a left black shoe. It is yours. Your very own. Do not lose it again or it will be lost forever, and blind men, you know, with only one shoe are regarded by the world as not only blind but mad and are picked up in the streets and destroyed like worn-out horses."

"Who's there? Is that you, Baltar?" I called up from the floor. No answer, only a low laugh, as though small rooks had fallen from a shelf within the cavern. A shoe dropped into the circle of my naked feet. The laugh thinned. The door to my room closed.

We have all felt that coldness. My body chilled and a fever of helplessness made my face flush. I finished my preparations impassively.

Again the whistle sounded and it was midday. Below the instruments hummed and voices rose and fell, as small circles of men danced and women stood about them clapping their hands, indifferent to rhythm.

The entrance door to Simon's suite of rooms was closed. It was locked. I had turned the handle.

"Come greet those who love you," I called through the keyhole. I said again, "Simon, our master and example, come greet those who love you." He had not answered my personal knock, three swift beats followed at an interval by a sharp rap. Again I said, my voice attenuated to a whisper, "Oh Simon, come answer my call to you." The lock was thrown and the door pulled open. "Let them be damned. Damned. Damned," he repeated. And then his voice steadied and the rage whimpered. "Nothing for them. I've done nothing for them. Ever. Believe me, never, ever. For myself. Only for myself." (And Simon thumped his chest—there were seven painful raps on that bony cavity, and with each rap the interval grew and the silence rose like a mountain between the murmur of the crowds without and the dead stillness of his rooms, and the rap of indignation lengthened into a muffled pound.) "I loathe them (*rap*). I despise their weakness (*rap*). I humiliate them (*rap.*) I deplete them (*rap-thump*). I suck them dry (*thump*).

337

I live through them (*thump*). I need them (*thump*). What's it for? I don't love them, those broken Jews. I hate them."

"Less," I spoke gently.

"Less?"

"Much less. You couldn't love them at all, you couldn't love me at all—us broken ones—were you not filled with loathing for yourself. Such a rage. Such a frivolous anger, Simon Stern. Listen to me. You're a runt, a *schmerl*, a young-old man. Your face is like a dried grape, no, a prune. Your arms are long and spindly. Some say like a monkey. Your body is pale and white, unhealthy like wood bleached in the rain. You're a sore, a boil. Isn't it true? Aren't you repulsive?"

I heard him gasp and he fell to the floor. I went toward him slowly, I let him suffer and then I bent down and held him in my arms and covered his neck with my kisses and my beard stroked his forehead. After some moments he subsided and the soft cries of bruised divinity passed into silent heaves.

The processional began.

The youngest of our holy congregation stepped out from the doors which were held open to the street, and by twos children, boys and girls holding hands, emerged, and by twos single men and unmarried women, and by twos husbands and wives, Halil Kantor and his wife from the tomb, Rivkeh (and before them the first-born, Abram, and their second carried in the older boy's arms), and many more, dozens, hundreds, streamed forth from the compound. With disjointed movements and solemn faces, feet stepped before feet as the processional music began, and then, as those who had stepped forth to the day of their congratulation—ascending the platform, standing before their places upon the benches that ran the dais, behind the dignitaries, coats fluttering, their skullcaps crowning wind-blown hair—the instruments struck up at a signal from the grandmaster of the festivities, Rabbi Steinmann, the sweet march in which Israelite youths and maidens come forward to greet triumphant Judas the Maccabee as he returns from his triumph over Nicanor, and then, voices intoning sweetly, silence fell upon the thousands who awaited to

"See, the conqu'ring hero comes
Sound the trumpets, beat the drums
Sports prepare, the laurel bring
Songs of triumph to him sing
See the godlike youth advance
Breathe the flutes, and lead the dance.
Myrtle-wreaths and roses twine
To deck the hero's brow divine."

What a miraculous folly, those words, happily lost to the
crowds—the little voices, not yet men, not yet women, commingled like the sweet-smelling petals of drying flowers,
swelled to salute the open door from which now stepped
forth Dr. Fisher Klay, his hand upon my shoulder, Rabbi
Steinmann beside the enormous Baltar, and after an interval,
distracted, his head raised high, like a boulder upon a hillock,
Simon Stern, forcing away a smile of pleasure, knowing that
it was he, the hero, for whom the celebration was done, but
knowing no less that his intentions were other.

"Greetings to you all. In this great city of peace and ease,
where so many millions of oppressed have gained their sanctuary and repose, we greet you and welcome you to our midst."
It was the Commissioner of Sanitation, reading from a typed
sheet. A musical salute. A blare of a trumpet, a pound of a
drum.

"It is no revelation to you, you Jews (Jews like myself) that
we are a hard-working, law-abiding community who know
only too well what happens when indolence and disorder
replace work and law. We get hit first. Now here, before us
(excuse me, behind us) is a testimony to the energy with
which Jews not only stick together but build for all bulwarks
against disorder." Feet stamped as the Deputy Mayor (the
Mayor was in Albany that day), a slight Jew with a German-
sounding name, in pinstripe and homburg, settled back to
his seat. A song. A shout broke from the back of the crowd.
It could not be heard above the wind.

Rabbi Steinmann introduced the secretary to the Jewish
Senator from New York, a young man one would gather from
his reedy voice, cadenced as an English lord's, mutant to
Harvard Square, who said, lightly, with splendid control that

only lust for Anglo-Saxonism could envy, "The great Senator from New York, a son and grandson of your very own people, is unfortunately not able to be with you today. He has a head cold and is running a temperature. But he has sent me, his executive assistant (my name, Rabbi, is Stebel, Leslie Stebel, and not *shtiebl*"—he nodded toward the Rabbi as he said this, his voice quivering with suppressed laughter, although he could scarcely have gotten the joke—"to bring you greetings" —he bent down toward his notes, presumably, for he paused and then sang out—"of great joy and salvation. Moreover, he has entrusted to me the good wishes of our benefactor, successor to the American father of the Jews who saved so many of you from poverty and blasted hopes, and moreover, worked until his tragic death to give rescue to your people, opening up the doors—wherever possible—to your fleeing and homeless ones. But that tragedy is done and you are all safe here in your own Lower East Side, and now, from our own Harry S Truman, President of the United States and heir to the mantle of our late beloved Franklin Delano Roosevelt: 'Distinguished sons of Israel, honored guests, revered benefactor and patron, Simon Stern, my wishes and greetings to you on the inauguration of the headquarters and domicile of the world-wide Society for the Rescue and Resurrection of the Jewish People' "—Voices called out "Just Jews," "Jews." "Excuse me— Jews. 'I know, as your President, of the trials through which you have passed, and it is one of my greatest satisfactions to know how much I and my predecessor Franklin Roosevelt were able to accomplish to effect your passage from the darkness of tyranny to the great light of rescue and freedom. Again all hail to you and your leader, Simon Stern. Yours, Harry S Truman, The President of the United States.' " Great applause and shouts. The Jews all loved Democratic Presidents. Only Simon Stern did not applaud, and although Fisher Klay and myself had begun to clap I felt Simon's body beside me inert and unresponsive. I stopped.

From the fringe of the crowd, beyond the rim of earshot, a mumble rose and closer came the sound of a cry, "Mur . . . mur . . . murd . . ." and approaching, the syllables collected until, from the occlusion of cries, came the word intact: MURDERER.

The young man, Leslie Stebel, stopped, and he turned around, and looked at Rabbi Steinmann. He had been heckled before but not this way. Stumping in Queens for the Senator he had felt the blood of anger against the Senator's ancestors, but not here among his own, and directed to whom? Harry Truman or, even worse, Franklin Roosevelt, the greatest President the Jews ever had, their best friend. He was undoubtedly appalled and he removed his tortoise-shell glasses and cleaned them, recomposing calm like folding a handkerchief. The voice cried closer, closer still, "MURDERER."

Simon Stern rose unexpectedly and went toward the microphone. Steinmann hastened to adjust it to his height, but Simon had still to strain his neck upward until it was bared and tense. "I do not greet you. This woman beneath us. I know her. Her name is Lubina Krawicz. You do not know Lubina Krawicz." Simon paused. Two members of the household staff of the Society reached Lubina, whose face, strained with rage, a patchwork of brown and white skin, her hands gripping the sides of a small aluminum frame with which she walked in public. They lifted her gently and one calmly covering her mouth moved her swiftly to the side of the platform and into the compound quarters. "You do not know Lubina Krawicz. I, however, know her. I know her well. And I will tell you her story. And I will tell you something of mine. And I will tell you about the Deputy Mayor. And about the Senator and his young assistant. And even about the President of the United States who has just spoken to us. I will tell you something about murder and I will tell you about murderers."

Simon spoke very slowly. There was none of the assurance of formed rhetoric. These were untouched words, fresh, unfamiliar—as though just removed from a hidden chest, they were unwrapped and offered to the ear for the first time. "It is me to whom Lubina spoke. I am the murderer. I am the murderer to whom she spoke."

"No," "No," "No," broke in cries from the multitude, and the policeman before the stand turned from facing the crowd to face Simon Stern.

"It was several years ago now. Lubina Krawicz lived, a cripple as you saw her, but at that time a beauty, a young woman of fair beauty and courage, and she lived alone in the house occupied by my mother and father and myself. Some of you here will remember my mother and father—may they rest in peace—and the house in which they lived, and some of you will surely remember Lubina Krawicz.

"It came to pass that through an inadvertence—I say that again—an inadvertence, an overlooking, a refusal to see, to pay attention, that a fire broke out in that building. Lubina Krawicz, already a cripple, was rendered an ugly and unsightly woman filled with rage, and my mother and father were burned to death.

"Inadvertence. Inadvertence." Simon cried out, his palms pushing against the air as though the density of its frigid mass was moving in to crush him. "Not paying attention. And who was he, my friends, who did not pay attention? It was I. I did not kill my parents as a killer kills." Simon's voice dropped to a choked whisper. "I did not set the fire. But I, it was I who killed them as surely as if I had lit the match, shorted the wires, overloaded the circuitry of their universe and flash, poof, incinerated. Burned to ash. Crippled.

"Who is ever the murderer? The ones we sentence and condemn? Not at all. The murderers are everywhere. They are the ones who do not pay attention. And they are all these on this platform. Everyone, a murderer. Everyone. No attention paid. They walk through their lives, their faces circled with a band, seeing only what they choose to see. Blind Nathan Gaza here, the blind man with whom I sit, with whom I take my counsel, he sees more than all of us, all of you.

"You are murderers, I am murderer. He, she, it is murderer. Mayor murderer. Senator murderer. Young Executive Assistant murderer. And even, think upon it, even the late President, with all his paralysis, murderer. Think about your own pain and don't see. Think about your own glory, your own power, your own genius, murderer. You do not see.

"We must learn to see as blind Nathan sees or we are all to remain murderers until the end, until the end of our lives, until the end of time, until the end of history, when the only ransom we will have is that someone blameless, someone who has risen beyond blame to blamelessness, will come to us, a redeemer, the *Meshiach*, may he come speedily in our time, for we need him to show us to see. Amen."

342

He, the murderer. Simon the murderer. The words swept from his mouth like the pebbles of a stuttering orator, suddenly transfigured. Did I know joy at that instant of his speech from the platform mount, his words flying upward to the microphone like hummingbirds and coming forth to them, to all of them like lightning bolts, his face flashing like that of Moses, glowing with self-recognition? Some did not understand and, frightened, threw paper bags with crusts of sandwiches and orange peels, threw packages of cigarettes, threw gnawed potatoes—a shoe was thrown. Simon was struck by something. He covered his forehead with his hands and grimaced with pain. Blood, not much blood, edged through his fingers and he was led away to the compound by Fisher Klay. Rabbi Steinmann restored a semblance of order. The limousines carried off the dignitaries, preceded by sirens and motorcycled policemen.

How splendidly deserted it was by late afternoon. The Society for the Rescue and Resurrection of the Jews had been inaugurated.

The settlement grew and flourished in the months that followed. A new year, religious and secular, passed and the spring of 1947 began.

The events of the inauguration were not discussed. That is to say, I realized that it was best not to pursue the significance of Simon's astonishing confession, nor were objections made (although one imagines curiosity was considerable) when Lubina Krawicz was installed in the chambers—a bedroom, sitting room, and bath—above his own. The newspapers had reported upon the celebration, but fortunately the proceedings had been anticipated by Steinmann's expertly worded press releases and none but the Yiddish press had regarded the occasion as being of sufficient note to send eyewitness reporters. For that reason the world uptown remained unaware of the extraordinary events of that day. The Yiddish press, however, was fascinated, and lengthy accounts of Simon's career were published. The leftist press regarded Simon's confession with considerably greater charity than the conservative religious papers. The former interpreted his misfortune as an unavoidable consequence of decadent capitalism, the latter

343

/

as attributable to his purported indifference to the ritual law. Whatever the musings of journalists, the fact remains that, if nothing else, the activities and founder of the Society were now subject to continuous scrutiny, and our press releases— the opening of our branch in London, the distribution of Simon's infrequent public addresses, the documentation of his wealth—were all duly reported. What was not reported, what could not be reported, since most of us were unaware, was the shift in the interior life of the Society. We were no longer single-mindedly engaged in charitable work, in ransoming through European agents the typical incunabula of our Jewish past—tractates, prayer books, volumes of *hasidus*, works of Jewish philosophy and codes of Jewish law—which had been stolen by the enemy to exhibit in libraries formed to document our degeneracy, or occupied even primarily in training and rehabilitation, although we sent many of our number to trade and vocational schools and, in due course, sent forth into the world able typists, mechanics, carpenters, and started on their way to university many others who would become doctors, lawyers, engineers, physicists, and mathematicians.

The surface shined with our useful activity, and the Society became the envy and admiration of charitable institutions and religious sects, each sending delegations to our headquarters to discuss with our accountants and business managers, our teachers, therapists, counselors the techniques of resuscitation we were employing with such apparent success. (Nightmares diminished, spitting on floors decreased, defecation in the corners of the buildings ended.) It would have appeared to the casual visitor that in less than two years sociality and ease had all but returned to our community. And it was so. But then it was not so. Smoothness and calm was restricted to the daylight hours, between the sounding of the morning call to rise and the evening hours when shadows gathered in the corridors. It was at night that the interior life of the community flourished, lectures, concerts, religious study and private interviews with Simon Stern.

It is all told by me with such matter-of-factness. Growth, success, expansion. I think back to these penultimate months and run my hands over their face trying to recover the crags and pits I had failed to sense at the time. It seems no less than I have reported it. There were no obvious signs, no further omens. My left shoe never deserted me again; Baltar lost no more at chess; Lubina was quiet in her rooms, listening to chamber music; Fisher Klay traveled throughout the country and abroad raising money for the Jews of Israel soon to be elevated to nationhood; Rabbi Steinmann studied the Kaballah and watched over the far-flung establishments of the Society; and Simon Stern, through accountants and lawyers, continued with half an interest to accumulate wealth. It was normal, all was normal and precisely its normalcy should have warned me, for it could not be that Simon Stern had become bored and unoriginal.

Messiahs are not revolutionaries.

They are, the real messiahs, those few, the single ones, all for the status quo, *the* status quo ante *however, when situated in paradise creatures were splendidly dignified and serene. Even after knowledge descended like a summer cloud upon their councils, causing them to cover (and, tradition believes, to dissimulate) their nakedness, they were still marvelously innocent. The tradition, always guarding against the future was unsubtle, for self-consciousness is no concession to finitude and death unless there be the sense of historic past.*

Paradise has neither history nor time. A silly myth-making to accuse those primal creatures of a knowledge which can be born only from acts committed as crimes. Nakedness no crime. And carnality. How? to innocent eyes. The psychology of the myth-makers is always to control births, restrict the consumption of food, prevent scarcity, diminish useless labor. Theologians are all social planners. I can't think of Adam and Eve as more than occasions for rescuing forgetfulness and loss, making memory memorial, time a frozen valley. The messiahs are only disrupters who seek to restore an ancient balance.

No less is it a perversity to imagine that messiahs are all gentle men, with delicate hands, and graceful beards, men who glide through the world hardly touching the dust of the road. It is the way with tough creatures that they arrange to dispatch their images of ransom and perfection to that corner of the universe where doves and pigeons coo (creatures who are, despite poetry, naturally fierce and tenacious).

The world breaks its pastoral messiahs, transforming them as did the Byzantines from tenderness into ferocious judges who sit astride the universe, reminding the arrogant that even they are under scrutiny and at the end of days will meet their judgment. Those are ancient images, the images we preserve like faded photographs to remind us of the bygone and forgotten, to remove on festive occasions to smile and whimper over old ideas and tired prophecies. It has been such a wild excursion, this passage of men through time. Nonetheless how much we would like (and arrange to satisfy the wish) that all the dead heroes and visionaries be remembered only by a few simple truths and apothegms, redacted into books where they can be hidden, their words flattened by lockets of hair and dead flowers. Do the words come off on rose petals or alter the color of hair? The words are limp like the bodies of the adored. O Protestant Christ of the Americas, sun-tanned. O Christ of the Catholics, crucified to humble the might of Louis and Charles. Would you, like an Emperor, tramp the snows of Canossa barefoot, barehead, to abase all your power before a fat man?

What a miraculous history of reversal. All the confusion of men who cannot get straight the simple message of the way. The progress of creatures toward their death is all. Civilization, an arrangement to quiet the discontent of creatures who rage against death and struggle to die. Because Simon Stern is not like those ancient images, he is disbelieved, he disbelieves himself. He does not recognize what men make of him and how he collects his own self like a mendicant with an alms bowl. But he does not know (a fact which I know and have always known) that he, no less than all messiahs, is a victim of historical memory.

How should a messiah behave? Now tell me. Do you know? You know only one thing: that he relieves your pain, your precise pain. He is messiah to your particularity. That and only that and for the sake of that you would hang up your crutch at his altar or offer a votive in testimonial thanksgiving. Particularity. Always particularity. To make this unbearable excursion along the way to death tolerable. Your needs are no more than what the world of thoughtful and discriminating men call "simple needs." They, those others, with vast skulls and im-

346

probable learning, appeal to the history of general truths. They speak quietly, their words minced and fine, of such vast needs as the surcease of pain, the remission of violence, the removal of hunger, the release from venom, rancor, fury. They want a world transfigured without changing the species. The same creatures with somehow new hearts and new perceptions. They are as smugly general as the others are pitiably particular. The way is finally more difficult. Not alone difficult. Improbable. Implausible. Not impossible. I would never say the word impossible, for that I have experienced (the impossible is not a general truth, but a judgment upon the particular and hence, logically, what is impossible to me though it save my life is not impossible to him whose special task is saving lives, who does it so well, so confidently, so casually it appears to us as miracle and on that we, I, believe).

The Messiah, you see, is a general truth whose very being depends upon particulars. He is a general truth, a general person, a general humanity, whom helpful thinkers (liberal and generous minds who are embarrassed by such unemancipated notions as messiahs) confuse with the Declaration of the Rights of Man, constitutional guarantees and lists of individual rights, imperial codes and rescripts which guarantee what men can never guarantee for long. Do you not see that messiahs are not general truths and men do not make messiahs? They can sit about their clubs and vote on his merits or qualifications, but they have nothing to do with the real fact. That my life was saved by a general truth? Can you believe that? That a very particular man, ordinary in his khaki trousers, saw me bowed before the gate reading prayers from a book I could not see. He saw me and took me by the hand. That is all there is to being a messiah.

The predicament arises when the particular man, saving the particular man, becomes a general truth; that is to say, when the particular man saves more than one particular man, when the act of saving is no longer an act, but the transmission of the account of an act of saving, when others are saved by hearing about an earlier salvation; when lessons, maxims, propositions are extracted from particular acts and made general truths; when legends are born and myths created; when life becomes art, we have to worry. It is then we are in danger

347

of getting it all wrong. All of the glory and catastrophe of history rests squarely with scribes and redactors.

It was better when nothing was written down. Our sages wrote nothing down for centuries. But then the ugly general truth became manifest. Note that the first books of the Torah (until writing became a priestly habit) are full of stories and accounts. Doesn't one learn enormously from hearing the direct, unencumbered declaration of the lives and deeds of patriarchs? Of a sudden, however, it becomes very grave and dark, lists of sins, inventories of requirements, detailed records of cubits and numbers, measurements and definitions.

It makes me sick that I am one of them, a redactor who has to make it clear and luminous with the precisions of the forgetful that thus and so is the right and proper way. Comport yourself before the Lord with modesty and grace. But why not, like the fathers of the faith, sing, dance, rage, shout, backslide, build, tear apart, cross through, wander freely, eat fresh manna, and above all, take the name of God directly into the mouth like breadfruit, without importunings and scribbles, without the intermediations of transcribers and second-generation poets.

A messiah is a miraculous conjunction of a time with an ashen face and the ingredient of foolish courage and intense concentration. They come together rarely. When they fail to conjoin, we are given other prodigies. Military heroes; revolutionaries with intense eyes; zealots and martyrs; imaginative presidents and representatives. Or we are given painters who observe the lineaments of privacy and transcribe the world to the edge of the canvas; poets who finish their poems and end with a generous bit of loving-kindness or just rage before some obscure relative, or dead parent; we receive philosophers who stand their ground by ingesting the ground of the world; and even, sometimes, we are given theologians who think that God is a substance they have identified for the first time. But we have few messiahs and we have few redactors. The few we have require epic poets, blind men like Homer, like myself.

Simon Stern examined all the things that passed through his life and chose from them those that could sustain the mark of his attention. He did not think himself indulgent or vain when he fastened upon the word of a conversation (a self-evident

word spoken in haste or enjoyment, a word like "responsible"
or "silence" or "charity") and would raise his face to the
speaker and ask him to be very precise, to clarify, to make
certain he had understood.

"Do you mean silence as in the silence of winds (which
make noise but carry peace if all else is silent before their
speech) or silence as a contemplative who hears nothing but
the boom and clangor of the ineffable, or do you mean, sir,
silence as in speech which says nothing and is thus accounted
as silent? What is this silence that you seek? It passes under-
standing? Good. It is a true silence."

Simon Stern required of himself that he try to understand.
He was never an intellectual. He tried only to ask the right
questions. Revelation, miracle? To ask the right question?
Imagine if you can a man who stands in the center of a square
and asks over and over again, measured, beaten out like gold,
a simple question such as, "Why do you make so much noise?"
He stands there, days upon end, weeks untold. In a month he
is passed by ten thousand men. Each sees him standing upon
his upturned eggcrate and hears him ask, "Why do you make
so much noise?" They laugh back at him. They ignore him.
But then, of course (you will have guessed it already), one day
a powerful man comes to the square to speak, a man of such
extraordinary power that he can only tell lies, and as the car
bearing this person of power passes through the square he
hears distinctly the quiet, measured voice, asking, "Why do
you make so much noise?" And instantly, from the quiet and
calm of the question, he sees what he is become, he breaks
into tears and he remembers the question of his mother who
spoke to him so often and said so gently to his molested face,
"Child, why do you make so much noise?"

Do you not think that the repetitive, undoubtedly deranged
questioner of the square has been a messiah?

No single messiah will make clear to you that the Messiah
exists, that he comes forth daily like dawn. He is not alone
what you need, nor alone what you desire, surely not he for
whom you lust; he is the one who compels you to raise a
finger toward the snarled web of what you can become. He is
the dream of becoming. But not any dream? Not the dreams
of your perverse heart nor your agitated passions. The Mes-

349

siah is not the Other who fulfills the proud self. The Messiah
is neither libertine nor puritan. He has no ethical wish. I
underscore that! Think of messiahs with admirable bodies
and cured form, with liberated flesh and ennobled intelligence
and you dream a false dream. Nor would the Messiah censure
you for it. Nor would God who judges both he and we in one.
Messiahs and doing good works are not the same. It is good
for the rhetoric of communities and the gathering of donations
that the good and true be with us or with them or with
another. No matter. All faiths are true insofar as ethics are
concerned. What faith counsels murder or rapine, praises
avarice and greed, commands corruption and underscores the
promise of cruelty and injustice? Think upon it. All command
virtue. God is the principle and cornerstone of preaching
virtue. But we know, when the liturgy expires and the faithful
recover the presence of reality as they bundle into their coats
and step out into the cold, that something else adheres to
the universe. Those houses of worship are no sanctuary from
the world. At the most, interludes. Nothing avails if you would
think God an ethical man, a just man, a decent fellow. He is
nothing like that. But as well he is no king of tyrants, no
many-headed beast who heaves and lusts upon the world.
Ethics has nothing to do with anything but what we wish to
preserve to priggish lust and moralized injustice. What men
actually demand of life is a bit more of seeing straight and
paying attention.

The Messiah touches the infant God whom we worship and
the lined face that we become. The Messiah is not goodness.
He is hope.

Simon Stern was not unaware that he was anointed. No finger
transcribed a mark upon his forehead nor touched his lip, but
he was aware. What it meant, however, he did not know. He
tried everything to find out. And he made desperate mistakes,
but the promise of anointment drove him toward his freedom
as surely as if he were a child who prophesied by the arrangement of his toys. Saving was his illusion, acting upon the world
and altering its arrangements; staying still, being there, the
simple fact of presence and movement among men, doing as
they believe themselves to do, eating, touching, feasting eyes,
hugging trees, smiling at clouds, describing circles in the air,

350

tying shoes, fastening windows, undoing knots, all these exhibitions of mundane similarity concealed from him as much as from others that all his gestures were suspended in a hesitancy, a species of reflexivity uncommon among ordinary men.

Besides these moments there would be vast leaps of excursus and invention, trying out upon the world the wrenched imagination, the ellipse of an intelligence thrust from its proper gravity. In such moments Simon was the horizon of popular legend—a demon, a madman, a theurgist who turned everything upside down, who made old things carry new definitions. There are many already. The most prescient and important were to come.

The first of those which I select was the celebration of the Festival of Purim, the last Purim before the destruction.

The streets were impassable. It was not yet sundown and already the streets were rising and falling to the pounding of feet and the cheers and shouts of children. They came from every section of the city, from all the outposts of the community. Snow had fallen two days earlier and the snow plows had only that morning come to our section of the city. A light rain had begun in the early afternoon and the snow was melting. It was no longer very cold. Neither was it springtime. But it was the time of rejoicing.

It was Purim, and Purim had a particular instruction for our community. Purim? Let me tell you very briefly, so you will understand both the actual significance of that ancient drama of Shushan, in the land of Persia, and its special significance to us, a community of remnants.

Purim. Purim makes no sense at all. It is a holiday celebrating craziness: a Jewish girl is taken by a non-Jewish king to be his concubine (already it's a bit peculiar—can you imagine pious Jews stroking their beards and meditating upon the divine truth of a mixed marriage, and that not even a marriage but the illicit concourse of a Jewish beauty and a middle-aged Persian king?). There is then a vicious adviser to the king who, angered by the bad manners of Mordecai, the guardian of the orphaned concubine, Esther, who had supplanted Vashti, the proper queen, seeks to kill him and, with him, all the Jews of the kingdom of Persia.

351

Esther, who, on the advice of her proud guardian, has not told the king (Ahasuerus is his name and it is he who always appears in the legends of necromancers and Indo-European mythologists) that she is Jewish (it being considered prudent, even in those days, to conceal such an ambiguous fact), is called upon by Mordecai to save the Jews. Cunning that she was, she cozens the king and wicked Haman to a feast, and there, having secured the favor of the king, no doubt, by heaving her breasts and casting lustful glances at him, receives the promise of anything she wishes. There and then she says that Haman is a monster, murderer (and an anti-Semite), who wants to hang her guardian, and destroy her people. The king becomes furious and exits. He comes back, and mistaking Haman on his knees pleading with Esther for Haman making advances to his beauty, orders him hanged and gives the Jews license to go on a rampage against the Persians. They do. Many gentiles are killed. The Jews are saved and the text notes repetitively that the Jews were very well behaved and slew their enemies without touching their goods (the opposite of what Haman had told his murderers they could do with the spoils of the Jews). The story is recounted amid feasts and drinking and rapine and lust and blood and slaughter.

It is a foul book of the Bible. Indeed, the rabbis were of many minds as to whether it should be recended into the canon of the Word of God. It was. Xenophobia prevailed against scruples or, perhaps more to the point, the Jews could not ignore the opportunity to include in their sacred history one document which made clear the hubris of their humanity. And so, at the same time that I cannot bear to read this book and have always refused commissions to transcribe it on parchment for use in the synagogue when it is read on the Festival of Purim, I cannot help but regard Purim as a triumph of the imagination. Here is a people who thinks it marvelous good fun to laugh at persecutors, to rejoice at the imminence of disaster, to relish a liberation in which not once is the name of God mentioned.

The Jews make a festival of recreation and abandon out of the downfall of a real, true-to-life anti-Semite. Anti-Semite? Haman didn't like Jews. Jews were separatist, private, exclusive. They didn't eat with their gentile neighbors. They kept their daughters and sons aloof from marriage with them. They appeared sometimes to be indifferent to the fortunes of their neighbors. They were regarded as fickle and untrustworthy citizens, and therefore advisers like Haman and after him thousands of princes, counselors, regents, kings, senators, presidents and potentates have seen fit to decide against them and to slay them. And the Jews make a holiday.

Do you realize in honor of Purim Jews are commanded to get drunk? To get drunk, mind you. Not simply to have a sip or a taste, but to get so drunk that when the names of Mordecai and Haman are mentioned during the chanting of the scroll they can't tell the difference. Also, Jews get dressed up, put on faces, costumes, masks—like a proper carnival. On Purim Jews pretend they're not Jews. For twenty-four hours they pretend that they are masters of casualness, that they haven't a thing on their minds, that for twenty-four hours God is off duty and has forgotten about them. Mind you, of course, *they* still have to pay attention. They can relax, fine, but they can't become forgetful. They still have to *daven*, and go to *shul*, and eat carefully, and be chaste—they can't get into real trouble, but they can cut up a little. And that's the real point. Escaping the decree of Ahasuerus without a miracle, just by cunning and cleverness and a little unabashed concubinage makes for Jewish joy. The Jews, forgive me, got away with murder— they escaped being murdered and they went out on the town and gave it back double. They were nasty and vengeful and they did it without God and they won. Ever since, Purim was a festival. It's the last time the Jews pulled it off. Millions dead later, they're still celebrating Purim as though it were yesterday, taking a day off from saying *Kaddish* to make a celebration out of the one really vulgar episode in their history.

But for Simon Stern, Purim was a sacred event. Simon regarded Purim differently than I. The afternoon before the eve of this Purim, he took me into a section of his library which he kept locked and showed me a book of photographs of a medieval monastery where a choir of dwarfs, dressed in costume, were dancing around a Maypole. While he showed me, and explained what seeing eyes could see, my hand rested

353

upon his own, which covered the top of the page. The faces of the dwarfs were obscured by the fingers of his hands which splayed the etchings, making the detail invisible. Like seeing faces in a forest. And then he slowly withdrew his hand, my hand with his own, and began to tell me in a voice charged with intensities of madness what I would have seen.

"All the dwarfs, Nathan, those dancing dwarfs, their feet kicking up in little shoes, their colored doublets puffed and swirling, are all wearing death's heads. And above them, reigning as their lord and king, is the mocking face of Satan. Now, that, Nathan, is Purim."

"Purim," I gasped. "Purim," he repeated, "the feast day of the Adversary. It is our apotheosis and it must be celebrated that way."

"But, Simon," I protested, "it isn't so. Purim is a feast of liberation, a celebration of escape. You make it an incantation to the Adversary. We want to forget him. We've seen him face to face. You haven't."

Simon was silent. "You're right. Of course you're right, Nathan. But the truth is always mixed. Of course. Of course. I have no right to force others to see the blackness I have before me. But it's there. Purim should warn us, not deceive us."

"Of what?"

"If not Haman, another drunken Ahasuerus. Who am I? Mordecai at the gate refusing to bow down? Who am I? Esther bedazzling, tricking, seducing? No." Simon paused. He seemed to be reflecting aloud, as though I were not there. "This year it must be different. So many things are different now. Soon we will be ready. But we are unprepared. This Purim it must be different. *It will be different.* The raggle-taggle of past years must go. It must be a show of unanimity, of our strength to resist, to die, to live again. They will drink as in the past, and they will revel and sing and masquerade as in all the years of their lives. But this year, something different. Something so that they will know"—and as he said this he tore the etching of the dwarf from the volume and in a voice hissing with decision—"that we must also rejoice in a dance of death."

Simon's resolve to transform us, to wither our ancient limbs

354

of submission and paralyze our habitual knee-bending to historical fortune, struck me then as uncharacteristically ungenerous. He doubted his vocation, but what hero is without doubts? What seemed incongruous, unworthy—in a word, mean—is that he forced us—we who had endured—to become the playing field of his caprice, fighting out on us struggles which were higher (and deeper, and therefore more obscure in origin and incitement) than we could comprehend, much less deserve. I felt again the influence of Baltar's advice that Simon train anger on his own.

Was it Baltar presiding over the congregation of our dwarfs? our Adversary? our rod of instruction? Baltar at my elbow, Baltar bringing internal cool into the warmest of rooms, taciturn, muttering Baltar, skulking in the wings of our universe. He spoke to none but Simon Stern; he spat words at Klay and Steinmann; he humored and seduced our company; but only to Simon Stern did he speak and to me, to me, for my blindness was a patent from heaven and the threat of another sight.

Many hundreds of people, as I have already said, those within the compound, visitors and friends, crowded the streets in the hour before sundown. Small bonfires burned in metal trashcans, and children, with masks of painted gauze clinging to their faces—the mustachios of fantasied viziers and the turbans of imperial regents—marched in mock solemnity about young Vashtis and Esthers, their costume gowns trailing in the melting slow. Ginger cakes stamped in molds of Biblical personages and steaming tea laced with brandy were sold by street vendors. The crowd continued to grow. The reading of the Scroll of Esther was to be at the hour of seven, and already the air crackled with noisemakers and the thump of small drums as children prepared to drown in noise the mention of Haman's name. It was all joy and exuberance, but for the expectation that an unknown sage, a *maggid,* an itinerant preacher, known only to Simon Stern, would speak at the conclusion of the reading.

The service began in the compound synagogue, a large but intimate space calm with white, the pews arranged in rectangles facing the centered *bimah,* behind which rose up the free-standing Ark of cedar wood. The synagogue was crowded, people standing in the aisles, children clustered in the center, a phalanx of noise, rattling their noisemakers, shoving each other, laughing and pranking. The heat of the room rose, despite the cold of the day, and foreheads glistened with perspiration. The service threaded the intimacies of nods and conversations, waved greetings and clattering clappers. The prayers were sung out, words shouted punctuated by the expectant squeals of the children. Friendly divinity.

At the conclusion of the service, Rabbi Steinmann, nodding to Simon Stern for permission, ascended the *bimah* and before him lay the Scroll of Esther, written by the hand of a North Italian Renaissance scribe, its letters marvelously tricked with discreet curlicues, its borders elaborated with the particular scenes which dominate the narrative of the book, and its opening sheet surmounted by enormously detailed and expressive impressions of the principal characters of the story but for the figure of Haman, whose head, in obvious irony, bore a high conical hat on which was written "Edom," the Biblical tribe which, in the imagination of the Jews, contained and exhibited all of Christendom.

Rabbi Steinmann, his voice gutted by decades of Eastern European Ashkenazic, sang the trope of the text with a strained eloquence. He sang it as a living text, intoning, caressing, raising his voice with dramatic intensity and hushing it as suddenly, obedient to the dramatic rhythms of the story. "Now it came to pass in the days of Ahasuerus." A storyteller's delight. What a calm and distinguished opening. Flat and resonant, he proceeded to the insult of Vashti, and again calm, with distinction: "Then the king said to the wise men, who knew the times." And Vashti was cast away and the virgins assembled and the orphaned Jewess, Esther, brought with other maidens to the pleasure of the King, selected and raised up, and the plot discovered, and Esther, informed by the attentive Mordecai, discloses the advice in Mordecai's name and the King is saved and Mordecai raised up and the Queen, the Queen Esther, further honored in the sight of the grateful king.

All this in attentive silence, whistles, noisemakers occasionally breaking the solemnity of the reading, but at the commencement of the third chapter of the narrative the hated name was mentioned. Rabbi Steinmann paused, looked up and smiled, and the noise of hundreds of clappers cracked through the synagogue and boos and hisses, amid nervous laughter, broke from the assembly. And so it continued through dozens of Hamans and the joy ascended and crested and the salvation of the Jews was announced with the hanging of Haman upon the gallows he had readied for the beloved Mordecai. Jeers broke like united thunder, a single clap, and the body of Haman fell limp into the imagination. The succeeding Hamans, the ordinary identifying mentions—the house of Haman, the gift of Haman's ring—were received with fewer shouts and congratulations, only the children continuing, mindless of the words, to stamp their feet and beat their drums.

The reading of the Scroll of Esther ended in a conclusion of sentiment and remembrance and so the Jews were commended for all generations to fast—as they had done on the day before the festival to commemorate the disaster averted and to celebrate thereafter the day of their natural remission and resurrection. "For Mordecai the Jew was next unto King Ahasuerus, and great among the Jews and accepted of the multitude of his brethren; seeking the good of his people and speaking peace to all his seed."

Rabbi Steinmann concluded the reading and returned to his seat in the synagogue facing the eastern wall. Silence fell upon the assembly and remained unbroken for some moments, rustling and straining, unnerved, the heat rising with the anticipation. It was the moment when the unknown *maggid*, "Simon's own *maggid*" as he was called, would appear and stand up before the congregation of the rescued and resurrected.

At the back of the synagogue a large figure wrapped in a black cloak whose hood covered his face, and supporting his weight upon a staff, moved slowly toward the *almemor*. Slowly he moved, his feet advancing in light slippers, the toes of which were curled and striped like the slippers of jesters and his stockings visible beneath his cloak, not white like a Hasid's, were a crisscross of colors. He moved unhesitantly toward the platform which supported the Ark of the Scroll until the congregation came to silence, smiles retained, faces bright with the hope of further delight and entertainment, for even great *maggidim* would be jolly on this most jolly of festivals. The *maggid's* face remained bonded to his chest, averted in the folds of his enveloping cloak, his body rising like a cenotaph draped in crepe.

"The words with which this sacred scripture conclude are these: 'seeking the good of his people and speaking peace to all his seed.' " The *maggid's* voice, vast, even, unmodulated, echoed throughout the synagogue.

"The paroxysm is done. The enemy is slaughtered. The many Persians are butchered by the beleaguered of our people. Haman hanged and Esther confirmed. Ahasuerus justified and Mordecai elevated to be the second, mind you, the second to the king of a nation which stretched from India to Ethiopia, numbering over 'a hundred and seven and twenty provinces.'

"It is well within the people called Jews, brought to that far-off kingdom in the time of Nebuchadnezzar. The first exile of the people. The people called Hebrews in the Land; called Jews by the nations of the world." The sonority of the voice, speaking a learned English, perfect, unaccented, of no place but a textbook or the bowels of the earth, broke into plain song, the meter of his words establishing a cadence without melody.

"Now then let us think first of this matter of names. Do you, gathered before me by your master and teacher, do you prefer to be called Hebrews or Jews?" The voice seemed familiar, a voice known, but still elusive. "I ask for hands in this matter. But before we vote on the election of your name, let me comment further. Hebrew—tribe name of the blood. Jew—spat out like phlegm. I prejudice your vote. That is permitted. I am a preacher with the right to influence your decision, to prejudice you, yes, to prejudice you. Vote then. Up with the hands. All hands. Children. Children. You, too, little ones, you may vote. Raise your hand. One hand only." The *maggid* was mocking the community, now snarling, now sniveling.

"Think about the sound. I shall say the sound. The sound I say is *Heb-rew.* The sound now is *Ju-Jud-Jude-Yid.* Now then, let us vote. Once more. *Yid.*"

Hands rose. Some hands. Very few. I felt Simon's arm rise.

It was scarcely seen, for he was blocked by the bulky figure of Rabbi Steinmann, who sat behind him. Where was Baltar? I did not feel his heavy breathing upon my neck.

"The vote. I shall announce the results at the end. I shall count slowly and announce. Now *Hebrew*."

Hands clawed at the heat, arms shot forward, upward, calling out to the great *maggid* to be counted.

"Splendid. It's obvious. This *shul* holds exactly eleven hundred and eighty-six persons. There are about a hundred of you standing. And the count. Clearly. Only eleven of you wish to be Yids. The rest want to be Hebrews.

"How easy it was to transform you," the *maggid* hissed hoarsely, his voice heavy with disgust. The voice was obvious now. Simon had kept his promise to transform us, to train his anger upon us.

"Spit a little on your name and you swallow it," the *maggid* continued, his voice rising in even stages, plateauing, rising again, until it would reach the elevations of clouds, thin air, breathless, seething vapors and currents, where blizzards and tornadoes have their beginnings. "You're alive today because you lick spittles. You're alive because you hid out in the folds of your spit and endured. But what did the Jews of Shushan and the hundred and seven and twenty provinces do? What did they do? They schemed against the nations and they triumphed, they tricked a king of the gentiles and they endured, they butchered the Persians and Mordecai became second in command. Now, what do you think of that? What's the point of being Hebrews—a tribe of the blood—if you don't even know what blood demands. No more for the moment about blood." The *maggid*'s voice collapsed and tumbled from the heights.

"About you? Have you a wish to be like the Jews of Persia? Then you must congeal like ice, not frozen with terror, but frozen with the energy of bodies rigid and condensed, ice-cold, the coldness of underground fasts where bodies await the skull measurers of the future to dig them up and identify, *Anthropus Judaeis*—the Jewish skull, adamantine, frozen, sockets of grief filled with the dust of Alexander's blackened fingernails, with the eyelashes of Hadrian, with the down of Napoleon's cheeks, with the wrinkles of Stalin's face and the hairs of Hitler's mustache—those detachable appendages of the powerful will wither and turn to dust and fill up the skulls of our dead.

"You cannot bear more this evening. I am not finished. I have just begun. But it is enough for one Purim."

The moans began in the gallery of the women—cries, and moans. What an insanity. Some men tore their garments in mourning and children hid their faces in their hands and screamed. The speaker, his hatred spent, stopped his mouth. His flailing arm went silent and grasped once more his staff and the cloak clasped to his neck fell open, and there before us was a figure of death, his garment appliquéd with bones, his face mask a whitened skull. Stunned silence interrupted by renewed screams, this time of horror and amazement, followed by the rage of the obsessed broke forth, and the figure, pulling the cloak about his body, moved proudly from the platform and slowly disappeared down the center aisle, faces turning away as he passed.

It was more than a quarter-hour before the young among our community struggled up from their seats and began to leave the synagogue. It was the end of Purim.

In the weeks that succeeded the festival the community, unnerved and agitated by the words of the *maggid*, went about its tasks sullen and unfriendly. Members who departed daily for their jobs in the large city beyond the settlement returned full of irritation and resentment, berating the subways and the filth of other men. The women, left home to tend the quarters or mind children, burst unaccountably into tears or held their charges with such ferocity that sometimes the healthy bustle of the daytime was saddened by the tears of little boys seeking to break away from the embrace of their mothers.

No one identified the *maggid*. Simon Stern would speak no more of him, turning away questions with annoyance. "It's all done. It's over. We've all seen and learned. That's enough for the moment." But it was not enough, really. Dr. Klay was very angry with Simon for permitting such a lunatic, such a tasteless frenzy, to be loosed upon people who had borne so much already. But Dr. Klay's anger was unavailing. There was no apology to the community. Gradually the agitation subsided, but it was never forgotten. The words of the *maggid*, dropped as seeds into the ready soil of the community, would soon grow forth, mutant and wild.

It was a Saturday night at the end of April, 1947, that I first heard unfamiliar noises and mutterings. Not unusually, our community was depleted on Saturday nights. The Sabbath over, families went to visit in other parts of the city. Some had relatives in Brooklyn and joined them for an evening of conversation. Many remained away overnight, returning late on Sunday. Yet others would go to theater and film, remaining afterward to sip tea and eat cakes at the late cafés of Yiddish intellectuals. After midnight on the eve of the first day of our normal week, our community was usually down to half-strength.

Earlier that night, amid the gathering shadows of evening, I had ended the Sabbath in the company of Simon Stern, Baltar, Rabbi Steinmann, Fisher Klay, and a curious assemblage of visitors, men in small fedoras, their sharkskin suits redolent with cigar smoke. These other guests at table—there were seven, I believe, all identified by the names of cities from which they came, were introduced to us, to Simon Stern, by Baltar. We did not understand what it meant to be named Sy from Newark, or Mac from Cleveland, or Jake from Chicago, but Baltar knew, and Simon acquiesced to the information, acknowledging at the conclusion of his introductions that he was grateful for their visit.

The table, for this, the concluding feast of the Sabbath, the mystic Third Meal which bids the bride of the Sabbath farewell, had been set for sixteen persons. The men clustered about its head, listening to Simon, who spoke softly and intently with them. Several women of the community poured wine and distributed the small tidbits of jellied fish and bowls of cold vegetables among the guests, returning to their places where they chatted among themselves, looking up and attending only at those moments when our voices were raised up in song or when Simon began to speak.

The words of Simon's allocution, the homily and its interpretation, which I remembered and transcribed immediately after the conclusion of the gathering, are as accurate as fallible memory allows. The verisimilitude of my recollection of the

361

homily and its interpretations is underscored, however, by the discovery of a meditation which Simon undoubtedly jotted down either shortly before or just after this Third Meal. It is the interior argument which he developed in order to justify to himself the pain he felt and the pain he wished to impose upon the world. A sad document, it was found among the papers which were retrieved by me several months after the end from a vault in a neighborhood bank where they had been placed, it would seem, only a week before the fire.

AN ALLOCUTION OF SIMON STERN

It would be traditional to speak to you of the portion of the Torah read this morning, to comment upon its intention and significance for us today, to establish correlations and contemporaneities between the leading forth of the Jews from the land of Egypt to the leading in of the People to the Holy Land which goes forward at this moment and will soon be consummated, may it be His will, in the national reconstitution of the Jewish people. And then, no doubt, having established such easily understood analogies between then and now, I could ascend the ladder of understanding to more subtle meanings, playing upon a syntax or an eccentricity of language, constructing dialectical castles which later, my ladders laid against their walls, climbing higher, I would set afire in order to fabricate out of the billows of smoke and flame even more ethereal and mysterious towers and drawbridges by which to lead you, to lead myself, to that perfect union of our souls in love to the beloved One whom we seek to meet and know. But I cannot do this, not to you, gentlemen, who visit us for this Holy Sabbath, who were called to the reading of the Torah, who chanted the blessings and then transmitted blessings to your wives and children and the prospering of your hand.

No. I could not, at this Third Meal of Holy Sabbath, misrepresent to you the truth of my feeling. I would dishonor you and dishonor myself.

I shall propose therefore a homily for your consideration. I will pause briefly after its completion and then I shall interpret its significance. Since I am the author of the homily and also its interpreter, you shall have to bear in mind the curious division in my spirit, one part adhering to a text (which I create) and the other to an exegesis (which, also, I create). But let me assure you of one thing. Although I have created the homily I have not determined its meaning. That will come after the pause in which we will all think together about its meaning.

The Homily of the Roses

It is said, if I recall the passage correctly, that one of our ancient rabbis was a gardener. I cannot remember his name. (I quote sources poorly. Since all of us, you no less than myself, are sources, it isn't relevant to remember the original. In any case, I cannot remember the rabbi's name and it does not matter. We have so many ancient teachers.)

The ancient rabbi raised roses.

He would go out into the desert each morning, and there, among the rocks, he would grow roses, sheltered from the heat, but nourished by the reflected light of the sun. He never raised very tall roses, nor were his roses very beautiful. They were stunted roses and all his roses were red, but their thorns were tough and fibrous, sufficient protection against the small lizards who made their home in the clefts of the rocks.

The rabbi raised roses with stubborn defiance and they responded. They were nourished by his quiet affection and they were hearty. Of course they would die. When they died, one by one, over each dead rose the rabbi would say one word of the *Kaddish*, scratching a mark in the sand until all seventy-five words had been spoken, and then, the *Kaddish* completed, he would gather the broken stems, the rotting petals, the dead buds and bury them in places on the mountainside along with seedlings so that other rosebushes would grow forth. In time the entire mountainside before his cave was covered with rosebushes.

You may well ask, Did that holy man ever pick a rose for himself? He did not. Picking was not the purpose. Planting and watching the struggle, saying the *Kaddish* and planting again was enough. That is the homily. Now, let each of us think about its meaning." Throats cleared, feet shuffled but no one spoke. After some minutes Simon began once more. "We have waited long enough. What do you think, sir from Chicago? You decline the honor. Or you from Detroit, no idea? You, Pittsburgh? You, Newark? None. Not any. Don't fidget. Give them some wine. All right. I will proceed.

Interpretation I

There are two possible meanings to the homily. The first is appropriate and correct, but not completely relevant. Like all interpretations the groundwork comes first.

In the case of the homilies of the rabbis (the lives of the saints, as the others call them) the first interpretation is founded upon actual history. Our rabbi—let his name, for the moment, be Yohanan ben Zakkai, a saint of a rabbi, a rabbi of a saint—lived in the times of the destruction of our Temple, that is the time of the Roman conquerors, those that are later called Edom (to signify Christians) and at that time called, simply, simplistically, Romans.

The Romans threatened to destroy us and, in fact, very nearly accomplished their objective. What were we then? We were roses planted in the craggy soil of the Holy Land, soil that could not bring forth without nurture, without water, without sustenance and care.

And we were roses of but one color. That signifies that we were united, but having only the strength of single-mindedness we were both strong and weak, strong in that we were determined, breathing with a single breath, an integrated people, but weak in that single colors define unanimity without the presence of antibodies, foreign agents, diversities from which resilience and tensility derive.

So. We were strong and weak. And red. Blood. Clear and simple. The Adamic color, the color of our soil, the color of our blood. Red. And strong though we were, we had the strength of knobbly men, bowlegged giants, powerful but without mobility and speed. And so we died. Picked off one by one. Our petals fell until by the time of Masada we were vanquished.

But then, let us say, the Holy One Blessed be He, had a kind of mercy upon us and loving our stupid loyalty, our single-mindedness, our sacrifice, our obduracy, having spoken over us prayers of mourning, he replenished us until from a single bush we covered the mountainside, as in fact we are everywhere on the face of the earth.

Are you any clearer? Cleveland, what about you? You should know my meaning? Squeezed by the Italians? Heh. No? Or you from Los Angeles? At last pushed out of the unions by able-bodied hunkies? What do you think? Nervous. Perhaps a little. Still no clear idea. All right.

Interpretation II

Let us update the interpretation. Let us make it real. It is our time, our palpable time, the time we can hear rumbling and taste bitter.

The same roses. But of weaker strain. The thorns less testy, less provocative. Few in number, no longer mighty, huddling together in the countryside, in sections of the cities, isolated, cut off from the side of the mountain. Granted the soil is indulgent, full of acid and fertilizer, and we have grown. We were once sixteen million. Now we are cut back to ten. We will grow up again.

But the thorns are no longer fibrous. Little brownish pockets on the surface of the green. Grasp them between your thumb and index finger and break them off clean, not a prick, no blood at all. Not their blood surely. None of their blood. But ours, red no less than before, pouring forth from myriad apertures, pouring, pouring. Yours as well as mine. And do you think your planting of green, your real green, your fake green, your backed green, your strong-armed green, will stop the flow of red?

Your money is no power unless your power be in blood. To fight red you must spill red and you must, knowing that you are separated and alone, combat their red with your own. Elsewise their viscous fluids, their sap, their watery corpuscles will dilute your red until it is no more, no more yours, no longer blood, no longer red.

And the earth will be replenished and no less than before a prayer will be spoken, but when the petals are gathered, and the stems, and the thorns, and the roots and all these are planted with a new seedling, the rosebushes that will grow up will be smaller with each generation, more stunted, more stubbly, until finally nothing but midgetry and dwarfdom will be seen in the land.

"Do you see now? You must supply us with everything we ask. We will stock and store. We will train and discipline. We will be your legions and your strength."

A grunt was heard from the table, and Cleveland rose and extended his hand not to Simon as I would have thought, for Simon sat back exhausted from his exposition, but to Baltar, who sat beside me. And Baltar returned the greeting, not touching the extended hand, for his own continued to rest like shovels upon his knees, but demanded, "When?" and the answer came from Chicago, who presumably controlled the delegation. "Tonight and for cash." "Done," Baltar replied and it was done.

It was late upon that Saturday night that I heard unfamiliar noises and mutterings. I had not really understood the homily of Simon Stern. I doubt Simon's guests understood, either, but for whom it was business and what they understood best they would receive. Now, yes, of course, I understand it clearly, in all its nuance, but then I did not. Now, having before me the document I append at this juncture, written in a nervous hand, a hand possessed as though the fingers danced and the veins hummed, a document of Simon's eccentric brain, the weaving of his strange and elliptoid intelligence, I understand clearly, but then, having nothing but the testimonial grunts and heavy breathing of seven strangers from beyond the pale of our settlement, I could not know the significance of what I had heard.

A Meditation by Way of Exegesis Upon the Homily of the Roses

I do not despise Christians (not Christians, Christendom), let me say for the record—but this is no record for any other but myself. Nothing I do has been casual. Not a single thing. I have done nothing in my life without circumspection, without going round and round—whatever it might have been—a dubious idea, a project, a device, a stratagem, it didn't matter —a dozen times to discover whether its flaw reflected the smile of my face, whether it cast a light in which I might see the cut-scar jagged smile of my lips. No. Christians are not despised by me casually. How can I despise them? I do not even fear them now. Not now. What can I fear from them?

Oh I cannot think any more. (Why did I begin this. There have been others with my millions—that baron who—fool— engineered the Jews to Argentina and negotiated for the deserts of Uganda and that Viennese journalist making promises to the Pope and fondling with the Sultan for concessions in the Holy Land—what were they doing? Did they not believe? No! What of it?)

I believe in you, Lord and Ruler, bloody King of the Universe. (Be silent, Simon, and write against the Christians. Leave Jesus Christ alone! Who can he talk to? Angels? Minions of the Deep World? Dead Son, Assumed Mother, Windy Afflatus of the Spirit? They don't understand, those people, those others, those Christians.) They don't understand how difficult it is to be God, how very difficult it is, and how sad and unrequited is such a power, coeval and conatural, God with God, forever and to the end of the World, this world, all worlds, without end, blessed and damned that he should have told us that he lives.

"If there was no God, man would have created him." Foolish tradition. Anaximenes to Voltaire and beyond. If we were bulls, God would be cow and so forth and so forth. Stupidity. *It is not so.* If God were God, incommunicate, the solitary, unspeaking, remote, distant, inviolate, unreachable, arcane, divine, divine, divine, neither making nor fashioning, neither desiring nor seeking, we should conduct ourselves ignorant of him. There is no reason why he should have come into our minds at all. None. Natural religion! Nonsense. All men know this and that, natural truths, natural virtue, natural persuasions. Not at all.

It is because God is a gossip, an uncontrollable talker that we know of him, and look what's become of us because we know. Now it is we who can't stop talking about him, all the time talking about him. But God could have spared us if he had not been vain, if he had been a successful narcissus who looked in the waters of Eden and beheld his face and was satisfied knowing that God is God is God is God and no more, no more. But the water was already filled with droppings and filth and it was muddy and he could not see himself and he was forced to act and therewith he called to an angel and the angel tried to brush the water with a wing and clear its surface. But the water was murky to its depths and God could not see himself and he meditated upon that fact for eons and in that time he made waters above the waters and waters beneath the waters in which to see himself, but still he could not, and at last, in desperation, for he missed the beholding of himself, he realized that he could never again see himself clearly, that the waters were muddied by the repetition of his face, that his face was imprinted upon the waters and the filth of the

367

image was the imposition of millions upon millions of his faces and so, at last, he made a new model that inaccurately would contain him and by its inaccuracy would correct the perfection that he could no longer behold and so he made us that we would be incomplete, inaccurate, angular, subtle, jagged, harsh, protrusive, recessive, reflecting myriad times all of the shades of his person, but that none of us would be him, only a part, a dimension, an incompletion of himself. That would have been enough, that we were this, that he might in an instant of his intelligence put all those billions of faces together and behold his own, undirtied and uncorrupt out of all the hundred billion billion billion of ours. And God, God, what did you do? You told us! You told us! Merciless narcissus! You told us that we contained you.

O my God, what a folly, and now I—and through the generations of man, others—must suffer a thousand deaths to tell them that it is only partially so, that we are not gods, that we are only broken pieces of glass, that we are nothing but slivers and fragments, and that it is you, only you, who contains and makes us whole.

God, why were you so vain?

Do, please, realize that Simon was not forcing his hand. He was not impatient with God. He had grown accustomed to his divagations and vanities. It was only that he wished to draw attention to God's apparent distraction, noting his busybody preoccupation with lesser issues. Simon was noting something in the world, a cloven passion whereunder good intention and honest will left men battered with rhetoric and promises, when what was demanded in the universe was rectification. But he was only a man, an inspired, glorious, wondrous man, but no less a man of normal complement and habituations, striving out of remarkable intelligence and clarity to insert into history something which was not clearly understood. It was the sense of our having had it and the desperation of our having had it, and the self-awareness that no one else really cared a fig for our having it, that moved him to act.

No wonder then that early on the morning of the first day of the week following the Third Meal I should have been raised from my light sleep by unfamiliar noises and mutterings.

I wrapped myself in my robe and slid my cold feet into slippers and slowly opened the door to my room.

"It's the blind man." A sawed-off voice which I recognized to be that of Chicago greeted me.

"Forget him. Down the stairs with you," I heard Baltar answer. I extended my hand into the passage and felt the bodies of perspiring men and the heavy wooden crates, banded with wire, which they carried to the bottom cellar, three floors beneath the compound. I counted the minutes until the first of the carriers passed me on his return and knew that they had deposited their boxes on the lowest level of the compound before the secret storage room. I stood for more than an hour in that corridor until the last of the deliverers had left, and then, suddenly cold, the heat of bodies and motion gone, turned to retire once more to my room.

"You saw nothing," Baltar spoke and a hand pincered my jaws. "You saw nothing. You will say nothing." He held me in his grip for more than a minute and my face began to ache and tears came to my eyes.

"Do I see, Baltar? Do I see? You know better than to speak of sight."

"You see everything, Nathan Gaza, but I see *you* even better." Baltar lifted me in his arms, carried me into my room, and threw me on the bed.

Each night the strange visitors reappeared. A few during weeknights and they came shortly before dawn. The large deliveries were always on the morning of the first day, after the Sabbath had declined into night. I counted eighteen shipments in all. The storehouse must be filled, the cut cedars now crowded by crude slatted boxes smelling of machine oil.

I knew. I understood and I feared.

The addresses which Simon delivered to our community on Sabbath afternoons when he would study with us before *Minchah* accented the unhappy turn of his imagination. News clippings of Kielce were posted on bulletin boards, although that massacre was many months old. Notices from German newspapers on the desecration of Jewish gravestones. Incidents of bedaubed synagogues and burned out *yeshivot*, acts of wanton anti-Semitic vandalism, assumed for him the station of a new conspiracy. Hostile churchmen, tales of insults and slights, restrictive covenants, diplomatic condescensions and rudeness surrounding the debates over the future of Palestine (now Israel *redivivus*), the vulgarisms of the English Prime Minister, the murder of British troopers by Zionist terrorists, all these became for Simon occasions for dilations of rage or exclamations of joyous assent. Of course, I can now, with the gentling wisdom of hindsight, recognize his conflicted mind, his enormous acts of salvation and their palpable ineffectualness. Nothing had changed in the world, although he had set out to change it. The resort to desperate measures—that suggested not Simon Stern but Baltar, and for that reason I resolved the week after the shipments had ended to confront Simon Stern with my anxiety.

It was Simon's habit to speak with petitioners after the hour of eleven at night. During the day, rising like ourselves at seven-thirty, he was occupied with the work of the Society, but at night, after studying and writing from the conclusion of dinner until the hour of eleven, he saw visitors.

I was his appointments secretary. It had become a complicated task. Visitors abounded, dropping in from strange places in the land, bringing children, and donations, asking for advice or for charity, which were usually dispensed by the bailiffs of our sagacity or of our petty cash with an even and unstinting hand. Not a month passed that we did not give away without question sums that mounted through several score benefactions to fifteen hundred dollars. But it was through me that all petitioners passed.

During the day I sat at a desk in a narrow room that commanded the entranceway to the compound and the stairwell that rose to his quarters. A major-domo, young Peter Narzissenfeld, who came to Fisher Klay from a small labor camp near Grodno, would pace back and forth before my desk, waiting for someone to ring the doorbell or knock upon the outer door. Narzissenfeld cocked an ear to the sound and would divine from the knock, the quality of the ring, its ease or agitation, its steady self-confidence or its embarrassed hesitation whether it was man or woman, donor or prospective recipient, a slummer, sightseer, tourist or someone troubled and preoccupied. He would call over to me: "Nathan, a woman, middle-aged, arthritic, and a young boy with acne." Invariably correct. Narzissenfeld had an infallible sense for disorder. Of course I could not check upon his accuracy. He could have lied. I suspect he did, but no matter. After they had come to my desk and I had disposed of their request, noting their petition, checking for an appointment with Mr. Stern or shunting them to a siding at which Klay or Steinmann would receive and give them refreshment, Narzissenfeld would whisper. "Right again. Swollen left hand and the kid smells from sulfur and ointments." Narzissenfeld had little wish to sympathize.

I might well have forgotten the events of April and May, but I was prevented. Baltar often came to my room and sat sullenly smoking a cigar, regarding me while I wrote or read in the system of Louis Braille which I had mastered. A quarter-hour, a half-hour, he would sit, regarding me silently, blowing smoke before me, and at the end when he would hit my knee or squeeze my shoulder or pinch my neck. I understood. More warnings, more threats. But I did not know why. Why the strange visitors? why the clandestine deliveries? At first I did not want to ask. It was an evasion, but I rationalized it. I couldn't see. Everything came back to that. What could I know? What could I understand about the night visitors, about the gentlemen with the names of cities?

My resolve to confront Simon Stern with my questions was strengthened.

The bell buzzed insistently. "It's a fat man with a sticky finger. Can't take no for an answer. Prepare a 'no,' Nathan." Narzissenfeld opened the door. A small breeze of June blew quiet warmth into the airless reception hall. I received it upon my face and warmed, turning toward the light like a plant to the sun. But the obstruction was formidable. A large man, a rumpled man in a suit draped like a winding sheet, filled the doorway, entered, and the door shut behind him.

"Who's there?" I rarely called out, usually allowing Narzissenfeld to announce the visitor to me. "Who's there?"

"Mr. Nathan," Narzissenfeld replied, whispering to me through a cupped hand, "it's a gentleman. He says his name is Gusweller and he has an appointment with Dr. Klay."

"Gusweller? You're not Jewish, are you, Mr. Gusweller?" It was a nervous question for me to ask.

The voice, laughing at my involuntary atavism, for I was not rude, replied, "No, sir. I'm R.C."

"R.C.?" I replied, puzzled.

"Roman Catholic. Uptown we say R.C. Parish of St. James the Less."

"Oh, yes. R.C. Very witty. It wouldn't do to say I'm J., would it?" I laughed, looking above him. What was Dr. Klay doing with a Mr. Gusweller, an R.C. Gusweller at that? I called Dr. Klay on the telephone. "Dr. Klay? We have a Mr. Gusweller to see you. You'll be right down? Good." He had been expected.

"Prepare a no." That's what Narzissenfeld would usually say. Sometimes a yes. But rarely. He loved visitors, but he didn't like them to get by him. He hated interlopers in his life, but he enjoyed the assault, the effort to poach and pry, as long as he knew that I made the decisions, that it was I, sitting at my large desk, several digits away from all kinds of help and assistance, employing willful muteness to flagellate my blindness, who could reduce undesirable visitors to humiliation and embarrassment.

"Prepare a no." It was easy. I had a technique for no which was incomparable. It was developed when I decided that conversation got me nowhere with strangers. (I have a voice. Of course. I am not mute as I pretend, but I have lost interest in speech.) I didn't like the outside world. I had too much work before me to bother with chatter and gossip. It was for this reason—my boredom with ordinary transaction in the world— that I developed a system of speech which raises all the basic questions without requiring that I speak.

I have prepared one hundred small flash cards, printed in Hebrew (for the modernists), Yiddish (for the traditionalists) and English for the everyday world. All conversation is really about functions of need: sleep, eat, relieve, lust, buy, destroy. Flash card: *Ritzoni l'echol. Ich vil essn. I want to eat.* A simple flash card like this held up at the right moment will produce enough salivary compassion in the beholder that he will answer straightaway: "Go ahead and eat." I go and eat. The conversation which threatened to begin ends. See how easy it is? One flash card, a few words, and a whole block of time is consumed eating. It takes few words to fill time. Flash cards cover the basics. They are printed up and distributed efficiently on my person. I always wear a double-breasted dark jacket with my corduroys. That gives me two inside pockets, two outside pockets and my lapel pocket. It works well.

Somebody comes to call whom Simon doesn't want to see. Narzissenfeld says "Prepare a no." First off, I produce easily and efficiently from my lapel pocket a flash card which reads: "I am Nathan Gaza." Absorbed. I flash a second card: "I am the scribe, record keeper, historian and appointments secretary of The Society for the Rescue and Resurrection of the Jews." Absorbed. Last lapel card: "What do you want?" This usually finishes them off. The visitor becomes flustered. He thinks I'm crazy. He thinks we're all crazy. He excuses himself and stands up if he was sitting. Or sits down in disbelief if he was standing. But it ends pretty quickly. If visitors aren't cool and persistent they've had it. Those who are get other flash cards. They ask questions for which there should be answers. Since most questions needn't be asked and those that are don't deserve to be answered, I usually remain silent to see if they'll press further. If they do, I use the flash cards in my rear back pocket. That's a hard pocket. Hard to arrange, hard to get to, clumsy and difficult. Disarming to strangers. They ask, "Tell me about the work of the Society." Usually journalists, charity workers, ladies with nothing to do. They get the slow rear-pocket treatment. I reach into the back pocket, twisting around in my chair, bending forward. I look like I'm scratching my buttocks. I'm not. I'm pulling out ten cards. They read in order of numeration: (1) Is that what you *really* want to know? (2) But why do you want to know this? (3) I don't know the answer. (4) I *really* don't know. (5) There's nobody here who knows except Mr. Stern. (6) Mr. Stern sees nobody from outside. (7) Mr. Stern is sick, tired, eating, sleeping, OUT. (8) Mr. Stern is *always* sick, tired, eating, sleeping, OUT. Why don't you let me help you. Very rarely, very rarely indeed, do I use the last two cards. Those cards are calling cards, printed differently from the others and carbonized for record keeping. They read: Mr. Stern will see ———— (print name) at ———— o'clock, ———— night (print date and day). Authorized signature (print). The last is self-evident. May the breath of heaven cease to blow through the body of ———— (print name).

Gusweller didn't get the cards. He didn't want to see Simon

Stern at all. That was unusual. It rarely happened that Dr. Klay or the other members of our governing secretariat had appointments with outsiders. Whomever they saw they were asked to see by Simon. Everyone wanted to see Simon first. If Simon had a crowded schedule, visitors got one of the others. Not unusually, then, I was curious about Gusweller. Dr. Klay appeared in a few minutes. He was dressed in his familiar grey. Narzissenfeld said in my ear, "In grey, beautiful grey, Mr. Nathan." Narzissenfeld snapped his fingers to signify elegance. He always snapped his fingers to indicate fitness and style, whether of dress or manner.

"Mr. Gusweller. Thank you for visiting me. Would you come this way. My office is above." There were no introductions. Dr. Klay clearly knew his visitor and expected him.

"Yes, sir," Mr. Gusweller replied, willingly.

"One moment," I said without premeditation. "Would you be good enough to sign our visitors' register?"

"That isn't necessary, is it, Mr. Gaza," Klay replied with irritation, using my patronym, an unusual form of address.

"Indeed it *is*, Dr. Klay. Quite standard procedure." It wasn't standard procedure at all, but I wanted to know more about our visitor. My stubbornness was not rewarded then, for I learned nothing beyond the name I had already mastered.

"Mr. Harold Gusweller." Narzissenfeld told me after Gusweller had disappeared up the stairs behind Dr. Klay. "What's a foreigner from uptown doing with Dr. Klay?" he added, mystified. I did not know but I determined to find out.

Later that afternoon I called upon Dr. Klay.

"I thought you would come," Klay said as I shuffled into his room. "Sit down, Nathan. We haven't talked in some time, although that's no fault of mine. I've tried hard enough." That was true. Dr. Klay had tried but I had not responded. I was too preoccupied to reply. I hated speaking idly, as I have explained. It was the beginning of my vows, although at the time I surrendered conversation I had no knowledge that I would continue the whole way, becoming finally before the end and the new beginning a proper Nazarite.

I sat down upon a low divan, a graceful shape covered in a cool linen fabric upon which I dried my perspiring palms. "I've come to ask."

"Indeed you have. About Mr. Gusweller?" I nodded. "Well then, what do you think? Why do you think? Let me tell you who Mr. Gusweller is and what he does. He is a private investigator, a detective, in a word. And why a detective, you will certainly ask.

"We conduct our lives virtually like monastic celibates, like nails grown back into our own hands, witnessing to our leader. He is our light. He is our teacher. But dare we admit to ourselves that he is also quite mad, magnificent, splendid, but mad. Genius-mad. But no less mad despite genius. God afflicts him with both genius and madness, and he lives out over us all the struggle with his twin derangements, that he is a light and torch to the exile of our people and no less a demon, an underside of divinity. Our sages called it, I believe, the *sitra achra,* the other side of God. He is a *sitra achra.* Our demon and our redeemer in one. Who is he, this Simon Stern, before whom we lay our life? Eh? Tell me? Do you know? you, his most intimate adviser, his ears, his artificial lung, his uncanny voice? Do you know? You do not. You know nothing about him and neither do I. I think we should know."

"What is to know?" I responded quietly. "What is to know but what you believe you know. Information is meaningless to belief. What will you confirm? What will you deny? That he is murderer? That he is not? That he is mad like the whorls of a tornado? that he is sane like its eye? What? What do you wish to know other than that he is, that he does, that he promises hope?"

"I wish to know facts. I am uninterested in the theory of his life, its glorious and eccentric configuration. I am beyond that. I have been beside him now for nearly six years. I changed my life for him. I came down into the encampment of this province for him. Do you think that's easy for a Viennese Jewish rationalist who was once a millionaire himself? I turned my coat inside out for him, wearing the sacking face out to the world, I, who had a whole life, but still a life without him, before him, before I knew him to be."

"But that's all different now. You have given yourself to him."

"Given, indeed," Klay snorted and I could hear him stroke his chin reflectively. "I have given everything, but have received these past months only the marks of his derangement."

375

"You know then?"

"What?"

"You know what's been going on? You figured out the presence of those strange visitors two months ago?"

"Gangsters. Every one of them a gangster. Yes, I knew. I could see them. I knew only too well. And we—his counselors —are displaced by Baltar, by crazy Baltar. Baltar's not only mad; he's a maniac. A real maniac. I want to know about them both. About Simon. About Baltar."

"Baltar too?"

"Baltar, most of all. I want a complete report. On everything Simon was. On everything Baltar is. Only then can we know what must be done."

"We? Do?"

"Only us. We, most particularly. Do you imagine, blind Nathan, that the work of redemption is done without the cooperation of the redeemed? I do not. It is no action of authority to which men submit when they are saved to themselves. Simon Stern can do nothing for us unless we will it. Baltar cannot harm us unless we allow it. That is the fact of the matter. Redemption is cooperative."

"European socialism, Dr. Klay. You make God and messiahs sound like collective farmers—joining together in some splendid plan for recultivating the species. Ecological spiritualism!" I replied with disgust, but I was investing my anger with wit, which more than blunted its effectiveness, for Klay sensed that my annoyance was more with myself for having done nothing while he had taken the initiative.

"You know better than that. That isn't why you're angry with me. You're angry only because I guessed your own mind. You know, blind Nathan, that Mr. Gusweller did not have to sign your book. Nothing is written down here. No one keeps track. Perhaps we should, but that isn't our free way. But you made him. You suspected. And you were right, however, my old friend—now we're together in this. We are conspirators, what? to save the saver."

"Save Simon?"

"Very much so. Let me admit that our inquiries into Simon Stern are a cover to the pursuit of Baltar. If anyone finds out, we announce our findings about Simon Stern. What is *ad majorem gloriam dei* in Hebrew? At all events my Jesuit mind works well. Viennese upbringing. *Cheder* and the Jesuits, my father and Ignatius the aristocrat. Ha. Well. At all events. Let Baltar find us out and we release our documents on Simon Stern. We announce his splendor and his glory, out of miserable beginnings he comes to us, titan of power, phoenix of spirit. But underneath where the worms collect, there we will find out about Baltar. Mr. Gusweller is assigning members of his staff to investigate Simon—his neighborhood, his old schoolmates, teachers, friends of the family. But Gusweller leaves for Europe tomorrow with letters of introduction I have already prepared to trusted members of our organization abroad, our skullduggers who still live in DP camps awaiting transit visas, to people who may remember Baltar from Ravensbrück, who knew him in Paris. Who knows what we will discover about our Rumanian friend, Janos Baltar."

My meeting with Dr. Klay was unsettling. Such mildness, such self-collection. "Terrifying" is more accurate. I was frightened. The limbo of weeks until Gusweller's return became wasted time. I scarcely left my room, occupying myself with note-taking in my blindman's language. Daily Baltar visited me and I felt his form like a giant bird. "Go away, Baltar," I would say without turning toward him. "Remember," he would admonish and depart.

Simon let me be. I saw him daily, of course, but my conversation was pared down to slivers of amenity and circumspection. I could not look upon his face. Not once, as it had been my habit since I came to know him, had I approached him and passed my hand over his face receiving for my comfort the reassurance of his giving flesh. I forswore it. Not that I was angry. Not at all, but I could not be reassured and I would have used that face falsely and there would have been neither warmth nor comfort in the gesture. Simon noted my withdrawal. When our brief communications ended each day and the list of appointments had been presented to him for approval or delegation, he would rise and accompany me to the door, standing patiently awaiting the passage of my hands. By the fourth day of my refusal he was content to open the door and stand aside as I passed through. Dr. Klay did not speak to me again of our common concern. Our civilities returned. I spoke a little, refusing still to speak idly, but I greeted him in the morning and wished him good rest at night. My beard began to grow, my earlocks to curl and ride along my cheeks. The penance had begun, my own consecration. It proceeded slowly through the devious ways of unknowing. Nazarite conceit, Nazarite self-containment, Nazarite vanity. It shall consume others, but it shall spare me. My work must go on. I must be spared to tell the story.

The heat of the city rose. Faces passed through our doors, and Narzissenfeld, open-necked, a chain of thin gold about his neck, was all coolness and bemusement.

"A sweaty palm print on the door." It was a telephone repairman come to inspect the central box located in the second basement. Later he became lost and was found wandering in confusion. Narzissenfeld was annoyed by the telephone man. But later a plumber came who claimed there was a leak in our basement. He was retrieved from the sump-pump, and his shoes tracked sludge to the door. Dried in the heat, sneaker marks imprinted the linoleum.

What was this? These tradesmen, these servicemen. The compound appeared to be in disrepair or so it seemed to my innocent imagination. During one day, that early day in July, a telephone man uncalled, a plumber unwanted. And then, not logical, the same telephone man returned the following day to repair what he had undone, for our phones seemed out of order; a hum and beep interrupting the flow of conversation prompted a formal request from Rabbi Steinmann that a repairman check our system. And then not one but three men in coveralls with phones in their back pockets and screwdrivers arranged like fountain pens along their chests returned and spent the day moving through the basement chasing the wires, unsnarling them, examining phones and connections, installing little devices which we thought would diminish the eerie electric hum which startled our older, untelephonic members. And plumbers and electricians and exterminators with pots of poison, and inspectors from the fire department. In the course of that week and the next, amid the unreasonable heat and the fierce whirring of our fans, the dirt of these servicemen left our walls covered with the graffiti of labor, handprints of grime and oil-soaked thumbs along doorjambs and electric outlets. We were wired and rewired, and our small brigade of watchers, uncurious, unsuspicious, allowed these itinerants to wander through our premises like generous helpers and Rochel, our chief cook, solicitously offered them iced tea and cookies.

What struck me as most curious was the change in the attitude of Narzissenfeld, our major-domo, our doorkeeper, our extra sense, who ordinarily guarded the entrance and exit of our domicile, lounging at the front door before I took my place at the hall desk, already eager, awaiting visitors, preparing the acerbities of his simple vocabulary, priming his third eye to guess and discern, to warn me and advise.

Narzissenfeld was always there when I arrived at nine in the morning. He would help me with the books I carried to the desk to study in becalmed moments. He would lay to my right hand, ordered neatly, the sharpened stylus with which I punched laboriously at my braille and the quills which on occasion I would set up with parchment and ruler to facilitate my scribal commissions, although I scribed then but rarely. Blind men, however miraculous their memory, are really blemished and are excluded by the Law from the fraternity of scribes. Although I knew the sacred five books by heart and could easily, faultlessly write an entire Torah, how could I guarantee infallible transcription of the holy words?—a fantasy, a galactic thrust of the unconscious, could so easily set even my perfect scribal memory to whirling distant thoughts and ascribing improbable words to the divine text. A perfect memory, but nonetheless an imperfect man. I gave up scribal work —being secretary to God—the day I interpolated in a recitation of names, commonplace in the book of the generations of the descendants of Noah, that of my beloved uncle, Moses Abishag. Indeed I thought him among the eternal blessed, but he was not redacted scripture. I surrendered then, honoring the given word as much as the imagined, for I was a scribe, not an innovator. Henceforth I became Simon's exclusive scribe and combined the two, divinity of impulse and innovation of recension. I scribed Simon's allocutions and dicta and treated them as I would have treated any writ to be preserved, consigning them to parchment, translating them faultlessly into a quasi-archaic, quasi-modern Hebrew, and using my pen and inks as I had been taught by my father decades ago to present the words of God to Moses.

Narzissenfeld was late. He did not appear until nearly ten o'clock and I was curious about his absence. Oversleeping, he apologized, but I thought otherwise. The life of Narzissenfeld was in the darting shadows of the animate and moving, not in the recumbency of shades and dreams. The second morning his lateness was more considerable, and I was struck less by its increase than by the more curious fact that he had come into the hall not from the inner stairwell but from the outside, unlocking the door, entering on tiptoes, soundless except to my ears, saying nothing for some time.

"Come now, Narzissenfeld. You tricked my eyes, but my ears don't believe you."

"I'm sorry. I had to go out. I was meeting someone," he stuttered nervously.

"I have no objection to your seeing someone, Narzissenfeld, but never try to deceive your friend, Nathan."

I had no cause for suspicion, but suspicion formed like a dust cloud at the periphery of my mind. Long low conversations with the plumber. Frequent pilgrimages to the basement to bring Rochel's offerings to the repairmen. Narzissenfeld was not the kind of man to entertain strangers and yet there he was, congenial, attentive, interested in the comings and goings of these servicemen. Young Narzissenfeld's morning absences continued, and no longer did he disguise to me that he was reentering the compound from the street. His explanations became more complicated with each lateness. A girlfriend with whom he took a coffee before she departed for work, but the implausibility of this friendship lay in the no less evident fact that Narzissenfeld saw her at no other time. He would pass his evenings, as always, within our quarters, although unlike his earlier habit—dominoes and endless games of hearts with a retarded child of one of our guests—he would wander the compound, opening doors that were closed, peering into closets, pacing the corridors that connected the four blocks which enclosed the inner courtyard and the stairwells that laced the buildings together. He seemed singularly preoccupied and distracted, intent upon something, but as he was neither very bright of mind nor knowledgeable, what he sought appeared to elude him.

So. Every morning, after *Shachrit*, after we had breakfast— a roll and coffee—I would go at eight o'clock precisely to the kitchen in the basement of the corner tenement of the compound and have another cup with Rochel, our chief cook as I have mentioned, but no less the grieving woman we had gathered to ourselves from the debris of Berlin, where she was born. When we came to know Rochel's diminutive person, small-boned, with tense, drawn face, relieved by warm hazel eyes and blond, almost flaxen hair worn short, like a page boy's, held in place by colored barrettes, she had grown accustomed to settled, introspective ways, aloof and distant. The one eccentric gesture for which Rochel offered no explanation was that in the kitchen which she supervised she kept a framed drawing—crude and naïvely delineated—of a young boy. To all our inquiries about the subject and the artist she replied disingenuously, "It's Yossl, my nephew. I've never seen him, but I made him up. He's beautiful, isn't he?" And that would be all.

Sometimes Rochel would be busy. Most of the time she was busy even if she wasn't. It was her way to be busy. Not with the busyness of the world. Not moving potatoes for the sake of reporting that she had relocated a sack of potatoes or examining tomatoes for the sake of announcing to the grocer that three were bruised. She had no need to make *things* responsible for her activity. She was busy in a quite different way. Simply that she, like myself, did not wish to talk. She could be sitting quite still, her head averted when I entered, and never turn to greet me. Unfriendly? No. Simply quiet, she had the habit of curling away from the world in order better to protect her private voice. On those days she would acknowledge me with an arm pointed over the double aluminum stove to a large pot of simmering coffee—pointed, I was told, like the ironic arching of a swan's neck, gentle but imperious. Some months before, when I first tested my privilege, I had approached her silently until I felt her warmth around me and, reaching out, had found her arm, arched and pointed, yes, correctly, like the graceful neck of a swan toward the coffeepot. That first time she dropped her habitual reserve and led me step by step to

the pot and told me that from that morning until my death—
may it be a century from then, she added—the pot would be
on the same burner, third on the top, and a cup and saucer
would be exactly six inches to its right on the counter. No
sugar or cream. Rarely would she talk, as I said, but that didn't
mean—not for a moment could it mean—that we did not
exchange affection daily.

Rochel would sit at the counter on a high stool. The fish was
in the refrigerator by that early hour; the carrots and celery
were chopped; the boiled potatoes were cooling in mayon-
naise. A cold lunch or a hot lunch. It didn't matter. By eight-
thirty in the morning, lunch was ready, the three girls who
helped her in the kitchen were already out of her way checking
linens or cleaning rooms, and Rochel would sit in the kitchen
reading German poets (her favorites were those twins of dark
imagination, Mörike and Hölderlin), or making notes in a
spiral-bound book, or else, hands folded in her lap, studying
rabbinic interpretations of the dietary laws.

When I entered for coffee I was, I thought, the first stranger
of her day—all her pots and cups and plates being her spotless
friends and companions. *"Sholem aleychem, tochterl Rochel,"*
I would say, and she would mumble a greeting and that could
be all, except for the swan's neck.

It was late in the month of July that I came for my morning
coffee and found that Rochel was not seated. When I went to
fetch my coffee I felt no alternation of light as an arm would
produce gesturing before the grey-black of my blindness. Nor
heat. Rochel was not there. I poured my coffee and waited.
Where was Rochel? A door opened and Rochel entered. She
moved slowly this morning. Her feet were in slippers. The
window was closed and the humidity returned and caked my
body like the fog of a steam engine.

"Rochel. What's wrong?"

"Reb Nathan. Forgive my absence when you came." She
spoke sternly like a ward nurse to a familiar patient.

"*You* should apologize? Rochel. I should be excusing myself
once in a while. Nonsense."

"I'm crying."

"I know."

"Yes, you do know, don't you?"

382

I was embarrassed how much I knew. Condensation forces me to pay attention. Having less to work with I extract more. But this particular morning, pride was excluded by her tears. She *had* been crying.

"What about? You're wearing slippers. Who died?"

"You've heard."

"How could I have heard?"

"That's true. The letter only came this morning. My nephew. The child of my husband's brother. The child of my drawing. He died." I heard her go to the sideboard and pick up the framed drawing and kiss it.

"I'm sorry, Rochel."

She continued as though she had not heard my sympathies. "He wasn't close to me. But he was the last. He had my husband's name. My name. And he's dead. Pneumonia. There were no other children. And so I'm dead." She dropped the frame, and the glass covering the drawing shattered.

"Rochel. Such an immortality!"

"Reb Nathan. You're blind. You're a scribe and therefore holy to some. You are the finger of Simon and for that alone precious to all of us. But you cannot feel everything. Some feelings you must leave to others."

"Yes, Rochel. Tell me."

"I have thought many times that people don't really exist. Only their names exist and their names are like so many ashes that fly up to God when they go down at last into the earth. I remember once standing at the electric fence that surrounded the camp at Majdanek and looking out at the crematorium when the smoke belched up white against a lowered sky and seeing patches of ash and thinking to myself that they were all names going back to God. Not bodies, not faces, not children or women or young boys or old men, but names. Yankel, Sarah, Moishe, Fritzi—just names going back to be remembered and used again. That idea was fine. It helped me for a little bit. But some months afterward a miserable Jew from Lodz died in his tracks one morning on the way to the quarry in which we dug and nobody thought twice about him. He was a louse to everyone. He stole bread from other prisoners and sometimes when he was beside himself with anger he would go over to some weak Jew and tip over his bowl of soup. But that miserable bastard liked me. I was likable. I was twenty-nine then, and I was very pretty and I had golden hair like an aristocrat. He liked me, and whenever things got very bad he would come to me and tell me sad stories about the poor people of Lodz or he would sing me songs in Polish or Russian or Yiddish and sometimes he would give me a cigarette or a potato. For nothing. For nothing. So he *was* a miserable Jew. And then he died. His heart gave out. And right where he fell, his fellow prisoners hacked open the frozen earth and rolled him in. And some of them—Jews who had slept next to him in the barracks, who knew he snored and coughed and blew his nose just like themselves—sniggered and one man made a mess into his grave. Do you know, Reb Nathan? From that moment on, I tried to remember his face and I couldn't. I wanted to remember his face, not his name, but his face. I rediscovered faces from trying to remember his. But all the others forced him out of my mind. Nathan. All I could remember was a face, you should pardon me, with shit all over it and that's not a face any longer. And so, what if Rabinowitz was his name. And so, what if God took back his name and the ash flew straight up. God would never know that Rabinowitz belonged to a sometime decent man with snow and crap all over him."

"So, does it follow?" I asked, knowing that it did follow in the strange logic of inversion which we had all mastered.

"Does it follow? Does it follow? Of course. My husband's nephew is dead. The nephew who bears my name. The son of my husband's brother. The son (I've never seen) of a brother-in-law I've never seen, of a husband dead five years, is dead himself and I remember a name. I never saw my little nephew. I don't know whether he was scrawny or straight, black-haired or brown, chiseled, pocked. But until this morning he lived there in Europe, a survivor, and I lived here and I thought of him and made him up every day and when his body was complete in my imagination I gave him my name and he became a real Yossl Pincus. And now he's a dead Yossl Pincus and his name has flown up and my dream of him is dead and he might as well be covered in snow and crap. Do you mind if I cry?"

"Rochel. Cry, sister. Of course cry. I should stop you? Fortunately, it's a half-truth."

She stopped crying and blew her nose. "And what's the whole?"

"There is a point when the name and the body meet again. You know God can read even what I've erased. It amuses me that the Law states that when a scribe, such as myself, writes the name of God and by accident misspells the name of God he must bury the parchment. Bury it like a dead thing. Like the dead. No, little sister, not like a dead thing, but like a holy thing. That's why the dead are buried, because they *are* a bit of God. Such a theology. But you understand. And if holy, not dead. Dead in the order of half-truths, but not really dead, not ever dead, and even though God has reclaimed the name, he knows where and when to restore it. Rochel. Stop chopping carrots and celery today. Chop an onion and cry. When you're finished I'm sure you can make up your mind what Yossl Pincus looked like and then you can give him his name once and for all." Rochel bent down. She kneeled upon the glass, which cracked like the backs of desiccated beetles, and tore the drawing of her nephew once, twice, repeatedly, until the boy had passed into confetti.

It helped a little. Within a week Rochel seemed back to normal. The quiet. The tough gentleness returned. It worked for a while. That is to say, I didn't pay attention to Rochel. Not that I ignored her. Picking one's way through the labyrinth of a compound with only a metal-plated white cane with a red handle doesn't give one the liberty to ignore anyone, anything. Being blind takes wits, and on the days I felt dull and incompetent I wouldn't even go to Rochel's kitchen. I was always afraid of falling down stairs or tripping over a garbage pail. I stayed put. It was early August now. You could never be certain of the seasons in the city. Dilapidated firetraps and piles of refuse don't put out buds or recall them. I knew the seasons were changing, as city Jews have always known simply by the portion of the Torah one had reached on Monday or Thursday or Sabbath. The closer you came to the month of Elul the closer you came to the New Year and the closer you came to winter rains. So it was nearly fall and my bones were cranky. The morning heat was the more oppressive as the day promised to be less bitter.

It was a morning early in August, the second morning in a

row, in fact, that my hour had passed and I had not descended into the basement of the corner tenement to visit with Rochel and take a coffee with her. But eight-thirty arrived and my automatic timepiece (a gift of Simon's) went off in my pants pocket, tickling my leg with its hum. I found some energy, and picking my cane from under the chair where it lay like a watchdog I went off to find Rochel, with the intention of actually speaking to her about the approach of the New Year and autumn cool.

As I approached the door to the kitchen (it was a wooden door sheeted with metal against fire but so incompletely nailed that the door never shut tightly, always leaving a crack at the bottom large enough for a mouse), I heard a voice within. It was not Rochel's. But it spoke with a tenderness that only Rochel deserved. "Little dear," the voice said. "Little angel," it continued, and the stately compliments came forward like operetta soldiers bearing boxes of chocolates and glazed fruits to a princess. Could I help but listen? Of course. But it was harmless. "Gentle mother," the muffled voice caressed. Surely it was Rochel who received them. Surely not her assistant, a wall-eyed girl with a mole on her forehead, who was mean as well as ugly. The low and indistinct voice, suffering from a nasal wheeze, perorated in conclusion, "Mistress of gefilte fish," "Genius of potato soup." There was silence, followed by a low moan and a cry of pleasure. I remembered those moans and cries. Again there was silence and the whimper of exhaustion. I tapped lightly on the door. It sounded far away. I tapped more loudly. I tapped loudly. I paused. I opened the door. A blind man entered the kitchen, where the smells of carnality mingled now with the aroma of cakes and freshly made coffee.

Who was Rochel's lover? It did not matter. It was enough that Rochel was loved. A body edged past me and a sleeve brushed my own. At the evening service in the compound synagogue, the nasal wheeze sat beside me. It had entered late and squeezed next to me. I did not understand then—it would be some weeks before I did—why it decided to confess: "It was I, Narzissenfeld." That was all he said. The wheeze and the voice and the love of Rochel belonged to Narzissenfeld.

Such strangeness. A girlfriend, indeed. Indeed. Each morning, then, he would make love to Rochel before I arrived,

386

and leaving by the delivery door of the pantry, return to the compound by the front door. My suspicions seemed to be unwarranted. Narzissenfeld, a young man of twenty-three; Rochel a mother of our family, not more than thirty-two, but grey-white like a blasted birch tree, and as proud.

I guess Narzissenfeld always made faces. At least, during the two years I had known him he was constantly molding and kneading his flesh, sometimes growing whiskers which drooped like a Chinese emperor's, or next allowing stubble to cover his chin, ragged like a beggar's, or yet, going from fixed steel spectacles to orbs of plastic in shades of brown, green, or red. When he wasn't putting on disguises, using the props of hair and eyeglasses, he would insert an index finger into his mouth and stretch his lip, or by tugging his ear with fury raise on its dry surface welts of bruised red skin. He grimaced menacingly; he laughed and spittle collected at the corners of his mouth; he could force his eyes to redden and tear; he hollered and his rubbery flesh, distorted by the ventral blast, assumed the shapelessness of a man trapped in a wind tunnel. That Narzissenfeld! He had no definable form. One knew that he was of a certain height, that he had arms and legs like other human beings. It was only that he had no reliable face.

It was, however, this very facelessness which had kept Narzissenfeld alive. He lost his face in the war. Or rather, let us be accurate, he sacrificed his face in order to survive the war.

Peter Narzissenfeld had been confined in a small concentration camp, established in late 1944, near Grodno. It was so small that it needed only one sadist of ordinary imagination, SS Oberführer Ehle, and a platoon of squadsmen with submachine guns to keep that little camp controlled and orderly. Two hundred Jewish men and a scattering of women would go out to the fields every day in that northerly waste of Europe to plant and harvest potatoes or care for the enormous herd of milch cows of the old baron whose estate had been expropriated to feed the Wehrmacht.

Weeks before Oberführer Ehle was charged with tending to the estates of the sick and slightly deranged baron, the country had been combed and Jews picked off the land like lice. It was then, the major transports over, the area cleaned, all able-bodied Poles deported to forced labor or shot, that the Protector of Poland realized that whole areas of Prussia were going untended—crops wasting, cows dying of illness, chickens being foraged by the peasants instead of being fattened for the army—and deputed various SS officers to set up camps ringing Prussia to the North Sea and into the Baltic countries to care for the land. Only Jewish misfits—too healthy to be killed or left behind because they were employed in the large cities as Jewish police, as medical orderlies, as functionary bureaucrats who knew the names and the faces of their town—these and stray women, and some young children who pleased their officers, were divided up and sent to these camps of the north. Peter Narzissenfeld was among them—no longer a boy, not yet a man.

The day of his arrival at the camp near Grodno, Narzissenfeld decided to become a woman.

I have simply announced that Narzissenfeld became a woman, but it must be explained, because only then will you comprehend why this thin and precise boy (who, in a snapshot he preserved throughout the years of his dispersion, is seen standing posed as a lad of thirteen, his hand resting upon a holy book lying closed upon a lectern, his shoulders covered with the drapery of a shawl, his forehead bristled with the armature of his phylacteries) should have decided in the fall of 1944 to assume the aspect of a woman, and why now, restored, he can only make faces, and be afraid.

It is often the case that the weak become women. It is not as often that women are weak. If, therefore, Peter Narzissenfeld, a young and underfed *bahur* from the ghetto of Riga, decided to become a woman, to put on the first face of what were to be scores of faces, the face of a peasant *shikse*, we must grant him a terror—a terror so profound that he would willingly surrender for a time all image of manhood to the suggestion provided by his weak and weightless form.

Terror in one so young is not formed of casual dismay. It could be, he once suggested, that he contrived his fantasy of death long before it became a real possibility.

When still a boy Peter had once helped his father, a bricklayer, raise up the walls of a building in his native Riga. It

was not uncommon for children of working fathers to accompany them to work, to soften hides and cut leather if
they were cobblers, to sort out rags and paper if they were
junk dealers, to mix the mortar, and pass up the concrete if
they were masons, as was Itzik Narzissenfeld. That particular
morning, Itzik had climbed up the ladder and was about to
begin his work, putting in place on the second story of the
building the dun-colored bricks that had been piled on a
scaffold the night before. It was at the moment of beginning
that he remembered that he had forgotten to fill his pail with
mortar. He called to his son below and threw down the
empty pail. Young Narzissenfeld happily filled the pail and
set forth to climb the ladder to bring it to his father. In his
delight and abandon as he neared the top, smiling all the
while to his father, who called out "hurrahs" and "well
dones," he missed his footing and toppled to the ground,
some twenty feet below. All the masons and carpenters
rushed to the unconscious form and, so the grown man of
faces recalls, the first voice he heard was that of an elder
mason addressing the sobbing figure of his father Itzik, "God
be praised he has the lightness of a woman. Were he built like
a man he would be dead." Is it a wonder that in the camp
near Grodno, separated from his father and mother, Peter
Narzissenfeld recalled from his deeps the wisdom of that
mason? He procured a skirt from an old woman, a blouse and
sweater from an SS officer who fancied his looks, and a ker-
chief to cover his long stringy hair, and converted himself
into a peasant girl—a peasant girl near starvation, to be sure,
but nevertheless a girl. It did not matter to him that all the
prisoners ridiculed him, slapping their sides with laughter
and disgust as he went out to the fields. It did not matter.
Their laughter helped them endure the bitter cold and his
impersonation amused Commandant Ehle and pleased the
officer whose friend he became. The war would soon be over,
he told himself as 1945 began; the Russian planes constantly
bombed and strafed the nearby roads and railway junctions,
the retreat of the German army began, and on the last night
before the camp was abandoned and the prisoners broke
from their huts into the fields to join the partisans, he had
plunged a knife into the back of the lieutenant who had pro-

tected him for more than four months. He had survived. He threw off his woman's dress, but when he went to find new clothing for his nakedness he could not resist putting on a pair of trousers so large and bulky that they doubled around his waist and about his neck he knotted a piece of string into a tie. The man of faces succeeded the peasant girl. The faces he would wear, even now in the security of our compound, would be as various.

The Black Fast of Av was concluded; our community was recovering itself.

A dull inaction had settled upon us as we prepared for and passed through the time of mourning. The Black Fast, as it is known, recalling that event, millennia past, when the seat of His glory was pulled from under Him and we, attendants at His throne, despondent and confused, were driven from the Land of our comfort and desire, had continued over the centuries to demand a dreary exaction from us. We, who had not beheld that glory nor served at His altar, were cast back upon florid dirges and unintelligible poetry, filled with obscure allusions and bizarre constructions, to stoke an imagination which had, of late, been fired by other fires, more real, more immediate and devastating. We had no poet to draw the analogy between that ancient destruction and the recent fire through which we had come. But the analogy was not lost on us, we who sat in our slippers, ash upon our foreheads and intoned, with Rabbi Steinmann, the threnody of Lamentations. But the fast was over—concluded not as was that of Yom Kippur with an assurance of having won out over the Angel of Judgment, but with a whimper as if the punishment were not yet done nor the destruction finished. We can make peace with God, we men, but with history who can make peace? We were as beset in the aftermath of the Black Fast as we were before. God promises, but history provides and what a provider.

It was therefore with joy that I, and with me, it is hoped, my fellow councillors, Dr. Klay, Rabbi Steinmann, and Baltar, who composed the Council of the Society for the Rescue and Resurrection of the Jews, were informed by message that we were to gather in Simon's study at 3 A.M. on the morning following the conclusion of the Fast. We were awakened from

390

our rest only a quarter-hour before the meeting was convoked. Narzissenfeld, message bearer, rapped on my door at that early hour, and in a whisper hoarse with excitement, called me to Simon's rooms. Minutes later we were seated around his council table. We were in robes and slippers, although Baltar's feet were bare. We sat, talking little, awaiting his appearance to us. We waited, but he did not come. We heard nothing from his room. Baltar went, put an ear to the door and shrugged. He seemed to be unconcerned. The others were quiet, weary from uncompleted rest. Only I, sensing that it was a time between times, a moment between the commemoration of a destruction and the season of reconsecration, conceived another purpose to Simon's convocation.

And of a sudden there came to my mind all the examples of our past in which at times such as these God kept us in impatience, calling us to be ready, demanding our presence, choking the breath of expectation by dilatory evasion, putting us off to watch us squirm under his scrutiny. And in the past we fled from him, taking up with other consorts, lighting fires before other divinities, rushing about madly to break the strain of his silence and divagation. It was such a time. Simon was keeping us waiting with a reason. I could not bear it once more and it was then that I whispered to Dr. Klay, whose eyelids drooped from fatigue, "Listen, Klay, don't you understand that Simon's the Messiah? Simon's the one we have awaited all these years. He's the Messiah."

Simon Stern did not appear.

After an hour, first one, then another of my fellow councillors returned to their rest. Only I remained. When all had gone and I was alone, embarrassed by my passion and my espousal, I felt his hand cross over my face, touching my vacant eyes, marking the crease about my nostrils, outlining the curve of my lips and coming to rest, index finger in solitude, upon the declivation between nose and upper lip where it is said an angel touched us to wipe away our remembrance of the supernal wisdoms which we had all once known but had to forget at birth that life might continue hard and wondrous.

Dr. Klay was not indifferent to the movement of strangers

through our quarters. Perhaps because his sense of private order had never been humiliated as ours had been, he regarded the infestation of our domicile with this plague of incompetents (for they never finished their work, the same faces recurring with unsettling frequency) as profoundly annoying, rather than suspicious. Once he accosted a telephone repairman and demanded his credentials, but he was apparently satisfied, albeit grudgingly, for the work of repairing our telephone system continued throughout August. Klay spoke with me one morning about these trespassers, complaining that he could not understand such open faces with red cheeks, the sandy-haired, white-shirted, neatly attired inspectors and foremen and their crews of earnest, industrious artisans, but it seemed more an aesthetic distaste than anxious wariness. Nor did Simon Stern understand, for his telephone worked perfectly despite his complaint that it seemed to emit an unfamiliar buzz at the beginning and end of each call, an irregularity which the company's repair department explained resulted from faulty wiring which they were trying to locate and remedy. In a word, all our executive suspicion was allayed by mechanical explanations and technical language, and the general community, our hoi polloi, were polite and yielding, content in our surrogate advocacy of their irritation. Narzissenfeld carried forward his pursuit of Rochel, his morning visits stretching beyond my own half-hour in her company. My concern for Narzissenfeld and his erratic comings and goings, contained by his improbable liaison with Rochel, was renewed by the hint of fear which entered his voice each time I mentioned Rochel's name, each time I noted his late arrival. There were mysteries and confusions in our habitation which I, for one, could not understand.

Baltar, unlike ourselves, however, was not content with mystery and confusion.

"Who are these marauders?" he screamed.

It was early in September and I had been napping after lunch. A week had passed without alien visitors, but as suddenly as they had vanished they had reappeared the previous morning. The congenial telephone repairman had returned, accompanied by two assistants carrying metal boxes filled with incredible equipment. There was a plumbing inspector who claimed our pipes were giving off a noxious odor, befouling to the neighborhood—with him was one assistant with a wrench. And a fire inspector and a functionary from the water department, and a deputy of the garbagemen's union who complained about the manner in which our garbage was prepared for collection (he asked to inspect the hall behind the kitchen where refuse pails were set out for midnight gathering); and a building inspector, and someone from the gas company about our meters. The list of complainers, inquirers, fixers was quite extensive. Some sixteen gentlemen visited our quarters. Several stayed an hour or two, questioning Rabbi Steinmann, or Rochel in the kitchen, or simply wandering with apparent aimlessness throughout the four corners of the compound. It didn't really bother anyone. Our community seemed perfectly willing to cooperate. They were accustomed to answering questions—the more peremptory the question the more unhesitant their answer. Some things were asked, for which no one had answers, and having demonstrated their ignorance of the answer, there was nothing to do but pass on. The inquirers were apparently satisfied (or else so profoundly dissatisfied) by the answers they received that they gave up asking them, and by the next day, although a number of repairmen returned, others had disappeared, permanently we hoped. We regarded these servicemen as distractions, gentiles with practical skills about which we knew nothing and cared less, but for Baltar these outsiders were a menace. He had a secret to guard which Simon knew, but which he alone had created. Only myself, besides Simon Stern, suspected the secret, and so it was that he came to me.

"Who are these marauders?" he screamed again.

"I am not frightened of you, Baltar," I answered calmly. "Dear Baltar. No man can frighten Nathan. You can take my life. That's all. You're welcome to it if you wish. So screams and shouts will get you nothing."

"Who are these marauders?" he demanded again, but more quietly.

"The workmen, the repairers? How should I know? Workmen and repairers, I imagine. Mending, fixing. Do you think otherwise?"

"You're clever, my friend. Don't you think I've observed them examining rooms, checking entrances and exits, knocking on walls. Not ordinary workmen. And I caught one drawing a map! I tore it from him. It was a complete map of the western section of the compound. They're spies. That's what they are."

Of course they were spies. I saw that clearly for the first time. And they had reason to spy.

"But why should they spy?" I asked disingenuously. "What would we have to hide? Eighteen shipments of what? What were those shipments—" I mused aloud. "More books? No, not likely. Or machinery—heavy enough for machinery, and the smell of oil and grease. But of course! What kind of machinery, Baltar? What kind of machinery would someone of your disposition favor. Ploughshares and pruning hooks that men learn war no more? I doubt that."

I should not have laughed, but I did. I laughed from terror, from the terror of what I had guessed. I suppose I had always known, but I had not dared to admit it. I had also resolved to speak with Simon, but that, too, I had not done.

Baltar's hands closed around my throat, smooth hands, and large. "Like a twig, I can snap your neck or, if I choose, wring it like a goose. I told you once that you saw everything. You do. But I warn you. This project is mine. I created it and I will not end it before it is begun. A hundred, a thousand, ten thousand of them and us I will take with me. Warn Simon Stern and you die."

Baltar released his grip and left me as suddenly as he had descended upon me.

The next day I would have come to Simon Stern, but it was already too late. I had waited too long (or perhaps there is no too long, too late, too early in the affairs of men, only an inexorable moment which is always the right time).

It was on the afternoon of September the 9th, the day after the repairmen had completed their second visit to our Society, that Mr. Gusweller reappeared. I called Dr. Klay, and Mr. Gusweller went up. He knew his way. But he was accompanied this time by an abbreviated gentleman whom Narzissenfeld nervously described as "compact, very compact, little eyes, little nose, little mouth and such a ridiculous mustache. Funny little man to work with the agent."

"The *agent?*" I said immediately, struck by the word. "He's not an agent. Why do you say 'agent'?"

Narzissenfeld's voice reddened with confusion. "Well, not agent, you know what I mean. He investigates or something, doesn't he?"

"Indeed?"

"What?"

"That's what I'd like to find out. What? What's going on with you, Peter Narzissenfeld?"

"I? I'm the man of faces, remember, Mr. Gaza? What can a man of faces be up to. I'm all show, all curtain. I'm a curtain raiser. I'm an opening note. My God, Mr. Gaza, what do you think I am? I'm nothing."

"Peter, my friend of faces, no one is no thing. Even a speck can blind an eye."

"I'm sorry. Whatever I've done, I'm sorry. I won't do it again. I'm finished doing it." Narzissenfeld began to sob. I stood up and pulled him toward me, holding his hand until his sobs subsided.

"What have you done, friend Peter?" I asked firmly.

"I can't tell. I can't tell. They'll send me away if I tell," he blubbered, his tears renewed.

"Who, Peter? Who has threatened you?" I persisted.

"Others, bigger than all of us. They threatened to send me back and they can do it," he said, pounding a fist on my desk like a child in helpless rage.

"All right, Peter. But you must promise me one thing: you will not speak to these others again without telling me first. Is that understood? Clearly?"

He nodded his head and began to rub his eyes with the backs of his hands.

A minute later Dr. Klay called me. I expected the call but was unnerved when the phone jangled. Klay spoke to me hurriedly. "Come to my room. Tell no one." I hung up, took my cane, dismissed Narzissenfeld who began to lock the front door against the evening and left my desk. As an afterthought I called back to Narzissenfeld, "Wash your eyes with cold water, Peter. They're red. I don't want people asking why Peter has been crying. Understand?"

"Yes, Mr. Gaza, and thank you for caring about me," and

improbably he came to me, took my hand in both of his and raised it to his lips.

Too long had he loved that lieutenant, I thought, with feeling for his confusion.

Mr. Gusweller, and his associate, whom he introduced as Pan, sat across from Klay on his divan, an uncomfortable arrangement, since it was less appropriate for formal visitations than for Klay's lounging reception of friends. But now, uncomfortable, their papers resting upon their knees, the visitors had no choice but to come to the point.

"I think I'll let Mr. Pan talk first. He's done the Simon Stern inquiry. It's fairly routine, but there are some interesting facts. Mr. Pan."

"I'm not going to review all the documents. They're right here, arranged in the chronology of his life, beginning with his birth certificate and brought up to date with an interview we had with your architect, Dr. Setzer. No point going through them. What comes across is already well known, certainly well known to all of you. An extraordinary man, it would appear. Did you know, however, that he once consulted a psychiatrist? Yes, right here. In black and white. We interviewed the gentleman. He's very old now, but still lucid. He had—the psychiatrist, that is—kept his notes on the interview. At first he denied that he had any knowledge of Mr. Stern. Scruples, you know. Secrecy of the confessional and all that, but we have our little ways. The doctor was an immigrant, most of those old psychiatrists were. Just had to mention that the Department of Immigration and Naturalization are always interested in annoying foreigners, particularly psychiatrists. It's not true, of course. But he listened, looking through his bifocals, bug-eyed with fear. He told us about the interview. Let me read it to you. I left out a lot of the technical talk. I didn't understand it, so I left it out, but the essence of it is here.

DOCUMENT #5
Interview with Dr. Gustav Bochenski

Yes, I remember Mr. Stern. A very ordinary little man, not undersized, really, but a trifle underfed. I thought to myself almost from the first moment I put my eyes on him that here's an ordinary man who's probably suffering from being an ordinary man. Stands to reason. But I had no idea until he began to talk how much he suffered.

He told me about his childhood and youth in the city; how he was a midget until he was nearly twenty and how he began to make money and how he had no conception of money as more than a means of compensating his parents. He told of making millions upon millions of dollars, but would add, pausing after the description of some giant exploit, that he bought his mother a dress or his father a pair of shoes or provisioned the table for a week. Those masses of millions came down to a few dollars of compensation.

There was a pattern, but there was no key. We need so much information, you know. So much information. And it was difficult for me to get information from such a strange person. You know he sent a limousine to bring me to his office. I charged him $250 for that interview. It took more than four hours up and back. It wasn't an unusual fee to charge for my time or to charge someone so prodigiously rich. Another compensation, particularly if our inquiry had gone on. But it did not. It stopped right there.

When he called me—he said from a telephone booth in the back of the storage room where he had his office—he said he was suffering from backaches which had begun after his parents' death. Backaches, and headaches (classic migraines), and worst of all, a recurring nightmare, in which he dreamed he saw the Ark in which the Jews put their sacred scrolls covered by a giant bat who sank his claws into the parchment and sucked out the words like blood. A word-eating vampire. Or let us say a vampire who sucked the blood of God. Now that's a curious dream to connect with the death of one's parents.

It was a fascinating interview. Not because the problem was unique. We have all the patterns. It's persons we lack. We know everything about the general order of delusion and neurosis, but what's the use of general knowledge.

How did he find out about me, you ask? Now that's also curious. I write often for psychoanalytic journals, and Mr. Stern had quite by accident, he insisted, read one of my essays, on religious delusions and divination, it was. At all events, he read that essay and thought I could help. We talked, as I said, for a long time and he told me many things about his parents [Dr. Bochenski consulted his notes at this point], "Father Abram" and "Mother Ruth" he always called them. He blamed himself for their death. "Inadvertence," he said. "Self-indulgence," "arrogance," "invulnerability," but mostly "inadvertence." Those were the words he used. I knew he really didn't want to be helped.

It's hard helping patients. They have to want to be helped, very badly want to be helped to be helped at all. What he really wanted was a chat. He wanted to be in touch with some expert who would hand him the solution and let him go off about his business. I couldn't do that. Of course I couldn't. But I told him he had some severe problems and only if he put them to work *for himself* could be gain some relief. What I meant was that you had to take guilt at face value. It's something you take very seriously or not at all. Too seriously and it ends up giving you all those symptoms. Not at all and you leave the superego like an unfed beast. So I said to him: "Mr. Stern, put it to work. Put that guilt to work. If you think you murdered (which you obviously didn't), do something for someone else, relieve the imagined guilt by taking on the guilt of others. It helps. It's still crazy, but at least it's useful for a change."

I went back uptown and about a year later he called to say he was being useful and the pains had disappeared and the nightmare hadn't recurred. He said thank you and sent me another check, which I returned to him.

Signed: Leopold Pan
Staff Investigator
Lubrice Detective Bureau

"So much for Dr. Bochenski. There's nothing else to tell you that you really don't know. We took about twenty depositions. They're all here, arranged in sequence. A very curious man, your Mr. Stern. But remarkable. Remarkable. Over a hundred million dollars. Remarkable."

"Thank you, Mr. Pan. You can go now. I have other things to discuss with our friends. More private. Much more private."

Mr. Pan obviously knew he would be dismissed. He stood up, and in a single gesture smoothed the hairs of his mustache, the front of his jacket and the fold of his pants (rather like washing himself), and shaking our hands departed. Fisher Klay told me about this gesture afterward, laughing I think a bit hysterically, for the other news we were about to receive was more than enough to oblige hysteria.

"Your colleague, Janos Baltar," Mr. Gusweller began, "is, however, rather a different cup, gentlemen, rather a different cup. I should say, thinking aloud, which is not my specialty (I'm a fact gatherer, not a judge of men) that Janos Baltar is one of the most frightening specimens I've ever encountered (and I've encountered quite a few). It's not that he's a murderer (which he is, a competent, skilled murderer, in fact, though the evidence would hardly be persuasive to a jury), but more improbably a religious fanatic.

"Janos Baltar appears to think of himself as a kind of inverted Christ, a crucified man who has the responsibility of opening up the wounds of the world and forcing them to bleed again.

"One of our informants, an interesting professor of art history, Wolf Kragun, attached to the Albertina in Vienna (that's a famous museum with one of the world's greatest collections of Albrecht Dürer), described our subject (whom he had known briefly in one of the camps where he served as official SS archivist and statistician) as a sadist, whose pleasure was to undertake the torture and then succor and ease the pain of the tortured.

" 'Baltar, for example,' Kragun explained to me, 'exactly in the spirit of Dürer's print "The Large Crucifixion," which depicts the suffering of Christ with angels holding cups to catch the blood which gushed from his wounds, had the habit of burning into victims the four wounds of Christ, and then as the blood would begin to flow and his victims groan in unendurable pain he would put a cloth soaked in vinegar upon them, he would bathe their heads, he would hold them in his arms until they revived or died. And then most curiously he would become deeply melancholic, weep pitiably, begin to recite snatches of Hebrew prayers it was not believed he knew and then disappear to sleep it off and, upon reawakening, have no recollection of the torments he had inflicted.'

"'You see,' concluded Professor Kragun, 'Baltar was only a half-Jew—his father was a Jew, but not his mother—he knew that according to the Jews he was no Jew, and according to the Nazis completely a Jew. In short he belonged to no one.'"

Gusweller paused, cleared his throat, tapped the ridge of his reading glasses and made himself as comfortable as possible, for the portion of the narrative he was about to unfold was, as will be seen, the most extensive. We, however, Dr. Klay and myself, were already rigid with stupefaction.

"Janos Baltar was born in 1902 or 1903 (birth records were somewhat casually kept in his village, and many pages of the large register in the town hall were all but illegible, soiled as they were with grease stains and ink smudges—our investigator was told that the town clerk was a slovenly man, an alcoholic who never entered birth and death dates unless thoroughly drunk), in the village of Kluzh in northwest Rumania, some sixty kilometers from the commercial center of Satu-Mare.

"Kluzh was a peasant village. It had a granary, a general store and a church—a modest affair with one stained-glass window and an altar whose only distinction was an eighteenth-century ciborium, stolen, we were told, from a bishop who had traveled through the area a century earlier on pilgrimage to a shrine of the Holy Virgin in Hungary. The population of the village was, in that attractive East European locution, numbered at 'a hundred and seven souls and eleven Jews.' As it happens, the family of Baltar was drawn from each, for his parents' marriage was never solemnized, and neither church nor synagogue could claim their registry.

"The father of Janos Baltar, Michoel, was both a lumberman and a drover who served the farmers of the area by collecting in his charge each spring the cattle and sheep they wished to sell and bringing them to the market at Satu-Mare where he would dispose of them. In the course of time, he became a rich man—that is, rich by the standards of poverty. He owned his own cottage and cattle pen, his own barn and fields, but this meant little more than that he was not bonded to Count Cescu, a nobleman who idled his time in Bucharest and, when he could afford it, Paris.

"All the lands from the hills behind Kluzh to the east until the banks of the Somes River which flowed through Satu-Mare were owned by Count Cescu. The Count (let us be explicit, for it figures in our narrative of the life and times of Janos Baltar) preferred the company of young men to that of young women, to that of women of any age, although his elderly mother, an obese woman with a persistent delight in laudanum, was always in residence at the manor house of the Count, covered with decayed clothing and a dozen Pekingese who yapped and spilled over her body (one indeed was found dead in the folds of her dressing gown where it had unfortunately burrowed while she slept) from morning until late at night.

"The parents of Janos Baltar—can one call them parents?—were forever screaming, cursing the time of their union, cursing the hour of their birth, cursing, it would seem, the moment of Janos' birth, for that birth consolidated before the world what simple lust had not previously demanded. Baltar's father, the Jew in Baltar's life, had come to Kluzh a young man of eighteen. He had been traveling in the company of Mendel Lieber, a Jewish lumber merchant from Hungary. An orphan, he had been adopted into the entourage of this merchant, who appeared in the village two years before the birth of Janos. The merchant had sought to arrange a lumber franchise with the Count, then a man in his early sixties, but the feasts and banquets which he organized in his honor were unappealing, centering as they did about the misapplied attentions of a variety of gypsy girls and singers whom he had brought from a neighboring encampment of the Kalderesh who traveled through that area of Transylvania. The Count, not abashed by his perversity, made it clear to merchant Lieber that not the gypsy girls but rather Michoel, father of Janos Baltar, was pleasing to his sight and that for the gift of him he would grant the franchise. Merchant Lieber was no less unembarrassed in making clear to his young ward that if he would consent to allowing the elderly Count to take his pleasure with him the Count would make him bailiff of the forests and establish him in the village, providing him moreover with the services of a pretty gentile girl who more evidently attracted him. The arrangement was accepted; the father of Janos Baltar would become the lover of the elderly Count, the franchise was arranged, the documents executed, the appointment of Michoel confirmed as bailiff and a sum equivalent to $1000 paid over for the purchase of a cottage, a hundred acres of good grazing land, and a small herd of cattle. On the night following the completion of these arrangements the Count summoned the young man to his bed. He arrived tardily, drunk, and beat the Count within an inch of his life. The Count left his lands early the following morning and did not return for more than a year, and then only to attend the funeral of his mother, who died suddenly and was buried with no less alacrity.

"By the time of the Count's return, Michoel Baltar had taken in concubinage the blond woman of his choice, bribed and humiliated into submission by Mendel Lieber before his departure for Keckskemet in Hungary where he made his home. The arrangement went passably at the outset. The villagers, enriched by the influx of lumbermen organized by Michoel to cut and transport the trees from the Count's vast forest acreage, were scarcely in a position to assault his liaison with the pretty Christian girl (who would have scarcely enhanced the reputation of any other peasant lad, for her virginity had disappeared some years earlier when the army had passed on maneuvers through the region). Despite, therefore, the protestations and disgust of the village priest, the unsanctified union of Michoel and Drina (for that was her name) was accepted.

"The Jews, however, were less than content with their union; for them, vulnerability being their life, the disgrace of such a perverse history and consummation was an unspeakable outrage. The Jews of Kluzh were but three families, not even a quorum being available for daily services and Sabbath. These Jews, only one of whom was a man of substance, for it was he who owned the general store and mead house, reviled Michoel, spitting unobtrusively as he passed and fingering their *kameot* beneath their shirts when they were obliged to come near his house. He was a disgrace to the Law, an insult to the blood and worse than a mere Christian, an

402

abomination, truly 'a crawling thing,' worthy of being crushed.

"The month of Count Cescu's return to his properties Drina became pregnant. The pregnancy was announced as a public event, Michoel making certain that all—Christians and Jews —became aware that their union, passing the boundaries of lust and desire, would soon be fruitful and multiplied as God intended, despite his refusal to allow the child to be circumcised, if it should prove to be a boy. He would have none of them, not he, but he would demand from them (since he was, second alone to the Count, the most powerful man in the village), the respect due him, his wife by consent, and their unborn issue.

It did not happen as he wished. As the months passed and Drina became larger, her wantonness became more exaggerated, her immodesty more patent, her bulging belly covered in summer by only the flimsiest of gowns, the outlines of her stomach and the shadow of her pudenda visible to public gaze through the thin muslin of her dresses. Michoel did not care, for by then he was carrying on an affair with another girl in the neighboring village. His tardy returns, his indifference to Drina made her even more suspicious of his movements. One day she went to a gypsy woman who told fortunes and learned that her suspicions were justified— Michoel was unfaithful, always unfaithful. As the time of her confinement neared she became fretful and melancholic, refusing to eat, and taking herself unaccountably to the village church for vigils and fasts. Her religiosity returned as a diversion from her rage, for undoubtedly she loved Michoel as best she understood that indefinable notion. The priest, delighted with her return to the Church, took the occasion to chastise her dereliction, exaggerate her sins, and calumniate the sensual Jews.

"Drina began labor on the eve of the Jews' festival of Passover. As we have said, there were only eleven Jews in the village of Kluzh, ten excluding Michoel. It was the custom of these Jews on the major festivals of their religious year to depart the village and go from there to the Rumanian city of Cluj, known in German as Klausenburg, the seat of one of the most revered of Hasidic dynasties, that of the Klausenburger, a saintly rabbi, we are told (whose son is now installed

403

in Brooklyn), to pass in the company of their coreligionists the most sacred times of the year. The Jews would seal their houses, bank their fires, and depart in the early morning in carts so as to arrive at Cluj by early afternoon.

"Drina labored through the eve of Passover and early on the morning of Passover day her son was born. Michoel had not been present for the delivery; indeed he had disappeared two days before and had not returned; undoubtedly passing the time in the company of his mistress in the neighboring village. Efforts were made to find him, but to no avail. At dawn, thinking her asleep, the midwife departed. Drina, weakened by her labor and loss of blood, was fevered. Undoubtedly she was fevered. She wrapped the infant and walked the half-mile to the church, where the priest met her—it having been arranged earlier in the day that she would come to him at an hour when she would not be observed. The priest baptized the infant, giving him the name Janos. As the service was nearing completion and the weakened woman was giving way to moans of pain and exhaustion, Michoel entered the church, and seeing what was going on, retrieved his son from the hands of the priest and taking from his pocket the knife which he habitually carried drew it around the praeputium of the infant, threw the foreskin before the altar and bathed the child's circumcised member in the fount of holy water in which he had just been inscribed in the name of the Father, the Son, and the Holy Ghost. Is it a wonder that in rage at this desecration the villagers should have burned to the ground the three homes deserted by the Jews, while Michoel stood before his own, shotgun in hand, drunk beyond comprehension, and fired salvos into the air as each house went up in flames?

"An auspicious beginning for Janos Baltar. My investigators were as disgusted by these findings as you must be. I was elsewhere discovering other curious details. A few more years of Kluzh and Janos Baltar will be launched upon the world, but for the moment we stay behind in that dismal village.

"After the burning out of the Jews, only the owner of the general store and tavern returned. And then there were four —the husband, wife, son of the general store and Michoel Baltar, father of Janos, who eight days after his violent circumcision, on the day, in fact, that he should have been circumcised according to the Jews, received the name Baalam from his father, who bent over his bed and taking his hurt member between thumb and index finger pressed from it a drop of blood which he put to his lips as he pronounced the name with which he was to permanently bedaub his son. Baalam the pagan recalcitrant, the cowardly God-fearer, was to be to the Jews what Janos would be to Christians—the mark of the half-man, the half-named man, the half-formed Baltar. But Baltar grew up despite the distortions of his beginnings, a powerful lad, so all recall, with the body of a lion and boundless energy and strength. Moreover he was a silent child, a child who scarcely spoke, who contained words unsorted and disarranged, refusing, it appears, to speak for fear that his words would tumble in disorder and confusion from his lips. When he would begin to speak, he would stamp upon the ground to summon concentration and his reddish brows would contract and force his speech, but what came forth, however calm his manner, was not the speech of men, but the speech of strange creatures. Is it a wonder that the villagers struck by such a mysterious sign should come to regard young Baltar as possessed, handsome of body but deformed by the insertion of some devilishness?

He grew up. One says that simply. There is no way to describe growth, the growing up of such an untamed and possessed child. Michoel and Drina scarcely attended to the process, their own lives centering upon alternations of embittered orgies of drink in which Drina came to participate as intently as Michoel and excursions of passion, wanderings forth, field and farm copulation, in which Michoel supervised Drina's seduction of the woodsmen and Drina observed Michoel and the mistresses of the villages.

"It is not unusual that Michoel Baltar, insensitive to the life of his son, should have been indifferent to the casual request made one day by Count Cescu that Janos be allowed to serve him as page and errand boy, dividing his time between life at home and a room over the stables of the manor. Janos was then a lad of ten years, tall for his age, strong, of a reddish cast and complexion, though his hair remained black and grew in curls which fell in a tangle and snarl, dirty with the earth, upon his shoulders. He looked more a gypsy than a Jew-Christian, more a wild creature than a young man. But presumably, given the Count's perverse ways, precisely that look of wildness attracted him to the boy and the offer of four gallons of distilled spirits and two chickens each month were attractive enough payment for the services of a useless son. It appears, however, that the Count was preparing for more than the seduction of the boy—that intention you will have already guessed. There was more, for he wished to repay upon the son what he did not dare to inflict upon the father who had beaten him a dozen years before. And so it happened that one night the Count's coachman and manservant came to the room above the stable, seized young Baltar while he slept, bound him securely, covered his mouth and brought him to the bedroom of the Count, who awaited his delivery. There the boy was thrown upon the bed, and while the Count watched, was beaten until the child's back was livid with wounds and blood flowed as freely as the tears which streamed from his eyes. Only when the boy fainted from pain and exhaustion did the Count undertake to rape him, it being difficult for an elderly man, a man already beyond the age of seventy, to have abused him while he was awake and struggling against his bonds. In the morning Janos found himself in a field miles from the Count's manor, beside the Somes River, with an elderly woman, her grey hair braided with colored fabric, her neck circled with necklaces of gold pieces, bending over him, applying poultices of cooling mud to his back and stroking his head with rhythmic gentleness.

"The gypsy woman, though she appeared to be very aged, was not older than sixty-five when our investigators found her in the encampment of the surviving Kalderesh who traveled the region from the Carpathian Mountains to Transylvania and by night into eastern Russia. She remembered the boy, for she had adopted him into her family and taught him the viciousness of the *gaje* (the term of opprobrium by which gypsies address the settled world of the outsider who know nothing of the right life of man, which is, according to them, to move swiftly as clouds, to travel as quietly as the hovering bird, to keep the honored counsels of the tribe, who know too well the treachery of men who claim wisdom and righteousness as a birthright).

"Janos (for he was called Janos by the tribe; the name Baalam, the half-Jew who could speak the word of God only when it was forced upon him, she did not know, Janos keeping that name a secret) became a circus acrobat and tightrope walker. The tribe earned its keep and travel documents by performing in small towns and commercial centers from Sevastopol to Bratislava—performing bears, jugglers, fortune-telling, and tightrope walking. Janos, because of his powerful frame, coordination, and concentrated composure, was ideally suited to become a tightrope walker, and walk he did, beginning fifteen feet above the ground until by his maturity (for gypsy boys were regarded as fully mature at sixteen) he was striding confidently, his hands gripping a slender balancing rod, fifty feet or more above the ground and there, high above the crowds of upturned faces, he allowed himself to speak to them, his speech flowing easily, with clarity and order, his songs of hate and loathing, cursing them, Christian and Jew alike, and calling upon heaven to hurl down upon them boulders and boiling oil and to release among them starved basilisks and ravenous griffins.

"As he would walk, one step moving gracefully before the next, beads of perspiration clotting his eyebrows, he would sing out 'Dear Lord of the Universe, punish them with fire and serpent. O delight me, dear Lord, by destroying them.'

"Janos Baltar became the principal attraction of the itinerant gypsy circus. He became the miraculous tightrope walker and his feats became more improbable—fifty feet became a hundred, became two hundred, and the balancing rod was replaced by turning leaps in the air in which he would ascend three feet into the heavens, turn his body and land reversing direction, or carrying a pack on his back when he reached the center of the wire he would remove a small table, attach it to the wire, set utensils upon it and begin to eat an elaborate meal, spitting out pits of cherries and herring bones upon the crowds below. He left the gypsies during his early twenties when an impresario from a Warsaw circus saw him perform and induced him to join his troupe as the star attraction. 'Miraculous Janos' he was called, and for a number of years more he moved through the north of Europe, traveling from Moscow and Leningrad to Lübeck.

"It happened one night when Janos was thirty-six or thirty-seven (that is to say, if we accept the date of 1902-1903 as his time of birth, in 1938 or thereabouts); he was performing in a small town in Lithuania, near the city of Vilna. His performance completed, he was sitting in his dressing room near the big tent when there entered behind him an old Jew, whom one judged from his fur hat, black silk coat, white stockings and patent shoes with silver buckles, to be a figure of considerable importance. This old Jew looked at Janos Baltar and said nothing for some length of time. Baltar pretended to ignore him, continuing to look into the mirror and bedaub his face with cold cream to clean away the make-up which he liberally applied to clown his features and hide from the menacing crowds below the strain of rage which still beset him when he walked the wire. The old Jew scanned his face, the reddish complexion, the head shaved clean, the stiff back, the curved musculature, the trim waist, the powerful biceps and thighs, the slender ankles and small feet, examining them without appearing to raise or lower his eyes, but attentive to every curiosity of his body.

"At last, after watching him for more than half an hour, neither having spoken nor acknowledged the presence of the other, the old Jew said distinctly in Polish, 'Miserable Jew.' Baltar tensed, hearing the words, but paid no attention, choosing to ignore for the moment the reference to his disgusting origins. 'Miserable Jew. See your forehead!' The old Jew lifted his silver-headed walking stick and pointed toward the mirror into which Baltar continued to stare. 'There, that pink birthmark upon your forehead. See there, not bigger than a starburst but ineffaceable. The thousand crossed lines of fate whirling upon your face. Die before you kill. Pray God to die before you kill.' The old Jew finished and lowered the menacing stick with which he had been circling Baltar's head with divinatory deliberateness, and muttering once more, 'Accursed Jew,' departed the tent. Baltar did not move. For hours he stared into the mirror, watching the small starburst grow until it covered his face, its tremulous shadows covering his cheeks, its sinuous tentacles spreading out until they covered his

408

skull and curved beneath his chin. He was found the following morning lying as though dead upon the earth floor of the tent, completely paralyzed and motionless.

"A sanatorium on the North Sea restored Baltar to health, his speech defect cured, his body released from the devils of his childhood. He spent more than eighteen months in that institution, receiving shock treatment, hydrotherapy, hypnosis and psychiatric interviews which were conducted in a spirit of genial cruelty, the director personally interesting himself in the case of the renowned circus performer. It was from him—the same doctor, Constantin Braunschweig—that we learned of the old Jew and his terrorization of Baltar. Dr. Braunschweig, deeply interested in race theory and purification, regarded Baltar's history as a splendid example of precisely the degeneracy and restoration which his political mentor, Alfred Rosenberg, obliged him to endorse in return for the annual state subsidy his institution received. Dr. Braunschweig, knowing of Baltar's questionable racial origins, nonetheless regarded him as having been winnowed of his father's impurities and restored by medical treatment to an Aryanism which could be prudently employed by the Party. It is no wonder that, with his doctor's recommendation and endorsement, Janos Baltar was admitted to the German army in 1941 and received the rank of noncommissioned officer.

"By 1942 Janos Baalam Baltar was to be found as a camp guard at Ravensbrück, where he distinguished himself for the sadism with which we began our narrative. During the course of his service in that infamous camp he was directly responsible for the torture murder of three inmates and the crippling of some score more, all of whom were found pierced with scalpel efficiency in the same manner as had been the crucified Messiah.

"Several months before the liberation of Ravensbrück, Janos Baltar disappeared. No trace of him was found, although it is known that he made his way to Vienna where we believe we can ascribe to him (for obvious reasons) a grotesque incident which offended the Cardinal Archbishop of Vienna and did little to restore compassionate good will toward those few Jews who survived and returned and were suspected of this blasphemy. On Easter Sunday of 1945, it appears, the principal altars of Vienna—the cathedrals and Baroque chapels of the city to which the faithful now came in renewed numbers following the retreat of the German armies—found the crucifix of the high altars desecrated. Upon the body of the limp Christ had been placed a photograph of a dead Jew, his feet, his hands, his side pierced in precisely the manner in which it was known Baltar tormented his victims. What was this? Was it the Jew reviling Christian for brutalizing Jew for crucifying the Christ? What a confusion. What a play upon the endless drama of the Passion. Most assuredly Baltar. Crazy Baltar. Cured by Dr. Braunschweig? Contained, but not cured.

"Baltar then made his way to Paris. There he concealed himself for nearly six months, living on scraps like a beggar, without papers, for he could not reveal his identity to anyone. During that time, living hidden away, he contrived to strengthen his old Jewish self, the dormant self which had been suppressed by Dr. Braunschweig. The Yiddish he had learned as a child returned, and working with diligence and application he learned enough of the Hebrew language, its liturgy, and literature to begin the dissimulation which brought him to your attention during the late summer of 1945, which brought him to you today.

"And so, in summary, who is Baltar? A homicidal maniac, nothing more nor less. A war criminal undoubtedly. Undetected it would appear, for he has been expert in putting on the disguise of his natal past and has remained unrecognized. He does not travel. He stays put. He has remained undetected until now. But, may I ask you, gentlemen, is it possible that you suspected nothing?"

We heard the question, but were so shaken, we could not answer. Mr. Gusweller had spoken to us for more than an hour. His voice had been flat and nasal, undistinguished, monotonous. What he described, not without flair, which I have but slightly improved in my recension, required no dramatic italics or apostrophes. Nothing. Not rape. Not breakdowns. Not murder. Nothing nettled his speech into those gesticulations of accent so common to ordinary men for whom such material is not ordinary and unexceptional. For detective Gusweller, Janos Baltar, monster though he knew him to be, was simply a few cuts above the psychotics and psychopaths with whom he conventionally transacted the business of his life.

"Thank you, Mr. Gusweller." Dr. Klay stood up abruptly and walked to the door, which he pulled open and then closed. There was no one in the hall, although Klay confessed later that he detected in the musty air a distinctive odor, lingering, like the echo of a screech owl in the night, upon the doorjamb and knob, an odor which has already been described. Had Baltar heard our conversation? It would not be known, although the fear that he had heard, even if nothing more, the mention of his name which occurred often in Gusweller's report, aroused in us a sense of urgency. Dr. Klay returned to his chair and sat down, patting his forehead with a handkerchief.

"Horrible?" Mr. Gusweller commented.

"Very," Dr. Klay replied.

"More than that. More complicated even than that," Mr. Gusweller observed, speaking slowly and in a voice so low as to be scarcely audible. "I shouldn't be saying this to you. But you should be on your guard. Very much on your guard."

"Of Baltar?"

"Naturally of Baltar. But not of him alone. It's a threatening world you choose to combat, and even the best-kept secrets are discovered."

"Yes? What secrets?" I interjected.

"I've said too much already. I think you're both honorable men. I'm not usually hired by honorable men."

"We thank you," Dr. Klay snapped brusquely, "but honorableness doesn't help us much, as you can see. We took a Baltar into our midst."

"Yes, that is the question I already asked. You did, and it is of Baltar that you should be afraid, for Baltar is mad and the outside world is curious about his madness."

At that moment we became aware, although I could not see the glance which Klay undoubtedly turned in my direction, that Mr. Gusweller was no simple detective. I knew even more than Klay. I knew of Narzissenfeld's slip. Detective Gusweller was an Agent, an agent for the outside world, undoubtedly a government agent, a double agent, a detective for us, a spy for them, and I realized that Narzissenfeld's knowledge of this duplicity meant that he, too, was being used by Gusweller to spy on us. Not alone Baltar, but all of us were endangered.

"Thank you, Mr. Gusweller. I think we have concluded our business. We will not see each other again."

"Perhaps not, but nothing is certain in this world." Mr. Gusweller stood up, shook our hands and opened the door. As an afterthought he called back to us, with a note of warning and authority unmistakable in his tone, "Gentlemen, do try and clean it up. Quickly. You haven't much time."

We knew we hadn't much time. The mysterious night deliveries. Three hundred cases of mysterious shipments. It all made sense at last. Arms, guns and ammunition, wrapped in oil soaked rags, awaiting the moment at which Baltar would begin his fantastic scheme of revenge, a warfare of vengeance in which all of us—Jews and friends, neighbors and strangers, enemies and partisans—would go up together, an immolation of the Lower East Side.

We determined to come to Simon. Simon came to us. Not ten minutes had passed since Gusweller's departure. There was a knock on the door and Simon Stern entered Klay's quarters. We stood up as was our habit when Simon entered our rooms. We owed him that respect, and even now, strained as we were by the knowledge that had been given us, we behaved from habit, for Simon Stern was honored in our eyes.

"I've come to speak with you. It makes me happy that you are together, that I can speak with you together. I have seen you so little in recent days. It perplexes me. I love and need you and you have avoided me. But I understand. The confusion of this time. It is hard traveling a straight path. The straightest of paths is difficult. How much more so when one comes to a fork and there are no signs, no indications. A choice must still be made. It may well be the wrong choice."

"We're glad that you've come to us, Simon," Dr. Klay replied warmly.

"I have come to give you news of great sadness. I am truly weary from sadness, but this sadness is greater yet than any I have had to bear. Not an hour ago, my friend Lubina attempted to take her life. Please, now. Don't speak. Say nothing. Listen. Let me tell you. She will recover. I found her. I called our doctor and he applied the antidote. She is now in hospital. She will recover. That at least is assured. It was not her time. But it is, most assuredly, our own. For she undertook to take her life out of fear and love for me."

Simon Stern never visited the rooms of Lubina Krawicz, unaccompanied. Not, at least, until the hour just passed. Not, at least, so far as I was aware. You might think that he took this precaution to avoid scandal, lest gossiping tongues speak the wickedness of which they are inordinately capable (and even more so out of the envy and outrage with which they greet irreducible mystery in another). But that is not the case here. It was not that Simon needed restraint from harming or humiliating Lubina or that he needed the presence of another to brake an indiscretion. Since it was always I, I alone, who accompanied him, my presence would serve as no rein to him, for what, indeed, could I have done if it were the case that Simon was aroused by Lubina's splendid ugliness. If Simon wished to kiss her or to place his hand upon her breast or even to lie with her, my blindness would have been no constraint.

I accompanied Simon Stern not to protect him from his desire, but in order to spare him hers. You know all that is known of Lubina already. Little is known. Simon did not confide the details of his feelings to me, and what was evident was apparent—Lubina was first a crippled friend and then a scarred and embittered enemy. Lubina both adored and hated Simon, called him beloved and called him murderer.

The quarters to which Lubina was brought after the festival of inauguration which marked the opening of the end were already prepared for her. Simon had known that she would come to him. Indeed there are to be found in the numerous memoranda which he sent to Mr. Setzer during the construction and decoration of the compound detailed descriptions of the secret quarters to be built above his own and it is clearly indicated that he expected it to be occupied by a woman. Mr. Setzer took this, disrespectfully, to mean that even Simon Stern was not made of wood, that his passions, however muted and concealed, existed as in other men and that above his quarters he would install some splendid creature about whom Mr. Setzer could only conjecture. Mr. Setzer replied to one of Simon's descriptions of these rooms that it was imprudent, considering the "undoubted beauty of the occupant that she have such a small and unprepossessing bed," for Mr. Setzer imagined that the bed assigned to Simon's recreation be vast as that given by King Solomon to his favorite. Simon replied sternly and with contempt that Mr. Setzer "should confine his fantasy to the details of brick and mortar and leave such idle speculation to the cinema." Mr. Setzer, chastised, made no further mention of his romantic imaginings, but stuck tenaciously to the rough sketch which Simon had drawn—rough indeed, for Simon could scarcely draw, but he made it clear nonetheless that behind his library wall, next to the small concealed room in which Simon kept his odd manuscripts, incunabula and writing desk at which he habitually composed his most mysterious texts (see the Appendix for samples of these), there was to be a small corridor with a stairway rising to the apartment in which his visitor was to be housed. The apartment, of necessity, was small, for it was designed to forestall the curiosity of those inhabitants of the next floor who would question why indeed, facing them, was a blank wall, whereas on other floors apartments could be found. Simon explained once, when he toured the entire compound before the inauguration giving its inhabitants a careful inspection of each other's quarters to promote conviviality and dispel complaints of favoritism, that indeed there was a room there, but that it was the continuation of his personal library and contained a room for private meeting and reflection. This was in fact the case, for the library did contain a small writing room concealed behind a swinging section of the library cases, and as for a room of meeting, it could not be doubted that the presence of Lubina Krawicz installed above was to facilitate private meeting. An accurate and innocent half-truth.

And so it was that behind Simon's desk, which was situated in the corner of his rectangular study at the juncture of his bookcases and the bank of windows which faced a corner of the compound, there rose a tapestry, a priceless tapestry, I am told, which depicts the medieval city of Beauvais, a tapestry which Simon had acquired through an agent from a South American collector several years before. The tapestry exhibits the city in gold, turquoise and rose thread, with battlements and turrets, soldiers in armor standing larger than its walls,

414

and miniature horses caparisoned and peaceful in their elegance. It is a splendid treasure. My hand has gazed it. It is twelve feet long and nine feet high, suspended from a runner that can be drawn only six feet, for the silk is so thick that it cannot be opened further. But that too complied with Simon's wish that the medieval city of Beauvais should drape portions of his library in order better to conceal the entrances to his secret chambers. Behind the arras then is the door in the library shelving which leads up two floors to the highest floor of the building where the quarters of Lubina were situated. The door cannot be opened from the inside. Lubina had demanded this. She had said at the very first meeting between Simon and herself in my presence after the accusation of the Festival: "If you wish me here, Simon Stern, keep me here, lock me in, keep the key. I want nothing more of the world outside, beyond these doors. It is beautiful, but it will be wise that you lock me from myself. If I had the choice, whatever my sensible wish, I would struggle down these stairs a thousand times to announce again and again my charge against you. Oh Simon, lock me up and keep me in silence." Simon obeyed her. A locksmith altered the arrangement that evening. The door was locked when Simon departed and the key was carried by him always.

Lubina lived in that visionary prison for many months. There was an abundance of elegant furniture, couches in rich fabrics, chairs with fluted backs and arms like embracing women, lamps of porcelain, and a small collection of Chinese jade bottles and plates, and the paintings were exquisite subjects of fantasy and sensuosity, a bowl of anemones by Odilon Redon and an Archimboldo depicting a grotesque head fashioned of vegetables, and a dramatic scene of espousal and disdain by Gustave Moreau. Dr. Klay, sufficed by a brief description of the complex psychology of the woman who would one day come to inhabit that room, had purchased wisely. The pictures did not seem of much value, since their aesthetic quality was diminished by their fantastic improbability, but to all reports they pleased Lubina, who began to think of her quarters as a magic land. Indeed the one recreation which she allowed herself other than reading and listening to music was the cultivation of an indoor garden which came to overgrow her sunny

415

and light bedroom. She claimed that she was content to be locked away from the world. She prepared her own food, occasionally asking that a special meal be fixed for her when she was particularly tired, and she professed excellent health despite the weight of her braces and the labor of walking. Her only act of anger (and that occurred the first day of her habitation) was to smash the two mirrors in the apartment. That was understandable, although I could not see how it was that, without mirrors, she was able to groom herself with such expertness as to elicit from Simon repeated avowals that he found her lovely.

It was Simon's custom, as I have said already, to visit her in my company. It was understood that on Friday evenings, after the benedictions of the Sabbath, after the meal had ended, after our songs of greeting had risen into the night, after Simon had given blessing to all those who sought it most particularly on that evening, I would come to his rooms, indicate that it was I by my particular knock, and together we would pull back the arras, press the button in the library wall, pass behind it into the cul-de-sac which it concealed, close the wall once more and ascend to the rooms of Lubina Krawicz. She would await us. It was the only visit she allowed. We would knock on her door and then unlock it. There we would find Lubina, dressed in a lounging gown about which her silk robe would be drawn, her braces hidden beneath its folds, and she would conduct us with regal grace into her sitting room.

"The greetings of the Sabbath to you, Lubina," Simon would invariably begin.

"And to you, Simon Stern. May you find some peace upon this Sabbath," she would habitually reply.

The greetings completed, she would bring from the sideboard to the small table that fronted her divan a tray with tea and cakes, a small glass bowl containing pistachios and glazed fruits, and a lacquer vessel filled with sweet-smelling dried flowers, and there for more than an hour, over tea and cakes, they would converse quietly. I would remain seated behind them, hidden by the shadows, recumbent and isolate in my own somber world and attend to the complicated rhythms of their dance.

"You seem well, Lubina. Your face is very lovely this evening. Permit me to say that to you."

"Anything can be hidden, Mr. Stern. Anything. I have managed without mirrors to conceal everything. I apply the paints of the cosmetician and feel the layers of white upon my face build until the tightened skin is no longer described by my fingers. I am finished when I have covered my face and hidden the scars you gave me."

"Please, Lubina, must you?"

"You know I must, Simon Stern. If not I, who else is there to remind you of your presumption? None of those others."

"I know it well enough."

"You cannot know, for you know nothing of the world. You cover yourself with Jews who have neither the wish nor the reason to tell you the truth. I alone must tell you. Dear Mr. Stern, every Jew needs, as you Jews say, his *shikse* to tell him the truth, and I suppose every *shikse* needs her Jew to hear it. It is an exchange of loving fury. Ah well, the world cannot do without us. Our eternal love and our eternal enmity. I feel more and more like a courtesan, an aloof mistress of memory who cultivates her rage like my plants are cultivated, by indirection and artificial light."

Each visit was the same, a perambulation through graciousness, edged with an unspoken sense of intimate touch (for all I know, they held hands while they assaulted each other, while Lubina assaulted and Simon received), and the stately pavane of rage, her murderousness cupped the grace and stature which suffering had conferred as a reward, and his endless guilt which most particularly in the presence of Lubina he allowed to be revealed.

"Again you demand it, Lubina. Every Sabbath eve for these many months you have forced me time and again to this point. And every Sabbath eve brought to this point I have assumed it again. 'Here is your guilt, Simon Stern.' You offer it to me as a treasure, as a votive gift and I take it from your hands, stroke it, touch it, embrace it, love it as my own. My own guilt. My happy, treasured guilt. I take it from you and I kiss it as I would kiss you, were you to permit it."

And again, invariably, Lubina Krawicz would laugh disdainfully, draw her feet together and the braces would sound a warning of her infirmity, and hearing it she would say, "And now the final indignity, Simon Stern."

"The final one. Yes. Will you marry me, Lubina Krawicz? Will you marry your Jew and become a Jew as he, so that the warfare can end?"

And again, replying in elongated phrases, her lips no doubt sealed to enact her contempt more powerfully, her words withdrawn like arrows from a concealed quiver, she would reply: "Submission does not end warfare. Neither does victory. Simon Stern. You learn nothing. Our ritual must go on until you do."

Lubina would then rise, profess her weariness, thank Simon for his visit, and bid us goodnight.

The ritual was unchanged. Week after week, from the first Sabbath eve following the inauguration until but recently, the ritual would enfold. At first they did not conceive their visits as ritual encounters, but gradually the style of their entanglement became clear, the tendrils visible through the disguise— snarled but visible, tangible, explicit—and seizing upon each, fingering its separateness, it would be woven into the intricacy which I have abridged here. The essential is apparent, and indeed were I as shrewd a prophet as I am a redactor of the past I would have observed then that they were playing out not alone a ritual but a homily of the universe.

The ritual altered.

The alteration of ritual, even a ritual as developed and habitual as that which Simon Stern and Lubina Krawicz had devised, is only that—ritual. It is the case that ritual, failing of liturgy, arranges at best the sinew and bone of men, obliging them to pass through orders of action, uncomprehending, yielding and resisting, fighting off passion and conceding to exhaustion. But ritual transported to liturgy, that's another moment. There, when liturgy arises out of the dry bones and arms are flung out and feet step forth and words—even the same words —tumble in a rush of feeling, ritual has yielded place and man lives. The ritual of Simon and Lubina, their drama of unconsummation, holding back both love and fury, was bound to spill out, to open forth from ritual into life.

The first to alter ritual was Simon, and for him the liturgy bent itself toward rage.

The Sabbath eve, three days before, we had passed up to

her quarters and once more she greeted us, her gown edged with lace, the chiffon I take to have been azure, for it was cool to my grazing touch as I shook her hands and blue was, in my sighted days, a color of cool and calm collection. I retired to my accustomed place and the ritual unfolded—exchange of greetings, offering and refusal of compliments, denial of beauty and accusation, reception of guilt, and then at the moment when Simon in the past would have taken upon himself the generous offer of guilt, elevating it like a monstrance to be beheld and then laid upon his breast until it fastened there and stuck, his language changed.

He began, as in the past, and I settled back to wait out the torture of his words: "Again you demand it, Lubina. Every Sabbath eve for these many months you have forced me time and again to this point. And every Sabbath eve brought to this point I have assumed it again. 'Here is your guilt, Simon Stern.' You offer it to me as a treasure, as a votive gift and I take it from your hands, stroke it, touch it, embrace it, love it as my own. My own guilt . . ." Simon faltered and stopped for a moment, and Lubina, perhaps leaning forward to stroke his hand, prompted him, "I take it . . . I take it." But Simon stood up and the chair upon which he sat toppled over and the dish of pistachio nuts and glazed fruits fell upon the carpet. He began to pace, nuts exploding under his feet. "But no more," he began with agitation. "No more. I will have it no more. You offer to me what is not mine. It is not mine. Yours. Most certainly yours, but not mine. Now admit this to me, Lubina Krawicz, did I desert you? No. I did not. Your own father deserted you, swilled himself like a swine, drank himself to despondency and abandoned you. Not I. You want me to punish. Indeed. We take it—I take it from you. We have—I have done that always. Taken the guilt from your world and laid it upon ourselves—myself. No more. Lubina. It's a farce. This is a farce. The arrangement of our game of love and hate. Oh Lubina, my dear friend, don't you see what is done by us? It's such an easy compliance with the world. You accuse me of murder and I accept the burden. I confess over the heads of thousands. I announce the principle of murder in the world. Inadvertence, I say, and I sound the emptiness of my chest, pounding the hollow cavity with my fist. So what, Lubina.

Always the same way. The world is unmerciful and the Jews announce the principle of justice. And so on and so on. Always the same. The world does—in its gentile fecklessness—and the Jews stand to the pulpit and pound the principle. Damn it. Done. Done. No more, dear friend. I come to you no more unless it be as dearest friends. I am done with our ritual."

Simon cracked pistachios throughout his exordium to Lubina, crying and beating upon the low table, and then he walked over and put his arms about Lubina and she wept, holding him in her arms. No further word, but the rustling movement of clothing and the indistinction of their tears and the cumbersome gestures of Simon falling upon the wasted body of Lubina. Simon did not say goodbye. There was no departure. He left and I followed. In our confusion the door was not locked.

"We did not lock the door after us," Simon said, addressing me. "I forgot and you did not remember. What happened? I can only guess. There is among us someone who wishes to destroy us? Who is this one? We know. Indeed, we know and we must confront him. He came to her, that one, just a short time ago. He came to her and spoke to her menacingly, threatening her with exposure, threatening me with exposure. She demanded that he leave. He did not. He sought, my friends, to assault her. The brutal boy. But she struck him and he left, enraged. It was an hour ago, that she called to me. She pounded feebly upon the floor. I did not hear her. Then, knowing that I couldn't hear her timid poundings, she began to throw from the doorway of her rooms to the floor below the crockery and jade bottles, the porcelain plates which stood upon the shelf before her door. It was fortunate that I went behind the arras for a book. I heard the shattering glass and went to her. The pills she used to stop the pain. The whole jar of pills—some thirty or more—she had swallowed and nearly a half-vial of iodine. And near her head upon the floor I found her message: 'Dear Simon. You are right. I was wrong. Protect yourself. Protect yourself. The world wants you by the throat. I cannot stay behind to see it.' No more tears, friends. It is the time to act."

Dr. Klay and I were silent, believing that Simon Stern had,

without us, come to the conclusion about Baltar to which we had already come. We would have preferred to have buried our intimate knowledge of Janos Baltar, as long as we were released from the menace of his presence. If he knows without our telling, so much the better.

"I have convoked the community to gather in two hours' time, at precisely eight o'clock this evening in the deepest vault of the compound. There, in the presence of all, we will accuse and we will pass judgment. Peter Narzissenfeld will hear our accusation and the people will decide his punishment."

"Peter Narzissenfeld?" we both replied in amazement.

"It was he. He was the boy who threatened Lubina Krawicz."

"Simon Stern," I shouted. "Listen to me then before you act."

"There is nothing that can stop me. Nothing. The summons to the community has gone forth. At this moment Baltar carries the summons to the community. All must be present. Men. Women. Even the children and babes. All must know and judge."

"I say again, Simon Stern, listen to us. You cannot recall the summons. Done. Agreed. But not Narzissenfeld. Not he. The judgment must not be upon him."

"Not him. Not him alone, you mean. Others."

"Not him," Dr. Klay said. "Narzissenfeld is an innocent. He is guilty, but he acts out of terror. His action is foolish, his motives naïve. His is no impurity but that conferred by his past. No, dear Simon, we ask you this, Nathan and I ask you this: before you pass judgment tonight, read this dossier. Read it, consider it and then decide. You will understand more than you know."

Dr. Klay handed Simon Stern the dossier. Simon acknowledged it and Klay told me that a look of exhaustion and confusion passed over his face, for the name "Janos Baalam Baltar" was typed upon its cover. Simon Stern left us.

We continued to talk. We continued to talk and to wait. Tonight the struggle would begin. But then, we believed that confronted with truth, truth comprehended within the bounds of the universe but not recognized nor yet encountered, Simon Stern would honor the truth.

The processional of feet, which daily approached the sleeping priests who slumbered upon their divans, their sacred clothing wrapped beneath their heads, awaiting the call of the officer of the day demanding that the key to the Holy Sanctuary be delivered and the worship center of the universe be opened again, passed through my mind as I prepared to descend into the cavern of the compound, that room of hewn stone which lay empty beneath the first and second basements to receive us. There, convened as did the Great and the Minor Sanhedrins in the ancient Chamber of Hewn Stone, which stood to the extreme north of the hall of priests of Herod's Temple, was the court of the community who would shortly hear evidence, examine witnesses, question the accused and pronounce judgment.

The intimacy with which Simon Stern conversed with our history, marvelous though it appears, was not without danger. It is often the case with figures such as he, from the very beginning until this moment, that what they know of history —its detail, its configuration, its portent—is more than offset by their ignorance of time. You might think that the one goes with the other—clasped hands and intertwined fingers. But it is not so!

Simon Stern, for instance, knew history, but time was like a diaphanous curtain no different from the blue, white, scarlet, purple drapery which separated the Outer Temple from the Holy of Holies within—a tissue of fabric, brightly colored and deceptive, which protected the interior psyche from the harsh light without. Simon wore no watch, carried no clock, observed no timepiece in his quarters. Every other instrument of measuring the universe he obeyed—of dictionaries and lexicons, atlases and gazetteers there was an abundance, of eyeglasses, magnifiers and binoculars a profusion, of systems of communication, microphones, speakers, recording devices, radio equipment our establishment was endlessly supplied, but all these aforementioned are devised to render space, to define its compass, replicate its occupancy—whether of word, sight, or sound. Time, however, the unnumbered beats of the brain pulse, the flutter of stomach demons, the buzz of flies in the heart, these locusts of the interior life were not noted by him at all. He abolished time by a fiat of will, but he did not abolish

history. Now, that amazed me. How was it possible to accom-
plish the one and maintain the other? Something would have
to be wrong. Not to know time, but to wear history as an
undergarment, to dress in history, to outfit one's memory with
the reconstructions and regenerations of historical appraisal,
to look upon history as though there, in it, was to be found the
key to the riddle, the key to unlock the Sanctuary. He abolished
time—that is, he did not care about mundane time. Not alone
that. Of course that, but many people accomplish such a dis-
dain, eating their main meal at four in the morning, breakfast-
ing at midday, lunching at suppertime, dressing for a stroll in
soft grey and kid gloves at daybreak, preparing to go out to
tea at an hour when most ordinary people are concluding their
matins. Not at all. Such simple reversals of order are accom-
plished efficiently by untraining the stomach and the bowels,
permitting those disciplined muscles to relax and release their
tyrannical hold over will. It is easy to break the prison routine
of the body. But that only effects the shucking of the husk of
time, its coarse materiality, but does little or nothing to silence
its hum and buzz in anguished conversation with death.

The miracle of Simon's indifference to time, his unfamiliarity
with it, is perhaps to be located in the fact that since the com-
munity had been gathered he had lost interest in death. I know
what you will reply, in disbelief: No one can lose interest in
death (without at the same time losing interest in life) or per-
haps, no one loses interest in death, only in the death of others
(never his own) or only in his own death (never the death of
others)—but that balance depends upon whether you think
such a one to be an artist of the digestive ego who encounters
life as an assortment of delicacies presented in simultaneity
(rather than in succession, digestion requiring, as we have sug-
gested, a sense of gastric time), or else a monster of sanctity
who spends his life contemplating the ecstasy of his death, but
no one of us can bear to smell the rancid breath of saints or
contemplate their filth (I cannot, but then my sense of smell
and contemplation is highly cultivated). No. It is not that
Simon Stern has abolished death (the sense of time he has
abolished, not time itself but the sensus temporis—*the warp*
and woof of that noumenon are come apart in him), but he has
lost interest in it. That means, factually speaking, that he con-

ducts himself as though neither life nor death were a miracle, a miracle of giving and a miracle of taking (back, away). He did not know that he would be born. He had no idea. It came unheralded to him (however much that prophet of Warsaw had announced his coming into our world). Since he did not reflect on his beginnings, he came to know of them only by reflecting upon the certainty of his end. He began as most men do, knowing of life by having knowledge of death. All those pithy apothegms: When does a man know that he is to die? When he draws his first breath. Or. It is the knowledge of death that makes man cry out at birth. Or. Every minute of life is spent dying. Or. It is because sleep is a metaphor of dying that I give my soul to God until I waken. I give my soul to God as a deposit. While I sleep God reviews my soul and by the cock's crow determines whether or not to return it to me.

It is a chancy business, conducting one's life as though it were a dance through a midnight garden in which death stalks us, striking first one then another marble statue, mistaking it for us, until the morning comes and we have survived, laughing at the river's edge, eating our fruit and drinking our wine until nightfall returns and the hunt and chase begin again. Of course, one day the skeletal angel will catch on, and like the cat who pounces upon the chimera and not its source, one day, emboldened, the game done, the trickery exhausted, the cat will find the hand, the angel the dying man.

Death no longer bothered Simon Stern. It will come when it is time. Presumably that was the point. Time and death numbered each other. Time ticked while death tocked. They were the cuckoo clocks of our generations, the one springing the catch that opened the door and the other marching out on its mechanism, a carved and painted little fool to croak and chorus what no man needed anyway to know. The time. And so what? The point is not that they are illusions. That's the philosopher's game, to parse the concept and pin its pieces to a display board, but the philosopher is called to die no less than I, no less than Simon Stern.

The ineluctability of the real, its inevitability in a word, is no reason for a man to consume his life fearing it. Even if time numbers death (and for that reason becomes itself a source of terror to men), it is insufficient reason for a man to struggle

424

against time or to curse death like an enemy. Simon Stern has managed to close the warfare with death by regarding himself as so conversant with the ways of God that death and death-lessness become interchangeable. Even if he dies, he presumes that it is no different for him to lose his body than for God to acquire one—what is so remarkable about a body that one should fear to lose it or wish to acquire it? It is a device of obscurantism. He believes, then, that to lose the body has no relation to the end of the work. He takes time back from history. There is no past that is real, no future that is portentous. For others, yes, for others who have known nothing about wearing history like a sackcloth, who are born with stocked memories like artificial pools in which choice fish are fattened for the chef's hook. But he, we, he contends, are not allowed to become individuals first and then men of history. We begin our lives in reverse. We are born with words put in our mouths, covered with honey it is thought, but only to sweeten the salt. He, we, he argues, are born already eternal principles, carrying in our mouths an endless obligation and an unforgettable treasure. It is no way for a man to live unless, of course, that man is allowed to forget. But we are never allowed to forget, not when we go to the bathroom, not when we eat, not when we make love, at no moment is it possible to put aside the knowledge of eternity. What a difficulty it is. Always carrying God on our backs.

There is, then, no way of closing the gap of history. No easy way, but there is a way. It is not simply the way of memory. Every society maintains an order of consensus, or else it would not long remain a society; but a society need not have a relevant history—that is, a history immediately relevant to its existence. Not quite so. A simplification. Of course it does, even if its memory is only of the day before the day of recollection. It remembers people who lived and died; buildings and houses, persons come and gone. These populate memory as one walks down a street in his own small society, creating and liquidating in the mind, building and destroying. But that is the small society. What of the large society, the millennial society, the society which endures through centuries, cut open and evis-cerated, closed up and healed, reconstituted and then ravaged once more—where society is a burn, an occasion which forces

425

history to have a consciousness, to recall itself, to think about its own existence and justification?

All the arguments for a philosophy of being, of discrete and static entities is part of the ongoing protest of men against history, a reality which obliges human beings to think about themselves and fabricate themselves from the fragments and broken recollections of what they were once upon a time, then, beyond the order of their everyday.

How can Simon Stern be believed—believed, that is, as one who never went through the agony but somehow managed to incorporate everything within himself—that is, the agony and the pain and the uncertainty and the horror and the disbelief —who managed it as a measure to complete himself without the suffering (the real actual suffering) but who chose, nevertheless, to surround himself with the sufferers, not to view them as objects nor to punish them by his existence, but only in order that he might share with them. He must pursue his disinterest in death to the end (the almost end—which would be his own death) in order to come back and be renewed and renew others. (I have read that the monks of Latrun are vowed to a silence interrupted but for the obligatory greeting, "Remember death." What a sholom aleychem!

The Messiah cannot himself suffer; that is why the Messiah ben David comes after the Messiah ben Joseph. The Messiah cannot be a self-tormentor but someone who can achieve that rising above the considerable order of natural torment, to arrive at a condition of near-complete self-knowledge (the instant before illumination, for there is no fulfilled illumination for the Messiah; no redeemer could have a perfect knowledge of his achievement, else he would not be able to complete the action of redemption—he must retain an ignorance of who he is and what he intends). Does the Messiah then know he is Messiah? Never. Absolutely share suffering without undergoing it? A contradiction? A possibility? Suffering is not connected with pain. There is suffering without pain, without diminution, without loss. It is a draining away of heart, a loss—a temporary loss or else all suffering would end in death—of the persuasion that outside of oneself there is the object, the person, that which confirms its relevance and rightness. Simon is able to suffer: why? Why should one want to suffer? why should one

426

be able to bear suffering? why should one be able to tolerate the suffering of others? There can be no reason other than the fact of having given suffering to another. Not willingly but involuntarily. The hardest guilt to bear is for the crime one could not have chosen to commit. If otherwise, one would be mad and forfeit the attention and solicitude of others. No one is interested in the maniac except insofar as he cares about his victims. No. The concern is other: the necessity of cutting back the psyche of the guilty to the issue of his guilt and our caring. That I live and another perish.

It was dark when Dr. Klay and I descended. The air hot and dense.

The passageway from the candy store, which abutted the cross street bounding the southern face of the compound, was concealed behind shelves stocked with tins and glass jars filled with sourballs and licorice braids. We had been instructed to enter the store casually without attracting attention. For almost two hours now the occupants of the compound had been going forth, taking devious routes, going in opposite directions, circuiting alternate blocks in order to enter Matsky's Candy Store from unfamiliar approaches to avert comment or observation. But I knew from Gusweller's generous warning that we were no longer unobserved, that if Gusweller the Agent had admonished us, other agents posted in windows of unrented apartments which faced the four sides of the compound were training spyglasses upon our entrances and exits. We were observed.

It could not be otherwise. The word had gone forth—how? Who can surmise, for we did not know the operation of their world—a tip, an anonymous letter, a hostile informant could have brought us to their attention; Mr. Chicago or Mr. Cleveland could have talked (an assimilated Jewish gangster?) and pointed the finger—"Listen. Mr. Agent Gusweller," he might have confessed, "those Jews on the Lower East Side are run by a saint and a maniac—one of them tells homilies and the other bought two million dollars' worth of guns and ammunition." (Wouldn't you pay attention?)

The buttons behind the jars of chocolate raisins concealed a dial panel which governed the electrical system, air-conditioning, fire doors and alarm system of this, the southern face of the compound, and its secret caverns and basements. While Dr. Klay pressed the buzzer and waited for the secret door to open, I conversed with Matsky, who offered me a sourball, which I declined. "Come," I heard Klay whisper, and I felt Matsky's hand touch my elbow in farewell. I followed the echo of Klay's voice which repeated the imperative, "Come, come, we're almost a minute behind schedule and the next to arrive will be here before we've disappeared." He took my arm and guided me into the passage, and the door closed silently behind us. There was no light other than a purple bulb toward which Klay described our movement. We descended toward its glow and I counted thirty-two steps to each landing, sixty-four until our feet touched the bottom floor, cold now with unheated stone and concrete as though we had reached the lowest level of a prehistoric cave. We walked for what seemed a street block and a steel door opened before us and a young guard queried our names and checked them against a list when we replied.

We were conducted to our places where we were obliged to stand. All stood. Behind us we felt the crush of bodies, straining against the gloom to fathom the intent of the congregation. None had been told the purpose of the summons. All were there, from babes sleeping quietly in their mothers' arms and toddlers playing among the rows of legs, crawling in and out as though the adults had been purposely arranged for nighttime games. But the adults, sensing the gravity of the call, were for the most part silent, whispering among themselves, although I could hear Shrieking Peshele, trying to catch the ear of her husband who was listening to another householder.

The room continued to fill. It could accommodate us all, the fullness of our complement, but it would be some minutes yet before the proceedings would commence. The room in which we gathered had been constructed of cut stone as were the passageways, but it was faced with black slate, which gave it a severe demeanor, particularly as the only light within the room was cast by thick candles arranged in two clusters at the front.

"It's almost eight o'clock," Dr. Klay whispered. "Where's Simon? He should be here."

Where was Simon Stern? He was our only hope. We knew

that without him Baltar would destroy Narzissenfeld. The community would condemn him, and even though only Simon could pass the sentence, whatever Simon's forbearance, the sentence would be severe—nothing less than banishment, which for Narzissenfeld would be tantamount to a sentence of death. In the past when Jewish communities (no less situated than we, islands in a gentile sea) policed themselves, traitors were punishable by death and though never condemned to death were often murdered. Narzissenfeld would fare no better. "Where is Simon?" I wondered aloud. Dr. Klay took my arm and answered, "I will protect young Peter."

We were not aware, until that moment, of Baltar's presence. He had hung in the darkness, his body clinging to the wall like a shadow, and then, unbidden, he was there, materializing from the grey blackness, his voice before me. "Simon Stern is not here. But he has ordered me to begin promptly. It is now eight o'clock. Klay, prepare yourself to assume the defense. But, Klay, I warn you, I spare no one."

"Bring forth the accused," Baltar ordered, and a door, obscured in the gloom, opened upon its steel hinges, and from the anteroom stepped Peter Narzissenfeld, blinking with fright. He wore this night a true face, the face beneath the faces of his disguise, a face littered with terror. He stepped into the chamber and the door slid shut behind him. For some minutes he stood there, abashed, his hands clasped before his waist, his face twitching with a remarkable spasm, his head bowed to his chest.

"Accused, stand forth to the chair of accusation," Baltar ordered, and Narzissenfeld shuffled toward the lone chair, the sound of his feet deadened by the slippers which he wore, the only token of his accusation and his penitential condition (it was only later that Dr. Klay told me that those slippers were Simon's own, that undoubtedly Simon had offered them to that poor unfortunate as a gesture, perhaps, of community with his penitence).

Janos Baltar commenced the proceedings.

The voice shall describe all. The voice, the absence of voice, the clamor and the silence. No more shall there be reliance upon the confirming testimony of my companions who describe all to me, for at this moment, the truth and the lie is voice, the carriage of voice, its intonation, its flood and restraint, its lash and its grace.

"Peter Narzissenfeld," Baltar began, snapping the name of the accused, "you stand before this multitude of your friends, all, brothers and sisters, who have suffered not unlike you and endured, accused of having aided the outside world, our enemy, serving it as agent in our company, spying out our just secrets and delivering your knowledge, whatever its truth and value, to them, that it may trap and dismay us, and bring us down once more to humiliation and disgrace. Not alone have you done this, but failing all, in frustration, you are accused of forcing your way into the quarters of an innocent, a woman disfigured by fortune, and threatened her, threatened our master and teacher and sought to enforce upon her tormented body your own lustful rage.

"You are accused of treason to us and the humiliation of an honored visitor to our company. What do you say to these charges?" Baltar withdrew from the side of the accused where he had addressed him as an intimate, his words rising to the remembered hiss of Job's commentator and falling into the cavity of his chest from which the words rumbled, low and forbidding, gathering force.

Narzissenfeld's voice began and stopped, a hoarse cry, of no word, but that of cry. Human cry? A wordless voice, individual, absolutely one's own, unduplicated and yet wordless. A cry. "Aaaaii. Me? Me?" His voice stammered, affrighted that he was alone, that none other had been traduced, that alone, he, of all his comrades, had betrayed the company. "What must I say?" he asked of Baltar, his voice clamoring to confess, flights of disturbed starlings rushing in a flutter from his mouth.

"Confess," Baltar shouted, "confess, confess."

Narzissenfeld blinked as he did most persistently when he was embarrassed. "But what? What should I confess, Mr. Baltar?" his voice whined, and his hands slapped his knees as though the words had to be struggled up through tightened gullet, pushed out against their will.

"Peter Narzissenfeld, you have heard the charge. You know the charge. Confess it and be done with it."

"Confess it, Peter," a woman's voice called, and I recognized Rochel's pleading.

"Ah, Rochel. Confess it," the poor boy began to cry, "confess it. My God, what have I done?"

"Shall we bring out the witnesses? We will call the witnesses. We know so much about you, Peter Narzissenfeld. We can bring the witnesses. We can offer not one but at least three depositions. We have found out everything. More than the two required witnesses, we have more," Baltar pounded out the threat, the insinuation to poor Narzissenfeld that he surrender to us and humiliate himself before us.

"Confess it," he continued to repeat to himself, the words mixed with tears. "I will confess it." His voice slid off and he paused. "I had no wish to harm you. You are my friends. I made faces for all of you. All of you have loved me. I was your friend. I made you laugh when you were sad. I pulled on my cheeks and slapped my neck until I raised welts for you. And I remember helping you to laugh when you were crying. I don't know why I made myself a fool before you, for so long to be a fool, to make you laugh when all I did at night was cry. Rochel, tell them, don't I cry a lot?" (Rochel answered from the dark room, "Friends, he's always crying.") "My heart is broken, too. I'm not saying it's a different heart than yours. It isn't. It's the same broken heart. I don't claim anything different for my heart. But I was exposed. I was different than you because I was exposed. Many of you are orphans like me. But you went out. Out there into the world to find your way and you came home every night and this was a home to you. But I was stationed at the door. I was the house guardian, the house fool. There I was, every day, standing with a blind man and telling him about the world as it came through the door. That's frightening. To know that there's a world outside and to be too afraid, too unsure to go to it, to stay put and describe the bits and pieces that blew in through the open door. All the people who wanted money, all the cripples who wanted a blessing, all the visitors who wanted Simon's secret. And I became very frightened. It was like being back in that camp when I wore a different disguise, when I knew that the world was frightening and all I could do was hide out from it. You don't know what such a fear is. When there is nothing real to be afraid of and you're still afraid."

"The point, Narzissenfeld. The point. Get on with it. The

431

point," Baltar demanded, his voice rising and falling like a hammer.

"Yes, the point. The point," Narzissenfeld repeated to himself, and his tears began again and his fingers snapped as if he were trying to remind himself to remember the point.

"All right," he sighed. "It began nearly three months ago. I don't remember the day. Nathan will know. It doesn't matter. This man came to see us. He wanted to see Dr. Klay. At the time I didn't know who he was. Just an outsider with an un-Jewish name. That's all I know."

"An outsider, was he? What did Dr. Klay want with an outsider?" Baltar questioned closely, but it was clearly irrelevant.

"I don't know. I don't know. I never found that out."

"What was his name?" Baltar demanded.

"Gusweller, Harold Gusweller. R.C. Gusweller, Nathan called him, but I forget why. His name was written 'Harold Gusweller.'"

"On. On. Hurry it up." Baltar sounded nervous, his voice became abrupt; the abrasive fluency, the dramatic tops and bottoms to his register which made his voice so unusually powerful, became clipped.

"This agent came down the stairs."

"Agent? Why agent? How did you know he was an agent?"

"That's the point, Baltar, you don't understand. He wasn't just an outsider. I made the same mistake once before and Nathan caught it, too. Nathan guessed. He must have guessed."

"A conspiracy? A conspiracy? Nathan, Dr. Klay, Rochel. It seems we have more than one traitor," Baltar snarled contemptuously, turning toward us.

"A minute," Dr. Klay interrupted calmly.

"You'll have your turn, Klay," Baltar replied, angry with the interruption.

"You wait one minute, sir," Dr. Klay replied, his voice marshaling an unfamiliar power of irony. "This boy has no protection. You appointed me to defend him. I'll start now with my objection."

"It's not the time for defense. This isn't a gentile court. It's our court. There's the accused. I'm the prosecutor. Simon Stern is the judge. It's that simple. We've discussed it all. The community will decide the verdict. Simon Stern will fix the sentence. That's all there is." Baltar replied. The smug satisfaction of having prearranged the process delighted him and he disclosed the preparation as though it should be completely acceptable because it had been defined by him and Simon Stern.

The community behind us stirred and several voices called back: "It's not the Inquisition." "We're Jews, Baltar." "Justice, justice." "Give him a chance." "Give Peter a chance." Baltar faltered before the calls of the community.

"All right, then. Let Klay begin to defend the accused," Baltar agreed, his voice unusually shrill.

Klay left my side and went to Narzissenfeld, with whom he spoke reassuringly, resting his hand upon his shoulder, his back averted from Baltar, but speaking loudly enough for all of us to hear his words.

"Calm, Narzissenfeld. These here, most of these here, perhaps almost all of these here *do* love you. Perhaps you have done wrong. Perhaps you have. But as you know, there is forgiveness for unwitting sin. It is more important that we find out not only whether or not you did what you are accused of doing, but whether you did these things with the intention of harming us . . ."

"No, Dr. Klay, no, you know that. I never thought of harm. I was afraid, I was very afraid," Narzissenfeld answered, his teeth clacking in terror, and once more he began to sob. "Oh God, I didn't want to harm anybody."

"All right, don't be afraid. Continue. Answer the questions he asks you."

"Now then," Baltar resumed. "Tell us about the Agent."

"Yes, the agent. He was an agent. The afternoon he left Dr. Klay the first time, he came downstairs. The reception hall was empty. Nathan had gone off. It was just before the end of regular visiting hours. The agent, Gusweller, said to me something like 'Young man, I'd like to speak to you.' I answered, remembering their earlier exchange, 'Okay, R.C., let's talk. Here I am. Peter Narzissenfeld at your service,' and I guess I did one of my bows like a cabaret waiter. 'Stop that acting,' he said gruffly. 'Not here, boy. Out there.' 'I can't, R.C., sir,' I answered. 'I have to be at my post until five-thirty, when we lock the front door and visitors use the night entrance. It's got a buzzer that rings upstairs and someone comes down. That's how it works,' I explained to him. 'All right, son,' he started again, 'but there, across the street and down two blocks is a little café where the wops drink coffee. It's a private club and the windows are all painted black. It's called the Taormina Social Club. Just say you want to see me. Come. There's something in it for you. And if you don't come, you're in trouble— so you be there.' And with that he drilled a finger into my chest until it hurt. He scared me."

"They offered you money?" Baltar asked quietly, hoping to trap him.

"He didn't mention money, Baltar. You're guessing," Dr. Klay objected.

"About an hour later, I guess it was, I slipped out after locking the door and putting on the night alarm. I walked out and down the street. It was the tenth time I'd been out by myself. (I'm twenty-three and it was only the tenth time I'd been out in the city—two blocks from home—since I came to you. I was always on duty, and even when I wasn't on duty I told myself I was. I couldn't admit to myself that I was just scared of the outsiders. I knocked at the door of the Taormina and a weasely face opened it just wide enough to poke his head out. 'You want?' I answered that I was to see Mr. Gusweller. 'Okay, kid,' he slipped through his teeth, and opened the door. I went in. Mr. Gusweller called to me from the back, where he was sitting with two other big men. I was afraid. I should have left right then, but when I turned back the weasel-faced man—he had a growth of beard, two, three days old, like he was sitting *shivah* —was watching me so carefully I became more scared. So I went over to them. Mr. Gusweller introduced himself and his two friends, and each of them reached to their back pocket, pulled out their wallets and flashed a picture card of themselves at me. I thought that was very funny and I laughed, and then one of them said, 'We're FBI.' "

There was a hushed murmur from the community as the letters F.B.I. were whispered in awe and fright throughout the chamber.

"Yes, FBI. I didn't know anything about that. And said it slurred like a word, 'Feebee,' and then they laughed and must have thought me pretty stupid. (And I am. That I confess.

You all know it. I'm pretty stupid.) Then one of them, the younger one, I forget his name, said to me: 'Son, you want to do something for us? We need some help in there.' I said, 'What kind of help, sir?' and he answered, 'We need information.' 'What kind of information?' I asked. 'I can tell you some, sir. I make faces. Baltar plays chess. Rochel is the finest pancake maker in the world.' 'Yes, that's good stuff, all that. Tell us about Baltar. We know a great deal about him already.'"

"They asked about me," Baltar said, his voice taut with anger. "Do you hear that? Even me. Next they'll be after Simon Stern and then all of us. What did you tell them?" he bellowed.

"I told them the truth, Mr. Baltar. I said you were our security. That's the expression, isn't it? You take care of us and make sure we're back safely and ask us questions about what we've seen and where we've been. You broke the nose of that Spanish man who tried to climb in a window last year. So I'm right. You're our security. You protect us. That's what I said. Well then, they went on and said they wanted to find out what's in the basement. I said left-over furniture—beds and cots and stools and tables. And that's so. And sacks of potatoes and onions and containers of flour and tins of coffee and tea. So there. That's what I said. And then one of them, a dark-haired man who kept running his fingers through his stringy hair, smoothing it back like a Latin, but with puffy little red lips. I've got to laugh at him. He wasn't convincing. And I didn't even get it. He said to me, 'Now stop this' (he used an unclean word) and then got angry at me. 'You're not as stupid as you make out. You couldn't be,' he said. And I said that I was. 'Brighten up,' he answered. 'Just brighten up. You be a little wise-ass,' he said and he took me by my shirt collar and lifted me out of the chair. The other man said 'Lay off the kid' and he put me back down. I didn't like him. 'We want facts. What you've told us so far anybody can find out, but we're FBI, get it. FBI. The President makes us Agents and we're the spy eyes of the country. Now listen, you either work with us or we get you. We'll send you the hell out of this country, back to whatever lousy country you come from. Right back.' I got scared. I didn't want to go back to where I came from. I would have once upon a time, but that was a long time ago when my father was still alive. But why should I want to go back? Why? So I said, 'Please don't send me back.' That's a movie line. I remember it from a movie we had in the recreation hall about six months ago. 'Mister, please don't send me back.' Remember? Well, I used that line, but I really meant it. It wasn't the movies. It was real life. And then the other agent, a fat little thing with fingers like baby wieners, wagged one at me and said, 'Listen, Peter, listen here, Peter, we know that the guys who run your little place there are storing about two million dollars in guns and ammo in the basement. Enough guns to shoot up the neighborhood. Enough dynamite to blow up a couple of blocks. Enough heavy stuff to take Union Square and hold it against a small army. Now, we don't like citizens with guns. We don't like it. And, what's more, it's against the law, against the American way.'"

At this point a kind of shudder tremored the room. Most of the community knew nothing about the guns, knew nothing at all. Baltar knew, we knew, and about fifty young men that Baltar had chosen and had begun to train in this very room. They knew; nobody else knew. "Pass over these details, Narzissenfeld. There's no reason to discuss them," Baltar commented nervously.

"I suggest there is," Klay demurred. "It is a fact that the agents claimed to know something very dangerous about our community and for that reason sought to recruit a spy. Whether or not there are these guns and ammunition hidden in our basements is irrelevant. What is relevant is that they were able to terrify young Narzissenfeld with this information. And I judge from the gasps of surprise and shock we have just heard from all of you that you too, every one of you, is shocked and afraid that this is true, that our Society is become a repository for weapons, a blind for some insurrectionary movement, a movement of well- and ill-intentioned fanatics and zealots."

"Continue, traitor," Baltar shrieked with disgust.

"Stop, Baltar. Narzissenfeld is no traitor until he is judged a traitor. You must stop that."

"Thank you, Mr. Klay. You're really helping me," Narzissenfeld said to Klay, his voice opening wide like a supplicating hand. "They said all those frightening things. I never touched guns. I was good with a knife. Very good with a knife. I killed one of them with a knife once. I had to. We all did. We all wanted to. I did. But guns? No. I hate guns.

"Then Gusweller spoke. He had been sitting quiet while the other two had taken turns with me. 'Now, here's what's up, Peter. We want to know first if there *are* guns and then we want to know where they come from. We think we know, but we need facts, as my friends would say, hard facts. And we want to know what your Mr. Stern and his sidekick (they called you a sidekick, Mr. Baltar)—and his sidekick, Baltar, plan to do with all the stuff. Sell it? Deliver it? Use it? What? Details. Details. We'll get men in there to find out and help you. Telephone men. Repairmen. All kinds. A plague of spies will get in. Tap the phones. Pick the locks. Spy out the land.' Just like our spies in old times. Spy out the land. He used that right out of the Bible. . . . I'm tired. I've been talking so long. I'm tired."

"Go on," Baltar urged, kicking at his shoe to prod him.

"They said if I did as I was told, they wouldn't send me back. They showed me pictures of piles of corpses they'd found in the camps. I got sick and went to the bathroom. I threw up. A few minutes later, Gusweller came in and washed my face with a paper towel and said it would be all right. (Since I was a child people have been saying to me that it would be all right and it still isn't all right. Damn it to God. It still isn't all right.) I went back home. Here. I went back here and tried to be a spy. I wasn't a spy. A few weeks afterwards I was called to the Taormina again. I had seen one of the agents every day. He was the telephone foreman. I didn't have a thing. I hadn't heard anything. I didn't know anything and they were very mad with me. They screamed at me and one hit me in the face. And then they told me about Lubina Krawicz. They knew all about her. They told me how Mr. Stern had killed his family by not paying attention, and how she had been scarred by Mr. Stern. But that I knew already, but didn't let on to them that I knew. They told me that Lubina knew everything, that she loved Mr. Stern, that she'd do anything to protect him and that I had to get in to see her. They told me they had the plans of Mr. Stern's quarters, that they knew where the hidden passage was and where I would probably find the release button. They said that if I didn't give them the information by this

437

coming week they'd come in here with a search warrant and clear it out. They said Mr. Stern would go to prison and that all of us would be deported. If I'm a traitor, then all *that* made me one. What was I loyal to—I mean, why be loyal to all you crazy people who want to take a chance on being sent away from this place? I wanted to stay and I wanted to save my friend Rochel. Yes, Rochel, that cook of ours, who has been my best friend here. So I gave in. That was four hours ago. You already know the rest.

"I got into Mr. Stern's study when he went downstairs to the dining room for tea. I found the release button and got into the passage, up the stairs and into her room. The door was unlocked. I turned the knob and went in. She was lying there on the floor naked. That's right. Absolutely naked except for her steel braces and a silk scarf over her face. She lay there and I knew she was alive because the silk scarf puffed and sucked when she breathed. I didn't even look upon her. I turned away. I didn't look upon her except that first minute when I came in the door. That half-minute. A quarter-minute. No. A blinking of the eye. Just a glance, like passing your eyes over the spines of books without being able to read the titles. That quick."

"Did she answer? Did the woman answer?" Baltar demanded rudely.

"No, not directly. She didn't answer directly. She was afraid of me. She thought I meant to hurt her. (I've only hurt one person in my life. I killed him. You know about that from my record.) But her, a woman, a crazy, naked crippled woman lying helpless on the floor, why would I hurt her? But she thought I would, and so she told me things about Simon Stern. She told me about the fire in which his parents died and how she got her terrible burns. Instead of demanding information I began to cry for her. Her story was so terrible. But she probably thought differently. She knew—I had told her—that I was working for the government, that I was a spy and that I was forced to spy. I begged her to help me spy. She wouldn't. What did she know? Only that she loved Simon. But she was, I guess, more afraid of me, me, the spy, than I was of her. So she did what she did after I left. Took poison. I'm glad she's going to be all right."

Peter Narzissenfeld had been standing before us, the flickering candles crowning his head with dancing shadows. He was weak from tears and confession. Dr. Klay urged him to be seated, but Baltar prevented it, requiring that he remain standing until the time of judgment came. Narzissenfeld continued to stand and Dr. Klay acceded.

"Is this all you wish to say, Narzissenfeld?" Baltar began. "Do you expect this company to believe that you told nothing, that none of our secrets were revealed to them? Do you expect us to believe that you were threatened, that you acted against your will, that your motives were innocent, your judgment infantile, your action simply foolish and naïve? Do you expect us to believe all that?"

"Yes *that*, if I understand what you're saying, Mr. Baltar," Narzissenfeld said quietly, his voice breaking from strain and confusion. "I am a simple boy. I am a foolish boy. A shorn lamb, that's what I am, a shorn lamb." Narzissenfeld's voice thinned like a curl of smoke. "I remember the lambs that I watched the *shohet* kill in the shed behind his house in Riga where I was born. The lamb was bound and the *shohet* carried it in his arms from the pen to the slaughterhouse. Once I watched the *shohet* carry a lamb in his arms from the pen into the yard to the place of slaughtering. Until that moment I had always watched the animals, for I was still a small boy and my eyes did not rise above a certain height to the face of the *shohet*. It was a hard time in Riga and the *shohet* had only three lambs in his pen to slaughter. Two he had killed before Rosh Hashana. It was now a month later and Succot was upon us and this was the last lamb. But I was no longer a small boy. When this happened I was eleven and my eyes roamed high and low. I was in the yard behind our little house and I watched the *shohet* through the slats in the fence. He came to the pen and led out the grey-white lamb and he took the lamb into his arms and my eyes rose to his face. I saw him cover the nose of the lamb with kisses and its eyes with kisses and I saw him bite it gently on its ear. And then I saw that the *shohet* was crying. It was his best-loved lamb. It was his last lamb for many months. I had forgotten about the face of the lamb, but I always remembered the *shohet*'s tears." Narzissenfeld returned, the reverie consumed, and blinking, seeing the dark before him, appealed to us.

439

"I'm asking for mercy. Have some tears for my face before you decide to judge me."

Narzissenfeld's last words were not without effect. He had spoken them very quietly. He had not cried while he spoke. The resignation to his fate was apparent in his virtually disinterested narration of the story of the *shohet* and the lamb. He was not even aware of how effective the story was, for throughout the hall sniffles could be heard, nose-blowing, and soft tears and suspirations. He had moved the community by his plea. Only Baltar seemed untouched by Narzissenfeld's appeal. He knew only too well how efficient was Jewish sentiment. Nothing like lambs and *shohetim* to move Jews—how literal was the imagery, an obvious transcription of the condition of innocent victim which most Jews regarded themselves to be. Of one thing there was no doubt. Narzissenfeld was an innocent victim.

"You have spoken well, accused," Baltar began, his words measured and even, almost casual and disrespectful. "Very well and we admire your words. They appeal to us, that core of grainy sentiment which makes our eyes fill with tears and our noses sniffle.

"There is no doubt in our minds that you were exposed, as you say, and vulnerable, as we recognize. But you have confessed. You have admitted the crime. You were terrorized into becoming our enemy, a spy against us. You told them nothing. We may believe that. We may accept the truth of that. You gave them no useful news. It is then not the crime of your action that we judge, but the crime of your existence that comes to judgment. The action was unavailing. They learned nothing they did not already suspect. And, given their insinuating presence in our company, their plague of spies come in the disguise of helpers and servicemen, they have undoubtedly discovered what they sought to find.

"The crossroads are come. They will attack us this coming week, you have said. You have told us more than you told them. You are a double and triple spy. Unwitting in all things and how unreliable. Neither a good spy for them nor a good friend to us. Yours is disorderly being, disarranged and out of place and of no good use to them, to us, to yourself. You should take your life and be done with it. But that is unlikely.

440

You are too weak for even that, that proud assertion. No matter. We will dispose of your inutility.

"It is clear, friends, is it not," Baltar said, turning from the accused to the assembly, addressing them like a cloud heavy with rain, "that a larger matter confronts us now. They come to rob from us all that we have, all that stands between us and the last violation of our pride. Indeed, most of you knew nothing of our storehouse of weapons. We had no wish to use them, but if they come to us in the week which has just begun, we have no choice but to oppose them, to make of them, of us, a pyre of energetic and unyielding pride. There is no question but that, judgment executed upon him, this poor fool of a boy, we must go forward to defend ourselves, to stand together against them. Judge him. That is upon you. Guilty, innocent. Of what crime? Treason to us his friends, his brothers and sisters, his fellow endurers. I say guilty."

Voices began to call out to be heard. But Dr. Klay fore-stalled the clamor. "It is my turn to speak. My turn now. I know that I am considered an aristocrat. Behind my back you call me 'the Jewish count.' I accept the description. What is Jewish aristocracy (and there is—I contend—excellent reason for imagining Jewish aristocrats) other than someone who disallows the persuasion of sentiment, who is not alarmed by gentiles nor stampeded by the fears of Jews. I refuse to lose my grip. And my contention, friends, is that that grip, that tenacity of will, is unmistakably Jewish. I, no less than you, have had the pistol at my heart. But, more than lose my life, I did not dare to lose my pride. I said on that occasion, in Vienna, in the days before my departure, to that disgusting young man who pointed his weapon at me, 'Is it I, sir, who threaten you? If so, please fire and be done with it.' Embarrassed, strangely, he turned away. My friends hailed me as as aristocrat. I stood my ground. I stood my ground. I shall stand it now before you, most particularly before you, Baltar . . .

"The issue this evening does not concern young Narzissen-feld. I would rap his knuckles; if he were smaller and more accommodating I would thrash his backside, but to call for such an innocent to take his life, to die because of a stupidity is not judgment but a criminality more disgraceful than that of which he stands accused. No. No. No. The issue here is between Baltar and ourselves, Baltar's intention, Baltar's vengeance, Baltar's own criminality, his indescribable talent and capacity for criminality and an inconsequential boy who has tripped his plans out of fright."

"Do you acuse me?" Baltar replied, unconcerned, his voice flat and disengaged. "Do you dare to accuse me, Jewish count? Where are *your* numbers?"

"Where are my numbers? Nowhere. And yours. Where are yours?"

"Here. Here. Look at my numbers," and Baltar rolled back his shirt sleeve, and indeed as we knew there would be, the numbers could be seen, the tattoo as permanent as that which rested upon the arms of all our company excepting Dr. Klay, Rabbi Steinmann, and Simon Stern himself.

"The numbers are false," a voice called from the depths of the room. "The numbers are false." And the crowd of people shifted and from the back of the chamber there pushed toward us a presence, still hidden by the undifferentiated mass of bodies wrapped and hidden in darkness. It was Simon Stern.

"Here, here, see them, see all these numbers. My numbers. My Ravensbrück numbers like all the rest," Baltar screamed, thrusting his bared arm before Simon Stern.

"Janos Baltar, they are false numbers. When you applied them I do not know. It doesn't matter. Vienna, spring, 1945 or Paris that summer? It doesn't matter, but they are false." The words moved out like the stateliness of players miming speed, exaggerated movement and rhythm, desperate slowness and deliberation.

Baltar came to rest before Simon Stern, his vast body forced to rest. For a moment he stood and then slowly, slowly, he raised his right arm above the head of Simon Stern, a clenched fist of iron, and poising it above his head, he held it there as time moved off, seconds beating their way into the past. The fist began to pound against the air, trying to force its way down upon Simon's covered head, but the air between the fist and brittle skull became as lead, heavy, impenetrable, and the fist beat against air in small motions of rage, smaller with each movement, until after some minutes the arm died from the air, dropped back to Baltar's side and his body slumped upon its knees before Simon Stern.

The voice of Simon Stern, more enormous than I had ever known, addressed that crumpled body, intoning a judgment we had in no way known or anticipated:

"Baalam ben Michoel Baltar, known to us as Janos Baltar, you are not what you have seemed. It was suspected long before this moment, but all things come to their proper place and time.

"The knowledge of crimes and deceits, crimes and deceits to which others more wise than I succumbed, are known at last to me. I can imagine the project of evil as readily as I dream the kingdom of the ransomed. They were one and indistinguishable. And I believed your use to them, a source of pure and energetic opposition against which to test out and plan. But you humbled me, and my invincibility shattered like a cheap armor. The violence of your youth, the disorder of your origin, the brutality of your growing up to manhood (who would not excuse these?), sorrowing with you for them as we sorrow with young Peter whom you wish to drive toward despair and death. But beyond madness there is still judgment. It does not matter to us that yours has been a grim and tortured life. Bear that yourself; contain it and we would support you, show you tenderness and succor. Turn that rage toward us, maim and kill as you have done before and we are left with no choice.

"You are banished, expelled, driven forth. From this moment, when the hour strikes the mid-blackness of this night, you must be gone, and in this place, guarding the entrance door to this establishment, there shall be one person, young Peter Narzissenfeld, armed with the last weapon we shall permit to us for our protection, and there with pistol and with knife he shall watch over us, your replacement, our security."

Simon Stern spoke with an even rhythm, neither moving nor observing the naked skull upon which his words fell. Baltar remained upon his knees throughout the judgment, but at the last he tumbled forward and his face struck the stone floor and he lost consciousness. None moved to assist him and the silence remained.

Simon Stern turned to us all, facing the community, for he had more he wished to say.

"Jews of the Society.

"You have not known until now that this room existed. It is our *Lishkat HaGazit*, a chamber of hewn and polished stone, which in ancient times, when the Temple of our manhood stood upon the holy ground of Mount Moriah in the city of our longing, was used by the seventy-one sages of tradition to pronounce judgment upon the guilt and innocence of all Israel and of mankind. There it was, in that ancient hall of assembly, that the great ones of Israel determined who shall live and who shall die, who shall be stoned, who strangled, who hanged, who beaten, and who driven forth from the favored protection of the People and the concerned wings of the Archangels.

"The Temple exists no longer. The Chamber is vanished. The Seventy-one Sages of Israel perished, many as martyrs. In the generations, numberless, which stretch from those days to ours, we have seen an endless horror. We have endured that horror.

"It is not possible for us to explain that in men which is called irrational, when men are seized by uncontrollable passion, when they lay over the universe their own unreconciliation. We are left with the irrational, unexplained, inexplicable. The irrational is just that—irrational. It is a private preserve of the spirit. Try as we have throughout all our generations to understand it, it becomes dust in our mouths, either a naked folly (the foolishness of the nations, as we say) or else by wit it acquires a semblance of reason, a burnished patina of the sensible and meaningful. Such semblances dissolve upon scrutiny. The irrational is irrational precisely because it is recognized by us that reason orders life, but can neither create it nor endure it.

"Is it fit that men should sit in judgment upon unreason? Indeed what is law, our own law, sacred though it is, but the judgments of men upon the unreason of other men. To be sure our law is a gift of God, a gift which descended upon fiery tongs to burn the tongue of Moses, to engraft upon him a burning wisdom which pebbled his speech until his death. He spoke and they danced about the calf. He destroyed the calf, killed the evildoers, and spoke again. And through all the generations of men there have been pebbled speakers who have tried to speak and who spoke well of what it was the Lord desired of us, and nonetheless, in every generation, there were enough—unrighteous they are called—who danced about golden calves and hugged the laps of idols and refused to hear.

"An endless altercation between reasonable requests and unreasonable replies. Has it been so hard, really, to do justice, to do mercifully and to do humbly that in every age of history the predominance should go to arrogance, cruelty and deceit? The untold irrationality of the heart, demanding all, deserving little.

"We are a community of endurers. 'Survivors' we are called, but 'endurers' is more appropriate. We are not survivors, for we did not survive. We simply outlasted. It is for this reason that we have banished statistics from our community. We do not mention that six million of our kinsmen perished. Why not? If it were in fact six million and one and we forgot him, that last one, in our calculations, we should have nullified the memorial we burn to the other six millions, and if one less than that number we shall have to account one of us as dead. But whom? The number in its grandeur makes the enormity no greater. In no way can we make over feeling into a number, and our community is founded upon feelings and not upon ideas.

"Baltar is banished, but the judgment of excision does not complete the work of judgment. The storehouse of arms existed. It surrounds us now. False. It is not the way. The task is not violence but our refusal to be violated. And that refusal as in the past has its own laws. Pride, pride, but we cannot take the world down with us in pride. We cannot even if we could. We cannot because we cannot. It is not principle that dispels fantasy but always and ever only reality that defeats it. We cannot crush the enemy. They will crush us and cover over our graves and we will be forgotten. The task of Jews is not alone that we should not forget, nor should we cause them to remember, but that we should never be forgotten. And to avoid that fatal decree, the ignominious insult of being forgotten after more than three millennia of our walking upon this earth, we must stay with what we have struggled to become—endurers who say over and again what must be.

"The arms will be removed this evening and tomorrow after the service of the morning at which in special celebration of this night the Psalms of Hallel will be said; we will begin all of us in joy to build in the open space surrounded by our walls a replication of the ancient Temple there to celebrate our worship, a consummated sacrifice, a Zion of our will."

Simon Stern finished his words and passed before the assembly and departed. Wordless and virtually without sound —only soles scuffling upon the stone—the community passed out behind him. Baltar remained in the darkness and was seen alive by us no more.

Morning came, and before its fingers spread upon the city, warming the cool of dawn which shivered in the courtyard of our encampment, the songs of thanksgiving had already joined the clouds. The workmen assembled before the open doors, flung wide to what had been, until that hour, a private garden to our habitation. The numbered stones and cut cedar beams withdrawn, the work began, and Simon Stern, his architect beside him, withdrew the plans long since drawn and well prepared for this occasion and directing our builders, laid down the cornerstone into the yielding earth. He blessed it and urged forward our hands.

I stood beside him through the days of toil. I never left his side, holding to his arm, my finger crooked into his belt, for I feared to lose him now.

The Temple rose. Our Temple rose, but we did not believe that we had changed the center of the universe, that by our decision the axial gravity of all things had shifted to our place. It was known to us that the whole was elsewhere, that imagination had designed the universe in other quarters, forming Adam from the dust of Mount Moriah, sending him forth from paradise to that place, whereupon he sacrificed a unicorn to him who had misunderstood a gesture, and dying had been buried on that self-same mount. It was there again that our terrestrial progenitor, Father Abraham, had brought his only son to burn him as an offering and for his steadfastness was given a ram in substitution, and there, yet another time, a king, the blessed David, established the Ark of the Covenant and to his son, wise Solomon, gave charge to build a temple in which to honor, celebrate, adorn and house an ineffable Name in an empty chamber.

In the course of time that temple was burned and built again, defiled and reconsecrated, expanded and destroyed once more. It did not seem to hold as history advanced.

The cubits measured, the scale reduction well devised, the foundations solid in the earth, the walls, the arches, the entranceways, the chambers, and the altars upon which our prayers would soon be offered rose up.

It was seven days from the conclusion of the New Year, two nights before the eve of our Atonement, one day before the festival of consecration, at an early hour of the morning, before the fringes of a prayer shawl can be seen held against the blue-blackness of the sky, that a glow was noticed in the Temple by the watchman of the night. He cried aloud in joy, but the glow was no miracle of investiture as for a moment he confessed he thought, remembering other miracles of dedication. His pause of faithful indecision was costly to us all. The fire puffed and sputtered from the center of the Temple where it had been started, and racing along conduits which had been well devised, a web of flame turned the inner courtyard, choked off from air and access, into an inferno. The Temple exploded first, and our people, warned by the sight within, fled outward to the city beyond. The Temple was destroyed, and by morning the retaining walls were all that remained of our habitation.

Epilogue I

"Come closer," a voice called to me, and I heard that voice, distant from my fingertips, and my cane tapped out a semicircle of incantation into which I walked, pressing toward the sound. I had passed through many hands, many arms holding mine, so many hands entwined with mine, guiding me to that time and place. I was an unfamiliar but gentle sight, a blind man with wild beard and untrimmed curls, a blind man with intention, not idling at corners waiting for solicitude, but stepping forward into streets, confidently, cars screaming to a stop, and as I crossed over a double street which appeared divided by a central promenade, an irate driver abandoned his car and cursing conducted me to safety.

"Come closer," the voice trembled on a breeze embracing

me, and I divined the distance, the voice more resonant, less hindered by buildings and the encumbrance of competing sounds.

It was autumn, and my cane struck upon a fallen leaf.

"Come closer." I approached the sound and a hand, stretched forth upon the greeting, took my own and drew me toward it. He drew me toward him and held me, bringing down my exhausted body beside his own.

"It is well now, friend," he began. "Do you know that I am nearing fifty years of age? I'm not old, perhaps a little tired, but not old. What do you think, Nathan? Was it worth it? I have no doubt. I have no doubt at all. It was worth it. Nothing really has been lost. Not even time, which some men think the greatest loss. I think we have learned immensely. And what's the point if not to learn.

"There's no way, I think, of reconciling men by keeping them at the borders of our lives. I thought that was the right way, holding every creature at the end of my stiff arm, my flattened palm pressed against them, imagining their obduracy when all along it was my own. I shall simply go among them now. I shall be who I am and I shall demand—if I demand anything again (and I know I will)—that they become human. If I learned one thing, I have learned who I am not. I am not God. I shall never try to be Him again, if it was He, in fact, whom I seemed to be. I am even with men. I no longer wish them to serve my suffering. I can do much more now. I am free to take on God Himself, since I know that I am not God. It will be a more equal combat and one I'm grateful to lose. Will you join me? I'm tired of this open place." Simon paused a moment and his body turned from me, but I felt his closeness about me. "Did you know, Nathan, that children feed the animals?" I did not know, for in my sighted days I had never visited a zoo where animals are caged.

We left our places in the park. Other men who had watched over Simon Stern during the three days that he sat before the lake joined us, and we made our way slowly through the walks of the park until we emerged into the traffic of the city. Simon often stopped, remarking on sights he had not seen, describing things to me that I had once known but long since forgotten about the ways of men in the large world.

Epilogue II

The years have passed since Simon Stern departed his confinement and joined himself to the large world. Many of those
years I spent in his company. We traveled throughout the
nation, we visited continents, we became familiar with many
communities of Jews, many communities of Christians, and
communities of other believers whose names I do not now recall. We found that they were not all the same, nor their
teachings identical, nor the sense of holy purpose which they
cultivated interchangeable. We knew before, we know more
profoundly now, that there is no general virtue, no general
truth, no general holiness. Everything is imbedded in particularity, and it is the felicity or abrasiveness of its particularity

that enables some human beings to honor age and murder children, to succor infants and beasts but to hold maturity in contempt. It is all different and our view is no less different. But Simon Stern, attentive now to his intelligence and feeling, makes himself ready for yet another moment.

The Society is not dispersed. The compound has been rebuilt, but its windows are somewhat larger and more light is allowed to penetrate its inner space. It flourishes, and Rabbi Steinmann has cultivated its easy domesticity. Most of the old survivors have departed and new ones have replaced them, but all return on the anniversary of our community's inauguration. We used to return to the Society each year during the first years of our wandering, but Simon has not been back for several years now, and on our last visit together in 1957 I decided to remain behind when he departed. I am now a man past my fiftieth year. I still walk confidently, but choose to stay put, in the new compound, to work upon the documents, to collate the resources of my narrative, to tell the story which you have just considered. The others. They flourish, some of them. Rochel is together with Peter. They have children and a gentle life. Lubina Krawicz died several years after Simon passed into what she called "the wilderness." Dr. Klay lives with us at the Society but maintains an apartment uptown where he has begun to entertain cultured friends from all over the world and to write a psychological biography of Spinoza (he finds it curious that Spinoza enjoyed incinerating spiders with his lenses; that fact obliged him to consider what it means to love God intellectually).

And Simon Stern? The messiah is a real moment, never a psychological conceit. I think of Simon Stern as one correct moment. There are many times that need messiahs, but time skips over the moment, and the messiah, waiting ready in the shadows, does not appear. I have told you the story of a fulfilled moment. It is when God flees that we have tragedy. But it is as well the occasion when genius, risking the little that a man can share, holds back tragedy until God regains his courage and returns.

It goes on like that. It is a story which blind men tell best.

Appendix

Selected Writings of Simon Stern

THE SCRIBE'S PREFACE

The writings which follow are selected from the considerable
body of scraps and notations which I remembered and transcribed after Simon Stern had spoken them to the community
or read them to me in private.

The writings are of two distinct sorts. A considerable portion are extensions and commentaries upon the opening chapters of the Book of Genesis, wherein God describes his creation
of the universe. What is notable about the commentaries of
Simon Stern is the unmistakable presence of a confusion, his
unknowing identification of himself with God, and his no less
profound awareness of difference and separateness from him.
It is as though Simon were attempting during those years

before he took up the life of a wandering messiah, to set himself in opposition and contrast to God, imagining Him, in some anthropomorphic simile, as inhabiting a house not unlike his own and ruling a far-flung universe as he administered the destiny of the Jews.

The last of the versions of the story of creation Simon dictated to me not long before the trial of Narzissenfeld, the expulsion of Baltar, and his death in the Temple holocaust. He seemed to understand, for the first time, that being a creative man is different from being God.

And the nighttime meditations, what of them? There something more relevant and immediate to the messianic sense is revealed. Messiahs happen to be Jews, but they take on so many different forms and save so many different persons that the messianic voice is without historical time or national origin or sectarian identity. Simon wrote meditations in the mode of Buddha and the Mahatma. He wrote in the mood of Dostoevsky and Bakunin, of obscure sophiologists like Valdimir Soloviev and public emancipators like Karl Marx. It did not matter to him who made life meaningful as long as they made it meaningful for someone other than themselves. And he wrote all these nighttime meditations as dramatic monologues in which the real tensions would emerge from the conflict between simple, confused humanity and the endless complexity of destiny. I have chosen these at random. They are all extraordinary, for they revealed to me that Simon Stern understood many psychologies other than his own. He stopped writing myths of creation and messianic bedtime stories when the compound burned. Now, much later than the time of my recension, he is what all men must become, creators and redeemers, the twin gifts by which heaven has rewarded human imagination, that it make alive and sustain the falling.

Nathan Gaza, Scribe

Creation I

There are two Biblical recensions of the creation of the universe. In the first, God is sovereign and alone and He creates with order and logic, proceeding from orbs and stars to plants, beasts, and the men who feed upon them. In the second, God has already lost His nerve, for apparently (if we read the text correctly) he consults the angels and having consulted does the work impetuously and, it would seem, in haste. There is no doubt that he formed his understanding of the Jews in the second of these creative ecstasies—impetuously and in haste. Inspiration without genius!

Creation II

God created the universe and left it to man to destroy it. I believe, however, that if we succeed (as perhaps we shall) in destroying it, God will create the universe again. The pity of the matter is that we can do without God. Folly can simply pass over wisdom, never noticing it (even if a blind man cared whether Kant's thaler exists, he couldn't see it to verify his care)—but God, the divine Narcissus, must always behold himself and he will go on, stamping very real thalers with his image, while we go on—no doubt ever more desperately— debasing them.

Creation III

"I said aloud, 'Let us create' (for I too am overcome with the joy to fashion and build), and the angels were silent. Thinking they had not heard, I spoke louder, 'Come, let us begin to create,' and still no angel moved, all rested, silent and hovering. I spoke this time in my power and majesty, but more precisely, for angels too are confused by abstraction: 'We will make man and in our image.' They shuddered and four angels approached and bowed before me, abasing their wings in the dust. 'Do you mean this?' they asked. 'I create and I destroy ten thousand worlds. Should I not mean this?' 'It is true,' they replied, 'but no man have you ever made until this moment.' 'All the more reason to make him now.' 'But his heart is evil from its youth, the sempiternal writing tells us.' 'How shall we *know* until he lives?' I replied. '*Know, know*, Lord. Your knowledge precedes life.' 'Wrong, wrong, angels; even for me it is in the living.' And I spoke to them no more and began the work of creation."

Creation IV

And God beheld what He had done and was saddened by His enthusiasm. I am not satisfied with what I am, He thought, and in my inventiveness and delight, I thought to make them like me, that seeing me within themselves they would wish for my company. And I, bored by my own entrancement, would be fulfilled by theirs. What mistake. Yes. Mistake. Angels, gather and hear that the Lord of the universe is saddened and contrite. Let us take counsel together and devise that my heart may be lightened. And there came forward an angel that proposed that they be punished for their insolence. And the Lord said: "Shall they be punished for what I have done to them?" And the angel was silent. And another said, "Let their way be made hard and perilous, that they have little time to think of you and desire that impossibility." And the Lord replied: "Their way is hard now and will, of nature, become harder." And yet another proposed making women barren and men without seed that the creatures perish in their generation; that the land not bear and they starve; that beasts ravage their villages and pestilence decimate their numbers. But to all these devices, the Lord was undisposed.

"Angels, you are vain. How should you not be? You are all mistakes of my devising and you echo the baseness that only idle virtue can imagine. But behold them. They are the mixture of earth and blood, red earth and drop of semen. They are life and you are only perfection. And is it not my pathos that I should be saddened by them and wearied by you? No, dear council of perfection, you cannot understand, for what they seek you possess. what they desire you cannot experience, what they earnest to become you only are. If they toil endlessly to reach me, making generation beyond generation, planting without harvest, building without completing, they too will tire and they will destroy themselves from unfulfillment.

"Why, why in my own folly did I put into them the notion

that they were gods?" The Lord groaned and the waters of the deep shuddered. "If they go on thus, wishing to be like me, they will not be like themselves and it is only having passed through a becoming to themselves that they can become like to me." And the Lord groaned a second time and there were floods and earthquakes and the moon faulted and the sun cooled.

"Six days have passed and before me the millions of ages of the generations of man pass and I can see what I have done." And the Lord groaned for the third time and there was a darkness upon the earth and man slept, and by the morning of his waking the provisions of the night had rotted and the fires in his hearth were banked and gone out and a cold sun rose and man cried for lack of food and warmth and the beasts, brazened, howled in the morning and came close to man and made ready to devour him. And the Lord repented of the excess that He had wrought in the heart of man and made manna to drip from the breadfruit trees and slow to collect on the leaves of plants and let bees make honey from the ooze of passion fruit and spoke: "And on the Seventh Day the Lord rested and caused man to rest from his labor, to be as Him who spoke and created the universe."

Creation V

It is well that our fathers did not know, in the time of their origination, the teachings of the Greeks or they might have imagined as did those other saints of Wisdom that the world is moved by love. The gods loving in the lemon groves, and the issue of their love, these wheeling planets, these cold stars, these heavy waters (the tears of unrequital, uncondensed to firmament, which, resentfully, wash over and over the surface of Creation, wearing it away), these monstrous growths of fiber and chlorophyll—succulents drawing water from sand and over the millions of years changing into flowers (they disguise themselves for the upheaval when they regress again), these animals and men, instinct into cruelty, instinct into intelligence into cruelty.

What did those Greeks imagine the gods did in their lemon

groves but sow disorder? It is other than this. The myth of my fathers is beyond the muting of fantasy. They had no inheritance of primordial myths and ancestral gods. To whom could they turn: the Chaldees, the Egyptians, rocky kingdoms and sandy principalities, where struggle made of death the consummation, and resurrection the promise with which to balsam death into something less grotesque and final than it is? They wanted no part of such extremities: neither fantasy nor desperation. They chose a hard and truthful way which is to reverse the course, to make childishness the beginning and maturity the end (unlike the Greeks), to conceive Creation the beginning, and death the consummate end (unlike the Egyptians). And the monument of their invention, those opening words wherewith at the beginning the Lord of Creation fashioned in the order of necessity the whole of the universe and concluded with the pacification of man.

(This pleases me. It is a more fitting beginning. Close to a philosophic anthropology which is needed: something to interpret to man—without the risks of artificial teleologies and mysterious entelechies—that his hard way, his relentless way, his painful way, is no act of love, but the trial to time, that God thinks less than we suppose, that He is orderly because in order there is—even for Him—the escape from thought.)

A Meditation of Baruch Spinoza
Before Retiring to Bed

I have ground today two lenses, completing one so that the lawyer may read his briefs without strain, beginning another for my own delight, that when the eye beholds a distant point, all light will flee from the superfices of vision, and aided by my device will reflect blue zenith with absolute and uncompromised clarity.

Today I have seen no one and none have sought my discourse. A bowl of soup I warmed myself. It is no distraction to argue with my adamantine mind. I have as well completed a letter to her Majesty, the Queen of Sweden, declining her kind invitation to winter at her palace and there instruct the members of her court in philosophy. I have done these two things, it may be thought, obedient to an impulse of the will. It is not so, for all that I have done is to find in reason what is already imprinted upon my nature. I am, alas, no different than my philosophy has made me, a mere example of thought reflecting its necessity. (I would have wished to sup with the Queen of Sweden, a gifted and intelligent woman, who would have relieved me of the dampness of this lowland winter, but that cannot be.) I am utterly serious and there is no frivolity in me. I cannot succumb to what my whim and fancy propose. Moreover, all that in me which, like the creatures of the species, is phlegmatic and seasonal, rash or intemperate, is to be suppressed, for I am—I must admit—*natura naturans,* a nature striving to perfection, without doubt, no less nor more than any other. But who tells me what that perfection is to be? See Ethics, Proposition X, and it will be clear. I must reread that work of mine, lest I forget from where my passions come and how to deal with them.

I put my hand upon my reason to restrain its excess, curb it, return it to the right well-worn course, where all the energetic stallions of whom Plato wrote with so much adoration are now reduced to pulling loads and bearing sacks of wheat and casks of wine. Yes, I have destroyed the credibility of my ancient tribal testimony and no longer do enlightened men here, in France, in England, read that Scripture with quite the surety and conviction that they did before my Treatise was passed abroad, but what has it brought me?—wisdom, yes, but I can no longer cry and my loneliness is sometimes beyond bearing.

A Meditation of Sabbatai Zevi Before Retiring to Bed in a Turkish Prison

Abject, I am victorious. Defeated and reviled, I will be remembered to eternity. And so what? Brocade and robes trimmed with sable in the morning, a spotted cotton kaftan at nightfall. Ridiculous how our fortunes depend upon the fanfare of man and the cooperativeness of God. Am I any the less a Messiah for having failed? And is Messiah accounted messianic for having put food on the table, wine in the grape, the Jews in their land, and the holy Torah in its proper place —the *aide mémoire* of revelation, a system of reminders, mnemonics, nursery rhymes so that each day we recall to ourselves the humanity we rush to forget?

They say that I hastened the end and that the end will not come until He elects its coming. True enough. But am I not Messiah for having been foolish (or courageous) to bring to God's attention what He has overlooked, perhaps even (and justifiably) forgotten. Well, I am not regarded so. Jews have converted to Islam and others (emulating yet another of my gestures), running across the border into Germany, have passed water in the Church. They are crazy. They think because I appealed to the Sultan and he gave me asylum and then later—a wily Sultan—obliged me to join his community or else cast me across the border back into the hands of my enemies that I recommend Islam as one more pressure point on the *corpus dei*. They think I worry about strategy. How they misconstrue me. No. It is more simple. What I have tried to do is to humiliate God into redemption. He cannot oblige us to the litany of obedience, break our spirits with the mortar of his wrath and grind us in the Exile without occasionally—I ask you, Lord, only occasionally—giving us some attention. You think the Torah was gift enough. Well, yes, in our own community, where it is honored, but our community is never our own. Are we more, therefore, than human, finally, more than human? We are not. We are extraordinarily human, marvelously human, consummately human, human supra human, but still human, knotted tissue and gnarled beyond imagining, bruised, contused, confused, but human, human. (Here I imagine Sabbatai Zevi might well begin to have a fit and fall upon the floor to foam and gnash, and a janissary with numb face and a scimitar in hand will enter his cell and place a gag into his mouth and lift him gently in his arms and lay him upon his cushioned bed and pour water flavored with sugar upon his face.)

Now I am recovered. I did not sleep as I had planned, but fumed and foamed as others had devised—my mother, that yellowed used parchment, who in the presence of my father's rage dropped me to comfort him, and the result, brain lesion and the Messiah.

In short, therefore, I am the Messiah—one among many it will be said, false and untrue, incomplete and penultimate, but dear children of Israel, will you ever unanimously, with a single and complete heart, honor one Messiah. Will there not always be one Jew, a handful of Jews, a whole community of Jews who will say—he isn't really Jewish, he isn't observant enough (or perhaps by then, he isn't unobservant and contemporary enough), his eyes are set too close together and his mouth is weak and effeminate, his clothes are badly made, he talks rough, he talks too kindly, he is obedient too readily or he is disobedient and thoughtless.

O God, not one, not a single one. Not ever one Messiah, though we dream and pray for him, believing in our prayer that we will have the courage to dare the impossible, to believe that one human being, all human and imperfect for his humanity, will so breathe the breath of God and so exude the perfume of perfection that all will bring themselves under his banner (that is why that other regnant faith made of the Messiah a progeny of God—I call it, *épater les Juives*—doing us one better and making of an impossible demand a believable one). Man will more readily swallow something ludicrous—that the Most Perfect devised with semen and egg to make something so grotesquely imperfect as man (and that without touching the maidenhead or breaking the membranous tissue and setting the ovulating universe to turn about itself); God sent doves into the womb and there came forth perfect man—perfect God, half and half, cream and butter from the same impure stock. Who can believe this? Millions upon millions. And we, with the logic of commandments and obedience, the stern way of our nature, the hard discipline of our humanity—where are we? Nowhere at all. Locked in at nightfall lest our reason and our lucidity crumble the phantasmagoric fabric of their belief—locked in, burned, tortured, recantation and destruction. And for all this I have come and by my excess and my madness, by that bridge that I throw between our dispassionate ways of peace and their mythic rejection of humanity, I am both Messiah and accursed. Neither can bear my instruction, for I disdain all of their fanaticisms, the fanatic self-indulgence of a vain and bored divinity, the delusion of a Christendom that cannot tolerate its ordinariness, and of the Jews, my own, who think the ordinary more than it is. Now, I say, is that not a Messianic view and am I not Messiah? (The Messiah at this moment, we suppose, weary and distracted, falls back upon his bed and sleeps. The janissary, confused now and uncertain, departs, stooping to avoid hitting his head on the archstone of the doorway. The wooden door, sheeted with worked metal laid on in strips and studded with bronze nails, screams shut. The Messiah sleeps at last.)

A Meditation of Simon bar Kochba Before Retiring to Bed on the Evening Before Battle Against the Romans

We shall lose tomorrow, this battle, like the last, will go against us, and ten thousand more will be lost. In the morning our troops will annoy and agitate the Romans, our archers will slay their forward guard, pick off their legionnaires, wing and maim them, but by noontime, their patience threaded, the cavalry will move around our flanks and encircle us in a wide sweep, drive us together, herd us to the river's edge and we will drink our thirst in blood by nightfall.

Our position is always bad, but we have no choice of position. This war is late in our day and positions of power are scarce in this isolated corner of the world. We fight alone against that tyrant. Tyrant? Their tyranny, not ours? Jews must always be free to elect their own tyranny. On Sinai we received tyranny with joy, bludgeoned and humiliated. Moses slew those who defected to the imagination of Aaron. He calls us free, our Lord and Salvation. He convokes our assembly in the desert beneath that stubbled mount and congratulates our good fortune. Had we not been forty years in that misery I doubt we should have succumbed any more than those others—Greeks, Egyptians, Phoenicians, Persians— to whom He had offered it before succumbed. Why should they, those others, with olives and wheat, cities and store-

houses, administration and culture, have taken upon themselves what was to be an onerous obligation? Had we choice?
No. Surely. The punishment was told before the prize, the
threat before the liberation. Had my ancestors thought of
the Messiah in those days when they bondaged to his service?
No choice theirs. How my friends, the Rabbis, delight in the
fancy of those Biblical words: "We shall do and we shall
hear." What they make of them, what, indeed? The will speaks
before intelligence reflects. In joy we hasten to obey before
we understand. Like a child anxious to please its father, they
rush to do before they have been told. Is this free service
or is this tyranny? The latter. In our terror of being returned
into the wandering we break our will to serve Him, and now,
our substance gone and our spirit humiliated, we give our
last breath to die for His sake. We slay the Roman tyrant,
but we are no tyrannicides, for our own yoke—the yoke that
we have chosen—is about our shoulders, and the single tyrant,
blessed be His name, Him we cannot oppose, Him we dare not
fight, Him we must slay and will not raise our wrath against
Him. (Simon bar Kochba sinks exhausted to his couch. The
oil light burning upon a rough desk where parchments lie
rolled and tied with leathern thongs flickers in the desert
wind. A soldier enters the tent and stands, looking down upon
the general who sleeps now, snores (yes, snores), and bows
his head in prayer, indeed, in adoration, for word has just
come to the camp that Akiba, Sage of Israel and Teacher to
all the Jews, has proclaimed this. sleeping general Messiah,
Anointed, Son and Servant to the Lord of Heaven.)

A Meditation of Michel de Montaigne
Before Retiring to Bed

Sanguinity: a cool and pensive disposition, distant from those
passions which heat the fluids of the body, condense them,
cool them, producing distillate liquors from which the spirit
draws a draught and then putting them aside sinks back into
torpor, languishes, sleeps with dreams. An unhealthy condition which I avoid by sanguinity, as I say, by calm and ease.
Consanguinity? I have none, for in playing upon this notion

I conclude that my sanguinity results from that interplay of cultures and kinds, features and temperaments, which my Spanish, French, Catholic and Jewish blood demands. Amusing, but I am told that I am Jewish. I learned this today, neither to my delight nor to my dismay, though some among my enemies will account my dissident imagination to whatever Jew there hides within my seed. I am a Marrano, my family having derived from Spanish Jews who were persuaded by an itinerant vagabond priest that it would be better to marry the Church than be burned by her. They decided, prudently, in her favor. This is a decision, no less free than others compelled by argument to an alternative less dolorous than its companion. But can it be that I am Jewish, that those Jewish elders who called upon me today to claim my affection, producing documents and genealogies, were speaking truth? Why presume otherwise? What can it mean to me that I am a Jew and not, as it is commonly supposed, a Christian like Christians, unbelieving and fractious, respectful of authority, disdaining of its presumption, tactful in the presence of public fools, truthful before the paper and the quill. What should it mean to me: a Jew amid the fortune of my maternal line? Those gentlemen are emboldened and rude to have told me this (must I now come to endorse the views of those who wish them exiled, for they are seditious of my rest, of my sanguinity, adding yet another strain to that fidelity of blood I call my own?), but they are right for speaking, are they not? They did not tell me of the consequence of their communication. They do not expect (surely) that I should enter Synagogue, observe their feasts and abstinences, do over my psyche, fit it out with heavy curtains and secret doors, burn the pictures of my mind and efface the images of divinity I have carefully described. So. So. What did they want but to destroy my sleep, for I cannot be party to their misery and I cannot speak more for toleration than I have done or write more acidulously of the King's fanaticism and the Church's pretense than has been my habit. It means nothing to me. But it ruins my rest. Sanguinity: it passes. Consanguinity: thick and sticky like a potion.

ABOUT THE AUTHOR

ARTHUR A. COHEN was born in New York City in 1928. He is the author of *The Carpenter Years*, a novel, and many other works on the history of modern Jewish thought, including *The Natural and the Supernatural Jew, Martin Buber*, and *The Myth of the Judeo-Christian Tradition*. His most recent book (with photographs by Philip Garvin), *A People Apart*, was nominated for a National Book Award in 1972. He lives in New York and is working on a new novel.

810 F

816